RAINBOW BRIDGE FARM

BY

LYNN ROBERSON

Llumina Press

REFERENCES

Go to Sleep my Little Pickaninny: Minstrel song of the late 19th
    century
Amazing Grace: John Newton
Mansion Over the Hilltop: Ira Stanphill
You Are my Sunshine: Jimmie Davis and Charles Mitchell
Down in the Valley: Traditional American Folk Song
She's Single Again: Charlie Craig and Peter McCann
Love me Tender: Elvis Presley and Vera Matson
What a Friend we Have in Jesus: Joseph Scriven
Jailhouse Rock: Jerry Leiber and Mike Stoller
All Creatures Great and Small: Samuel Taylor Coleridge, James
    Herriot
The following are legends and folktales I have heard all my life.
    The original authors are unknown:
The Doodlebug Chant
The Foxglove Legend
The Legend of the Devil's Tramping Ground
The Legend of the White Rose
The Rainbow Bridge Poem
The Indian Legend of the Rainbow
The Snowdrop Legend
The Dogwood Legend
The Jacob's Ladder Legend
The Big Fish Story
The Ghostlight Story
There are many Southern euphemisms and short rhymes included.
To the best of my knowledge, they have simply been handed down
through the generations by mouth, and have no recorded origins.
                                        —Lynn Roberson.

MISS VELVIE

"If wrinkles must be written upon our brow, let them not be written upon our heart. The spirit should never grow old."
—James A. Garfield

J oanna Morgan was holding a beagle while her friend Denise gave him an injection. The young women looked up at the sound of screeching tires. A bright, lime-green Suburban was pulling into Denise's driveway. As it came closer, they could see a sign that was painted on the door.

YOU KILL IT—WE STUFF IT
HAWKIN'S TAXIDERMY

The truck skidded to a halt and two women got out.

"Denise, I wanna talk to you!" the taller woman demanded. Penetrating, slate-gray eyes glowered at them, like those of a ferret. A sickly, jaundiced complexion encased a hollow temple and angular features that flowed down to a turkey-like neck. Orangish-brown hair with a hennaed cast bristled down around her collar. Dirty nails tipped rawboned hands and spindle-shanked legs protruded from a dirty pair of baggy, denim shorts. Heavy men's brogan boots covered her feet as she marched across the ground with heavy steps.

"You ain't got no right tellin' people they can't have a dog," she glared at Denise. "Look Agnes, that's the one he wanted."

The other woman didn't say a word, she just gave Joanna and Denise a hostile look. Rather squat and extremely full-bosomed, her round cheeks were flushed and her heavily rouged lips seemed permanantly pursed. Broad-shouldered and bull-necked, her long, black hair hung to the middle of her back in tight little sausage curls.

"What are you talkin' about?" Denise, still kneeling by the dog, looked up.

"You know damned good and well what. Eldridge Evans come over here to get that beagle yesterday. I had told 'im he'd make a good squirrel dog, he's one of my best customers!"

"Well, that would be an awful home," Denise defended herself. "All he thinks about is huntin'. He's got a yard full of dogs, all chained up, starves 'em to death, and never takes 'em to the vet. I heard he'll shoot 'em if they don't hunt good."

"So?"

"Well, my goodness! That's the reason we started the Beagle Brigade in the first place. There's so many poor huntin' dogs that are neglected and abused around here."

"You give me that dog—right now," Hilda demanded. "I'm gonna take 'im to Eldridge."

"Well," Denise got to her feet, holding the dog in her arms. "I don't know. I really wouldn't feel comfortable givin' 'im one of the dogs I foster."

"You're gonna be sorry!" Hilda bellowed as she turned on her heel and stomped away. "Come on, Agnes. Let's go!" The stocky woman followed, running to keep up with her. They got into the truck and pulled off, kicking up gravel as they went.

"Who in the world was that?" Joanna asked.

"Hilda Hawkins. And 'er sister, Agnes. They're crazy!"

"What's she got to do with it, anyway?"

"She's been involved with the beagle rescue for a long time," Denise explained. "Most folks are afraid of 'er." Putting the dog down on the ground, Denise scratched him behind the ear. "Don't you worry, boy. I'd never let anybody like that man have you."

"Hey, Jo! You 'bout ready?" The women turned to look up as a shiny, black Ford pickup pulled into the yard.

"I'm gonna haf'ta go, Neecie," Joanna said. "We're cookin' out on the grill tonight. Why don't you come?"

"I might ride over."

A wiry young man climbed down from the passenger seat to let Joanna in and she scooted over beside her husband, Randy. Johnny-Vernon Bradley slid back in and grinned down at her. He wasn't exactly what you would call handsome, with his hook-nose, thin, mousy hair and the close-set eyes that always seemed to be squinting. Yet, women seemed to be drawn to him. His best feature was a generous mouth, always turned up a little at the corners. And when he smiled, his entire face beamed so hard that his eyes crinkled until they almost disappeared.

"Whoo-eee!" he howled as he waved at Denise through the open window. "Pee on the fire, call the dogs, and let's go!"

"We're gonna run by Food Lion," Randy said. "Get some of them steaks they got on sale."

"Hey, baby!" Johnny-Vern leaned out the window a few minutes later and waved at the pretty blonde that was coming out of the store. "I may not be Fred Flinstone, but I bet I could make your Bed Rock!"

"Shut up, Vern!" Joanna dug an elbow into his rib cage as the young woman threw him a scowl and hurried to her car. "You're gonna get us all shot one of these days."

"Hey, what's that old lady doin'?" Randy asked as he nodded towards the other side of the parking lot, behind them.

Joanna turned in time to see a scrawny puppy skitter across the asphalt as an old woman tried to catch it. Her back was bent and twisted and she walked with a pronounced limp, but she obviously wasn't going to give up.

"Come on and let's see can we help 'er," Joanna urged. As the threesome approached, they could hear her talking.

"Come on, little feller," she coaxed in a gentle voice. "I ain't a-goin' to hurt you none. I just wanna help you. Ain't you cold and hongry?"

"Hold on there and we'll help you," Joanna called. "If we can ease 'im up into that corner between the two buildin's, I think we can get 'im."

"Oh thank you, honey," the old woman responded. "Lord have mercy, I been out here nearabout an hour, tryin' to get my hands on the pore little thing. I just can't stand to see nothin' homeless."

They cornered the puppy and Joanna picked her up, the little body quivering as she held the dog close against her chest and the brown eyes looked up at her warily. The long, honey-colored hair was matted with cockleburs and beggar lice and angry, raw spots covered the little body. Joanna handed her over to the old woman and the gnarled fingers stroked the shivering head as she uttered soothing sounds. "You'll be all right now, Velvie's got you, and I won't let nothin' bad happen to you. Don't you wanna go home with me and get all warmed up and have some supper?"

Twinkling blue eyes peered up at Joanna as the old woman hugged the puppy to her bosom, the way a mother would clutch an infant. "I want to thank you young folks for helpin' me like that. Most folks think I'm just a crazy old woman, but I ain't never cared what people think. I been helpin' animals all my life, and I ain't stoppin' now. By the way I'm Velvet White, but most folks call me Velvie."

The slight build suggested a fragility that the impish face denied. Despite the furrows that the years had plowed across the cheeks, she wore a hint of rogue and delicate pink lipstick. The snow white hair was carefully done up in finger waves on the sides and pulled back into a thick chignon. The finely chiseled bone structure hinted at a beauty that had slowly faded, but would never completely disappear. Liver colored age spots marched across her neck and arms.

The old woman held the puppy out to look at her. "This little girl looks like she's got some cocker spaniel in 'er. Just look at them long, wavy ears and that feathered coat. Don't know what she's mixed with, maybe feist or hound?" As she gathered the dog close again and continued to stroke her gently, the little tail began to thump. "See there, it ain't so bad, you're waggin' that little nub at me already. Anyways, I appreciate the help from you young people."

They watched as she limped over to an old gray hearse. Most of the paint had peeled off and rust showed through. The driver's side was battered with dents and long scratches. Still holding the puppy, she began to load her groceries from a nearby cart.

"Let us give you a hand there, ma'am," Randy said as he and Johnny-Vern walked over and began to stow sacks into the back of the old vehicle. Joanna noticed there were a lot of dried beans, bargain brand macaroni, and the only meat she saw was a package of pork knuckles. But there was a great deal of pet food. There were several fifty pound bags of dry dog food and she wondered how the old woman was able to lift them. There were also large bags of dry cat food and entire paper sacks full of canned food. Joanna also noticed a sack of cracked corn and two bales of hay in the back of the hearse.

They stood watching as the old woman drove away slowly in the strange looking vehicle, cradling the puppy on her lap. Joanna thought of her often over the next few weeks, then the incident slowly faded from her mind.

Joanna didn't see the old woman again until a blazing hot day in late July. The sun was beating down unmercifully, melting the pavement, so that her Reeboks were sticking slightly in the soft asphalt as she crossed the parking lot at the grocery store. The hearse was loaded down with supplies and Miss Velvie was trying to get it started. Joanna could hear a grinding noise as she turned the key in the ignition. Before she could get across the parking lot, the old woman got out and raised the hood. She looked up as Joanna approached.

"Hey there, honey. Looks like I got trouble."

"Let me run call my husband. He'll come help you, if I can find 'im.'"

"Well now, ain't no need in all that. I got some jumper cables. If you could just pull your truck up here and give me a charge, I believe that would do it."

Joanna pulled up and jumped out. "I'm always scared I'll hook 'em up wrong."

"P'shaw. Ain't nothin' to it. Just negative to negative and positive to positive. Like this right here." Taking the wires, she connected them with confidence. "Done it a million times, I reckon." The old vehicle started and she raced the motor.

"I'm gonna follow you, make sure you get home."

"I'll be fine, but I'd love for you to come visit. And you could stay for tea."

They veered off the blacktop onto a gravel road and followed it for a few miles, then turned into a long driveway lined with mimosa trees, the blossoms swaying in the gentle breeze like feathery, pink, powder puffs. A faded sign hung at a haphazard angle; MIMOSA PLANTATION. Joanna could see a huge, old Victorian-style house where steep gables and elegantly arched turrets soared up into the treetops. The verandah came into view, embellished with graceful, curving gingerbread trim and spindlework.

"Gosh-a-mighty!" Joanna exclaimed as they got out. "You must love livin' here."

"That I do, child. I grew up poor, raised on soppin' bread and gravy, in a two room shack. I never thought I'd live anywhere like this, until I met my husband and he brought me here to the town of Whipoorwill Springs. We lived here with 'is folks and they treated me as if I was their own daughter. They're all buried right out there in the family plot," she pointed to a small square out in the field, enclosed with an iron ornamental fence. "I declare, sometimes I just can't wait to get up to Heaven and see 'em all again." She looked up and smiled. "If I climb into Heaven, thou art there. That's from Psalms 139:7-11."

"Ma'am?"

"From the bible, don't you know? Look-a-yonder, there's some of my little friends comin' out now."

Joanna looked around and animals were beginning to appear all over the place. Dogs of all breeds, and no breeds in particular were barking. Curious kittens peeked from the screened porch and cats peered down from lofty perches on the roof. Joanna could see now that the exterior of the grand old house was in a state of disrepair.

"That there's Isabel," the old woman pointed to an aged golden retriever that led the pack in spite of a slight limp. "Some young boys beat 'er with sticks, broke 'er leg. The dog-catcher run 'em off and brought 'er to me. I got a splint on 'er. That leg healed up just a mite crooked. We're both gimpy old ladies, ain't we, Izzy old girl?"

Close on Izzy's heels was the puppy Miss Velvie had rescued. "Here's little Amber, ain't she lookin' better? And growin' up a storm!"

"How many dogs you got? I can't hardly count 'em all."

"They's fourteen of 'em. Folks are always askin' me why I want so many dogs, but they didn't none of 'em have nowhere else to go."

Beaucephus here came from the prison," she indicated a bloodhound. The pendant lips and wrinkled forehead lent a look of perpetual sorrow to his face, but the thick tail wagged with joy. "He was too slow to track and they were gonna put 'im down, but one of the guards snuck 'im out. Made a jailbreak, they did!"

"What about the cats? Looks like they're hidin' everywhere."

"They's twenty-three. That litter of kittens was dropped off at the end of my path."

"I can't tell them two apart," Joanna leaned over to caress two golden tabbies.

"That's why I call 'em Pete and Repeat," the old woman giggled.

"That there's Ishmael," she pointed to the black and white cat that had remained alone on the rooftop. "Named 'im after the outcast in the bible, 'cause the other cats won't have nothin' to do with 'im."

"Here's little Bump-Bump." Joanna gasped in surprise as she looked down at a beige-colored cat. "She was born that-a-way, with no back legs, but it ain't never bothered 'er one bit. You ought'a see 'er out there, hoppin' around with the pet rabbit. She's mighty special, ain't you, dear heart?"

"What in the world?" Looking out behind the barn, Joanna saw a strange animal in the pasture. "That ain't a camel, is it?"

"It sure is. Old Clyde, he stays out there with the goats. We saw 'im at a circus nearabout thirty years ago and they were beatin' on 'im, near starved 'im to death. I got Willie to buy 'im and you never saw a sweeter critter! I even rode 'im a few times. Don't you know that was a sight, Willie on 'is high-strung thoroughbred, with me and Clyde pokin' along behind?"

Joanna smiled at the thought.

As the old woman opened the door, a tiny, cream-colored terrier trotted into the room, standing on her back legs, begging to be picked up. "Hold on, Doo-Dad, let me put my bags down and I'll hold my baby girl."

Joanna looked around the kitchen where wicker baskets and bunches of dried herbs hung from massive wooden beams. Apothecary bottles filled with liquids of all colors sparkled in the sunlight that danced across a shelf over the stone sink. Alongside one wall an old-fashioned Coca-Cola box hummed and a butter churn squatted in a corner.

Miss Velvie led Joanna into the spacious living room, where one entire end wall consisted of a stone fireplace. Gold-leaf horses flew across the old, chipped ivory background and a heavy set of brass horseheads held a row of books.

Joanna's feet sank into the Aubosson carpet, the once vibrant colors now faded and worn. A petite, gray-striped cat reclined on the triple-back settee, the green eyes looking up at the women sleepily. "This is little Abby, my tabby," the old woman picked the cat up. "You're my sweetie-pie, ain't you Abby?"

Over the settee hung a painting of a handsome young couple in a continental filigree silver frame. The woman's light golden hair fell in long, loose waves around the alabaster skin of her face and bare shoulders, cascading downward over a dress of white lace. The handsome young man looked down at her with deep affection.

"Miss Velvie, is that you in this picture?"

"Yes, child, that's me and my Willie."

"You were so beautiful, like a movie star or a fairy princess!"

"Willie used to call me 'is white velvet rose," her eyes took on a faraway look. "My middle name's Rose and he thought that little sayin' was so clever. Oh, how I did love that man, he was so good to me. And the animals he had to put up with! He'd say, 'Now Velvie, I don't want to see that damn dog here when I get home.' And when he'd come in, he'd just shake 'is head and say, 'Well, I see that damn dog's still here,' and go on in the house.

"You want to see the upstairs?"

"Yes ma'am."

"Willie's granddaddy built this house, before the civil war," the old woman chattered as they started up the spiral staircase. She opened the doors to what had once been romantic bedrooms, the walls covered with faded cabbage roses and antique four-poster beds on the scuffed hardwood floors.

"Now here's somethin' really special," she said as they climbed the stairway once again, and it gave on a gigantic room. "This used to be the grand ballroom. Then, Willie got 'im a sideline as undertaker and we used this for the services. Mama would play the piano there, and sing The Old Rugged Cross, I can just about hear her now.

"That old car I drive, that was the last hearse my Willie owned. Seems like it's a special connection between us. And besides," she grinned. "It comes in mighty handy for haulin' my animals in. I couldn't never get 'em all in one of the newfangled economy cars. Now let's have our snack."

Joanna took out Coca-Colas while Miss Velvie put fresh-baked cookies on a plate and carried them to the porch. Kicking off her shoes, the old woman tucked one foot underneath herself and smiled with a faraway look in her eyes. For a moment, Joanna caught a fleeting glimpse of the girl who had lived here with her loving husband.

Joanna bit into her cookie and a flood of warm, sweet sensation filled her mouth. Bits of toasty pecans blended with a fudgy filling, topping a flaky crust. "M-m-m, what is this, Miss Velvie?"

"Chocolate pecan pie bars. And don't let's tell nobody, but they got a tad of bourbon whiskey in 'em," the old woman giggled.

They watched the kittens skitter across the floor, chasing each other and climbing on the chairs. Lavender petunias cascaded down from hanging baskets and zinnias peeked up gaily from planter boxes. Joanna closed her eyes and breathed in their sweet fragrances, listening to the creaking of the old swing. Instantly, she was transported back in time. Back to her childhood, back to her own grandmother's porch and a sharp wave of unexpected nostalgia overwhelmed her. She got up and walked over to a little table that held a wooden box, carved with an ornamental pattern.

"This is beautiful, what is it?"

"Oh, that's my bible box. I like to sit out here and read it, of an evenin'. That little church at the edge of the woods yonder, that was my church.

Papa donated the land and the men built it with their own hands. Oh, we had some good times there! And the singin', why you never heard such in your life!

"Then the young people got to goin' to the fancy church in town, or maybe just quit goin' at all. Anyways, it got to be where it was just us old folks, then they got to dyin' off like flies. For nearabout ten years, it was just me and the preacher. And then, I'll be danged if he didn't pass away. Nowadays I just sit on the porch of a Sunday mornin' and have a little service of my own. The animals gather 'round and I sing a little and pray a little and it's right nice. But I miss goin' to church so much.

"How 'bout you, honey? What church you go to?"

"I used to go when I was little, but...I don't know. I'm not sure I even believe in God."

"Oh, honey! Me and you got to talk! Without the Almighty, we got nothin'. It's Him makes everything possible. Why, everything you see around you, He made it and give it to us! And all the love you've ever felt, you know, from different folks, that comes through Him."

"I don't know, it's just hard for me to believe. A God that loved us wouldn't let bad things happen."

Miss Velvie looked at her. "What kind'a things?"

"Well..... you know. Just bad stuff."

"Somethin' real bad happen to you?"

"Yes ma'am."

"What was it?"

Joanna walked across the porch and picked up a kitten. "I don't know....I...I don't really want to talk about it."

The old woman pulled a can of Tube Rose snuff from her apron pocket and dipped down into it with a blackgum twig, packing a little behind her lower lip. "You want to help me feed up?"

"Yes ma'am." Joanna followed her to the garage where she filled buckets with dog and cat food, then started out to an open shelter. Three sides contained a wide shelf-like area that held cool whip bowls and aluminum pie dishes to feed the cats in. Underneath were containers for the dogs.

"Willie built this for me to feed up. Caught me on the low roof, there over the side porch feedin' the cats and said I'd break my fool neck. What he never knew for a long time was, I'd still sit up there with the cats, it was such a nice secret place and you could look down of folks without 'em knowin'. But one time, I saw somethin' that embarrassed me awful!"

"What was it?"

"Well, the menfolks got to drinkin' and had 'em a contest. Hung a bucket on their tallywhackers and tried to see who could carry the most bricks in it without the bucket fallin' off!"

The old woman started to giggle. "I thought I'd just about die. Tried to shrink myself up and hide. But I did peep back. And guess who won the contest?"

"Who?"

"My Willie!" Miss Velvie threw her head back, clapped her hands together and laughed.

"And nobody knew you saw 'em?"

"Years later, I finally told Willie. He just said since I was watchin', he was mighty glad he was the winner!

"Now I got to do my doctorin'," she declared. Joanna followed her back to the kitchen where she took some leaves from an ancient borax tin and crushed them with a pestle. She mixed in a little water and heated it over a low flame until it had a pasty consistency.

"This is rosemary leaves, it's for Rounder. He's nearabout sixteen and the arthritis plagues 'im. Come on here, boy and let's get you fixed up."

"Gosh, you're just about a veterinarian, you know so much."

"Oh, no. But days should speak and a multitude of years should teach wisdom. That's Job 32: 7-9. Anyhow, you got to be careful with home remedies, some can be highly poisonous."

"Miss Velvie, do you reckon you could sell me some of that stuff you used on that puppy? My friend, Denise, she runs a rescue group for beagles. She's got a dog with skin problems and she's tried everything."

"I'll give you all you can tote. I take sarsaparilla rootstock and boil it, then strain it. It's an old cure Mama Martha taught me."

Joanna took a mason jar filled with the concoction to Denise, but her friend was skeptical. Velvety brown eyes looked up at Joanna over the spectacles that were sitting on her nose as she sat at her kitchen table, doing paperwork. She frowned a little, her milky white skin surrounded by the glossy, black hair that turned under in a simple pageboy style.

"Just give it a try. That puppy didn't hardly have no hair and now she's shiny as a new dime."

Denise agreed to try it and it worked. "I can't hardly believe I found somethin' that helps!" she exclaimed later.

"Ride over there with me to see Miss Velvie later this evenin' and we'll get some more."

"I can't, I've got papers to grade for class tomorrow. Besides, I'm babysittin' for my sister."

"Bring the young'uns with us, they'll have a time over there."

"Well now," the old woman opened the screen door a little later. "Who do we have here?"

"I'm Petey!" the little boy answered as he clambered onto the Coca-Cola box. "And that's Kayla. She's bashful." The little girl peeked out from behind Denise.

"You know, I've got some things around here, that I've been lookin' for a little boy and girl to give 'em to." Miss Velvie left the room for a moment.

"How would you like to have this?" She thrust an old-fashioned bubble-gum machine into Petey's arms.

"That's my favorite!" he shouted.

And this is for you, honey," she handed Kayla a kewpie doll.

They went outside just before twilight, to sit on the porch. Kayla plucked mimosa blooms and pretended they were powder puffs.

"Hey, you young'uns come over here," Miss Velvie bent to pick up a piece of pine straw. "Let's catch us a doodlebug! Y'all know how to do that?"

They shook their heads and gathered close around the old woman, eyes wide with interest. "Here's a doodlebug house, see that little hole there?" They nodded and watched as she carefully lowered the straw into the tiny burrow. "Now you got to blow on it, kind'a easy and make it wiggle." Petey got down on his hands and knees and began to blow for all he was worth, his short blonde curls nearly laying on the ground.

"Now we got to leave it be real still and say a special chant,"

Doodlebug, doodlebug; come out, your house is on fire!

Before they finished the third round, the straw began to wiggle, and quick as a wink, Miss Velvie snatched it up, with the doodlebug clinging tightly to it. The children gasped in amazement, they had seen a mysterious creature charmed right up from the bowels of the earth. They grabbed straws and ran to find their own doodlebug holes.

"Don't y'all hurt 'em now, if you catch one! Be easy with the little fellers."

"They loved that, Miss Velvie," said Denise.

"Oh, well! When we was little, we didn't have all that store-boughten stuff to play with. Had to make up stuff, but you know, I can't imagine havin' had more fun."

They sat on the porch visiting, long after dark, while the children chased fireflies.

"You know," Miss Velvie began. "Papa always said he used to know a man that crossed 'is bees with lightenin' bugs."

"Do what?" Joanna asked.

"That way they could see to work at night," Miss Velvie giggled. "And he made a double crop of honey!"

When Kayla grew tired, she climbed up to be rocked, along with the calico kitten and fuzzy puppy the old woman was holding. Miss Velvie began to croon.

Go to sleep, my little pickaninny
Brother Fox will catch 'im if he don't
Slumber on the bosom of old Mammy Jenny
Mammy's gonna switch 'im if he don't
Hush-a-hush-a-hush-a lu-lu-lu-lu
Underneath the silver southern moon
Hush-a-bye, rock-a-bye, Mammy's little baby
Mammy's little Carolina coon

"What's a pickaninny?" Petey wanted to know.

"Well, actually, it's a little colored child," the old woman answered. "I remember, Mammy Jenny that used to help us, she sang that song to all the children around. It didn't matter to 'er whether they were black or white. When Willie was gone off in service, I'd get to cryin' on 'er shoulder, she'd even sing it to me, a grown woman." She smiled at the memory. "Always teased me 'bout my blonde hair and called me 'er vanilla pickaninny."

Joanna was transported, once again, back to her own childhood, to her grandmother's porch, remembering happy times of days gone by. Miss Velvie was indeed, pure unadulterated magic, a breath of fresh air in their lives, a link with the past.

"Just remember," the old woman smiled down at the three sleeping forms that lay in her lap. "Always watch over the young'uns and the animals."

TOO HOT TO HANDLE

"It is better to be alone than to wish you were."
—Unknown

"Miss Velvie, would you ride with me over to Denise's house?" Joanna asked. "One of the dogs they rescued is sick and the vet can't find out what's wrong, throws up all the time. I bet you could help 'im."

The old woman agreed and Joanna picked her up the next day. She was standing on the porch, patent-leather purse hanging from the crook in her arm and a canning jar in her hand.

"The boys are cookin' a brunswick stew over at our friend, Stumpy's," Joanna said. "Let's stop by there and get us a bite to eat."

"You ladies get down and come on in here," Stumpy called as Joanna and Miss Velvie stepped out of the truck later. The cool shade of the lean-to shelter felt good as Joanna's bare feet worked throught the perfectly raked sand.

Stumpy was sitting in a ladder-back chair under the shelter of his old breezeway house. As usual, a wide grin stretched across the ruddy, moon-faced features, dimpling the pudgy cheeks. The short, stocky legs barely reached the ground as the heavy brogans tipped the chair back. An old redbone coonhound lay by his feet as he gazed out across the pasture at his little herd of ponies. Joanna often thought Stumpy bore an amazing resemblance to his shetlands, with his short, stocky build and chestnut colored hair.

A man was on the back porch, bending over and the women could tell he was concentrating on doing something. Then they heard a high-pitched peeping.

"What's that you got there, Haywood?" Joanna called.

"Oh, it's a little baby duck," the salt and pepper haired man looked around. "Got stepped on, leg's broke."

"I got some finger splints in my truck, where I broke my finger a while back," Joanna said. "I bet they'd fit perfect, I'll get us one."

They got the splint on and the duckling was able to stand. They watched for a few moments as he hobbled around, picking at grain the ponies had scattered.

"Now if we could just make it waterproof," Joanna mused. "He could get out there in the pond and go on about 'is business."

"Get my pocketbook out of the truck, honey," Miss Velvie said.

Joanna brought the old woman her purse and she rummaged around in it for a moment, then pulled out a tube of poly-grip.

"I don't think this here duck's got no false teeth, ma'am," Stumpy said.

The old woman carefully squeezed the ointment from the tube and smoothed it around the duck's leg. "We're gonna fix it so this little feller can go swimmin'."

She held the duckling while the poly-grip dried, then handed him to Joanna. "Go stick 'im in the pond and let's see what happens."

Joanna lowered him gently to the water and they watched him swim for awhile. Then Stumpy came down to the pond with a handfull of corn and called, "Here Duck! Duck! The big, white ducks waddled up into the yard, while the wild mallards hung back shyly, their dark green heads skimming above the water like velvet globes.

Joanna scooped the injured duckling up and inspected the splint.

"Dry as a bone! You're a genius, Miss Velvie!"

"P'shaw," the old woman smiled. "That's just makin' do with what you got."

"Jo, there's some of those little chocolate Yoo-Hoo drinks in the 'fridgerator," Stumpy said. "Get one for you and Miss Velvie, the stew's almost ready."

Joanna brought the old woman a drink, then settled her petite form into an old metal glider. The coon dog jumped up beside her. The heavy red head felt warm in her lap as he stretched out to let her scratch him.

Suddenly, a bright red Dodge Ram truck swung into the driveway and they heard Johnny-Vern Bradley whoop into the evening. He sauntered over, nursing a plastic cup filled with Jack Daniels.

"What's that there dog's name, Stumpy?" Johnny-Vern asked.

"That's old Lick-ems," Stumpy answered. "When he was young, he sure could lay a whippin' on a coon."

"I'd like to be a coonhound, if I could lay up in a purty lady's lap like that, and get my belly scratched," Johnny-Vern yelled as he stretched one wiry leg up to prop on the cement steps.

Joanna looked up at him, her pretty face lighting up in a grin as the sunshine picked up the soft highlights in her long, auburn hair, violet eyes sparkling. "Well, Vern. There's a lot of women around here that say you're a dog!"

Haywood placed a pan of corn on the table. Stumpy grabbed an ear and tore into it.

"Hey!" Randy shouted. "You got the missed-meal colic?"

Stumpy just looked up and grinned, kernels of corn clinging to his face.

Haywood's wife, Viola pulled up in a white Buick. "One of you boys come tote this pot of baked beans; it's heavy."

Johnny-Vern and several others jumped up and nearly ran each other over getting to the car. And it wasn't the beans they were interested in, but Viola's friend. Tall and willowy, shapely, tan legs stretched beneath tight shorts and short, blonde hair curled softly around the delicately sculptured face.

"Molly, this is Stumpy, said Viola.

The blonde woman extended a well-manicured hand and Stumpy shook it, as he stammered, "It's right nice to m-meet you ma'am."

"Well Viola, you didn't tell me he was such a cutie pie!" Molly said, as Stumpy blushed.

Later that afternoon, Denise took Joanna and Miss Velvie down to a row of pens behind her house. "Here's Barney," Denise pointed to a scruffy beagle that was hurling himself against the gate in excitement.

"Well hey there, old feller, let's see if we can get you fixed up a little bit," the old woman pulled a syringe from her purse, measured some of the potion from the jar and squirted it into the dog's mouth.

"What's that?" Denise asked.

"Slippery elm, a concoction we used to make for upset stomachs."

Sure enough, the medicine worked and the vomiting stopped. Soon, Miss Velvie was going over to help Denise on a regular basis. "Come on and give me a little sugar," she would urge as Petey and Kayla ran into her open arms, smothering her with hugs and kisses.

Joanna began to see a red corvette sitting in Stumpys yard. A caption was painted down the side in curlicued letters, outlined with gold paint:

TOO HOT TO HANDLE!

"Belongs to that gal, Molly," Randy explained. "I believe old Stumpy's in love."

Molly came in one Saturday afternoon while the men were there.
"Stumpy, this bunch of drunks has got to go!" she stomped across the yard.
Stumpy's mouth dropped open. "Honey, y-you oughn't to talk like that."
"I mean now," she retorted.
"Boys, I'm sorry, but I reckon y'all better go," Stumpy said.

Joanna and Randy pulled into Stumpy's driveway one afternoon, where several pickups were parked.
"That Molly, she's mean as a junkyard dog," declared Haywood. "I'm right sorry Viloa brought 'er over here."
"Hey, y'all know why Stumpy's smarter when he's havin' sex with Molly?" Johnny-Vern howled. "It's 'cause he's pluggd in to a know-it-all!"

Joanna and Miss Velvie were on the way to help Denise when the wind picked up and the sky turned dark. Just as they pulled in and hurried to the house, the rain began to patter down.
"Granny Velvie!" Petey called as he came running to the door. "We're gonna help Aunt Neecie walk the dogs. You want to help us?"
The storm only lasted a few minutes and they went out to the kennels. Petey was stomping in a mudpuddle when Miss Velvie said, "Well, look-a-yonder!"
They turned and looked up to where she was pointing in the sky.
"A rainbow," she said. "You know, this place here is nearabout like Noah's ark, with all these animals."
"What's that?" Petey wanted to know.
"Back in the old days of the Bible, God told a man named Noah to build this great, big old boat, big enough for two of every animal in the world. Then he sent a flood, rained for forty days. Washed away everybody but Noah and 'is family. And the animals, of course. And when it stopped, there was a beautiful rainbow in the sky. Y'all know what it meant?"

"What?" asked Kayla.

"It was God's promise, that everything would be okay. I do set my bow in the clouds, and it shall be a covenant between me and the earth. That's Genesis 9:13."

The men were cooking hamburgers on the grill that Sunday afternoon when the red sports car pulled in at Stumpy's. Molly got out and glared coldly at the men when they greeted her.

"That's my grill and I'm takin' it home right now!" she declared. Looking around wildly, she spied a heavy towel, wrapped it around the grill handles and thrust it into her hatchback, spilling a couple of the burgers. Leaving the trunk open, she got into the car and pulled off. The men stood watching as she drove swiftly down the highway and turned onto the interstate, with white smoke trailing out behind the car.

"Ya-Hoo! Too Hot to Handle!" Johnny-Vern bellowed. "She sure did put the right name on that car."

Stumpy just continued to play cards, never speaking one work about the incident, just trying to smile a little at all the teasing.

The corvette continued to sit in the driveway and the men steered clear for awhile. When they saw Stumpy down at Homer's store, he didn't have much to say. He would get his moon pie and a Coca-Cola, but he never stayed to settle down around the old wood stove and visit.

He came in one Saturday morning, got his snack and turned to leave. Johnny-Vern called, "Hey Stump! Me and Randy was just gettin' some ribs to cook. Let's do it at your house."

"I dunno boys. How 'bout lemme take a rain check?"

"Oh, come on, man! We'll leave a'fore she gets there, we won't get you in no trouble."

Stumpy finally gave in and in less than an hour, they had the ribs sizzling over the charcoal. As the day wore on, more of the men stopped in. By the time the food was ready, Stumpy was well on the way to being inebriated.

Haywood drove up with Macey, his Golden Retriever standing on the toolbox. She jumped down and ran over to sniff Lick-ems, they were old friends.

"What's that place on Macey's ear?" Randy asked, looking at the angry, raw ulcer.

"Danged if I know," Haywood answered.

"Looks like some sort of fungal infection," Randy mused.

"Hey! I got somethin' in the house there, y'all can use on it," Stumpy declared. He got up and returned in a few minutes with a tube of monistat cream.

"Hey, that's some kind'a female medicine, you ain't puttin' that on my dog!"

"Oh, just relax. It's for yeast, and that ain't really nothin' but a fungus. It's bound to work. Just don't y'all tell Molly, 'cause it's hers!"

Stumpy forgot the time, and before he realized it, the red corvette was pulling into the driveway.

"Oh, Lordy," he began to sober up quickly. "I'm sorry boys, but y'all better go."

"Don't pay her no never mind," urged Johnny-Vern. "It's your house, not her'n."

Molly got out and stomped over to the shelter, eyes glaring wildly. "Thought I told you there wasn't gonna be no more parties 'round here! Get these drunks out'ta here right now, Stumpy!"

"Now hold on honey" he replied. "They ain't doin' no harm."

Then Molly saw the half-used tube of Monistat cream, lying among the leftovers on the picnic table. "Just what the hell's been goin' on around here?" she wanted to know. "Y'all had a woman over here while I was gone, didn't you?"

"Ain't been no women here, I swear! We were just usin' it on Haywood's dog."

"Yeah, she prob'ly looked like a dog. I can just imagine!"

"We'll be seein' you, Stump," Haywood called, as most of the men got up and hurried towards their trucks. Soon, only Randy and Johnny-Vern remained, waiting to see what would happen next. Molly had gone into the house.

Suddenly, the back door flew open, and she was standing on the back porch with a broom in her hand. "Get 'em out'ta here, all of 'em, right now!" she shrieked. Lick-ems jumped up and started off the porch with his tail between his legs, but he was almost fifteen years old, and he didn't move fast enough. Molly brought down the broom with all the force she could muster, and the old hound cried out in pain. He ran over to Stumpy with blood oozing from his mouth. Stumpy bent over to examine the dog and when he straightened up, there was something no one had ever seen in those benevoloont blue eyes before...pure rage.

"That's it, lady!" he said through clenched teeth. "Hit the road, and don't you never even think about comin' back 'round here."

"I ain't goin' nowhere," she began, but he cut her short.

"I mean it. Get out. Right now. I ain't never hit no woman before. Leastways, not yet." With that he brushed past her and in a few seconds, kitchen goods began to fly out the door; pots and pans, plates, a coffee maker. Then everything went quiet for a few moments. Suddenly, clothes began to fly out the door. Then, came a handmade afghan and a picture of Molly. The solid brass frame shattered on impact.

Molly stood watching, speechless.

Randy and Johnny-Vern sat at the picnic table, snickering under their breath.

Finally, the storm ceased and Stumpy appeared on the porch.

"Go on, get you stuff and get! And if you ever set foot back in this yard, I'm callin' the law."

"But I can't get all this stuff in my car," Molly whined. "I'm really sorry, and I won't say anything about your little get togethers from now on."

Stumpy looked at her coldly. "Get!" he repeated.

"But my stuff..."

"Get what you can. The rest of it'll be piled by the road. You can rent a U-Haul, or whatever, but I'm gonna tell you one more time, don't you ever come back on this property."

Locking the door behind him, Stumpy called Lick-ems.

"I called Doc Cooper when I went in, and he's meetin' me at 'is office. You best be gone when I get back." Putting the old hound into his truck, he drove away.

Lick-ems had a dislocated jaw, and was placed on soft food and pain medication. True to his word, when they got home that night, Stumpy piled Molly's belongings by the roadside and she came to get them the next day while he was working. It had rained during the night, and what wasn't ruined was a soggy mess.

When Joanna told Miss Velvie what had happened, she shrugged and said, "Well, I'm mighty sorry it happened, but it's better to dwell in the corner of a housetop, than with a brawling woman in a wide house. That's Proverbs 21:9."

Now, once again, Stumpy's house was a place of friendship and camaraderie. Unless it was planting time or harvest season, there were always a few extra vehicles in his yard on weekends. A leisurely game of setback was going on one Saturday afternoon when Haywood remarked, "You know boys, it's mighty peaceful around here." He looked down at Lick-ems, lying between Stumpy's feet. "I reckon dogs are better'n women sometimes. They like for your friends to come see you."

"Hey! Y'all know the two best things about dogs?" Johnny-Vern howled. "They don't get upset when you call 'em by another dog's name, and they just love heavy pettin' in public."

Now, the broad smile was back on the round face and the blue eyes twinkled with quiet good humor. No matter how much he was questioned and teased, Stumpy only addressed the matter once. "The look of the puddin' ain't always the taste."

MOSES

"Love is the river of life in the world."
—Henry Ward Beecher

Joanna and Miss Velvie gathered herbs from the riverbank while the boys splashed around in the icy shoals at the bottom of the boat ramp. Suddenly, they heard the rumble of fourwheelers. One by one, they appeared over the crest of the hill...the Reckless Rebels. One big red Honda never slowed down, but splashed into the water, sending up huge waves. A black and white Border Collie sailed off the back and jumped around gleefully in the water.

"Wildman!" exclaimed Randy. "I didn't know y'all was ridin' today."

"Shucks, we rode all night, man. Ain't never been to bed yet."

"Wildman, you ought'a be more careful with Wrangler, there," Joanna admonished as the fourwheeler floated a little ways downstream. "He's gonna get hurt on that thing one of these days!"

The handsome, russet-haired young man looked up at her from where he sat, neck deep in muddy water and grinned, ruddy cheeks aglow with good humor. "Aw, he loves it. If I made 'im stay home, he'd pine his'self to death."

A pretty young woman drove up, her long brown hair flying out behind her. A heart shaped face framed dark sloe eyes, which gave her a slightly oriental look. The petite, but full shaped body was dressed in a light denim jacket and tight fitting faded jeans. She wore a pair of crimson snakeskin boots, and looked as if she belonged on the cover of Vogue magazine.

"Hey Wildman, who's that doll baby?" Johnny-Vern asked.

"That's Candice McClain. She's Tansey's cousin from Raleigh."

"Man, she's purty as puddin' pie, ain't she?" asked Johnny-Vern.

"She's a real, live city girl, with manners," Wildman declared. "Not like that hooligan cousin of 'ers. But she's doin' right good drivin' that fourwheeler."

Johnny-Vern stood up, dirty water trickling off his skinny body, bald spot gleaming in the hot sunlight and walked up to the bank. "Hey baby! You know why I'm like milk? 'Cause I'll do your body good!"

"I don't think so," the pretty girl answered, as she looked at him disdainfully.

"Tell 'im girl!" screeched Tansey Moody as she drove up alongside her cousin. She wore plain wranglers, scuffed brown boots and a tee shirt with a barrel racing emblem. Her strawberry blonde hair was pulled back into a casual ponytail with tufts straggling loose here and there. Freckles marched across the mischievous face and the little pug nose turned up as she whooped.

Whooo-eeeeee!
Don't worry about the mule goin' blind
Just lean on back and hold the line!

"Hey, Tansey," Johnny-Vern yelled. "Why can't you act like your cousin here?"

"Johnny-Vernon Bradley!" she retorted. "You know you and that beer bottle you're holdin' are a lot alike. Both empty from the neck up!"

"Y'all stay and eat with us," Randy said, as Tansey splashed water on Johnny-Vern. "We're gonna run up to Homer's store and get some chickens."

Everyone wanted to stay, so Randy and Nollie dried off and headed for the store, while Haywood got the big grill going. A black-capped chickadee perched on a cattail at the edge of the woods, singing in a high wavering call; "drink-your-tee, drink-your-teeee!" Brightly painted gourds hung from poles and a purple martin soared down from one, gorging himself on a gigantic mosquito. Squirrels scampered back and forth at the edge of the forest, gnawing on bright yellow cobs of corn that were skewered onto ten-penny nails high on the tree trunks.

The men were back in short order with the chickens and the aroma drifted tantalizingly through the air. Wrangler had tired of playing in the water and was lying in the cool shade of the big oak trees that surrounded the shelter.

"Y'all boys look in the cooler there and get you a Natural Light," said Randy. "We got a'plenty and they're good and cold."

"Ain't you got no Budweisers?" asked Wildman. "Them Naturals are just too weak for a real man."

"You're too picky," laughed Johnny-Vern. "Don't never thump no free watermelons, boy!"

"Hey, y'all come on and let's take a little spin while the food's cookin'," yelled Dallas. "Randy, you and Jo can take my fourwheeler and I'll ride with Nathan."

"You want to?" Randy asked Joanna.

"I'm not gonna leave Miss Velvie."

"P'shaw!" the old woman said. "Go ahead honey. I'll help Haywood with the cookin'."

"Hey, I wanna go!" yelled Johnny-Vern. "How 'bout lettin' me ride with you, Miss Candy Cane?" Hey went up and put an arm around Candice.

"Don't put your hands on me, please!" was the response he received. "And it's 'Candice McClain', not Candy Cane!"

"Aw now, come on and be nice. I figgered you' be sweeter than your cousin. I went to the clinic last week for a tetanus and she jabbed that needle in hard as she could. She's one sadistic nurse!"

"Hey, Vern," yelped Tansey. "You know why dogs are better'n men? 'Cause the worst social disease you can catch from 'em is fleas. More'n I can say for you!"

Tansey looked at Nollie. "You wanna ride with me, Mr. Nollie? You're 'bout the only man in this here crowd that acts like he's got a lick of sense."

"I don't know, Tansey," Nollie answered with a pronounced English accent. "They say you drive that machine like a wildwoman. I'm mighty old to be bouncing around on that thing."

"I'll look after you, Mr. Nollie. We'll go 'long easy."

"Promise?"

"Cross my heart and suck my gizzard
Cut my hair with 'lectric scissors!"

"Come on, Vern. You can ride with me," called Shelton.

"You're too ugly," came the reply. "But I might as well, looks like you're the best offer I got. Whoo-ee! Pee on the fire, call the dogs, and let's go!" He climbed on and they were off with a great deal of rumbling and blasting of motors and barking dogs, Wildman and Wrangler in the lead

Tansey did a wheelstand, nearly unseating Nollie. The fine, pale hair that he usually wore smoothed across his forehead whipped back in the wind and his eyes grew large as he grabbed her around the waist and hung on for dear life.

They took a path through the woods and fell into single file, slowing down to dodge pine limbs and thorn bushes. Finally, they came out into a huge, open field. "Let's go down to the Honey Hole!" yelled Dallas.

"What's a Honey Hole?" Candice wanted to know.

"It's a clearin', way back yonder in the woods," answered Johnny-Vern.

The engines revved up and they were off again, fanning out to drive through the field, kicking up dust until the riders could hardly see each other. Upon reaching the far side of the field, they started back into the wetlands and it soon became damp and swampy. Green sprigs of fern cropped up here and there among the dead leaves scattered beneath the tangle of scrubby pines and underbrush. As the path narrowed into a tunnel-like trail, they had to ride single file again, until they came out into a small, grassy meadow. A small herd of deer leapt through the air and dissappeared into the woods. "What beautiful place!" exclaimed Candice. "You're all are so lucky, living here in a place like this. Some of those people up there in Raleigh would give anything to be here."

Joanna looked around, seeing the familiar territory through new eyes. The ground sloped away gently and bright green grass covered the bowl-shaped swell of the valley. Wrangler was running through the purple allysum that floated over the entire surface of the dell like lavender fog, stopping now and then to wallow among them. A magnificent sycamore tree reached upwards with gnarled and twisted branches. In it's deep shade, olive green moss pushed it's way up through the rich ebony soil, and the thin-edged smell of dirt mingled with the soft fragrance of grassland and wildflowers. Joanna drew in a great lungfull of the sweet air, savoring nature's perfume.

Nollie reached down with a soft, plump hand to pick a long, leafy spike of bell-shaped pink blooms. "You ladies know what this flower is?" he asked as he offered the delicate plant to Candice, his slate-gray eyes smiling up at her.

"That's foxglove, ain't it?" responded Tansey. "Like they make digitalis from?"

"That's correct, but do you know where it gets it's name?" Tansey shook her head.

"Evil fairies created them for foxes to wear on their paws, enabling them to sneak up quietly on their prey!"

"Nollie was a professor of folklore over in England," Tansey explained as she put an arm around his shoulder. "That's how he knows all that stuff. Not to mention why he talks so funny!"

Wildman broke in. "Let's get on back down to the river, them chickens are prob'ly done by now."

Denise was sitting with Miss Velvie when they got back. "Randy, do you know anyone that would sell us some land real cheap?" she asked. "The volunteers down at the Beagle Brigade have finally raised enough money to put up some more kennels, but my place is really too small. We need more room."

"Well honey," Miss Velvie piped up. "I've got all that land. I'll give y'all a piece of it."

"We'll be glad to pay you."

"P'shaw! Y'all keep that money and use it for them animals. For food and vet bills and such."

"That sure will help," Denise said. "There's only a few of us. We'd like to hook up with a big group, you know like the ASPCA or a humane society, but the closest ones are in Raleigh."

They were just sitting down to eat when a battered old Thunderbird came down the hill. A grizzled, slovenly looking man was driving and a heavyset woman sat beside him, her gray hair hanging down in lanky, greasy strands around her beefy shoulders. They slowed a little as Randy waved and the man nodded his head. They drove down to the boat ramp and the man got out, carrying something that looked like a burlap bag.

"Who's that feller?" asked Haywood.

But no one knew who they were and everyone was concentrating on their plate, piled high with steaming food. They were digging in when Candice yelled from the riverbank, "What are you doing? What's in there, it's moving!"

The old Thunderbird was backing slowly up the ramp. As Joanna watched the car turn and speed away, she could see Candice in the water, trying desperately to reach a brown object that was floating downstream in the swift current, but it was getting farther away. Now it floated into a turbulent patch out beyond the craggy rocks that divided the water as it rushed around them in the never ending effort of descent. It caught in a whirlpool and disappeared from sight, to resurface a few yards down.

"Help me!" she screamed as everyone ran up. "There's puppies or something in that bag! Something alive! I can't get them!"

Wildman dove into the muddy waters and came up several yards out, cutting through the water with clean breast strokes. As the others watched breathlessly, he gained on the object, slowly but surely. At last he grabbed it and began to fight his way to shore, but the current was too swift to come back against it.

"Hold on, Wildman! We'll get you," yelled Haywood, as he began to maneuver his boat down the ramp and the other men rushed to help him. In a matter of seconds, the boat was launched and they were off. As the boat pulled alongside him, Wildman handed up the bag and grabbed the side of the boat to haul himself in. As they pulled back up to the ramp, Wildman was struggling to open the bag.

"Kittens!" he exclaimed as he peered into its depths. "I was out there, riskin' life and limb for a bunch of cats! I don't believe it," he said in disgust.

"Let me have them," said Candice as she grabbed the sack. "Three of them. But it looks like it's too late. They're dead already."

Joanna lifted one of the bedraggled little bundles, a black kitten with white feet. She massaged the tiny chest, stopping every few moments to cup her hand around the little face and blow, hoping to get some air into the lungs. But it was no use. The tiny form lay still, muddy water from the river dripping onto her lap. "Roanoke River water," she muttered. "The River of Death. The Indians sure named it right."

Try this one and see if it'll do any good," begged Candice, as she handed Joanna a gray tabby.

"Let me see 'im, honey." It was Miss Velvie. She looked up at one of the girls, who was still holding her drink, along with a drinking straw, still in it's paper wrapper. "Gim'me that straw!" she demanded, and carefully inserted the tip into the tiny mouth. Fifteen chest compressions and two quick breaths, just like cardiopulmonary resuscitation on people."

"You're just wastin' your time," said Wildman. "You can get a cat most anywhere if you want one, they're all over the place."

Candice's eyes met the old woman's and she continued doggedly. But as she kept working, Joanna began to think how right he was. Then, just as the old woman stopped, Joanna thought she saw a tiny movement, a spark of life. She looked down and sure enough, the little chest was moving, ever so slightly, in and out, in and out. A miracle, no matter how small, was taking place before their eyes and they were restoring a life which had been snuffed out too quickly.

"I think he's alive!" Joanna cried, just as the little mouth opened and water surged out onto Miss Velvie's palm. The kitten began to cough and opened his eyes. Precious little blue eyes, oh, they were so sweet!

"Gve 'er the other one and let 'er try again," Joanna said. The old woman gently placed the straw inside the little mouth and gave a couple of quick breaths, stopping to massage the chest. She worked and worked, but to no avail. Finally, she stopped and asked for the third kitten. Again, she labored over him with no results.

"Poor little things, it just seems such a shame. They never had a chance to grow up or play or anything, it's so sad," said Candice as she cuddled the one kitten that had come back to them. They carried him up to Randy's cabin and dried him off with a dishtowel. In no time at all, he was sitting up shakily, trying to balance himself, and began to meow pitifully.

"He don't look no more'n a couple of weeks old," Miss Velvie mused. "Surely they ain't old enough to be weaned yet. Haywood, y'all got any canned milk 'round here?"

"Yes ma'am, here's some right here," he pulled a can of Pet milk from the cabinet. "Even says it's for pets!" he laughed.

"How 'bought Karo syrup? You got any of that?"

"You know we got that, it's the secret ingredient in Johnny-Vern's barbecue sauce."

"Let's see, how can we get it in 'im?" the old woman wondered. "We need one of those tiny little nursin' bottles."

"How 'bout a syringe?" asked Haywood. "Nollie keeps some in 'is truck to take 'is insulin. He's diabetic, you know."

"Get us one, Nollie, and we'll give it a try," Miss Velvie answered as she mixed the milk and sat it on the stove to warm. Candice held the kitten on her lap and the other girls crowded around her, staring raptly at the bedraggled little creature. Joanna drew up warm milk in the syringe and carefully put a few drops onto the little pink tongue. Before long, the kitten was lapping up the milk hungrily.

"The Karo syrup's supposed to give 'em quick energy, from all the sugar that's in it. They make milk supplements, but this'll do in a pinch. And it's a whole lot cheaper."

Miss Velvie looked down at the kitten. "She named him Moses, sayin' I drew him out of the water. That's Exodus 2:8. That would make a good name for this little feller too, don't y'all think?"

"How about that, little guy?" asked Candice as she stroked the damp fur. "That would make a good name for you, let's call you Moses." The kitten looked up at her and mewed loudly in agreement.

Moses grew rapidly, bursting with health and vigor. He always came with Candice when she visited Tansey. His muscles rippled beneath the gleaming coat as he would walk across the room, looking disdainfully at the other animals. Other cats avoided him and more than one dog yelped and backed away when the sharp claws raked their tender noses.

"That cat's spoiled rotten!" exclaimed Tansey. "Get's his way 'bout everything. Eats out of a bona-fide crystal dish and got a little dollbaby bed with a lace canopy where he sleeps in the daytime. Shucks, when I go somewhere with Candice, she makes me ride in the back seat so's Moses can sit up front and feel the air conditioning better! Old Moses will just be chillin' and Candice leaves me sittin' back there by myself. Acts like 'er cheese done slid off 'er cracker!"

"Well, he deserves to be spoiled a little after all he's been through," her cousin defended herself.

"Yeah, Candice has got a boyfriend, one of them fancified city boys," Tansey said. But since that little cat come along, he has'ta get 'is own supper and fend for hisself. When it comes to old Moses, that feller sucks hind tit!"

NOW, AND BACK THEN

"To keep the heart unwrinkled, to be hopeful, kindly, cheerful, reverant; that is to triumph over old age."
—Thomas B. Aldrich

Miss Velvie stood in her yard, watching with Joanna and Denise as Randy pushed a tree over with the bulldozer. Behind him, Tansey maneuvered a small tractor, leveling the land until it was smooth as a dinner plate.

The contractor should be here early in the mornin'," said Denise. "He said once he gets the foundation laid, it should only take a few weeks to get the whole buildin' finished."

"Randy says him and the boys can put the fence up," Joanna said.

"We never could have put up a little buildin' like this without your help, Miss Velvie," Denise said. "Gettin' the land free left us enough money to do it. We're gonna start takin' in all breeds now and some of the girls are fosterin' cats they've rescued."

"You know, I've got some cedar posts out behind the barn," Miss Velvie offered. "And there's a big pile of wire. Might be we'd have enough to do the whole fence."

"I want to bring some of the dogs as soon as I can," said Denise.

In less than a month, the small building was completed. The girls hauled animals in until every dog run and every cat cage was occupied.

"Oh!" Tansey exclaimed after they had the animals settled in. "I almost forgot. I got us a sign made up." Going out to her truck, she returned with a large sign to hang over the door. BEAGLE BRIGADE AND SMALL ANIMAL RESCUE it declared in bold letters.

"Now it's official!" Denise said and they all let out a cheer.

"Miss Velvie, why don't you and Jo come to church with me this Sunday?" Denise asked. "The way Jo can sing, I been after her forever to join the choir."

"I might just do that, child. It would be so good to be in a church full of folks again. Let's us do it!" she looked at Joanna. "Let's go this Sunday!"

"I don't know," Joanna hesitated. "You know how I feel about church and all."

"Oh, honey!" Miss Velvie exclaimed. "How am I gonna get through to you?"

"I don't know," Joanna mumbled.

"Forsake me not, O God, in mine old age, when I am grayheaded, until I have showed thy strength to this generation."

Joanna couldn't refuse the old woman. When she went to pick her up, Miss Velvie was dressed in her finest white suit, made of velvet material, and a matching, veiled hat strewn with delicate roses. A gold and pearl stickpin adorned the front of the suit, twisted roping surrounding a rose of the most delicate shade of pink. "Why Miss Velvie, you look beautiful!" Joanna exclaimed as the old woman slid into the truck and smiled at her shyly.

"It's been a mighty long time since I dressed up like this," the old woman admitted. "This was Willie's favorite outfit. When he first bought it for me, way back yonder at the Sears and Roebuck, he give me this pin to go with it. Said it was just perfect for 'is white velvet rose."

They were a few minutes late and services had already begun. "Now, where's the amen corner?" Miss Velvie asked. "That's where I like to sit." The younger woman didn't know what she was talking about and headed for for a seat near the back, but Miss Velvie had other ideas. "Come on, let's get up to the front. Ain't hardly nobody up there. I don't know why everybody wants to sit way back here." So Joanna followed her to the front, where she settled down happily. She waved at Denise, who was sitting in the choir.

The minister nodded and smiled at them as he continued services. Whenever the old woman agreed with something, she'd shout out, "Amen!" or "Hallelujah, brother! Tell it all!" Joanna could feel the amused eyes of the reserved congregation on them, the Methodist church had never had anyone this outspoken before.

When the minister finished reading over the sick list on the bulletin, he asked, "Now, is there anyone else we should add to our prayer list that I'm not aware of?" Miss Velvie stood and said in a loud voice, "Preacher, I'd like to ask prayer for Victor Newman."

"Who?" the minister asked.

"You know, Victor Newman, on the Young and Restless. He's down with heart trouble, in fact they don't know if he's gonna make it or not. But, you know sometimes prayer works miracles, so we need to remember 'im."

Joanna thought she heard the familiar grinding of teeth mixed in with a few stifled giggles behind them, and looked over her shoulder. Sure enough, there, two rows behind them, sat Hilda and Agnes. As the sermon progressed, she remembered different remarks she'd heard the old woman make. She thought things on television were real!

With the exception of Hilda, everyone welcomed the women and were gracious to Miss Velvie, never mentioning the incident. "Please come back and worship with us again, we were so glad to have you," they were told over and over, as they stood outside the pew, visiting. Joanna overheard Hilda whisper to Agnes, "That old woman's plumb crazy, they ought'a do somethin' with 'er." Joanna shot her a hard look and Hilda slunk down the aisle to go out the side door, while everyone else waited in line to greet the minister.

"You know, they're some mighty nice folks, but they sure do worship right quiet," Miss Velvie said as she got into Joanna's truck. "I didn't hear not one person scotch the preacher! Why, a body could fall asleep in there."

"Miss Velvie," Joanna didn't quite know how to approach the subject. "Don't you realize that Victor Newman's not a real person, it's just a television show?"

"Oh no, honey! He's real, all right. They can't put nothin' on there ain't true, they'd get sued! Just like in the newspapers and magazines and all."

"No ma'am. It's playactin', like in the tall tales of the old days."

"Well, I don't think so. You can make up stories and tell 'em 'round home and friends and all, but if you put it on television, that's different. You talk to a lawyer, he'll tell you."

Joanna gave up and listened to her chatter on for a few minutes about the complications of Victor's life. "That Nicky is one lucky woman, to have a man like him, I think he's just the bee's knees. You know she used to be a stripper, before she married 'im. 'Course some called 'er a floozie, but she weren't a bad girl, just high-strung and full of life. But I tell you one thing," she grinned. "If I was a good many years younger and could get out there to Hollywood, she'd have some competetion on 'er hands. That Victor is some kind of fine! I've had a secret crush on 'im for a long time."

"Miss Velvie! I do declare, I'm surprised at you, thinkin' about a married man," Joanna teased.

When they got back to the old woman's house, Joanna noticed her television set. It was an old black and white floor model zenith, perhaps thirty years old. "Do you watch your show every day, Miss Velvie?"

"Oh yes, I wouldn't miss it for the world! That's why I like to be home every day at lunchtime." Now Joanna recalled various times when the old woman would turn down invitations to go somewhere in the middle of the day. A plan began to form in her mind.

"Look, Miss Velvie's got a birthday comin' up soon," Joanna confided to Tansey. Let's all of us get together and buy 'er a VCR, so she can tape her soap operas."

"What a good idea!" Tansey agreed, laughing a little when Joanna told her how Miss Velvie took everything on the shows for the gospel. "Let's throw 'er a surprise birthday party."

Everyone except Hilda wanted to help. "If y'all really want to do somethin' for that old woman, you ought'a put 'er in a nursin' home!" she exclaimed. "She's crazy!"

"Hey Neecie! Where are you?" Joanna called one evening as she entered the rescue.

"Back here," came the answer.

Joanna followed the sound of her voice towards the dog runs.

"Can you help me give some medicines?" Denise asked.

"Sure, just show me what to do."

The women tried to talk while they worked, but the noise made it nearly impossible. Denise had to shout out directions as they gave immunizations and wrote down dates.

"Oh, look!" exclaimed Joanna as they came to a run with a shaggy white dog. The white was splotched with irregular brown markings, and a dark line extended from the corner of one eye like Elizabeth Taylor's heavy eyeliner, giving her a delicate look. Beside her lay a tiny, white ball of fluff.

"That's Dixie," said Denise. "A lady found 'er out on the highway. She's the sweetest dog you ever saw."

"She just had one puppy?"

"No, there were four, but the others died. Doc couldn't figure out what was wrong. She's got plenty of milk. Maybe bein' out, lost and starvin' like she was had somethin' to do with it. I got to give this one an antibiotic."

Joanna's face clouded over for a moment. She cradled the tiny figure gently as Densie administered the injection, then placed a tender kiss on top of the fuzzy head. Placing him back on the blanket, she gave the anxious mother a reassuring pat. "We're not hurtin' your baby, girl. We're just tryin' to help 'im."

When Joanna arrived on the following Saturday, Denise asked her to start walking the dogs while she helped some people with an adoption. After they had gone, Denise put a leash on Rufus, a deerhound mix and went to join her.

"When I looked in the run at Dixie, I didn't see 'er puppy," Joanna said. "I know he ain't been adopted has he? Ain't he too young?"

"Yeah," Denise sighed. "When I got down here yesterday mornin', he was dead. Doc had told me he might not make it, but he seemed to be gettin' stronger every day."

"Oh no! Poor Dixie, 'er last baby!"

"Yeah, she's right pitiful. She's just layin' in the corner, whimperin'. I've tried to spend a little time with 'er, but there's so much to do around here."

Another family came by and Denise was busy with them for a half hour. Then, Miss Velvie came in and they headed back to the runs together.

Joanna was siting in the run with Dixie and tears were running down her face as she stroked the silky head over and over. When she saw the other women approaching, she got up quickly and brushed the tears away.

"Don't worry honey," the old woman said. "Dixie will be okay."

Tears came into Joanna's eyes again and her bottom lip trembled slightly. "I know, it's just so sad."

"Let's see here now, little girl," the old woman knelt down on the blanket beside the dog. "We'll get you straightened out, best as we can." She touched one of the swollen teats and milk came pouring out. She turned to Denise. "I brought some sage, that'll get 'er dried up. We got'ta be careful though, it's toxic if you use too much."

Dixie's milk production did decrease and in a few days, it had stopped completely. But the little dog continued to be depressed. Whenever Joanna came in, she would always head straight for Dixie's run and spend most of the time with her.

"Hey Neecie, see how Dixie acts with this little stuffed animal I brought 'er?" Joanna asked. It was a fluffy little brown teddy bear that squeaked.

"I've been noticin' the way she cuddles with it," Denise answered. "I believe she's substitutin' it for 'er baby."

Joanna came to Denise a few weeks later and asked, "Do you think I could adopt Dixie? I've gotten so attached to 'er, it's gettin' to the place where I can hardly bear to leave 'er here when I come."

"I think it would be a match made in Heaven," Denise replied.

When Miss Velvie's birthday arrived, Joanna took her out on an errand. Dixie sat between them, peering out the windshield with interest. When they returned, the old woman exclaimed, "Lord have mercy! What're all those cars doin' at my house?" When she got out of the truck, everyone came running off the porch, crying; "Surprise Miss Velvie!" Happy birthday!"

"Why, I haven't had a birthday party in years and years!" she exclaimed. "What fun!" She put on a birthday hat and blew out one of those little party favors that curls up, while the others started to carry food into the house. Everyone had made something to bring, and there was a big, homemade devil's food cake, filled with birthday candles.

"You know," the old woman said. "Every time I have devil's food cake, I think about the time we went to see the devil's trampin' ground, over near Siler City. There's a circle, where nothin' won't grow, they say the devil's flamin' feet just charred the earth. I was plum scared to death. Had a terrible nightmare, I remember. Willie was gone and Mama had to come in and sleep with me, that night. And me, a grown woman, married and all.

"Course, after you get old as me, you ain't scared of nothin'. I ain't even afraid of the devil no more, since I got saved. Y'all remember the day you got saved?"

"Well, I think that's somethin' that happens gradually, over a period of time," said Denise.

"P-shaw!" exclaimed the old woman. "Some things, you remember exactly when they happened. Like the day you graduated high school, you recall that, don't you? And special times, like your weddin' day. That's how it is when you really get saved. You don't never forget it!"

Joanna just listened quietly without saying a word.

After the birthday dinner, they went into the living room to open the gift. Miss Velvie sat in her favorite rocker and the children gathered at her feet. When Tansey laid the big box in her lap, they jumped up to help her tear the paper off as Dixie sniffed at it with curiosity.

"What in the world?" Miss Velvie held theVCR up and looked at it. "I sure do thank y'all, but I think you're gonna haf'ta tell me what it is."

You can tape your television shows with that thing," Joanna explained. "If you're gone somewhere, it records 'em, and you can play it when you get home."

"Well, what'll they think of next? It'll be just like at the picture show, I'll be watchin' it when it ain't really happenin'. And I can watch it over and over!"

Randy and Stumpy came in, struggling under the weight of a huge box.

"We got you a new television too, so's the recorder will hook up to it," Joanna explained. "And it's in color!"

They got the recorder hooked up and tried it out. As they played it back, Miss Velvie clapped her hands in delight. "Glory be! Ain't it a caution? I just can't get over these new contraptions they keep comin' up with. Now I can go on about my business and come home and watch The Young and Restless, won't never miss a thing!"

"And you can rent movies to play on here, too," Joanna said. "Down at the video stores, like Blockbuster."

"Well, you know, I've heard about that, but until now, I didn't never really understand just how it worked. I think I'll go down there, first thing in the mornin' and see if they've got Gone With The Wind. That's my favorite, you know. You think there's a chance they might have that?"

"Yes ma'am, " Joanna confirmed. "I've rented it myself."

"Oh, what fun!" the old woman smiled and clapped her hands. "Why, I believe this is just about the best birthday present I ever got."

The group went outside just before twilight, the adults sitting on the porch while the children ran around in the yard. Dixie curled up by Joanna's feet. Miss Velvie pulled out her snuff can and started dipping. In a little while, Petey came up to sit in her lap.

"Miss Velvie, you always smell like flowers and Juicy Fruit chewin' gum," he said as his chubby arms clung to her neck.

"Well, that's my signature perfume, Tea Rose," she said. "My Willie gave me my first bottle on our one-year anniversary and I been wearin' it ever since. He always said a rose should smell like a rose. And as for the chewin' gum," she grinned. "I always keep a pack or two close by." Reaching into her apron pocket, she pulled out two sticks of Juicy Fruit. "Take your sister a piece now." Petey scrambled down and ran to share his treasure with Kayla.

"Tell us some more stories, Miss Velvie," urged Denise.

"Let's see, now. Well, there was the one time my Willie got jealous."

"What happened?"

"Well, I'd been drivin' his car all week. He'd been in the field with Papa, too busy to take me anywhere. Anyways, he come stompin' up to our room one night, all in a rage, hollerin', throwin' lamps and breakin' stuff.

"Mama heard all the ruckus and come up to see what was goin' on, but he'd locked the door and wouldn't let 'er in. I was kind'a cringin' back in the corner, not knowin' what was wrong, and Mama was steady knockin' on the door. I'd never seen Willie like that, he was like a pure wildman or somethin'. He just kept stompin' around the room, goin' on a tirade, don't you know? All I could get out'ta him, was some nonsense about how he couldn't trust me.

"Finally, Papa come in downstairs and heard all the fuss. He come up beatin' on the door and it won't no timid little knock like Mama was doin'. He went to poundin' on the door with 'is fist, cracked the two-inch wood right down the middle, he did. 'William White,' he shouted. 'You open this door and I mean right now!' Willie finally went over and opened it and Papa grabbed 'im by the collar. It was the onliest time I'd ever seen Papa lose 'is own temper, and I was scared somethin' awful. I thought for a minute there he was gonna give Willie a whippin', grown man that he was.

"Papa made Willie tell 'im what was wrong. 'Velvie's got another man,' Willie kept sayin' over and over. Papa and Mama told 'im they knew that couldn't be true, they knew I wouldn't do nothin' like that.

"Well, there's a letter down in my car. It's got 'er rose perfume on it, and it says right there, on the front, Lover Boy, big as you please."

"Well, sir, I got to giggling, sittin' there in the corner and I couldn't stop. When Papa and Mama wanted to know what was so funny, I could hardly tell 'em. 'Let's go down to the car and get that letter, and I'll show y'all,' I said.

"We all went down together and Willie pulled that long envelope out from under the front seat where he'd found it. I told 'im to open it up and read it out loud. He looked at me real funny but he done what I'd told 'im.

"He took out a sheet of paper and began to read. To this very day, I remember every word.

Lover Boy:
"Male adult cat. Gray. Long-haired. One year old. Presented by owner for neuter. Procedure was accomplished without difficulty. Lover Boy is a very pleasant patient and I hope to see him again on a regular basis."
—Milton Joyner, DVM

"Well, sir, you could've knocked Willie over with a feather. He just stood there with the silliest grin on 'is face for awhile. We all got to laughin' and couldn't stop. Purty soon he apologized to me and we all went on back in the house, where Willie helped me and Mama clean up all the stuff he'd broken up in our room. Just imagine, the only male that ever came between me and my husband was an old tomcat!"

"Oh, Miss Velvie!" exclaimed Tansey. "Is that really true?"

"Cross my heart," the old woman said. "And hope to die. Stick a needle in my eye!"

"You know," began Joanna, one hand resting on Dixie's head. "We don't hardly even need television with you around, Miss Velvie. You're more entertainin' than anything I've seen in a long, long time."

PABST BLUE RIBBON AND PIZZLE-GREASE

"Knowledge becomes wisdom only after it has been put to practical use."
—Unknown

"Randy and some of 'is friends are gonna come move the posts and wire over to the rescue this weekend," Joanna told Miss Velvie.

"Well, stop by the house when you get here. I'm gonna cook a big dinner for y'all."

The men showed up bright and early Saturday morning. Joanna could hear them in the kitchen with Randy while she was in the shower. After she'd gotten dressed, she went in where they were having coffee.

Randy had hooked up his biggest flatbed trailer and they all piled into the crew-cab truck. Johnny-Vern and Wildman sat up front with Randy, while Nollie and Joanna took the rear seat. Haywood and Stumpy followed them.

"God-a-mighty!" exclaimed Johnny-Vern. "I ain't gettin' out'ta this truck, we're liable to get eat alive!" He peered down at all the barking dogs surrounding the truck.

Miss Velvie came out the back door, shooing dogs away. "Y'all get down, they won't hurt you none. Randy, you might wanna go ahead and pull your truck 'round behind that biggest barn yonder. That's where the posts are."

Joanna walked around behind the truck, just as Randy was getting out. "Boy, that's a pile of money there in those posts, Miss Velvie. You sure you wanna just give 'em away?"

"Sure as God made little green apples and worms to eat 'em up," she answered. "They been just a'sittin' here all these years, ain't doin' nobody a lick of good. Why, if them dogs can get out and run around, that'll be payment enough for me. I hate to think of 'em bein' cooped up in them runs all the time."

The men had begun to load the posts as the ladies talked. "Danged if these things ain't heavy," Randy groaned. Y'all womenfolks are tryin' to kill us."

After they'd finished moving everything to the rescue, Miss Velvie invited them in to eat. They all trooped into the big kitchen and washed their hands. "You boys go on in the dinin' room there and set down," the old woman instructed. "Me and Jo, we'll bring the food in. Here honey, take this bowl of collards."

They went back and forth, carrying fresh vegetables, hot buttermilk biscuits and a big platter of southern fried chicken.

"Now here's a bowl of bull-dog gravy and some homemade peach preserves, and can you take this pitcher of tea?"

They finally sat down to the mahogany table, covered with a hand embroidered linen cloth and porcelain plates, rimmed with gold edging. The oversized tulip bowls of the goblets tapered down to graceful stems. "Papa Frank always said a workin' man should have a big tea glass, not one of them dainty little things where you haf'ta fill up every time you take a swallow," Miss Velvie declared. "Now would one of you boys kindly grace the table? I usually do it, but it ain't fittin' for a female to do it when there's menfolks here perfectly capable to head the table."

"Randy, Johnny-Vern and Wildman grinned at each other, then looked around sheepishly, clearly embarrassed. "I'd be honored, Miss Velvie," Nollie began. Everyone bowed their heads.

"Dear Lord, we thank thee for the bountiful harvest this kind lady has prepared in order to nourish our bodies, just as you nourish our souls. And we are ever grateful for the coming together today of the people, in order that we may perform a deed that will make life better for a few of the creatures you send down to fulfill our lives. Christ's name. Amen."

"Amen!" Miss Velvie repeated. "It's been a mighty long time since there was menfolks 'round this table. Why, it's just like the noonday workin' dinners we had, way back when we'd ring the big dinner bell and the men would come in from the fields. I didn't think I'd ever see such again!"

Nollie and Joanna began to eat. Stumpy lowered his head close down to his plate and began to shovel in food as fast as he could while the other men continued to look around abashedly, feeling out of place.

"Well, you boys dig in, don't just sit there like a bump on a pickle!" the old woman urged. Once they began to eat, they didn't slow down for quite some time.

"I declare, I'm about to bust, Miss Velvie," Stumpy declared a little later. "This is some mighty fine eatin'."

"Y'all be sure and save room for some dessert now," she instructed as she went over to the sideboard and removed the glass dome from a plate. "This here's hummingbird cake, got bananas and pineapple, toasted walnuts and cream cheese, it was my Willie's favorite. And this is fresh lemon," she removed the top from a pie pan. Creamy meringue stood up in perfect peaks and little slits of transparent yellow shone through like topaz jewels.

Miss Velvie wouldn't let Joanna help with the dishes. "Naw, you young'uns just go on and get to work on that fence. I got all day long to clean up."

As she followed them outside, they noticed a goat lying down, moaning a little. "Why, somethin' must be wrong with old Grover," declared Miss Velvie. "He's always up eatin', unless, he's sick. Get up here, Grover! What ails you?"

But the goat refused to move and the old woman opened the gate to go into the pasture. She knelt down and placed her hand on him. "I declare I believe he's got a fever."

"You want us to take 'im in to the vet for you?" Randy asked.

"No son, but I tell you what you can do. Run down to the store and get oh, about three of them six-packs of beer. Get that Pabst Blue Ribbon brand, folks don't drink that much no more, and it's the cheapest."

Randy looked at Joanna, as if he hadn't heard right. Old women talking about being in the presence of alcohol; his own mother would have objected strenuously. He didn't know whether to carry out the request or not.

"Go on," his wife urged. "Whatever she says, just listen to 'er. She usually knows what she's talkin' about."

"'But what's she gonna do? Feed that goat eighteen cans of beer?"

"I dunno, just do like she says."

While Randy and Johnny-Vern were gone, the old woman rummaged around in the garage and came back with a large paper bag, which she put on the ground beside the goat.

The men were back in a few minutes with the requested items. "Now put two packs in your cooler there and bring me the other one," she instructed, as she pulled a plastic bag and some tubing out.

"Now open them beers and pour 'em in here," she instructed, holding the bag.

"What in the world?" asked Johnny-Vern.

"We're gonna give Grover an enema," said Miss Velvie. "This cold beer'll bring that fever down. And it'll relax 'im too, 'cause he'll absorb some of it through 'is intestines."

Johnny-Vern looked at Randy and they both began to snicker.

"I know y'all think I'm crazy, but it works wonders," the old woman said. "And it don't cost hardly nothin'. Now you boys hold 'im down to where he can't move. She greased the end of the tubing with vaseline and slid it into the goat's rectum.

Grover let out a tremendous BA-A-A-AH! as the cold liquid entered his intestines, then settled down. Each time a can would be emptied, there stood Nollie, popping the top on another one. Within twenty minutes, Grover had settled down peacefully. When the men let him up, he got to his feet slowly and looked around. He wobbled a little and shook his head, then began to graze. He fell over a few times, but it was obvious that he felt better already.

"Well, it did seem to work, Miss Velvie," said Randy. "But what's the other two six-packs for?"

"Oh, that's for us to drink. You always get kind'a hot and sweaty out here workin' on a goat. Papa Frank taught me that little trick and that's what he always did when he got finished."

"Yes ma'am!" shouted Johnny-Vern. "Randy told us we'd like you!"

"Why Miss Velvie, I didn't know you drank that stuff!" Joanna exclaimed in what was only half mock surprise.

"Oh, a little taste now and then never did hurt nobody," she said with a twinkle in her eye. "Long as you don't overdo it." In fact, I got some scuppernong wine in the house, if you fellers would like to have a little sample."

"Did you make it?" Randy asked.

"Sure did, right from that vine you see yonder. Papa used to let me watch 'im fix it up. Always told me not to tell Mama, though. She'd have had a pure fit if she knew."

They followed the old woman back into the house and she led the way to the parlor, where she pulled a solid silver cask out of the cupboard. Taking shot glasses out, she passed them all around. After the men had all been served, she lifted a glass to her own lips, smacking loudly.

"Right good, if I do say so myself!"

Johnny-Vern plied the cask again and again. The men were enjoying the amber liquid, but Miss Velvie refused. "No sir, one's my limit," she declared. "That's some right potent stuff."

They soon saw that she was telling the truth. In a short time, Johnny-Vern and Wildman were well inebriated.

"Hey, Miss Velvie!" shouted Wildman. "You got a cure for bald spots? Old Vern sure could use it."

"Come to think of it, I sure do. It's an old remedy of Mama Martha's and it used to work right good." She looked at Johnny-Vern. "You wanna give it a try, young feller?"

He looked at her, cross-eyed, barely able to stand up. "Give what a try?"

"You know, put some hair on your head."

"Might just as well. Man, if I had a little more hair, I'd haf'ta beat the women off with a stick!"

"Come on in the kitchen and we'll see what we can do."

Johnny-Vern followed obediently and sat down at the kitchen table, allowing her to tie an apron around his neck. Randy and Wildman stood in the background snickering, but Nollie sat down across the table. Miss Velvie rummaged around under the sink and finally pulled out a jar. Putting on a pair of yellow latex gloves, she dipped one hand into it and pulled out a handful of greasy, whitish gook. She carefully smoothed it onto Johnny-Vern's bald spot and began to massage it in vigorously.

"What is that stuff, Miss Velvie?" Haywood wanted to know. "It sure is yucky lookin'."

"This is pizzle-grease, son. I've seen Mama use it many a time. We had one old colored woman that worked for us, Mammy Jenny, 'er name was. All her hair had fell out and she had been bald for years. Wore one of them doo-rags all the time, don't you know. Mama got 'er to usin' this treatment every week and before long, she had started growin' hair."

"Exactly what is pizzle-grease made from, ma'am?" Nollie asked.

"The main ingredient is fat that's boiled from a hog's tallywhacker. You take that and mix in some good strong lye soap, barberry root and just a drop of turpentine. Then you cook it down, simmer it on low heat, most all day and this here's what you end up with."

"From a hog's what?" asked Johny-Vern.

"You know, his private parts."

"Hey! Vern's got hog jism on 'is head!" sang out Wildman.

"Huh? Is that really what's in this stuff, Miss Velvie?" Johnny-Vern asked.

"I'm afraid so, son." Now the old woman looked a little upset, as if perhaps she had done something wrong. "But, land sakes! It's been boiled, all the germs ought to have been killed out of it."

The kitchen chair fell over backwards as Johnny-Vern jumped up and headed for the door. Yanking the apron off, he ran for the garden hose and quickly doused his head with the cold water. He was drying himself off with the apron when everyone came out.

"What's the matter, man?" yelled Randy.

"Y'all got that old woman doin' voo-doo and stuff on my head. Probably cooked it all up ahead of time and planned a joke on me. I know how y'all are!"

"Man, I swear, I didn't know a thing about it. Miss Velvie's for real, it won't no joke."

Johnny-Vern got into the truck and slammed the door. "I'll just wait for y'all out here."

"Lord have tender mercy upon my soul," Miss Velvie said. "I believe that young man's upset with me."

"Oh, he'll get over it, ma'am," Nollie reassured her. "Don't worry about him."

"Well, we didn't get much done today," said Randy. "But I'm plumb wore out. Let's get on to the house."

"I sure thank you boys," Joanna said as the men headed for their own trucks. "That's gonna save us a heap of money." Everyone said their goodbyes except Johnny-Vern, who was still a little miffed.

A week had passed and neither Randy nor Joanna had heard from him. Then, she was out in the yard one evening when she heard a truck coming up the path. It was Johnny-Vern.

"How you doin' tonight, Jo?"

"Good! How 'bout you?"

He looked sheepish. "You reckon' you could get me some more of that stuff?"

"What's that?"

"You know, that cream Miss Velvie put on my head."

Joanna looked up in surprise. "What're you gonna do with it?"

He stepped down from the truck and bent down, lowering his head, running a hand over the bald spot in back. "Look-a-here."

Little tufts of fuzz were sprouting from the shiny scalp. Joanna rubbed her fingertips over it. It felt like the soft down on a baby duck but it was coming in thick and curly.

"I'll be danged if that potion didn't work! I don't know why I'm surprised, everything else she does works."

"You think you could get me some more?" he asked again.

"I don't see why not. I'll go by there tomorrow."

Miss Velvie was delighted. "Lord have mercy, I thought that young man was mad at me and I hated it so bad! I knew it'd work if he just gave it a chance, but I really didn't think we left it on long enough that day to do no good. The way he took off out'ta here, I didn't think I'd be hearin' from 'im again. I should'a never told what was in that ointment."

"Don't tell nobody," Johnny-Vern begged when he came by to pick it up. You know how that bunch is, they won't never lemme hear the end of it."

Each time Johnny-Vern's supply ran out, Joanna would get more for him. "You're amazin', Miss Velvie," she said.

"Days should speak," the old woman began, then Joanna joined in, laughing. "And a multitude of years should teach wisdom!"

They kept the secret between the three of them. But everyone soon began to notice that Johnny-Verns's bald spot was disappearing.

"Boy, that must be some powerful stuff that old woman put on Vern's head!" Haywood exclaimed. "A one-time treatment that cures baldness. She needs to put that stuff on the market, she could get rich."

They never knew that Johnny-Vern was continuing to use the concoction every week. And if he hadn't been cocky enough before, he grew steadily worse. But when he got too bad, all Joanna had to do was threaten to divulge his secret, and it worked like a charm. He still dated a different woman almost every week and showed no inclination to commit to any of them.

"Miss Velvie," he would often say, "All them other girls are just to pass the time. You know you're my one and only, my special sweetheart!"

THE COLD-HEARTED HALF

"Our task must be to free ourselves from this prison (separateness) by widening our circle of compassion to embrace all living creatures."
—Albert Einstein

"Hey, Jo," the voice on the phone was high and frenzied. "I just saw somethin' awful. I know you work at the animal rescue, so I figgered you'd know what to do."

"Why, what's wrong, Darlene?"

"It's a neighbor of mine, down the road yonder. He's got Pitt Bulls that he breeds, I think he sell 'em to folks that fight 'em. Anyway, he's got a litter, ain't even got their eyes open yet. The Mama dog's real sick, she's got a hurt leg and I think maybe it's done gone into gangrene. He said it got all wrapped up in the chain and that's how she cut it. Said the stupid dog should'a had better sense, that she done it to herself."

"Sounds like she needs some antibiotics. If it's gangrene, she might lose that leg."

"But he won't take 'er to the vet! I told 'im she was probably gonna die if he didn't do somethin' and he said he didn't care. I even asked if I could take 'er and pay for it myself, but he said no, he needs 'er there to nurse the puppies. Said it don't matter if she dies, she's real old and he's plannin' to keep one of the female puppies to breed. He said she ought'a live a couple more weeks, and by that time, the puppies are gonna be old enough to eat on their own, so it wouldn't matter!"

"I guess the animal control people would be the ones to handle this," Joanna responded. "Lemme see if I can get ahold of 'em." But she was unsuccessful. It was Friday night and there was only one officer that covered the entire county. So she called Denise.

"I don't know exactly what to do, either. I'll call one of the board members and see what they say."

She called back in a few minutes. "I talked to Sylvia, the president, but she said there ain't nothin' we can do. Said they don't like to get in the middle of nothin' like this, 'cause folks get mad at 'em if they try to help in cruelty cases. Said they're scared to upset people, 'cause if gossip starts goin' around about 'em, they might not get as many donations."

"Well, God-a-mighty!" Joanna retorted. "I'd think folks would be more inclined to give to an organization that would get involved."

"Me too, but that's sure what she said."

"Maybe I could go talk to the man," Joanna suggested. "Me and Darlene, we'll go over there first thing in the mornin'."

Joanna picked Darlene up the next day and they headed for the man's house.

"Just around that curve yonder," said Darlene. "The first house on the right."

They pulled into the driveway of a ramshackle bungalow, whose paint had long since peeled away. One of the front windows was broken, and covered partially with a ragged piece of plywood. Several junk cars were parked, jacked up haphazardly on cinder blocks and tall weeds sprouted up around them in profusion. And everywhere you looked, there were dogs on heavy chains, all pit bulls, barking and growling at the girls as they stepped out of the truck. Even though it was the height of summer, there was no shade for any of the animals, and several were simply chained to wooden posts, with no kind of house or shelter. Some of the dogs had no water, and those that did had filthy containers of various description, old kitchen pots, a rusty bucket and a paint can. All the dogs appeared to be undernourished and there was no food in sight. They were standing in their own waste and the odor was almost unbearable.

"Back here, Jo," Darlene said. "He's got 'er behind this little shed, so nobody won't see 'er I reckon."

A wave of nausea swept over Joanna as she rounded the corner and spotted the dog. She lay on her side, suckling the puppies, breathing in pants and gasps. The wounded leg stuck out stiffly, three times it's normal size and chunks of tissue that had fallen away lay on the ground nearby. The dog looked up warily, fear in her eyes.

"It's all right, old girl," Joanna crooned to her. The dog tried desperately to rise, as she cowered away, but her weakened condition wouldn't allow her to.

"Okay, easy now," Joanna backed away. "Calm down and hold still, girl."

She turned to Darlene. "You won't jokin' when you told me you seen somethin' terrible!"

The girls went around to the front of the house, and started up the steps, nearly falling when one of them gave way. They knocked on the door, and in a few moments they heard heavy footsteps approaching from inside. "Yeah, who is it?" a loud, gravely voice asked.

"It's me, Darlene, Mr. Daughtery,"

"What you want, now?" he asked as he opened the door. Joanna looked up to see a heavyset man with a long, scraggly beard framing a heavily-jowled face. He was wearing a dirty tee shirt that stretched across a pendulous belly and muddy hazel eyes stared out at her malevolently over a wide, flat nose and thick, blubbery lips, giving him a frog-faced appearance. The sour odor of unwashed skin rose from him as he stood, scratching his abdomen, faded navy jogging pants pushed down, so the skin was showing.

"Hey, Mr. Daughtery, I'm Joanna Morgan. We wanted to offer to help you with that sick dog, thought maybe you'd let us take 'er to the vet, if we'd pay for it. Of course, we'd take the puppies and bottle-feed 'em for you, so you wouldn't haf'ta worry 'bout that."

"No."

"Why not?' If it don't cost you nothin', I don't see why you won't let us help 'er."

"Because. I don't know that I'd get them puppies back. They're valuable animals, I get a lotta money for 'em, and I ain't havin' the likes of you to steal 'em!" He slammed the door in their faces.

"Come on, Darlene," she grabbed the younger girl by the arm. "Let's pull the truck around back and see if we can get 'er in there."

But when the girls pulled around to the shed, the man was standing there with a shotgun. "Y'all ain't takin' my dogs, I done told you that."

Joanna sat there for a moment, the engine idling.

"Jo, let's get out'ta here," Darlene begged. "I'm scared."

Joanna slowly backed the truck away, until she could find a space to turn around. Looking back over her shoulder as she pulled onto the highway, she could see the man, still standing there, holding the gun.

"I guess there's nothin' we can do," said Darlene.

"We got to think of somethin'," Joanna replied. "There must be some way to help that poor dog. I swear, it just ain't right for no livin' thing to haf'ta suffer like that."

When they arrived at Darlene's house, Joanna wanted to use the phone. "I'm gonna call Tansey," she declared. "Maybe she knows of somethin' we can do."

"Let's steal 'em!" Tansey declared.

"Huh?"

"Well, ain't nothin' else workin'!"

"It's gonna be hard to do, I think he's gonna be watchin' like a hawk for us. And the minute we set foot in that yard, all them dogs are gonna go to barkin', so you know he's bound to see us."

"Well, maybe we could distract 'im, somehow."

"How would we do that?"

"I dunno. He ain't seen me. Maybe I could go up and get to talkin' to 'im, you know, maybe ask for directions, or somethin'."

"I don't think that'll work. Old Frog Face is mighty unsociable. I don't think he'd talk to you for two seconds."

"I got an idea that ought'a work."

"What is it?"

"You'll see, he's a man ain't he?"

"Yeah, but what are you gonna do?"

"I'll be at Darlene's house in about an hour, you'll see then."

Forty-five minutes later, tires squealed as Tansey's truck turned into the driveway. Joanna and Darlene looked on as a blonde woman stepped out, but it didn't look like Tansey. She wore a skin-tight red dress, cut low in front. So short that it barely covered her thighs, she had difficulty getting down from the tall truck. Her hair was teased up high, sticking out in all directions, like a punk rocker, and her face was heavily made up. Bright red lipstick was slathered onto her mouth and thick rouge caked onto her cheeks. Dark blue eyeshadow covered her lids and enormous gold earrings swung from her earlobes. Half a dozen necklaces hung around her neck, as she reached up with long, bright red fingernails to push them out of her way. Gold sequined, six inch heels teetered dangerously, threatening to overturn her, as she marched across the yard on legs that were sheathed in sheer, black pantyhose that had little rhinestones embedded in them.

Joanna understood immediately. "Girl, if you don't look like a floozy, I ain't never seen one. I didn't know your boobs was that big, though."

"Oh, It's my sister's push-up, padded bra from Victoria Secrets. Does wonders, don't it?"

"You can say that again. Boy, I wish Johnny-Vern and them could see you, you wouldn't never hear the end of this. But I reckon you ought'a be able to hold that feller's attention, for sure!"

"Okay, y'all wait 'till I get inside the house, before y'all pull in. Then try to get the dog fast as you can and get out'ta there."

Joanna parked a little ways down the road, then she and Darlene got out to stand behind a crepe myrtle bush and watch. Tansey got out of the truck carrying a six-pack of beer, and smoking a Virginia Slim cigarette. "Yoo-hoo! Anybody home?" she called in a sultry voice.

The door opened the door a slit, then the man stepped out in surprise. "Well, hello there, purty lady," he said in a pleasant voice. "And what can I do for you?"

"Hi! I'm Ree-Ree Rogers and I'm gonna be your new neighbor," Tansey cooed as she stood there, smacking a huge wad of bubble gum and blowing smoke in the man's face."

"It's nice to meet you, honey," the muddy eyes slid over the slender body, as if they were mentally undressing her.

"Yeah, I'm gonna be movin' in that little trailer, across the field there, and I'd kind'a like to get acquainted." Tansey ran the hand holding the cigarette suggestively down over her bosom and across her right hip in a smooth motion. "I don't know nobody 'round these parts and it's gonna be lonesome," she stated in a low, breathy voice, as she winked up at him. "You know what I mean, Jelly-Bean?'

"I think I do," he grinned, showing a row of rotten teeth that make Tansey stifle a shudder. "It'll be right nice to have a neighbor like you. I ain't had me no lady friends in a mighty long time."

"Well, I got a six-pack here, I thought we could drink it and talk a little bit. I wanted to see if you could recommend a good plumber, 'cause I got to get some work done before I move in. And you know how it is, when workmen see a lady that's all by herself, they automatically take advantage of 'er. I figgered you might know somebody that works cheap. How 'bout lettin' me come in and we'll visit for a spell?"

"Why, shore! Come on in here, but you'll haf'ta excuse the mess, though. I kind'a been down in the back lately, and I ain't been able to do too much cleanin'."

He turned to move a box out of the doorway, so that Tansey could step in and she looked back over her shoulder, making a sweeping motion with her hand. "Go for it!" she was saying.

Joanna and Darlene lost no time in pulling around behind the shed while Tansey had the man's attention. Again, the dog cowered back in fear as they approached.

"Careful Jo, she might bite us," Darlene cautioned.

Reaching down slowly, Joanna let the dog sniff the back of her hand for a moment, then stroked the head gently. Some of the fear went out of the dog's eyes and she licked the woman's hand tentatively.

"All right, girl. We've got'ta lift you up, now. I know it's probably gonna hurt that leg, but we got'ta get you out'ta here." Looking around, she spied a small sheet of half rotten plywood.

"Hey, Darlene. Let's see can we slide 'er onto that board, then lift 'er up."

Mice and spiders scurried everywhere as they moved the piece of wood, and laid it flat beside the dog. Then, ever so slowly, they pulled her onto it. The dog moaned pitifully, and Joanna looked down. Her paw had separated from the leg, and was still lying on the ground, stuck tight in the pool of yellowish drainage. The dog made no move to bite, but looked around frantically for her puppies, whining deep in her throat.

"Oh, God!" Darlene exclaimed, then she leaned over and vomited onto the ground.

"Come on, Darlene, we got'ta get 'er out'ta here," Joanna urged.

Knees buckling, the girls gently lifted their burden into the back of the truck and slid it forward. The dog continued to whine until the puppies were placed beside her, then she stopped and nuzzled them, making sure they were all there. "Don't worry, girl, we got your babies," Joanna assured her. "We ain't leavin' 'em here." The dog closed her eyes wearily, as they began to suckle with little smacking noises.

"Let's get out of here," Darlene said. "I think I'm gonna be sick again."

The girls didn't breath easily until they had made it out of the driveway and started down the road.

"Now what're we gonna do?" Darlene asked.

"Let's get 'er to the vet right away."

They were just getting out of Joanna's truck at the animal hospital, when they heard a vehicle approaching and looked up to see Tansey coming into the driveway on two wheels. "God!" she shuddered. "I feel like I got cooties and crabs and everything else a body could catch. He was disgustin'!"

Tansey forgot her aversion as she looked down at the dog, still lying in the truck bed, the swollen leg with the missing paw stuck out as she suckled her little family. She lay completely still, her eyes filled with pain and bewilderment.

"Oh you pore thing!" Tansey exclaimed, as she reached down to pet the smooth head. "She's gonna be mighty lucky if she don't lose that whole leg." She turned back to the dog, "It's gonna be all right now, sweetie, we'll take care of you. Don't you worry, that feller won't never get 'is hands on you again."

Joanna and Tansey carried the dog in, still on the board. Darlene followed behind, with the three puppies in a box, trying to keep them close to the mother in order to reduce her anxiety.

"What in the world y'all got there?" asked Courtney, the receptionist. She listened as the little group told their story, then said, 'Y'all come on back here and let's get 'em out'ta sight. If that man finds out they're missin' he's probably gonna come here."

She led the way to an exam room and the girls laid the dog on the table. She looked around anxiously until Darlene took the puppies out of the box and placed them beside her. Once again, she heaved a deep sigh and closed her eyes.

They only had to wait a few minutes before Dr Cooper came in. The kindly old veterinarian looked down at the dog and shook his head. "I see a lot of neglect," he admitted, "but this is really bad. Looks like that leg's been infected for a right good while." They big hands probed and examined with an incredibly gentle touch.

"Bonnie," he called to the technician. "How 'bout gettin' a temp on this dog, and draw some blood. I want a complete blood count and a panel seven." He turned back to the girls.

"The rest of that leg's gonna haf'ta come off, unless we put 'er down. Before y'all decide what to do, let's run some tests and I can tell a little more about what shape she's in." He opened the dog's mouth and examined her teeth. "Looks like she's mighty old."

"She is," Darlene answered. "The owner told me she was at least fourteen years old, said he'd had twenty-some litters off her. Said he knew she won't gonna live more'n another year or two."

The veterinarian shook his head as he reached down to give the dog a gentle pat. "We'll take care of you, girl. You just rest now." He looked back up. "I got a couple of clients out front, but we need to get those test results, anyway. By the time I finish up, Bonnie should have 'em ready, and I'll be back in."

He was back in a half hour. "Girls, these tests don't look too good. If she was a young dog, I might say we should go ahead and amputate the rest of that leg and try to save 'er, but I'd almost hate to put 'er through it. She's mighty sick and I don't even know if she'll make it if we do the operation. I'm gonna leave it up to you girls, though."

They looked around at each other and Darlene reached down to stroke the dog's head. "We want to do whatever you think, Doc," Joanna murmured. The others nodded in agreement.

"Well, I think it would be the best thing for her if we put 'er down now. How 'bout the puppies? Could y'all bottle-feed 'em?"

"Yeah, we can do that," Tansey said, her voice choked with emotion.

"All right. Do you girls want to go on out?"

"I kind'a hate to take the puppies away," Joanna said. "That seems to be the only thing that fazes 'er, is when they get out of 'er sight."

"All right." The doctor started to fill the syringe he would use, when Darlene's knees buckled and she fell down.

"Tansey, can you take 'er out?" Dr. Cooper asked.

"Come on honey," Tansey took her by the arm. "Jo'll stay with 'er. It ain't any need in all of us bein' in here."

Joanna put her hand on the brindled head while Bonnie held her. As she looked up at Dr. Cooper, she thought she saw a tear swimming in the brown eyes behind the wire-rimmed glasses. "I'm sorry we couldn't do more to help you, old girl," he murmured, "but this is the best I know to do for you." He gently inserted the needle into the dog's front leg and depressed the plunger. It took a few seconds, then Joanna felt the dog shudder, and lay still. The puppies were still trying to nurse as she and Bonnie lifted them back into their box.

"I'll never understand how people can be so cruel," Dr. Cooper said, as he stood for a moment, looking at the dog with pain filled eyes. "Long as I been doin' this, you'd think I'd be used to it by now." He turned on his heel and quickly walked out of the room.

"How much we owe y'all, Courtney?" Tansey asked at the front desk.

"Doc said don't worry about it, this one's on us.

"Why don't you go on and take 'em home, Tansey?" said Joanna. "I'll run to the store and get some milk. You got any of those little nursin' bottles?"

"I think so."

Joanna and Darlene got the supplies, then went over to Tansey's. They heated the milk and filled the little bottles. Soon the puppies were slurping greedily.

"I just wish we could'a saved the Mama dog, too," Darlene said as she looked down at the puppy she was feeding. "I feel so bad for 'er."

"Well, you really helped 'er," said Joanna. "She must have been sufferin' so bad. I'd hate to think she'd just keep layin' there like that until she finally died. You know she's bound to be better off."

Tansey's dogs began to bark and Joanna looked out the window to see the bright, lime-green Suburban coming up the path.

Hilda and Agnes got out and came to the door, knocking loudly.

Joanna got up and opened the door.

"I heard what you done this mornin'," Hilda cried in her piercing voice. "And I want you to know you ain't gonna get away with it, you're gonna give them puppies back to that man."

"Like hell I am," Tansey puffed up. "You're crazy!"

"You're makin' the rescue look bad, like we're activists or somethin', and I ain't gonna stand for it."

"You don't even know the circumstances here," Tansey tried to reason with her. "That man let that Mama dog lay out there with an infected leg until her foot rotted slam off! A friend of Jo's even offered to take 'er and pay the vet bill and he wouldn't let 'er. I ain't gonna stand by and watch nothin' like that go on and not do somethin' about it."

"It was none of your business. If people hear about this, they'll get mad at us and they might not give us donations. We need all the money we can get."

"Well, money ain't worth a damn if you're gonna let a dog suffer like that one did!"

"Are you gonna take them puppies back to that man or not?"

"When the devil's dick turns into a popsicle, I will!" Tansey retorted.

"Come on Agnes," the taller woman turned on her heel. "Let's go." She turned to look at Tansey. "I'm reportin' you to the sheriff's office."

"Go ahead and call," Tansey shouted. As they were pulling out the driveway, she ran inside the house to make her own phone call.

"Come on, let's load those pups up and get 'em out'ta here," Tansey called to the other girls. "I don't know whether the law can take 'em or not, but let's don't take no chances on it."

"Where are we goin'?" Joanna asked as they clambered into the truck with the litter.

"Miss Velvie's. She's gonna keep 'em there 'till we find out what's what."

The old woman gathered all three of the puppies to her breast at once. "You pore little babies, Velvie will take good care of you." She looked up at the girls. "I'll hide and feed 'em as long as need be."

"That damn Hilda," fumed Tansey. "One of these days!"

"Now honey," the old woman soothed. "He that is slow to anger is better than the mighty. Proverbs 16:32."

Tansey gave the old woman a hug. "I sure do appreciate you doin' this."

"I'm glad to help out," she called as they drove away.

"Might as well go on back to the house and get it over with," Tansey sighed. "I know durn good and well Hilda made good on 'er threat to call the law. She just loves makin' trouble."

"Who in the world is she, anyway?" Darlene wanted to know.

"Ain't much of nobody, if you ask me. Her and that sister, Agnes own Hawkin's taxidermy. They opened it up a couple years ago. Ain't neither one of 'em never been married, or really had a boyfriend or nothin'. Hilda's too mean for anybody to want 'er, I reckon and that Agnes does everything Hilda tells 'er to. Agnes always acts kind'a like she's got the man-fever, but I don't think Hilda has ever let 'er date anybody. They're a weird pair!"

When they got back to Tansey's, a deputy was just turning around in the drive.

"Afternoon, Tansey, Jo," the clean-cut young man said as he unfolded his tall frame from the low seat. "How y'all doin' today?"

"A whole lot better now that I see you, Tony," said Blanchie.

"What you mean?"

"I figgered somebody from the force was comin' out to pay me a visit, and I'm mighty glad to see it's somebody I know."

"Yep, I hated like the devil to come out here, but I didn't have no choice. We got a report about y'all stealin' some dogs and hidin' 'em out over here."

"Damn right we did!" Tansey exploded as she explained what had happened.

"Don't sound like you girls got nothin' to worry about," the deputy soothed her. "The only thing I can see you did wrong was, you really should'a called us. Pore Albert, the animal control guy, he's worked slam to death, and he can't answer every call, so we kind'a fill in some. 'Course, a lot of the guys don't really want to mess with animals, but any time y'all need help, call me."

"So you don't think we're in any serious kind of trouble?" Joanna asked.

"Naw! Fact is, I'd be mad if y'all hadn't done somethin'. I'll go by there and talk to that guy. If he's plannin' on pressin' charges, I'll nip that in the bud right quick."

"I sure appreciate it, Tony," Tansey reached up to give him a quick hug.

"Don't mention it."

In a few weeks the puppies began to eat and Miss Velvie asked what the plans for their future were.

"I reckon we're gonna haf'ta find homes for 'em," Tansey answered. "It ain't gonna be easy, though. You know so many of the folks around these parts that want Pitts only want to fight 'em. We're gonna haf'ta be mighty careful who they go to."

"Well, I know a lady that specializes in rescuing Pitt Bulls. She's helped me a couple of times before."

"Great! Who is she?"

"She don't want nobody knowin' who she is. But if you want 'er to help, I can ask 'er for you."

"Is she somebody you really, really trust?"

"You bet. She's been helpin' stray animals for many, many years. More years than you been here on this earth, I dare say."

"Good. Call and see will she help us."

The anonymous advocate did indeed, end up taking the puppies and placing them. Miss Velvie went with her to visit them in their new homes and reported back to Tansey that they were in good hands. The girls had just had their first lesson in what would prove to be a very long battle, not only with outsiders, but those that had taken the pledge to help the animals.

SADIE

"Women and cats will do as they please, and men and dogs should get used to the idea."
—Robert Heinlein

"Oh, my gosh! Ain't they just the most precious puppies you've ever seen?" squealed Sadie Shaw, as she picked one up and gave him a kiss on the nose. "Your fur's so soft it feels like cotton. Did you know that? What a sweet baby!" The collie mix puppy responded by grabbing one of her long flaxen curls in his mouth and tugging on it. "Ouch! That hurts, you little scoundrel," she laughed as she folded her long, slender legs to sit on the kennel floor.

"Yeah," Joanna answered. "They ought'a get homes real quick, 'cause they're so cute. Everybody wants 'em when they're little round fuzzballs like this. Gracie Love brought 'em in. They belonged to her neighbors. They were gonna call animal control to pick 'em up, and she just couldn't stand it. She took 'em to the vet and got their shots done, and even took the mama dog in and paid to have 'er spayed. I wish it was more folks like Gracie around."

"Well, I'm sure glad she didn't let nothin' bad happen to you little guys! Now we've got'ta find good homes for y'all." Sadie stroked each of the puppies a few times before she opened the door to let them scramble into the outside run.

It turned out to be a busy night, and five of the eight puppies were adopted, along with one of the large dogs, and several kittens. "Sadie, I don't know what I'd have done without your help tonight," Joanna said. You're a lifesaver, girl!"

At that moment, the door opened and a tall, gangly-limbed young man walked in with a dark scowl on a gaunt face that was pitted with pockmarks. The high, boney forehead sloped down to reveal protruding, yellowish horse teeth and a few day's growth of dark beard marched across the drawn, sallow cheeks. Close set, beady eyes shifted suspiciously around the room.

"Sir, we're just fixin' to close up, but what can we help you with?" Joanna asked.

"Jo, this is my husband, Walter-Ray," Sadie interrupted. "Hey, honey! I was just gettin' ready to head on to the house. I thought I'd stop and pick us up a barbecue plate on the way."

"You need to just git on home," the hard, steely voice responded. "I ain't hungry. I been there at the house almost three hours, waitin' on you. I seen your note on the table, but why didn't you tell me this mornin' where you was goin?"

"I didn't think I was comin' tonight," she answered. "I was supposed to baby-sit for Cindy but 'er meetin' was canceled, so I decided to come on out here 'cause I knew Jo didn't have nobody to help 'er tonight. Come on back here and let me show you somethin' while you're here. We got the cutest little puppies! I was thinkin' maybe we could adopt one of 'em."

"Naw! You can just get that idea out'ta your head right now, you ain't bringin' none of these mangy dogs home. And you don't need to be comin' out here, no more neither."

Sadie turned and said, "Jo, I'd better go, but I'll give you a call."

A week want by before Joanna heard from her. "Sorry I haven't called sooner," she said. "I'm not gonna be able to come out to the rescue as much as I'd planned. I'm just so busy, what with work, and keepin' house and all, it don't leave a lotta time."

"That's okay," Joanna answered. "Just come when you can."

Sadie showed up a few weeks later on a Saturday morning. "Walter-Ray had to work this weekend, so I thought I'd come see if y'all need some help."

"Well, of course we do, we never turn down any offers of help!" exclaimed Denise. The two of them headed for the dog kennels to try and walk a few of the dogs before things got busy. Joanna started giving medicines, and Miss Velvie came in to help her. They were nearly finished when people began to arrive at ten o'clock.

When it did begin to get busy, the girls came in to help her with adoptions. Several large families came in at one time, and it was really noisy, with all the excited children trying to make themselves heard over the barking of the dogs. Joanna's nerves were frayed, but she was elated, because the animals seemed to be getting exceptionally good homes. She was talking with the Averys, and hoped they would choose one of the dogs.

"We had a terrier for almost fifteen years," Mrs. Avery was telling her. "She slept in the bed between us every night, and was spoiled rotten! She came down with cancer a few years back, and we did everything we could, even took her up to the veterinary school in Raleigh. We adopted 'er from a shelter up in Virginia when we were visitin' my mother, and now we'd like to help another dog that needs a home."

"I sure would love for y'all to get one of these," Joanna answered.

"I think the kids have finally picked one out," Mr. Avery announced.

"That's Trudy," Joanna informed them. The sleek, tawny body wriggled all over as the little boy picked her up and she tongue-bathed his chubby cheeks.

They went into the office and began filling out the forms, while Mr. Avery was busy looking through his billfold for his driver's license. One of the little girls held the puppy on the plastic leash they had provided. Sadie was looking through the cabinet for a sample bag of treats and toys when they heard a crunching noise.

"Trudy, have you found some dog food in here, you little pig?" Joanna asked, as she peered underneath the table where they were filling out the papers. To her horror, she saw a bag that had been torn open.

"Oh God! That's a herbicide that Randy left down here for us to put on those weeds out back!" She pried Trudy's mouth open and saw a few green granules stuck to her tongue.

"Miss Velvie!" Opening the door Joanna shrieked for the old woman.

"What's wrong, honey?" Miss Velvie poked her head out of the cat room.

"It's Trudy, she ate some poison!"

"All right, now. Just calm down. First thing we need to do is find out what kind. Let me read the ingredients on the bag there."

"Y'all put 'er up here on the table, and let's get some of this in 'er," the old woman instructed. Sadie lifted the little dog up to the table, where she continued to jump around, putting her front paws on everyone's chest, trying to lick all the concerned faces.

"Is my dog gonna die, lady?" the little girl asked as she looked up at the old woman.

"No sweetie," Miss Velvie answered. "She'll be okay. This here medicine's gonna make 'er throw the poison up, but it's lucky we caught it, do it could'a been mighty bad. But, don't worry, we'll get 'er fixed up."

Drawing the dark liquid up in a large syringe, Miss Velvie double checked the dosage. "You girls see if you can hold 'er head still and let me get this in 'er." The puppy grimaced and tried to wriggle away, but Sadie held her tight, and they slowly forced the medicine down her throat.

"We best take 'er on outside," Miss Velvie said when they finished. "She's gonna start throwin' up in about five minutes." Sadie carried Trudy outside and gently set her down on the grass. The little girl held onto the end of the leash as the puppy romped around, acting completely normal.

"What was that you gave 'er, Miss Velvie?" Joanna asked.

"It's a syrup made from elkweed. Acts like an emetic, you know induces vomiting."

Just as Joanna started to get up from her position on the grass, Trudy stopped and put her nose to the ground. The little stomach began to heave; in and out, in and out, and that familiar pumping noise started and the vomiting finally began. When she was finished, the onlookers could see the undigested green granules among the stomach contents.

"She ought to be fine now," Miss Velvie patted the shaggy head.

It was a few weeks before Sadie came in again, but Joanna took her to do medicine rounds. They gave several parvo immunizations and a couple of the dogs were on antibiotics. Bo-Bo, a boxer-mix, had to have ointment applied to an eye infection. He danced around the kennel and jumped on the girls with that zealous spirit which all boxers seem to possess. "Thank goodness you're here," Joanna panted. "You ought'a see me tryin' to do this by myself sometimes."

All but one of the dogs were due for wormer. Joanna watched as Sadie estimated their weights and measured out correct dosages. A litter of kittens had to have antibiotics for a respiratory infection, and a litter of puppies had to be dipped for scabies.

"This pink stuff, is this the amoxicillin?" Sadie asked.

"Yep. Draw up a half a milliliter in that syringe and give each one of 'em." She placed the tip of the syringe into the medicine and aspirated slowly until she had the correct amount.

"You're a natural at this," Joanna told Sadie. "You did real good givin' those shots, and folks usually have a lotta trouble learnin' how to draw medicine up in the syringes, it's a little awkward holdin' the vial and the syringe at the same time."

"I'm gonna start tryin' to come out more often," said Sadie. "I really like learnin' about the medicines and all. I wanted to go to school to be a vet, but you know how it goes; fall in love, get married, get a job." The pixie-like face clouded over a little. "Marriage sure ain't what I thought it would be like, though. Walter-Ray was so sweet when we were datin', but now he just seems angry a lot of the the time, especially when he gets to drinkin'. He stays out half the night with his buddies, but he wants me sittin' right there at home, waitin' for 'im when he gets back."

"That's how a lot of these redneck country boys are, honey," Joanna said. "If you let that foolishness get started, there ain't no changin' 'em, and they make your life miserable. You better nip it on the bud while y'all are still young."

"I don't know what to do though," Sadie stated. "Walter-Ray gets so mad that I find myself goin' along with what he wants. When he gets to hollerin' and cussin' it just tears my nerves all to pieces. Sometimes I go two or three nights and don't get a wink 'a sleep, on account of his temper tantrums."

"I hate to tell you this, sweetie, but it probably ain't gonna get no better. There ain't no turnin' these ol' boys around, they're hardheaded."

"I don't know," she answered. "Maybe I'll be able to find a way to change Walter-Ray. I'm sure gonna try, 'cause I do love 'im."

Sadie's sister, Cindy came out one Saturday with her boys to see about adopting a puppy. The children were very active, but Joanna noticed that Cindy watched them carefully and repeatedly warned them to be gentle with the animals, when they handled the small puppies.

"Maybe you ought'a think about gettin' somethin' a little bigger, then you wouldn't haf'ta keep your eyes on 'em every second. How about Broady, there? He's about six months old, so he's really still a puppy, but he's one rough, tough dude. Him and your boys would probably make a right good match." Joanna opened his gate and he barreled out to greet the children, who immediately began to wrestle with the slick, black bundle of energy.

Cindy ended up adopting the lab mix and she began to talk about her sister as they filled out the papers. "Sadie sure loves it out here."

"We have a good time out here," Joann answered. "And it's the best feelin', helpin' these animals find homes."

"Walter-Ray don't hardly let Sadie go nowhere without 'im bein' right up under 'er. I know she'd come out here nearabout every day if he'd let 'er, but that boy's mean as a blacksnake! She wants a dog so bad, and he won't let 'er get one. Shucks, we always had pets when we were growin' up, even if it weren't nothin' but keepin' one of Daddy's old coonhounds in the house and dressin' 'im up in our doll clothes.

"Sadie can't even go nowhere with me and the boys without Walter-Ray flingin' a fit. I done told 'im off a few times, myself. Daddy says she can move back home any time she wants, but as long as they stay together, he ain't gettin' in the middle of it. Says she burned her own ass, and she'll haf'ta sit on the blister."

The next weekend Sadie came out and it was a quiet day, so the girls spent some time with the animals, and enjoyed each other's company. They were sitting outside with three of the dogs that they had just finished walking, when a black pickup pulled into the drive.

"Oh, God, that's Walter-Ray," said Sadie. "I wish he'd leave me alone, just for a little while. He can't stand for me to be out'ta his sight more'n five minutes, and I'm sick of it."

She got up and walked over to the truck as it came to a stop. "Hey honey," Joanna heard her say. "I thought y'all were workin'."

He glared down at her. "You can't do nothin' but stay out here all the time, can you? You need to come on to the house and fix me some dinner, I'm goin' huntin' with the guys this afternoon, and I wanna eat before I go."

"I fixed a casserole before I left this mornin'," she answered. "It was supposed to be for supper, but you can have some of that for dinner. Just heat it up in the microwave."

"I want you to come on to the house," he answered. "And I mean now, not in an hour."

Sadie's shoulders slumped in familiar defeat and she walked back over to where Joanna sat on the ground with Oscar. "Tansey, can you take Bo-Bo? I reckon I better go, do we're gonna have a scene right here."

Tansey took the dog, and watched her walk quickly to her car and get in, and the anger welled up in her.

"Hey Walter-Ray!" Tansey called out. "What do you think, Sadie's meetin a man out here or somethin'? It's just us womenfolk and dogs!" In answer, he sped out of the parking lot, kicking up gravel.

"Tansey! You shouldn't have said nothing' to 'im," Sadie giggled. "Now he's never gonna want me to come back."

"He needs his scrawny butt kicked," Tansey yelled back. "You ain't done nothin' wrong. You're gonna be miserable all your life if you stay with 'im."

"I dunno. I'll figure out a way to change him, one of these days," Trudy responded as she got into her car. "I'll see y'all later."

"Boy, I feel sorry for her," said Becky, a young volunteer. "I don't know if I ever want to get married, if that's how husbands act. I wouldn't never let no man tell me I couldn't come out here."

"Well, it ain't always that easy," Joanna answered.

"Wonder why she wants to stay with 'im anyway?" Tansey mused. "He ain't nice, he ain't rich, and he sure ain't handsome. He's nearabout ugly as a lard bucket full of armpits!"

"I got'ta agree with you there, Tansey," Joanna giggled.

So that was the way it went for awhile. The girls wouldn't see Sadie for a few weeks, then she would come back, and Joanna knew she wanted to be there more often. Sometimes Walter-Ray would call and tell her to come home and she seemed afraid to defy him.

"Sometimes he can be so sweet, he's always buyin' me presents; real expensive stuff, too. Last time we had a fight, he bought me a new livin' room suite, but we didn't really need it. I'd whole lots rather do without all that stuff, and just get along better, you know, have some fun together. I don't know whey he gets so upset about me comin' out here!"

Sadie came in one Thursday evening.

"Hey girl!" Joanna called out. "I won't lookin' for you tonight, but I sure am glad to see you."

"From now on, I'm comin' whenever I get ready," Sadie answered. "I'm gonna try to come at least once a week."

"Good! Did you finally send old Walter-Ray on down the road?"

"No, but I sweetened up his attitude some."

"How'd you accomplish that?"

"You know how he's been acting, right? I finally had a belly full of it. You know that elkweed stuff?"

"Yeah, the emetic, that induces vomiting. What's that got to do with it?"

"He threw one of his tantrums last weekend. Came in late Saturday night, drunk as a skunk, cussin' and carryin' on somethin' awful. I'd fixed some spaghetti for supper and he didn't like it, so he threw 'is plate in the middle of the livin' room floor; right on the new carpet! I wanted to just jack 'is jaw, I was that mad. But what I did was, I slipped some of that elkweed into 'is bourbon!"

"You didn't! " Joanna shrieked in surprise.

"Yeah, I did. Remember, Miss Velvie was tellin' us it was good to have around if you got kids or pets? You know I keep Cindy's boys right much, and they just get into everything, so I got some from 'er. Well, all of a sudden, I got the idea to give Walter-Ray some of it. That old whiskey tastes so bad anyway, he didn't never even notice it.

"And a few minutes later, he went to pukin' 'is guts up, told me he thought he was dyin'. He crawled around on the floor, moanin' and groanin', upchuckin' all over the carpet and I had a time not to let 'im see me laughin'. I might as well to clean up what he's done eat, as to just let 'im throw it in the floor on purpose, right?"

"Sadie! I can't believe you did that!"

"I know," she replied. "I was startin' to get kind'a scared, when he kept on throwin' up. I thought for a few minutes there I was gonna have to take 'im to the emergency room, and I was gonna be in trouble for attempted murder, or somethin'. I even got to feelin' sorry for 'im, I ain't never seen nobody that sick before."

"Probably all that liquor made it worse," Joanna said.

"He thinks it was the alcohol what done it," Sadie confided. "Says he ain't gonna touch it, no more."

Walter-Ray did stop drinking and his attitude changed a great deal. Sadie seemed happier than she had since Joanna had known her. When the girls took Miss Velvie to the Texas Steak House, she went along. A couple of rounds of margaritas loosened their tongues and Sadie disclosed her story to the little group.

"You go, girl!" hooted Tansey. "You sure fixed im! I hated the way he was always followin' you around, with 'is hindparts on 'is shoulders. He reminded me of a booger you can't thump off!" As Joanna slid down her chair and lay there giggling under the table, she vaguely heard the waitress asking if she was all right.

"Give us a quote for this one, Miss Velvie," Denise begged.

"Well, let's see. I know, "A merry heart doeth good like a medicine.""

Proverbs 17:22.

But then, Tansey really summed it up for a lot of women with her country girl philosophy, "That there's why I ain't got me no husband, ladies. Dogs are a heck of a lot easier to train!"

LAZARUS

"And he rose up from the dead."
—The Bible

"No, I just heard somethin' that really upset me," Denise confided over the telephone. "Courtney said they had a seein'-eye-dog that was brought in today, down at Dr. Cooper's. The owner died and the family wants to have the dog put to sleep. He ain't sick or nothin'. Apparently, they just don't want to be bothered. How in the world can they do somethin' like that?"

"You know how folks are," Joanna sighed. "Always want to take the easy way out. But you know, we did some adoptions Saturday, opened up a couple of runs down at the rescue. I don't see why we couldn't take this dog. If we can just buy a little time, I bet one of the agencies for the blind would love to have 'im."

"That's what I was thinkin', but I didn't realize we had an openin'. You want to let's call Doc and tell 'im?"

"Why not?"

"We've got a problem," Courtney explained later. "The family won't agree to puttin' the dog up for adoption. Mr. Cox said it was his father's dog and he didn't want anybody else to have it. I could hear Doc, back in his office on the phone, practically beggin', but he couldn't get anywhere."

"Well, there's nothin' we can do," Joanna tried to console Denise.

"I know, I just feel so bad about it. I can't get it off my mind."

"Guess what, Jo!" Denise gushed over the telephone the next day. "Courtney called and said for us to come get that dog!"

"Great! Those folks must have finally changed their minds."

"I dunno. She said to wait until they closed. Asked if we could bring that truck of Randy's with the camper shell, 'cause they didn't want nobody to see 'im."

The receptionist rushed to open the door when Denise tapped on it that night. "Come on back here," she instructed, as she led the way to the kennels and opened the door to release a beautiful German Sheperd.

"Y'all wouldn't never believe what happened!" Courtney spewed out. "That Mr. Cox, he insisted on comin' down here this mornin' to watch while the dog was euthanized. Well, sir! Doc had 'im layin' up there on the table and gave 'im the injection. He put 'is head down and closed 'is eyes and let out the biggest sigh you ever heard. Me and Bonnie, we both got to cryin'. You know, just snifflin' a little bit, we couldn't hardly help it. Anyway, after the guy left, Doc called us back in there. He told Bonnie to check for a heartbeat and while she was gettin' the stethoscope in place, he got to grinnin'. Turns out, all he done was give 'im enough to knock 'im out! He come to in a couple of hours and been right as rain ever since."

"I guess you girls know how important it is that nobody finds out about this, don't you?" the elderly veterinarian poked his head into the doorway.

"We won't tell a soul, you old rascal!" Denise declared as she rushed over to give him a hug. "You're somethin' else, you know that?"

"Well, I don't know if I did the right thing or not," he answered. "I could get in an awful lot of legal trouble if this gets out. I don't mind tellin' you, I didn't know if I could actually get away with it or not. I kept wonderin' what I was gonna do if that guy wanted to take the dog with 'im. You know, a lot of times, clients want to take a pet home and bury it. I purely broke out in a sweat while I was standin' there thinkin' about that. But I should'a known that would be too much trouble for that feller." Dr. Cooper reached down to pet the dog. "Good thing for you, ain't it boy?"

Later at the rescue, the girls got the dog settled into a run. Joanna gave him a little food and he wolfed it down while Denise got a thick blanket for bedding. Denise lingered in the run, scratching the dog and murmuring to him, "We've got to go, boy, but I'll see you tomorrow. Don't worry, you'll be safe here."

Denise already had the dog out when Joanna arrived at the rescue on Saturday morning. Petey and Kayla were with her. They were romping across the back field with the dog. Just as Joanna walked over, Tansey drove up.

"So that's the dog y'all brought out from Doc's place?" Tansey asked.

"You ain't said nothin' to anybody about 'im, have you?" Denise asked.

"Naw! You know I can keep a secret, Neecie." She turned to the dog. "What's your name, big feller?"

"We don't know," Joanna answered. "Courtney said the people didn't ever tell 'em."

"Maybe we ought'a call 'im Lazarus," Denise suggested. "After all, he arose from the dead. Almost."

"That would be perfect!" Tansey agreed. "How about it, Lazarus?" The dog didn't pay any attention, as he lay on the ground with Petey and Kayla sitting on him.

The girls soon realized they had a problem. If they contacted one of the agencies for the blind, they were running the risk of revealing what Dr. Cooper had done. So they decided to remain silent and try to figure out what to do. Meanwhile, Hilda was beginning to complain because the dog seemed to be difficult to place.

"It's so frustratin'," Denise said. "Here's Lazarus, a really special animal and we've got to keep our mouths shut about what he can do."

"I swear, the big dogs are just so hard to find homes for," Joanna said. "Maybe we can find somebody to foster 'im." But they had no luck and Lazarus remained at the rescue.

A few months later, Tansey called Joanna with some news. "You're not gonna believe this, but we had a blind girl come in the clinic today. Me and her got to talkin' and she was tellin' me how bad she's been wantin' a guide dog. Says she's on the list, but it may be a couple of years before they have one for 'er. What do you think?"

"What a coincidence!" exclaimed Joanna. "Do you think she would keep it confidential?"

"I believe she would, once she knew the stakes. She seems to be a mighty sweet girl. Why don't we get Neecie and go visit 'er?"

The girls went to meet Amanda Starling that weekend. The white clapboard house was edged with colorful flowerbeds and the lawn was neatly manicured. "Looky there," Tansey pointed to the spacious back yard which was surrounded by chain link fencing. A smiling brunette woman opened the door and recognized Tansey. Leading them into the den, she called out, "Amanda, we've got company, honey. It's that little nurse from the clinic and some of 'er friends."

The slender figure sat on an oversized sofa, a book of Braille resting in her lap. Slate gray eyes stared straight ahead unseeingly, but they were softened by long, curving lashes. Mid-length hair of honey blonde curved across the porcelain cheek and Joanna thought she looked a bit like a gentle fawn, nearly lost in the vast cushions that surrounded her. At first her manner was subdued, no doubt wondering why her nurse had come to visit. But as they talked, she became more animated and her voice was clear and distinct. Her father came in from the garage and joined them.

After talking with the Starling's for a little while, the girls looked at each other and nodded.

"Amanda, I'm gonna tell you why we're really here," Joanna began. "Tansey thought you'd be interested in gettin' a guide dog and we've got one that needs a home. Looks to me like you two would make a perfect pair."

"You're kiddin'!" the girl gasped. "It's too good to be true."

"We need to keep it quiet, though." Joanna explained what had happened and the Starlings seemed to understand the need for confidentiality.

"Amanda's still goin' to have to go up to the blind school, though," Mr. Starling interjected. "And I guess the dog would have to go with 'er, you know how they work dog and master together. I'll call Monday and see what we would need to do."

The school scheduled Amanda and Lazarus to go three weeks later. They suggested that the dog not be placed with her until that time, so he remained at the rescue until the day before departure. Denise and Joanna met them there that evening.

They settled Amanda into a chair in the little waiting room and Denise brought Lazarus out. The big dog seemed to sense that something was different about the girl, because his playful demeanor changed. Walking slowly across the floor, he laid his head in her lap and stood, still as a statue. As delicate fingers stroked his ears tenderly, Amanda's face lit up in a radiant smile.

"Just think, Lazarus, you're gonna be my very own dog! I've wanted one for so long now, I can hardly believe it's finally comin' true." The big dog just continued to stand, motionless as the gentle hand caressed him over and over.

When the Starlings were ready to leave, Amanda hugged Joanna and Denise. Her mother watched, moist-eyed as she stood with her husband's arm around her. "How can we ever thank you girls?" she asked.

"Oh, you already have," Joanna answered. "Givin' that guy a home is the best thanks we could ever ask for."

They were gone for nearly a month but Amanda called Joanna the moment they returned. Bursting with excitement at her new-found freedom, she stayed on the line for more than an hour describing the training center where the animals and people worked together.

"And it worked out perfectly," she finished. "I'm gettin' back just in time for school to start next week. I can hardly wait to go so Laz can meet all my friends. And I bet they're gonna all be jealous of me. I'm gonna be a senior this year, you know."

When Joanna called at the end of the week, Amanda was still just as optimistic as ever. "Everybody just loves Laz," she gushed. "One of the guys in my English class brought 'im one of those thick doggie beds and the boys take turns haulin' it from room to room. Laz just lays right on it all durin' class and everybody thinks he's the coolest. I think when they pick the most popular student for the yearbook, it's gonna be a dog instead of a person!

"But you know, he's got some kind of infection in 'is gums and we can't get it cleared up," she continued. "And nothin' seems to help. He's had all kinds of medicines and shots, but it won't go away."

"I know somebody that can fix 'im up," Joanna responded. "Why don't I come get y'all and we'll go see 'er?"

Joanna picked Amanda and Lazarus up and they headed for Miss Velvie's house. With Lazarus sitting tall between them on the truck seat, Amanda chattered happily about school. "I'm plannin' to go to East Carolina University in the fall," she informed Joanna. "I'm goin' into the Social Work program. I'd like to be a social worker for the blind, like Michael Griffin. He's blind, too, you know. He helps so many people and I wanna be just like 'im."

"Well now, I believe we can get your dog fixed up," Miss Velvie informed Amanda a little later as she peered into the big mouth.

"Oh, good! What can you give 'im?"

"A little herb called tormentil. I'm gonna give you a liquid tincture and he'll need three drops twice a day. It's purty strong stuff. Come on in the kitchen and let me fix it up."

Joanna seated Amanda at the big table and Lazarus lay at her feet. They talked while the old woman put a pot of water on to boil, then she got a paring knife and started cutting the slender stalks with tiny yellow flowers."

"That looks like blood runnin' out when you cut through it," Joanna said as she watched bright red liquid draining down the sink.

"That's why the old folks used to call it bloodroot," Miss Velvie answered. "I was always fascinated when I watched Mama fixin' it. Jo, pour us a glass of tea, will you honey? This heat's makin' me mighty thirsty.

"That sure hits the spot. I declare, it's mighty warm for this time of year. If this keeps up, my hens will be layin' hard-boiled eggs!"

"Is this Joanna Morgan?" a cold, steely voice came over the telephone later that night.

"Yes it is."

"This is Simon Cox. You don't know me, but that dog you've got belonged to my father. He was supposed to be put to sleep! How dare you, and that...that so-called veterinarian. I'm calling the state tomorrow to report him and I hope he loses his license. You people have a lot of nerve!"

"Now hold on just a minute, Mr. Cox and let me explain. The dog is with a girl that really needed 'im, she's blind, too...just like your father was. I bet he'd be real happy at the way things turned out. And Doc's so good-hearted, always tryin' to help somebody, I hate to see 'im get in trouble. Won't you reconsider?"

"He's not the only one that's in trouble young lady, you better be worried for your own sake. I'm going to take you to court, you and that entire animal organization you work for!" He slammed the telephone down so hard it made Joanna's ear ring.

A patrol car pulled into the yard the next day and Tony got out. "Jo, I swear, I hate like the devil to haf'ta do this but I've got'ta ask you some questions. There's been a complaint that you stole a dog that was down at Doc's."

"What if I did?"

"The only thing I'm much worried about is Doc. You know, bein' a licensed vet and all, it could have some impact on 'im."

"How in the world did they find out, anyway? Didn't hardly anybody know and I'd bet my life, they didn't say nothin."

"I know exactly who's in on it with you and you're right. They ain't said a word. It was Hilda."

"How'd she find out?"

"She had set up a hidden camcorder and got y'all on tape. The guy brought it in and we had to sit down and watch it. And everything's on it, where y'all were talkin' about keepin' it a big secret to keep Doc out of trouble."

"That's all she lives for, is to stir up trouble!"

"I know it," Tony nodded.

"But there's one thing I don't understand. Why'd she wait so long to do anything about it? It's been over two months, now."

"She told Cox she'd been tryin' to reach 'im. Seems he'd been gone on some business trip. Works for one of them big pharmaceutical companies."

Tony got into his patrol car. "I'll keep you posted if I hear anything."

Denise called in tears Sunday morning. "Jo, have you seen the paper yet?"

"Why, what's wrong?"

"There's an article about us, right on the front page! There's a big picture of me and Lazarus, in color and everything. They must'a lifted it from that video, because it's right there in the waitin' room. The headline says, "Animal Advocates Abduct Valuable Guide Dog" It makes it look as if Lazarus was a highly prized dog and we took 'im away from somebody that cared about 'im. What in the world are we gonna do?"

Tansey knew what she wanted to do when Joanna saw her that afternoon at Miss Velvie's house. "I'm gonna kick 'er skinny butt!" she declared.

"Now, don't say that, honey," Miss Velvie murmured. "Fightin' don't never help nothin'. Remember, he that is slow to anger is better than the almighty. Howsomever, I'm nearabout to get to the place where I'd like to watch you do it, though. I'm beginnin' to think that girl's lower than a doodle-bug. Lord have mercy, I just wish that Hilda could behave 'erself."

"I'm beginnin' to think that won't never happen," Joanna said.

She went home that evening, thinking that things couldn't get any worse. Until Tansey called.

"Turn the local news on! Damned if that bitch ain't got us on t.v. now!"

Hanging up the telephone, Joanna hurried to turn the television on, flipping through the channels until she reached the local station. There she was, big as life on the screen, kneeling down beside Lazarus as Amanda stroked his head. Denise and Tansey lingered in the background, huge smiles on their faces. Amanda's parents came into view for a moment, then disappeared from the camera's focus. Then Joanna heard her own voice.

"We've got'ta be really careful not to let this get out, now. If the former owners were to find out, I dunno, it might cause a lot of trouble. 'Specially for Doc Cooper. So don't let anybody know where we got this dog from."

Suddenly, the picture changed and the local reporter's face came into view. "And there you have it, ladies and gentlemen. This scene came to you from the Beagle Brigade and Small Animal Rescue and the people you saw were among their most active volunteers, who allegedly stole this expensive service animal. And as the tape indicates, our local veterinarian, Dr Cooper was involved. It has been suggested that these people sold the dog for a very large sum of money, which they have used to line their own pockets. Those of you who have pets may want to take precautions, because this is a frightening scenario, that the local organization which was founded to help animals may actually be exploiting them! And now for the weather."

With shaking hands, Joanna turned the television off and sat down, staring at the blank screen. When the telephone rang again, she barely heard it.

"You know what we need to do?" Tansey screeched over the wires. "We need to get on t.v. and tell 'em the truth. That's the only thing I see to let folks know what really happened."

"Maybe you got a point. But we need to ask Doc."

The girls were there when the veterinarian arrived the next day. Joanna thought how old and tired he looked as he trudged across the parking lot, head down and shoulders stooped.

"Mornin' girls," he said looking at them with troubled eyes.

"Doc, I know you saw the news last night," Joanna said. "And the newspaper."

He just nodded.

Tansey thought maybe we ought'a get to the media ourselves and tell the truth."

Dr. Cooper looked at her and his eyes brightened.

"I don't see how it could hurt nothin', it's already out that we took the dog without the owner knowin'. Seems like to me we just got'ta let folks know what really happened. But I wanted to talk to you first."

"You know, you girls may just have an idea there. I don't like a lot of sensationalism, but they really made us look like criminals."

"Great!" Tansey shouted. "I'll go call the station right now."

A reporter came out to the animal hospital late that afternoon and everyone met them there. The girls stood to the side and watched as the old veterinarian stood before the camera and told the public what had really happened.

"So you see," he concluded. "We were only tryin' to help that dog. I did somethin' I've never done before, in all my years of practice. I was dishonest with a client. For the first time in my life, I did not respect their wishes. But I was gonna be forced to euthanize Lazarus, a fine animal, one that had done so much to help his master. That dog did not deserve to be killed. I do have to put down a lot of dogs, simply because they are homeless, but so many people would have loved to have Lazarus. I may be guilty of wrong-doing, but I believe it would be a sin to murder an animal that can be of such great service to a human-being."

"And this is Amanda Starling, the young lady who received the dog," the camera swung over to where Lazarus sat by Amanda's chair. "What do you have to say?"

"I'm really sorry they got in all this trouble, but I just can't tell you what it has meant for me, the freedom I've experienced for the first time in my life," the slender hand reached down to rest on the dog's head. "And what seems even more important, I love 'im so much. Lazarus is such a good dog, I can't bear to think that he could have been killed."

"What about the claims that you profited financially by this?" the reporter asked, as they focused on the veterinarian again.

"Those charges are absolutely unfounded," Dr. Cooper said. "All you haf'ta do, is come look at my tiny clinic or my battered old pick-up and you can see money is not so important to me. In fact, I'm gonna have to pay a right hefty fine...over a thousand dollars, but I'm still glad we did it. And as for these girls, why there's no one on God's green earth that could ever convince me they would do somethin' like that. You want to know why?"

"Why is that, Dr. Cooper?" the reporter asked.

"I'll tell you why. Because every time I turn around, these girls are pickin' up stray animals and bringin' 'em in to the clinic, tryin' to help 'em. And that rescue group never pays for it, they pay it out of their own pockets! Between the three of 'em, they've spent more money on raggedy old strays than a guide dog would ever even cost. I've even seen 'em pay the bills for other people's animals sometimes."

The camera quickly panned over to where the girls were standing.

"What about it ladies? Do you have anything to say on the subject?"

"I sure do!" Tansey declared as she pushed her way in front of her friends and grabbed the microphone from the reporter. "The first thing I want to say to all you people out there, is let's all start a collection to help Doc pay off the fine, just drop it off at 'is office. I didn't know nothin' about it until just now, but here's twenty dollars to start it off!" she turned and shoved it at the old veterinarian who stood there, surprise written across his face. "He did a good thing, and he shouldn't haf'ta pay for it!" And as for you, Hilda Hawkins," she looked directly into the camera. "I'm 'bout sick of you causin' trouble. Get ready, 'cause you're gonna tote an ass-whippin' tonight girl! I'm on my way to your house right now!"

Denise and Joanna grabbed Tansey as she threw the microphone down and started for the door. "Fool!" Joanna exclaimed. "You can't go beat 'er up right after you announced it to the world. She's probably on the phone right now, callin' the law."

Denise called Joanna the next evening. "Guess what! Courtney just told me people have been comin' by all day, makin' donations. One lady came in right at closin' time and Courtney told 'er they had already taken in enough to pay the fine. She wrote 'em a check anyway ... two hundred dollars! Told 'em to use it to start a fund to pay the medical expenses for homeless animals. Said anybody kind as Doc deserved a little help and she's gonna start a campaign to raise more for 'im."

"How 'bout that," Joanna responded. "Looks like Doc's gonna come out on the good end!"

"Yep. I'd sure like to see the look on old Hilda's face when she finds out."

Joanna was at Miss Velvie's a few days later when the Starlings drove up. "We just wanted to bring you a little gift for helping Lazarus," Mrs. Starling said. "Amanda said you wouldn't accept the money we sent, so I hope you can use this."

She handed the old woman a large wicker basket, tied with a pink bow and filled with toiletry items. There was a box of White Shoulders dusting powder, a matching bottle of lotion, a pair of fluffy bedroom slippers, bath sponges and scented soaps.

"Why thank you kindly," Miss Velvie opened the powder and sniffed. "This always was one of my favorites, Mama used to wear it and it smells just like 'er."

"Miss Velvie, that stuff you gave us worked like a charm," Amanda declared. "Laz feels so much better and he's eatin' good again." The big dog sat calmly by his mistress, ignoring all Miss Velvie's animals.

In the following months, the Starlings came by occasionally to visit the old woman and she developed a very close relationship with Amanda. When the first of June arrived she told Joanna she wanted to attend the girl's graduation.

"Amanda's gonna be the class valedictorian," Miss Velvie said. "Let's see if Denise and Tansey can go with us, too. And let's ask Doc. I got a little surprise planned."

"What is it?"

"Oh no, you'll haf'ta wait 'till graduation night and see. If you tell, it ain't no surprise."

They were all seated in the auditorium with Amanda's parents on graduation night, waiting for the ceremony to begin. At a quarter before seven, Miss Velvie nudged Joanna. "Come on and let's go find Amanda," she whispered. As Joanna held her elbow, the old woman made her way down the aisle, carrying a large bag of white plastic.

"Amanda," Joanna called when they spotted her. "Miss Velvie's got somethin' for you! Hurry up, I been dyin' to find out what it is."

As the girl started over, the old woman opened the bag. There, nestled on a hanger inside, was a strange looking replica of her graduation gown. But the navy satin had a strange shape to it, short in front, long in back and only looked as if it would be long enough to fit a toddler. Then she pulled out a smaller version of the graduation cap, complete with the golden tassel. And it had a strange looking chin strap.

"This here's for Lazarus," the old woman declared. "I figgered if he was gonna walk across that stage with you, he might just as well have 'is own graduatin' outfit!" All the students gathered around to watch as Joanna put the gown over the dog's head and draped it back to fall across his hindquarters.

"Fits right good, don't it?" Miss Velvie asked. "I used Izzie as a sort of model, she's just a wee bit smaller than Lazarus. I made 'er try it on for me so many times, it got to the place where she'd run and hide if she saw me take it out."

One of the girls picked up the cap and put it on Lazarus, adjusting it carefully so that it sat jauntily on his head.

"I was the eyes to the blind," murmured the old woman. "Job 29:15. That's you, old boy."

Following the introduction, Amanda was called up on stage to make her speech. A gasp of amazement rippled through the audience as she started confidently up the steps, the loyal dog guiding her swiftly. The two navy gowns moved in unison, as the golden cap tassels swayed and bobbed. Amanda's parents looked at each other, then Mrs. Starling leaned over and gave Miss Velvie a hug. "We wondered what you had in that bag," she admitted.

Five full minutes passed before the applause began to slow down. People were clapping, stomping their feet and letting out rebel yells.

When the noise finally stopped, Amanda's voice rang out clear and true over the microphone, as her canine companion sat looking up at her. She spoke of the usual matters that are brought up at graduations, such as college and plans for the future. But at the end, she had a few special words of gratitude.

"First of all, I want to thank my parents, who have always encouraged me to be like any other normal kid. Everything they do is always for me and I love you, Mama and Daddy. Secondly, I want to thank all the teachers and classmates who stood by me through the years. And last, but not least, I want to thank the people that made it possible for me to have Lazarus." She reached down and ran her hand over one of the silky ears.

"They'll never know exactly how much they've done for me. Jo? Can y'all stand up?"

Slowly and self-consciously, they stood; Joanna, Miss Velvie, Denise, Tansey and Dr.Cooper.

"How 'bout a big hand for 'em?" Amanda requested and the applause started again. This time it was deafening, as a few of Amanda's friends stood up on their chairs and other teenagers jumped up and down on the bleachers in a frenzy of excitement.

"A-Man-Da! Laz-A-Rus! A-Man-Da! Laz-A-Rus!"

"I declare," Miss Velvie exclaimed. "I'm nearabout proud as a dog with two tails!"

Amanda continued when the noise finally quieted down.

"I just can't tell you how much it's meant to me to have Lazarus. It sure was my lucky day when you saved 'im. He's made my senior year so special and we're gonna be together for a long, long time."

Joanna looked around at the others as Miss Velvie clasped her hand tightly. Dr. Cooper was smiling as Tansey hugged him tightly and Denise was dabbing at her eyes.

"It was worth it all!" she thought.

HOOD ORNAMENT AND STRIPPER

"The great pleasure of a dog is that you may make a fool of yourself with him and not only will he not scold you, he will make a fool of himself, too."
—Samuel Butler

"Hey, Randy! You'uns load up your hosses and come on over Saturday," Uncle Otto said. "We got a big ride planned and we're gonna cook down at the Sugar Shack." Randy and Joanna had stopped at Homer's to get a couple of steaks and he was inside talking to the other elderly men who liked to gather there in the evenings. We're gonna have a large time!"

"I got to work, we're tryin' to get finished plantin' down at the Simmons farm." Randy said. "But we'll ride over when y'all come in."

Trucks and trailers were scattered all over the pasture when they finally got to the shack that afternoon. A couple of the big, fancy rigs had tarps stretched out to form a shady sitting area and some of the small trailers had tents pitched beside them. As they came closer, they could see that Otto and most of the other riders had already come in. Randy ambled over to the pig cooker and Joanna went inside the shack to see if she could help Aunt Emma, who was peeling a big pot of potatoes and onions. The women put them on to boil, then went outside.

"Uncle Otto, I'm gonna run down to the river and get Haywood," Randy said. "I think him and Nollie are down there."

"Go get 'em, we got a'plenty food here to feed the whole dang town!"

"Come on, we'll ride with you, Randy," Joanna called. She slid into the passenger seat, while Tansey and a few of the other girls climbed into the back of the truck.

As they started down the path, riders were still straggling in, a few at the time.

Johnny-Vern was coming up the dirt road, riding between two pretty girls. When he saw the newcomers, he loped over to the truck on his flashy black and white paint stallion. The slight, wiry body sat so relaxed in the saddle that he seemed almost an extension of the horse.

"Hey, Randy, where y'all goin'?"

"We're gonna run up to the river, we'll be right back."

Johnny-Vern sailed from his horse and landed in the bed of the truck.

"Hey girls," Take my pony on in, will you? I'm gon'n ride with 'em."

One of the girls caught the paint by the reins and the horse followed them on towards the Sugar Shack, as Johnny-Vern sat down and put his arm around Tansey to settle down for the short ride. When they got to the river there were several trucks parked there and they could see a few of the men sitting under the shelter. Randy pulled the truck up alongside.

"Hey, Jo, I was lookin' for you," declared Eldridge Evans as he got up off the glider and started towards the truck. Black eyes scowled out of the hatchet face as he stood, legs set wide apart and hands shoved deep into the pockets of his faded coveralls. "I got a puppy here and if you don't want 'im, I'm gonna call the pound to pick 'im up."

"Don't do that !" she exclaimed. "Can't you keep 'im until we get an empty run at the rescue?"

"Naw, I'm sick of messin' with 'im. I gave three of 'em away, but I can't find nobody to take this last one, he's the runt of the litter and he acts crazy as a bedbug."

"Don't even think about it!" warned Randy as his wife started over to Eldridge's battered old Ford truck to look in the dog box. "He ain't goin' home with us."

"Well, I ain't leavin' 'im with Eldridge! You know what the pound has to do with 'em." Joanna opened the gate and a blur of black and white flew by. The puppy sailed off the tailgate like a high diving board and hit the ground running in circles. The sleek little body looked like a Jack Russell, but the head resembled that of a Collie, with tiny little flop ears. He zoomed around like a windup toy stuck on high speed until he spotted Haywood's Golden Retriever, Macey, trotting up the path and sailed on her, yipping like an angry hornet. The big gentle dog looked down, perplexed, as she stepped over the puppy and continued on her way. He grabbed the fringy tail and set his front feet, but Macey just dragged him along like a water skier behind a houseboat. He growled and shook his head as he was towed along.

"You're one bad dude, ain't you little guy?" exclaimed Johnny-Vern. "Kind'a like me, you're scrawny, but you sure are tough. How would you like to go home with me?"

"Shucks, Vern! You can't even take care of your own self, much less a dog!" Tansey exclaimed.

"Aw, it wouldn't take much to look after im, he's a tough little feller. He could hang with me all right, couldn't you, boy?" The puppy wriggled and licked Johnny-Vern in the face, yipping with delight.

"You best take 'im on this evenin', if you want 'im," said Eldridge. "You wait 'till, tomorrow, it's gonna be too late, he'll be down at the county pound."

Still holding the puppy, Johnny-Vern climbed back into the truck bed and the girls gathered around to stroke the slick fur. Erin cried out as the sharp teeth nipped at her fingers.

"You wanna go home with ol' Vern, puppy?" Tansey asked. "Man, you got a hard row to hoe if you're gonna survive livin' with that party animal."

When they got back to the Sugar Shack, Johnny-Vern climbed out of the truck, holding the puppy. "Hey girls! Come look what I got here!" The women swarmed over to the truck like bees to honey.

"All right, ladies, one at a time," he beamed. "Y'all can all have a turn rubbin' the little feller. In the meantime, if any of y'all want to practice by caressin' me a little, don't be shy about it. Step right on up." He put his arm around the blonde girl holding the puppy. "You'll haf'ta come over to my house and visit us sometimes, darlin'. That way, why you can have us all to yourself."

Joanna and Randy didn't see Johnny-Vern for a while and Joanna wondered how the little dog was doing.

Vern's havin' a ride at his place this weekend," Randy said when he came home one night. "Uncle Otto and Aunt Emma are bringin' the wagon. You want to go?"

"Yeah, that's always a good ride."

"Vern said to bring our bathin' suits. He's gonna take the big grill down to the old gravel pit and Marvin is gonna meet us down there with chickens to cook."

The yard was full when Randy and Joanna arrived on Saturday morning. Horses were tied to trailers, saddled and ready to go, as their riders lounged around waiting. They saw a crowd gathered around Brandon Tanner's flatbed truck and started over after unloading their horses. Jerry Lee Lewis was blaring out of the huge speakers about great balls of fire and Brandon was using the truck bed for a dancing platform. The pointed toes of his western boots flashed through the air at eye level so swiftly that they were almost a blur, as he ground his hips suggestively and played an invisible guitar. "Whoo-ee! Go man!" yelled Randy.

Joanna stepped into the little log cabin that Johnny-Vern had built himself. The interior was just as rustic as the outside, with rough shelving installed, instead of cabinets. Dirty clothing was strewn all over the living room and Playboy magazines littered the floor. Several glasses sat on the end table by the sofa, half filled with remnants of soft drinks and empty beer cans covered the coffee table, but she felt at home here.

Peeking into the kitchen, she spotted a stout man cutting up chickens. "Hey, Marvin!" Brown eyes looked up at her, swimming behind the thick lenses of his glasses and the handlebar mustache turned up in a grin. He wiped his hands and grabbed her in a bear hug.

Where's Vern?"

"Took the truck down to the back pasture to get 'is horse. He ought'a be on back any time now."

"Yee-Haw!" a voice whooped and Joanna looked out the window in time to see the black and white paint coming into the yard at a fast lope. Johnny-Vern pulled him to a sliding stop and sat easy in the saddle as the stallion reared up to paw at the sky with his front feet. When he came down, Joanna saw a little black and white head peering out of the saddle bags.

"That fool! He's got that dog up there on that horse, prob'ly scarin' 'im to death."

"Naw, he loves it. Vern rides 'im like that all the time."

She stepped out onto the porch. "Hey Jo! Come on over here and see little Stripper. He's growed since you seen 'im last, ain't he?"

The dog sat in the saddlebag, quivering with excitement as she walked over. "Where'd you get a name like Stripper?" she asked, stroking the slick head.

"Oh I don't tell nobody that, I like to show 'em," Vern answered mysteriously. "Maybe you'll see later on today. All right, folks! Pee on the fire, call the dogs and let's go! Y'all head 'em up and move 'em out!"

Everyone mounted up and they set off at a leisurely pace with Johnny-Vern leading the way. The little dog yelped happily as he swung to and fro in the saddlebag. As the paint settled into a smooth, steady jog, he climbed out to ride high behind the saddle. They made quite a sight, the high-stepping black and white stallion, with the tiny black and white dog perched on his back. Girls were constantly riding up to make a fuss over Stripper. "See here?" asked Johnny-Vern. "He's my chic-getter! Womenfolk just love this little guy."

Joanna heard the sound of a vehicle approaching behind them, and turned to see Haywood's pickup coming. Nollie was with him. Johnny-Vern pulled his paint up under a pair of huge old oak trees and reached deep into his insulated saddlebag. "I believe it's 'bout time to take a drink," he declared as the truck pulled alongside and Haywood cut the motor off. Johnny-Vern pulled a two liter Mountain Dew bottle from the deep insulated saddlebag opposite the side that Stripper had been in.

"What do you have in that bottle, Johnny-Vern?" asked Nollie.

"I mixed Early Times in and put it in the freezer. The bourbon keeps it from freezin' solid and bustin'. Get you a taste." He passed the bottle through the truck window. After passing the bottle around to some of the other men, he pulled a small cup from the bag. "Here you go, little buddy, I ain't gonna forget you," he said as he poured a few drops in and offered it to Stripper, who was now sitting in front of him on the saddle.

"Vern!" Joanna screeched. "Don't be givin' that dog liquor!"

"Aw, it's just a little bit, it ain't gonna hurt 'im none. He drinks it all the time."

The little dog barked down at Haywood, who was sitting on the tailgate with a bottle of Jack Daniels, trying to mix it with seven up. "You beg all you want to, dog," Haywood said.

"Your eyes may shine and your teeth may grit, but none of my whiskey will you ever get!"

A few minutes later the riders set out again. The sun was hot, beating down on their backs and Joanna began to think how good the cold water of the gravel pit was going to feel. Suddenly, her horse pricked his ears and looked up sharply. Coming down the path from a house was a young man, riding a sorrel horse that looked to stand well over seventeen hands tall. The body was lanky and lean and the stride was long.

"Calvin Cole," called Johnny-Vern. "I didn't know you rode. You go buy yourself a horse?"

"I sure did. Pure thoroughbred, he is, and he's fast, too. Paid three thousand for 'im. I wanna race somebody."

"Why don't you race 'im, Jo," Randy asked. "Bounty used to be a racehorse, didn't he?"

"Ain't no way. If I was to open this sucker up, he'd go crazy. You know how hard I had to work, tryin' to calm 'im down to make a trail horse out'ta him."

"I'll race you," Tansey rode up on the big Quarter Horse/Appaloosa mix. "Old Cloudy here can run a little bit." She pulled her horse up alongside the thoroughbred, who stood nearly a hand taller than Cloudy.

"Y'all see that field of frazier firs, where Marvin's Christmas tree farm starts?" Johnny-Vern asked, and they both nodded affirmatively.

"Let that be the finish line. Ready, set, Go!"

Cloudy crouched down and sprang out with his hind legs like a jack-in-the-box, as Tansey crouched low over his neck like a real jockey. The Thoroughbred got off to a slower start and it took him a couple of moments to reach his stride.

"Come on, Tansey!" the other girls were screaming at the top of their lungs. "Go, girl!"

The others could hardly see the Thoroughbred for the cloud of dust that Tansey and her horse had left him in, but he slowly began to gain ground as they went up the road. The man was leaning back in the saddle, holding on for all he was worth. They were slowly inching up, now they were only a length behind. Just as the Thoroughbred's nose pulled even with Cloudy's hindquarters, they crossed the finish line. Tansey pulled Cloudy to a sliding stop, but the Thoroughbred continued on down the road for a hundred yards before he could get the long legs slowed down. Tansey had gotten back to the others before Calvin had turned the big horse around.

"You know why I picked that spot for the finish line, don't you Tansey?" asked Johnny-Vern.

"Naw, why?"

"Well, 'cause it was 'bout a quarter mile from where y'all started off from. I figgered Cloudy would get off to a quick start, what with havin' Quarter Horse in 'im. And you know Thoroughbreds are for long distance runnin'. If y'all had gone the whole mile, you'd have been the one ended up eatin' some dust."

Finally, the riders saw the long path that led to the gravel pit. "Y'all walk your horses and cool 'em down, now," called Uncle Otto. "They're gonna want a drink when we get to the water. We got a good two mile to go back in the woods yet."

When they spotted the water, Johnny-Vern urged the paint into a gallop and splashed in, with Tansey close behind. The water was deep and within a few steps the horses were swimming. Stripper perched in front of Johnny-Vern on the saddle, barking in a frenzy of excitement.

"I'll race you 'round the float yonder, Tan," Johnny-Vern called. He had anchored a big raft about a hundred yards out. They struck out for it now, the horses swimming neck and neck. Tansey gained slightly and took the inside as they began to turn.

"Come on, Vern!" yelled Randy. "You ain't gonna let no girl beat you!" But the paint was already giving it all he had and Tansey reached the shore a couple of lengths ahead of him.

"That's okay, we'll get you next time," Johnny-Vern said as he shook the water out of his eyes. "Hey Marvin, you got that grill fired up yet?"

"Yep, the coals are just about ready. I was just waitin' for y'all to get here afore I put the birds on."

"You ladies can go change into your bathin' suits over behind the bushes yonder," Johnny-Vern said. Several of the girls tied their horses to trees and wasted no time in getting ready.

Amy picked a dandelion and sat down on the tailgate of Marvin's truck. Gazing out across the water, she took a deep breath and blew across it, scattering the feathery seeds into the air.

Nollie walked up and sat down beside her. "Now young lady, would you like to know how long it'll be until your wedding day?"

"How can you tell that?"

"By lookin' at that dandelion, where you just blew the seeds off. Now all you have to do is count how many are left, and that's how many years it'll be before you get married."

"Oh, Mr. Nollie! You're just makin' that up."

"Nope, it's an old folk legend. And look here." He reached down to pick a buttercup and hold it against her throat. "Your chin is turning yellow. That means you like butter."

"That's right, I do!"

Joanna stepped slowly into the cold water. Oh! It felt so good. Randy came behind her splashing, then grabbed her, dunking her completely under and she came up sputtering.

"You look like a wet muskrat, Jo," Johnny-Vern called from the shore, as she struck out swimming for the middle of the pit. The other girls followed and climbed up onto the raft.

"Stripper, come on boy!" called Johnny-Vern and the little dog jumped in without hesitation. When they reached the float, Johnny-Vern stretched his arm down and pulled him up, where he ran around shaking the cold water everywhere and making the girls squeal. Several of them stretched out flat on their stomachs to let the sun beat down on their backs. The others sat and talked quietly.

"Jo, you still wanna see how my dog got 'is name?" Johnny-Vern asked.

"I sure do."

Johnny-Vern motioned to Amy, who was lying closest to him. "Stripper! Get it!"

The little dog trotted over and grabbed the string holding her tiny bikini top together. With a quick jerk, he snatched it completely off and carried it proudly to his master.

"Hey! You little scoundrel! Darn you Vern, gim'me my top back, right now, do I'm gonna kill you - graveyard dead!"

"How you gonna kill me? You can't even sit up. You're at my mercy now, darlin'."

The other girls descended on Johnny-Vern, took the top back and pushed him off the float. He landed with a great splash and came up sputtering. One of the girls was helping Amy tie her top while another stroked Stripper's head. "How come y'all droolin' all over my dog and bein' mean to me? He's the one done it."

"Just 'cause you told 'im to," Joanna answered.

"See there Stripper, you don't never get in no trouble, it's always me that gets the blame." Johnny-Vern pulled himself back up onto the float and put an arm around Amy. "Come on, darlin' and take a little ride with me. Now we done got cooled off, I'm ready to get back in the saddle."

The others stayed on the float and watched them go down the path, riding double on the paint, with Stripper sitting proudly in front of his master on the saddle.

Johnny-Vern and Amy were just coming back in when Haywood called from the shore. "Hey, Randy! Marvin wants me to run up to Homer's and get some slaw. You wanna ride with me?"

"Wait for us, we wanna go!" Joanna dove off the float behind Randy, followed by several of the other girls. They climbed into the back of Haywood's truck, still wearing their wet bathing suits. Tansey was dragging behind with one foot on the bumper and Joanna reached down to pull her in as they started down the path.

"Y'all wait up! I'm goin', too," called Johnny-Vern. He handed Stripper up to one of the girls as the truck stopped and she clutched him tightly. "Go easy, Haywood," he said as he hopped onto the hood of the truck. "I'm gonna ride up here."

"Hey, Vern!" yelled Tansey from the truck bed. "I bet you won't take your clothes off and ride naked up there! I double dare you!"

"How much you wanna bet?"

"I'll put twenty bucks on it."

Clothing began to fly through the air. One cowboy boot landed in the truck bed, the other went into the ditch. His chambray shirt caught on the antenna and Randy reached out to grab his jeans as they flew by the cab window.

"What about them drawers?" Tansey yelled. "You got'ta take it all off before I pay up!" A pair of red boxer underwear flew back into the truck bed and hit her in the face.

"Whooo-ee-eee! Pee on the fire, call the dogs and let's go-o-o!" screeched Johnny-Vern as he crouched naked on the front of the truck, the wind blowing his hair back.

"I reckon he showed you, didn't he?" Randy called back through the open sliding window as Haywood accelerated and nearly threw Johnny-Vern off. "He's gonna get that twenty bucks!" Johnny-Vern tightened his grip on the grill as the truck blasted through the quiet little streets, the girls whooping and hollering, with the loud mufflers blasting. Revival services at the First Baptist church were just letting out and the ladies strolled along the sidewalk, some going to their cars, others setting out for the short walk home. They looked up in shock as the truck roared through with Johnny-Vern sitting on the hood without a stitch of clothing.

Stumpy and Lazy Ingram were coming out of the store when the truck pulled into the parking lot. "Hey, Haywood! Where'd you get that ugly hood ornament?" yelled Stumpy.

"That's exactly what he looks like, a hood ornament, with that skinny little body sittin' up there," screeched Lazy.

Johnny-Vern jumped down and put his jeans on. "Where's my other boot?"

Haywood looked up to see a cruiser from the sheriff's department turn into the parking lot and pull up beside him. Two deputies got out and walked over to the truck.

"Evenin', Johnny-Vern, Randy. How y'all doin' tonight?" the younger one asked.

"Purty good, Tony," Randy answered. "How 'bout you?"

"Well, we had a complaint called in a couple minutes ago. Some guy's been ridin' round naked on the hood of a fancy truck, with loud mufflers. Crowd of folks ridin' in the back, too. Disturbin' the peace 'round here a little bit. Y'all wouldn't happen to know nothin' 'bout that, would you?"

"Who, us?" Johnny-Vern asked. "You know we wouldn't do nothin' like that!"

"Yeah, when I heard the description on a loud truck full of screamin' women, I figgered I'd find you in the middle of it," the deputy laughed.

"Who called y'all?" Randy asked.

"The preacher's wife," the deputy chortled, then straightened his features, trying to look serious. "But really, Johnny-Vern. "Y'all can't go 'round doin' stuff like that!"

"Okay, I'll see if I can't get this crowd straightened out." Johnny-Vern turned to look at all his friends, still in the truck bed. "I'm ashamed of y'all." He hooked an arm around the deputy, turning him back towards his car. "You can dress 'em up, but you can't take 'em to town."

"Seriously, you guys give us a break!" the deputy laughed. Randy got the slaw and they headed back to the gravel pit. The rest of the evening was uneventful and everyone kept their clothes on.

Randy came in from the river a few nights later. "Eldridge heard about how Vern's got that dog trained to pull women's clothes off," he laughed. "Now he wants 'im back."

"Over my dead body!" Joanna snorted. "He was gonna let the pound put 'im to sleep, just 'cause he was too danged lazy to find 'im a home."

"Can't you just picture old Eldridge pullin' that trick?" Randy asked. "Ain't no women nowhere likes him, the old blackhearted scoundrel! Vern wouldn't let nobody have that dog, noways, that little sucker's got a home for good. They're kind'a like a team."

THE GREEN-EYED MONSTER

"You can't perfume a hog."
—Lewis Grizzard

"Hey! Y'all heard what Hilda and Agnes got?" Tansey yelled as she started into the kitchen where Denise and Joanna sat, drinking coffee.

"Nope," Joanna answered. "What's up?"

"They done bought 'em some horses!"

"What, just some ponies, or somethin' to keep around the house for pets?"

"Naw! High dollar horses! Told Uncle Otto they wanted to start ridin' with the crowd some on weekends. And y'all know how he is, always makes everybody welcome. He told 'em to come on over to the shack this Saturday."

"I didn't know they rode."

"They ain't never rode that I know of. They bought 'em from that Wheeler guy and Hilda told 'im there was some folks around that thought they know everything 'bout horses, and she just thought they'd show 'em somethin. Reckon she was talkin' 'bout us?"

"Oh, she wouldn't say that! She ain't that mean."

"Not to your face, she ain't. But it sounds just like 'er. You don't know 'er like I do."

"Well, maybe if they start ridin' with us, we'll get to be better friends. You know how you get to talkin' and havin' such a good time on the trail. I feel kind'a sorry for 'er. Seems like nobody don't like 'er much and I thought maybe that's why she acts like she does. I think she's one of them people that trys so hard to get attention that they turn folks off."

"I don't know, maybe you're right."

The Morgans and Tansey both arrived early Saturday morning and had their horses saddled up before anyone else showed up. The girls were sitting on the long picnic table, watching rigs pull in, when they spotted Hilda and Agnes towing a tag-a-long two horse trailer.

"Dang!" exclaimed Tansey. "They done got that trailer painted lime green, just like that truck!"

Joanna had turned around, talking to Aunt Emma when Tansey elbowed her in the ribs. Holding a hand over her mouth to stifle her giggles, she pointed to Hilda, who was getting out of the truck, wearing a huge, lavender colored western hat, made of velveteen material. A big, purple feather swept back from silver conchos the size of silver dollars, and the bushy red hair stuck out beneath it like a lion's mane. Agnes was dressed entirely in white, with sequins and pearls on a shirt that was so tight across her huge bosom that it pulled open between the buttonholes. A shiny rhinestone band adorned the white western hat and her coal-black hair hung down around her back and shoulders in tubular curls like fat little sasauges. Gold and silver embellished the high-heeled white boots and the white jeans were tight as could be.

"You ever seen anything like that in your life?" Tansey snickered. "Hilda's hat is so big, she looks like a skinny old rabbit under a collard leaf! Them purple jeans are so baggy, it looked like a whole family of hillbillies moved out'ta the seat.

"Hush up before she hears you, Tansey," Aunt Emma scolded.

"I got'ta admit, them outfits are somethin' else" Joanna said as she looked down at her faded wranglers and tee shirt. "I always thought my plain old black Stetson hat was purty sexy, but maybe I ough'ta put me some big rhinestones and feathers in it.

"You do and I ain't gonna be seen with you," Tansey declared.

Hilda went around and opened the trailer door and there was a trememdous commotion. Uncle Otto went running over to see what was wrong.

"Hold on there a minute! Let's close the door until you'uns get those hosses untied," he instructed. "Here, lemme help you ladies," he reached in through the opening in front to loosen the lead lines. "Okay, go ahead and open 'er up now."

Two Tennessee Walking Horses backed out. The larger horse was a palomino, golden muscles rippling in the sunlight, and the long white mane flowed down onto the sturdy neck. The smaller horse was a sleek black, more daintily built. At the sight of the other horses, they became agitated and the women could barely hold them.

"God-a-mighty, Hilda!" Tansey exclaimed. "That's one good-lookin' horse you got there. You want me to hold 'im while you saddle up, or you gonna try to tie 'im up?"

"He's all right," Hilda answered. "I'm gonna tie 'im to the trailer, if I can get 'im over there. Get my saddle out of the tack compartment," she ordered.

Tansey opened the door and pulled out a heavy mexican saddle, complete with covered stirrups and fancy silver studs. "Dang! You gonna show us up with this here parade saddle, ain't you? All we got is old workin' saddles." Hilda shot her a dirty look, but didn't say anything. Joanna could hear her grinding her big, yellow teeth, in that perpetual habit she seemed to have.

They never were able to tie the horses up, but had to stand and hold them until the others were ready to go. When the crowd finally did pull out, Hilda and Agnes were up front, leading the pack, front feet of the Walking Horses lifting high to paw the air, and hind end shuffling along to keep up. Unable to hold them back, Hilda and Agnes stayed far ahead and were constantly circling back to where the others were.

"Them Walkers are purty, but they sure ain't no trail hosses," Uncle Otto said. "They belong in the show ring, them gals are gonna have a miserable ride." When they would stop, the Walking Horses would fidget around, tossing their heads, ready to go.

"Look out Hilda!" Randy exclaimed. "Get that horse out'ta that field, do Clinton won't let us ride through here no more. You're tearin' up 'is peanuts." She finally had to get off the horse and hold him to keep him off the crop.

Meanwhile, Agnes kept trying to urge her horse closer to Johnny-Vern. He had pulled a fifth of burboun from his saddlebag and was passing it around. "Can I have a sip of that?" she asked. He handed her the bottle and she turned it up, making a face at the strong taste.

"Let's move 'em out!" Uncle Otto called from the wagon, and the riders headed back to the path.

"Look-a-yonder," Randy said as he rode up beside Joanna. "See how Agnes keeps circling back and ridin' beside Johnny-Vern. She's gonna drink that whole fifth if he don't watch out."

Joanna began to notice and, sure enough, each time her horse pulled ahead, Agnes would turn him in a wide circle until Johnny-Vern came even with her again. Amicable as usual, he kept passing her the bottle and it looked as though they were having a conversation.

"Hey, Hood Ornament!" yelled Randy, as he loped up alongside them. "Got a new woman, don't you?"

"Where?" Johnny-Vern looked around.

"Right there, beside you, man. Agnes!"

"That's right," Agnes nodded. "Me and Vern are gonna be an item, and everybody might as well know it."

"Do what?" Johnny-Vern looked around. "Naw, Agnes, I already got a girlfriend, I'm spoken for." He dug his heels into the paint stallion and took off. "Hey, Uncle Otto! Wait for me!" In seconds he had caught up to the wagon, swung in, and tied his horse behind.

Agnes looked at Randy. "He really likes me, he's just shy is all."

Randy turned back to ride with Tansey and Joanna. Agnes put her horse into the fast running walk that ate the ground up. She quickly passed the wagon and caught up with Hilda. The trio watched as they struggled to hold their horses down to a slow pace, but they continued to shuffle along, constantly turning back to ride in big circles until the others would catch up with them.

As Tansey rode by the wagon, Johnny-Vern sailed out and landed on the back of her horse. She pulled to a stop to wait for the others to catch up.

"Whoo-ee, Tansey!" exclaimed Randy. "You're brave, girl!"

"What're you talkin' about?"

"You ain't heard? Agnes has set 'er cap for old Hood Ornament here. And what a cap she's got! What about it, Vern? You're gonna have women fightin' over you."

Tansey half turned to look back at Johnny-Vern. "Brother, you'll make it with anything, won't you? God-a-mighty, boy! I know you ain't got no taste, but can't you do no better than that?"

"Don't listen to him! He's crazy. You know how he is, always got'ta make a mountain out of a molehill. I ain't done nothin' but give 'er a drink. That gal's ugly as a lard bucket full of armpits! I ain't messin' with 'er."

"Yep, I can see it now," said Randy. "Y'all will make a right cute couple."

"Yeah, Vern!" Tansey chimed in. "Maybe she'll let me and Jo be bridesmaids.

The wagon pulled up beside them. "Which way you'uns want to go?"

Uncle Otto asked.

Why don't we take the dirt road and cut through the Neville farm?" Randy asked. Can you get the wagon through there?"

"Yep, I think we can make it."

The riders didn't see Hilda and Agnes for a while, then they came to a small creek and there they were, watering their horses.

"Whoo-ee, this here shade feels mighty good," said Uncle Otto. "Randy, get that bucket out'ta the back of the wagon and get some water for these mules, will you?"

Everyone watered their horses and stood around for awhile. Every so often, someone would let out a yell, and go galloping through the water, splashing all those nearby. Aunt Emma got into the back of the wagon and opened a huge picnic basket. Soon, everyone had a piece of fried chicken or a ham biscuit and they all munched away happily.

Suddenly, they heard a little shriek and Joanna turned just in time to see Agnes going down into the water. She had been standing her horse in knee-deep water when he decided it would feel good to cool off completely. His knees buckled and he almost came out from under her, as she began to kick wildly. But it was no use, and he went down, rolling over onto his side. Agnes fell, but caught herself before she went under, watching her ridiculous hat float downstream.

"You okay, Agnes?" Randy asked.

"I'm just fine!" she retorted, grabbing her horse's reins and trying to mount. The horse danced in circles and she couldn't get her foot into the stirrup. The white pants were wet and began to draw up, becoming even smaller.

"Hold 'er horse, Vern and I'll help 'er on," instructed Randy. He tried to push her up, but she was awkward. Her fancy belt buckle hung on the saddle horn and stopped her progress. Randy pushed and shoved until Agnes was in the saddle once more.

Snatching back hard on the reins, Agnes dug the bit deep into the horse's mouth. He squealed and reared up. She kicked him with her cruel spurs and he spun around. Snatching a whip off the saddlehorn, she began to beat the horse.

Tansey ran up and grabbed the reins. "Quit beatin' that horse! What's wrong with you?"

"Get your hands off my reins!" Agnes shouted. "Just look what that stupid horse did to my new outfit."

"Well, hell! He was just tryin' to cool off," Tansey responded. "Ain't no need in whippin' him that way. He didn't know he was doin' nothin' wrong, he was just hot."

Agnes raised the whip and brought it down again, aiming at Tansey this time. Tansey caught hold of the whip, turned and threw it into the water where it sank from sight.

"Come on, Hilda. Let's go!" Agnes called.

They dug their heels into the horses and started up the path.

"I better not see you treatin' that horse that way, no more!" Tansey called after them.

The others didn't see Hilda and Agnes again until they got back to the shack.

Tansey had tied her horse to the trailer and was unsaddling him when Agnes walked around the front of the truck.

"You need to stay away from Johnny-Vern!" Agnes said.

"Huh?" Tansey turned, leaving the loose girth hanging beneath her horse. "What're you talkin' about?"

"I done told you once. He's gonna be my man and we could have a good relationship, is you just leave 'im alone."

"Well hell, honey! Go for it. Vern ain't my boyfriend. He ain't never gonna be nobody's boyfriend, least not for just one woman. Don't you know he's just a whorehopper?"

"You just shut your filthy mouth! I'm not gonna listen to nobody talkin' about my man that way!" Taking a step forward, Agnes slapped Tansey hard across the face.

Tansey gasped as her hand flew up to her burning cheek, hardly able to believe she had been struck. Then she flew on Agnes like an angry little wasp on a bull, knocking her to the ground. Agnes put out a beefy fist and grabbed Tansey's shirt, tearing it open down the front. Tansey reached out and tangled her fingers through the long sausage curls, making Agnes scream out in pain.

"Hey, you girls stop that!" Uncle Otto yelled as he and Joanna tried to seperate them, but it was futile. "Randy! You'uns come give me a hand, here," he called. Randy and Johnny-Vern came running around the trailer and saw what was happening. Johnny-Vern grabbed Tansey and pulled her off Agnes. Randy and one of the other men grabbed Agnes, each holding an arm.

But Tansey twisted out of Johnny-Vern's grasp and flew at Agnes again, knocking her away from the men. Randy tried to grab them, but they rolled over and over on the ground, horses dancing above them. Now they were under one of Uncle Otto's big mules and Tansey had Agnes pinned firmly to the ground, sitting across her hips. Suddenly, the big animal raised his tail and let fly with a stream of watery, greenish feces. It fell directly into Agnes' face and she sputtered and choked, nearly drowning in it.

"Ha-a-a!" Tansey screeched as Agnes bucked underneath her, trying desperately to get away. As she flailed her arms around, the mushy green mess spread until the white outfit was covered to the waist.

It took three of the men to finally pull Tansey off her. She kept struggling to get away, but Agnes just lay there exhausted, covered with the green muck. By now, Hilda had arrived on the scene and she started to help Agnes to her feet. But she drew back when her hands touched the stinking slime Agnes was covered in. Agnes rolled over and came up on her knees, buttocks high in the air, and finally struggled to her feet.

She turned to face the onlookers, cheeks flaming red. "She's crazy!" She pointed at Tansey. "I don't know why you like 'er so much!" She turned to Johnny-Vern. "You could have a real woman like me!" She stood there for a few moments, covered from the top of her head to her waist in the green manure, the white satin shirt now the color of the grass beneath her feet.

"Come on, Agnes. Let's get out'ta here," Hilda urged. They stomped off to their rig, where the horses were loaded and waiting, got in and drove away.

"Whoo-ee! I hope them women don't come back no more," said Uncle Otto. "I believe in bein' neighborly and all, but they're plain crazy. I saw 'er jump you, Tansey. What in the world ailed 'er, still on 'er high horse about Vern, claimin' he's 'er boyfriend?"

"That's exactly what it was!" Tansey exclaimed, still shaking with anger. "She's crazy, I wouldn't have 'im if he was the only man in the county! No offense intended Vern, you know I love you," she put an arm around him and gave him a hug. "But you couldn't hang with just one woman if your life depended on it."

"No offense taken, Tan," Johnny-Vern responded as he hugged her back. "I love you too, girl."

"Whoo-eee! Won't she a sight, all that fresh, green manure all over 'er?" Uncle Otto asked.

"That she was," Tansey began to giggle. "What you been feedin' that mule, Uncle Otto?"

"Oh, he's been out in the pasture, on that alfalfa grass. And I had gave 'im about two gallons of mineral oil last night. Looked like he was tryin' to colic, and I wanted to loosen 'im up some."

"You loosened 'im up, all right," laughed Johnny-Vern. "He was loose as a goose! I ain't never seen a hoss shit that much in my life. Poor old Agnes, in 'er fancy white suit. I don't reckon it'll ever be white again."

"Nope, said Randy. "I think Agnes was what you would call green with envy!"

ROXANNE

"The only immorality is not to do what one has to do when one has to do it."

—Jean Anovilh

"We're gonna have a big birthday bash for Stumpy this weekend," Randy informed Joanna when he came in one night. "We're plannin' on havin' a pig-pickin'."

"Good! I'll call the girls and we'll fix some other stuff. I might make one of them coconut cream pies that Stumpy loves so good."

"Ask Aunt Emma if she'll make some slaw."

"Okay."

"And guess what! Johnny-Vern's gettin' a band. Said it's some guys he knows and they won't charge nothin'."

Saturday dawned bright and clear and the grills were already started when the sun came up. Joanna was back and forth all morning, taking pies and running errands.

Around noon, more people began to arrive. Uncle Otto and Aunt Emma drove up and he lifted out a huge stewpot, filled to the brim with sweet, juicy slaw. Aunt Emma was holding a seven-layer chocolate cake. "Randy, get those containers of tea, will you, honey?" she called as she carried her cake over to the long picnic table.

Tansey came in with two huge bowls of potato salad and several watermelons. Denise and Sadie brought a birthday cake and a strawberry pie.

"Hey, who asked them two to come?" Tansey asked and Joanna looked up to see Hilda and Agnes pull into the yard.

"Oh, you know how it is around here," Joanna answered. "You ain't got'ta wait for an invite to nothin', you just hear somethin's goin' on, and you show up."

"Well, that's fine for most folks, but you know how they are. Anywhere they go, they're gonna try to start trouble, you just mark my words."

"Hey, Vern!" yelled Randy. "Your girlfriend's here!"

"Where is she?" Johnny-Vern responded. "Just let me at 'er!"

"There she is, right yonder, gettin' out of that lime-green Suburban. Old Agnes, she's lookin' for you, all right."

"Aw, shit! Let me get out'ta here!" Johnny-Vern headed for his truck, jumped in and screeched off in a cloud of dust.

"Dang, he really is scared of Agnes, ain't he?" Tansey asked.

People were sitting around on lawn chairs, picnic tables, and bales of hay; some still eating when the band started to tune up. They were set up on a large, flatbed trailer that the men had pulled into the yard.

"All right, Mr. Stumpy!" the lead singer cried. "This one's for you, let's get this party started!"

Happy Birthday to you
You live in a zoo
You look like a monkey
And you act like one too
Happy Birthday to you !

Too shy to dance himself, Stumpy took some good-natured ribbing as the band broke out in full swing and people began to dance. He sat contentedly, watching and smiling as the party wore on, sipping on his ever present cold beer.

"Hey!" he called out to the band. "Can y'all do some Conway Twitty?"

"Sure enough. What you wanna hear, brother?"

"Don't matter, long as it's Conway."

"Well, Hello Darlin'!" they began.

"Hey, where's Vern got off to?" Joanna asked Randy. "I ain't seen 'im for awhile. It ain't like him to slip off while a party's goin' on."

Randy just shrugged his shoulders as if he didn't know, but something in his smile told Joanna different.

A half hour later, Joanna saw Johnny-Vern's truck pulling back into the driveway. He drove around to the end of the trailer bed where the band was playing and she could see that he had a large object in the back of his truck. Looking closer, she could see that it was a gigantic birthday cake, made of sturdy plywood. She watched as he went up and spoke to the lead singer and the band stopped playing. Johnny-Vern stepped up to the microphone.

"Stumpy, my old friend, some of us guys got together and got you a little birthday present. You always tell us not to get you one, 'cause you don't need nothin', but you're gonna like this here present. And I can guaran-damn-tee you that! Haywood, you got your truck up there in position? Good. Shine your spotlight over here. This here is Roxanne! Hit it, boys!"

The band began to play Hard Hearted Hannah and the top of the cake blew off, sending up fireworks and sparklers into the night air. Slowly and sensuously, bending and swaying like a dancing cobra, a young woman emerged. A wild mane of copper-colored hair whipped around as she moved her head from side to side and full, sensual lips pursed as she undulated with the music. The ample breast tapered down to reveal a wasp-waist and long, coltish legs that moved with graceful abandon. The gold-sequined bustier sported silver tassels, that swung in circles as she moved.

Stepping gracefully out of the cake, she danced and writhed, slowly making her way to the stage in front of the band. For a few moments, she simply danced, swaying her hips and shaking her breasts sensuously to the beat of the music.

But suddenly, she reached down and tugged at the gold scarf that was draped across her waist, revealing a matching thong bikini bottom. "Uh-oh! Come on, Mama!" Uncle Otto exclaimed. "I think it's time we'uns better be goin', do you're gonna see somethin' you don't want to see."

Aunt Emma blushed a little as she followed behind him. "You young folks take care now. Don't none of y'all be drivin' home tonight, if you been drinkin'," she called. Uncle Otto shooed her into the truck and pulled off.

Meanwhile, the young woman danced slowly over to Stumpy, who sat still as stone in his lawn chair, mouth dropped open and eyes bulging out. She bent over to shake her now bare breasts in his face and he tipped the chair over backwards, landing with his heavy brogan boots sticking straight up in the air. The girl never stopped moving, but swayed in circles as she moved around behind Stumpy and he lay motionless on the ground, looking up in awe.

By the time the dance ended, Stumpy had managed to sit up, but he remained on the ground, looking up at the girl.

"Hey, Stump! You're gonna get you some poon-tang tonight, ain't you, boy?" yelled Johnny-Vern, as the girl led Stumpy into the house, and he looked back with a grin that stretched from ear to ear.

"Well, I never!" Hilda exclaimed. "Y'all are all just a bunch of heathens, the whole lot of you. You shouldn't even be allowed around decent people."

"Oh, be quiet, Hilda!" Tansey retorted. "Stumpy ain't had no female company in a long time, you ought'a be glad for 'im."

"We ain't gonna stay around no crowd like this, that has to have a hussy like that one in there. It ain't fitten! Come on Agnes, let's go."

"But Hilda, I didn't get to talk to Johnny-Vern yet. He just got back to the party and I don't want to go."

"Get in the truck, Agnes."

The girls could still hear them as they walked around the house, towards the driveway, Agnes pleading to stay and Hilda snorting in disgust.

Nobody saw Stumpy or the girl for the rest of the night. When Randy went up on the porch and started into the kitchen, the door was locked. He and Johnny-Vern went around to the bedroom and beat on the window, but complete silence greeted them. Haywood got his shotgun out of the truck and discharged it under the window, but even the tremendous boom got no response. They finally went back to listen to the band and around two in the morning, they called it quits and everyone went home.

"How much did y'all haf'ta pay that girl?" Joanna wanted to know the next morning.

"Well, we took up a collection," Randy said as he looked at her sheepishly. "You know it was a bunch of us guys went in on it together, it won't like I had to pay for the whole thing or nothin'."

"How much?"

"A thousand dollars."

"A thousand! God-a-mighty!"

"Now, don't carry on. I didn't put but twenty-five in the pot."

"A thousand dollars! That's a lot of money!"

"It was gonna be three hundred for an hour, so we decided to do it up big and get 'er for the whole night."

"You mean she stayed over there all night?"

"Yep, now don't you know Stumpy woke up a happy man this

mornin'? Shucks, it was nearabout worth it just to see the look on 'is face, boy was he surprised! I'm gonna ride over there and help Haywood clean up. You wanna go?"

"Dang right I do! I wanna hear what Stumpy's got to say this mornin'."

Stumpy was sitting under the lean-to when they pulled in, talking to Haywood.

"You old dog!" Randy called. "How'd you make out last night?"

"Right good, right good," Stumpy grinned up at him. "I want to thank you boys, that was the best birthday present I ever had!"

"Stumpy!" a feminine voice called from inside the house. "How do you like your eggs, fried or scrambled?"

"What? Is that gal still in there?" Randy asked.

"She sure is," Haywood snickered. "Stumpy's gettin' his money's worth. Or our money's worth, I should say."

The screen door opened and the lovely face peered out, framed by a wild shock of hair, flowing loosely down over one of Stumpy's work shirts. "Oh, I didn't know you had company. Don't you folks want to stay for breakfast?"

"I'll take a cup of coffee, if you got one," Haywood answered.

Randy said nothing, but looked at Joanna.

"I reckon we can get somethin' to eat, if you want to," she responded to his silent question. "Get back a little dab of that money you spent," she teased. "You need some help in there?" she called to the girl.

The pretty head peered out again. "Do you know where Stumpy keeps the fryin' pan?"

"Look in the little pantry, there off the side of the kitchen," Joanna answered as she started up the steps.

"That Stumpy is just the sweetest man," Roxanne said as they worked in the little kitchen. Joanna couldn't help but think she was even prettier close up. Deep green eyes peered out underneath long, feathery lashes and the porcelain skin appeared almost translucent, glowing in the early morning light, even without makeup. "It's been a mighty long time since anybody treated me decent, like he did last night. He was so polite and acted like a real gentleman, not at all like the guys I'm used to. In fact, he seemed downright bashful."

"That's Stumpy, all right," Joanna responded. "He can be mighty shy around women."

"You girls got that food about ready?" Randy called.

"Hang on, we're gettin' ready to bring it out, now," Joanna answered. "Come here and get this plate of sausages." He reached in to take them from her. "Wait, take these biscuits, too."

"Y'all made homemade biscuits?" Randy asked in surprise.

"Yep, we been workin' hard in here," Joanna answered as she turned around to wink at the other girl. "Ain't that right?"

Roxanne nodded in agreement, as she wadded up the package the frozen biscuits had come wrapped in, and hid them behind her back. The girls got the rest of the food and followed Randy down the steps to place it on the long picnic table.

"Gosh, this is like somethin' you read about," Roxanne said as she sipped her orange juice and looked out across the pond, where the ducks swam contentedly. "Sittin' right out here, lookin' at all the animals and smellin' the fresh, country air while you're eatin' breakfast. Here you go, boy!" She reached down to offer Lick-ems a choice piece of bacon, then fondled the soft, pendant ears as he licked her hand."

"Well, it ain't nothin' fancy." Stumpy began. "But I like it out here. Purty much got everything I need." He stopped to reconsider for a moment, then grinned. "Except for a woman like you. Even my dog like you a whole lot better than my last girlfriend. Ain't that right, Lick-ems?" Now, it was her turn to blush.

"You know, when I was a little girl, I always imagined I'd grow up and live somewhere like this, with animals all around, everywhere. Guess I should have married a farmer," she said and Joanna thought she detected a wistful hint of seriousness as the girl joked. Then, the calm was shattered as Johnny-Vern's truck turned in.

"Whoo-eee! Pee on the fire and call the dogs!" He got out, stopped and looked at Roxanne incredulously. "Dang, girl! You still here?"

"Still here," she answered as he walked over to put an arm around her.

"Well, maybe you and me can get together. I could give you a ride home and you could invite me in for just a little while. How about it?"

"I'd prefer to have Stumpy drive me," Roxanne said, as she stood up and moved away from Johnny-Vern.

"Yeah, Vern!" Stumpy answered. "Why don't you get lost?" He walked over to put a protective arm around the young woman.

"Okay!" Johnny-Vern stood back. "I got the picture. But my birthday's comin' up next month, and I wanna make sure y'all don't forget it." He winked at Roxanne and she couldn't help but smile back.

"Don't pay Vern no attention," Joanna urged. "Any woman he sees, he acts just like this. Boy ain't got a lick of sense."

"Come on, if you're goin' with me, Jo!" Randy called. "We got to get that fryer back to the river."

"All right, hold on. Roxanne, we'll see you around."

A few weeks later, a strange car was sitting in Stumpy's driveway when Randy and Joanna pulled in. "Wonder who that is?" Randy mused.

"I don't know. But that sure is a fancy car. Ain't it a Porsche?"

"Yep. Hey Stumpy! Whose fat ride is that sittin' out yonder?" Randy called as he opened the kitchen door.

There, at the table sat Stumpy and Roxanne, and the smile on Stumpy's face told how happy he was to see her again.

"Hey, boy!" said Randy. "You're grinnin' like a bucket full of possum heads, what are y'all up to?"

"Aw, we're just sittin' here, drinkin' coffee and talkin' a little bit. As if it was any of your business!" He turned to Joanna. "Come on and sit down here with us, Jo. That hooligan husband of yours, well he can just get lost."

"Roxanne, I was just fixin' to ride over to the animal rescue." Joanna said. "You want to go with me?"

"I sure do!"

"Come on. We'll be back in a little while, boys."

Once they got to the rescue, Joanna saw that the girl was a natural with the animals. She held a dog while Joanna gave him an injection, then helped her change a dressing on a cat's hind leg. "Poor little baby, it's gonna be all right," she murmured in the fuzzy yellow ear as she stroked him gently.

"I'd like to come sometimes and help out," she told Joanna on the ride home.

"How about this Saturday?"

"Okay, I'll be there," she promised as Joanna let her out at Stumpy's house.

On Saturday morning, Roxanne was busy walking the dogs while Joanna and Tansey talked with people about adoptions. Finally, the rescue cleared out and Joanna called her in.

"Come on and let's take a little break. I'll get us a drink out of the coke machine. What kind you like?"

"Anything that's cold will be good."

The girls were sitting in the little office when the door opened and an elderly lady peered in.

"Can we help you, ma'am?" Joanna asked as she tried to see what was in the basket the woman was holding.

"I....I don't know. I hope so. You see, my little dog is sick." She pulled the little blanket back and a fuzzy white head peered out. "I was wondering...that is..if you might..." the trembling voice trailed off and she just stood there for a moment, her lip quivering as though she might burst into tears any minute.

Joanna went over and caressed the little head. "Come over here and have a seat," she invited and the old woman sat down, dabbing at her eyes with a lacy handkerchief that she pulled from her sleeve.

"I'm sorry. I don't mean to act so silly. It's just that my little Snookie here, needs surgery and it's going to be very expensive. I don't know where I'm going to get the money to pay for it."

"We could take you to see Doc Cooper," Tansey suggested. "I bet he'd let you pay for it on time."

"No dear. I know Doctor Cooper, and you're right. He always let's me charge if I need to. But he can't do the procedure. He's the one referred us to the big vet's hospital up in Raleigh. And you have to pay flat out cash money."

"What's wrong with the little guy?" Tansey asked.

"It's a herniated disk. And it's causing paralysis in the hindquarters. Snookie can't walk, he's dragging his back end and it's just awful."

"Gosh," Joanna murmured. "I wish there was some way we could help. Maybe we could do a fund-raiser, or somethin'."

"That's very sweet of you, dear, but I don't think we'd have enough time. If the surgery isn't done within the next week, they're afraid it may be too late. Snookie will probably be crippled for life."

"How much is it gonna cost?" Roxanne asked.

The old woman shook her head slowly. "They say it's going to be at least a thousand dollars, maybe more. It could be up to fifteen hundred."

"Goodness!" Joanna exclaimed. "That is kind'a steep."

Roxanne said nothing, but got up and went out the door. She returned in a moment, holding her purse. Removing a soft, leather wallet, she pulled some money out, counted it, and handed it to the old woman, whose eyes widened in surprise. One hundred dollar bills, ten of them altogether, sat in the woman's trembling hand.

"Here's my phone number," Roxanne said as she wrote it on a pad from the desk. "If it's gonna be more, I want you to call me. Okay?"

The old woman reached up to hug her. "I just don't know how to thank you," she said. "How will you be able to pay your own bills?"

"Don't worry," Roxanne smiled. "I don't have that many bills, it'll be fine."

The woman picked up the basket and started out the door, then turned to look back. "You'll never know how much I appreciate this."

Roxanne walked over to give her a hug and said, "Let us know how little Snookie gets along."

"God bless you, dear. You're an angel."

On the following Tuesday, the old woman called Roxanne. The surgery had been successful and the little dog was recovering nicely. "Thanks to you, my baby can walk again!" she declared.

The next Saturday morning, the girls rushed to clean the runs before they opened. At ten o'clock, people were waiting in the parking lot.

"Can you start walkin' the dogs?" Joanna asked Roxanne. "Me and Tansey can wait on these folks, then we'll help you."

"Okay. Come on, Gambler. You want to go outside for a little while?"

Suddenly, the door burst open and Hilda marched in. She stood there, glaring down at Joanna and Tansey, who were seated at the desk, filling out the adoption forms for an elderly couple.

"What's SHE doin' here?" Hilda demanded.

"Who?" Joanna asked.

"You know who, that...that..hussy out there!"

Joanna looked out the window. "Well....she's got a dog on a leash, and she's walkin' along behind 'im. I believe that's what you would call walkin' a dog!"

"You're such a smart alec! She's got no business bein' out here, she'll give us a bad image."

"She ain't hurtin' nothin'," Tansey broke in. Won't gonna be nobody but me and Jo here today. We can't hardly do the adoptions, give the medicines, feed, clean the runs, and walk all these dogs by ourselves. And

I ain't seen you down here doin' it, so you need to just quit complainin'!"

"But she's a prostitute! That's gonna make us look bad."

The elderly couple, who had been staring in bewilderment finally decided they had seen enough. The woman stood up and handed the puppy back to Joanna.

"Young lady, I think we'd better go. Come on, Harold!" she beckoned to her husband, as he looked out the window, straining to catch a glimpse of Roxanne. "I said, COME ON!"

Now look what happened, all because of her!" Hilda declared. "That little dog lost a good home, all because you let the wrong caliber of people volunteer."

"Well, God-a-mighty!" Tansey exclaimed. They wouldn't have never known it, if it won't for you and that big mouth. That girl might be a hooker, but she's worth more than ten of you!"

"Just suppose we might have somebody to come in that's seen 'er workin' and knows about 'er."

"Well, hell! If they've seen 'er workin', they were in the same place she was in! And in that case, they ain't got no room to talk about nobody! Think about it!"

"You're just makin' excuses. I'm reportin' this to the board!"

Just then, a dog yelped and caught their attention. There, standing in the doorway, was Roxanne, holding the end of the leash, with tears running down her cheeks.

"Oh, Rox, I didn't know you were there," Joanna tried to smooth it over. "Don't worry about it. She treats everybody this way."

Roxanne said nothing, but turned and took the dog back to his run. Hilda stalked out and Joanna ran to catch Roxanne. She found her sitting in the run with the dog.

"Don't pay her no never-mind. She's always tryin' to stir up trouble, one way or another."

Roxanne stood up and looked at Joanna with eyes full of sorrow. "That's the way it's always gonna be for me, no matter where I go. People just don't want me around."

"Oh, come on! Everybody hates Hilda's guts, she's an idiot!"

"So how come she's still around?"

"I guess 'cause everybody's scared to say anything to 'er."

"Well, Tansey certainly wasn't!" Roxanne started to giggle. "She was givin' her what-for."

"Come on and I'll help you walk the rest of the dogs."

"I don't think I'm gonna come back," Roxanne confided later, as they were getting ready to leave.

"Oh, don't let old Hilda run you off!" Joanna exclaimed.

"I don't know, I think I may do you more harm than good."

"I've got somebody I want you to meet," Joanna said. "Come on, let's walk over to Miss Velvie's."

"Hey, there, Jo!" Miss Velvie greeted them. "I see you've got a little friend with you."

"Yes ma'am, this is Roxanne."

Well, come on in, honey. I've got some fresh baked double-almond coconut bars, come on and let's get some."

"No thank you," Roxanne resisted. "I'm really not hungry."

"Oh p-shaw," Miss Velvie said. "You can eat this stuff, even if you ain't hungry. Come on, now. Jo, get us a Coca-Cola." She laid the rose covered porcelain saucers on the table and filled them with the individual cakes, the powdered sugar sprinkled on top giving them a festive appearance. "Now sit down, and tell me what's been goin' on."

As they ate, the girls told her about the terrier puppies that had been adopted. "Folks sure like them little dogs," Joanna stated. "Wish the big ones could find homes that easy."

"I'd love to get a dog myself, but my apartment lease has a clause that says no pets," Roxanne confided. "I've never had any kind of pet, but I love all animals."

"You didn't never have any while you were growin' up?" Miss Velvie asked. "A body would think you'd been around 'em all your life."

"My grandfather always had a lot of animals. You know, huntin' dogs, cows and pigs. I used to make pets out of all of 'em. But then, after he passed away, I didn't have much chance to be around animals. My Mama and I moved to the city and she had a struggle just lookin' after me. It was real hard for her."

"When did you move back here?" Miss Velvie wanted to know.

"When Mama passed away. I was fourteen, and I came back to live with my Mama's cousin, but I hated it there. She always acted like I was a burden, and I ran away when I was sixteen. Went back to the city. I guess that was when I really started messin' up my life, and it just went downhill from there." Tears started to form in the big eyes once again and threatened to overflow.

"Well, honey, it can't be as bad as all that," Miss Velvie soothed her. "Why, a purty little thing like you, you ought'a have the world by the tail!"

"No, I've been awful bad, and now I have to pay for it," Roxanne said as she looked down at the table.

"Things are bound to get better," Miss Velvie insisted.

"You don't understand," Roxanne blurted out. "I'm a hooker!"

"A what?"

"You know, a prostitute! A lady of the evening, or however you want to put it. Just about the lowest form of life on earth." Now the tears were running freely down the translucent cheeks.

"Oh, honey! It's what's on the inside that really counts, don't you know that? You don't seem like a bad person to me. Sounds like you did what you had to in order to survive, is all."

"I don't deserve to be around decent people."

"Now why in the world would you say that?"

"Hilda came down today," Joanna answered bitterly. "And she had to put her two cent's worth in."

"Oh," Miss Velvie nodded her head. "That explains it," she sighed. "I hate to talk down about anybody, but that Hilda, she makes everybody feel bad. Don't pay her no attention, honey."

"But everything she said was true!"

"Now you listen to me. They's some folks that don't feel good about theirselves and they always got to be puttin' somebody else down, 'cause they think that makes them look better, or some such nonsense. Ain't nothin' to it! Why, child, we ain't none of us free from sin!

"And as for that prostitutin' business, here's the way I look at it. They's a whole lot of women that uses their body to get what they want. Even married ones. Yes, it's the truth! I've heard 'em talkin' about 'cuttin' their husband off,' if he won't do so-and-so, like they want 'im to. And you know what that means. Sex! Seems to me like it's kind'a the same thing. Only difference is, you're doin' it with more'n one."

"I never thought of it like that," Roxanne sniffled.

"Now don't get me wrong, I ain't sayin' that I approve of it. But it don't mean you're a bad person. You just need to get your life back on track. And we could help you, if you want. Why, with that purty face, you could probably be a model! There's plenty of things you could do."

"You really think so?"

"Honey, I don't think it, I know it. We'll help you. 'Two are better than one; for if they fall, the one will lift up his fellow. But woe to him that is alone when he falleth; for he hath not another to lift him up.' That's Ecclesiastes 4: 9-10."

"But I don't have any skills," sighed Roxanne. "Don't even know how to type."

"You could go back to school," offered Joanna.

"I don't know how I'll be able to afford to live anywhere if I'm workin' part-time at a minimum wage job."

"Well that's easy!" exclaimed Miss Velvie. "You can stay right here with me and it won't cost you nothin'. I rattle around this big old place by myself like a pea in a jelly jar. Now dry up and let's go out there and feed up."

Roxanne smiled through her tears and got up to clear the table. Later, in Joanna's truck, she confided, "You know, maybe Miss Velvie's right. I guess I could do somethin' with my life. I just never had anybody to encourage me before."

"Well, you do now," Joanna grinned back at her. "We'll all help you."

It sure is good to be around folks like y'all," Roxanne said. "A lot of folks are mean, especially other women. Usually, when I'm around other girls, they don't want to have nothin' to do with me."

"Well, shucks! They're probably jealous. 'Cause they don't look good as you do!"

Roxanne smiled. "Oh, you're just tryin' to make me feel good."

"Naw, it's the truth."

Two weeks later, Randy, Stumpy, and Johnny-Vern took the truck and moved Roxanne's belongings to Miss Velvie's.

"You said you wanted to live somewhere you could have animals," Joanna teased as they tried to make their way through the menagerie of cats and dogs.

"Get that dad-blamed dog out'ta here!" Randy exclaimed as he tripped over Beaucephus and dropped a big box on the ground.

"Lord have mercy, sounds just like old times around here," Miss Velvie clasped her hands, threw her head back and laughed. "Son, you sound just like my Willie." Roxanne and Miss Velvie followed Joanna and the boys out to the truck when they were ready to leave.

"Thanks for everything, you guys!" Roxanne called after them.

Joanna looked back as they drove off. The last thing she saw was the two of them standing on the porch, waving with one hand, the other arm clasped around each other's waist.

KIM

"Standing in the middle of the road is very dangerous; you could get knocked down by traffic from both sides."
—Margaret Thatcher

"Hey, Jo, Tansey!" Johnny-Vern drove up while the girls were out in the yard. "What kind'a puppies y'all got at the rescue?"

Joanna leaned against his truck. "Let's see, we got a couple lab mix, seems like we always got those. Everybody 'round here gets labs, then lets 'em breed and the poor pups usually end up at the pound, or dumped out by the side of the road. And we got some Border Collie mix, they're gonna go fast, 'cause they're so young, cute little fuzzballs. There's one litter, I don't hardly know what to call 'em, heinz fifty-seven, I guess. Gonna be medium size, short hair, tan color. Why, you want another dog to keep Stripper company?"

"Naw, it's for my girlfriend. I wanna get one and surprise 'er. It's a birthday present."

"You know good and well I ain't gonna send no dog off to be a gift. We done that one time. A man got a puppy for 'is wife and it turned out she didn't want it. A good while later, we found out she had given it away, went to a really bad home. We didn't find out until a neighbor called in a complaint about a dead dog. They moved out, left 'im on a chain and he starved. From now on, I want to meet the person that's gonna be the owner. Bring your girl down to the shelter and let 'er pick one out herself."

"But I told you, I wanna surprise 'er!"

"Tough titty, said the kitty, but the milk's still sweet!" Tansey yelped. "We can't help what you want, Jo's done told you she ain't doin' it."

"Come on, Jo! She's real special and I think I could really get to 'er, by bringin' 'er a fuzzy little puppy."

"Yeah!" Tansey retorted. "Get in 'er pants, you mean."

"Oh, come on, y'all make it sound like that's all I ever think about."

"Well, it is!" Joanna laughed.

"And you know I always help you do stuff for the animals and all."

"I know that, and I love you to death for it," Joanna admitted. "But it don't matter. I got to think about the dog. Suppose she done somethin' like that other lady?"

"She wouldn't never! She's the kind'a person that's always pickin' up strays and findin' homes for 'em."

"I tell you what. Let's us make up a gift certificate and you buy it for 'er. What day is 'er birthday?"

"Next Friday."

"All right, I'll meet you down there Friday evenin', how bout 'round seven?" He nodded. "Don't tell 'er where you're goin', just that it's a surprise. You could even put a blindfold on 'er or somethin', women love stuff like that. Makes it more romantic. 'Course, knowin' you, you'll be draggin' out the handcuffs and black leather and won't never make it there."

"We'll get there. It does sound like a right good idea! I like it. If she's blindfolded, at least she'd haf'ta be holdin' on to me tight and all. Let's do it."

"All right, and if she don't pass the application, I can just refund your money."

They arrived Friday promptly at seven and Joanna could see why Johnny-Vern was so attracted to the girl. She was slender and moved with a willowy grace. Short black hair curled softly around a fresh, young face with a pert upturned nose. Dark brown eyes smiled as she glanced around at the three cats that were sharing the office with Joanna while she performed some paperwork.

"Jo, this is Kim Collier," Johnny-Vern introduced them. "Ain't she purty?"

"That she is," Joanna agreed.

Kim confided, "Johnny-Vern said he had a big surprise. He's been actin' all mysterious, keepin' it a big secret." She grinned up at him.

Joanna reached into the drawer and pulled out the certificate, which she had wrapped in shiny, foil paper. As Kim opened and read it, tears started to form in her eyes. Joanna and Johnny-Vern broke out with the birthday song, and she reached up to give him a hug. "I think this is the most thoughtful gift anyone's ever given me," she said.

"I wish I could take every one of 'em," she said. "Even when I think I've found a good home, I still worry about what might happen' to 'em. Up until a few months ago, I lived in an apartment that didn't allow pets, but now that I'm in my own house, I think I'm ready for one of my own. Or two! Or three!" she laughed.

"The only thing," Joanna said. "You ain't got a fenced yard, and a big dog really needs that. What about a little one, that could stay inside? That would work out better."

"Sounds great. Let's go look at 'em."

Going back to the kennel area, Joanna began to show her a few dogs she thought may be suitable. Kim had to stop and speak to each one, giving it a gentle pat on the head.

"What about little Demon, here?" Joanna asked, taking a six-month Jack Russell mix out of his cage. "Him and Stripper would just about be twins." The black and white body wriggled and squirmed with excitement as she handed him to Kimberly. He licked her face, then jumped out of her arms and ran in circles, making them burst into laughter.

"Acts like he's possessed, don't he?" Joanna said. "And he's kind'a destructive. You're a regular little devil, ain't you, Demon?" The tiny dog answered by flinging himself upwards and landing at her waist, where she grabbed to keep him from falling.

"If you decide you want this little feller, you better go on and get 'im tonight," she cautioned. "When we open up in the mornin', everybody's gonna want 'im. I guarantee you, he'll be the first one that gets chosen. Everybody wants a little toy breed like this. I wish the big dogs could get homes so easy."

"Me too," Kim agreed. "I wish I could take one of those, you know, one that nobody else wants, but I guess you're right. It wouldn't really be fair to 'em, not to have a fenced yard, where they can run around in. I just love this little guy, but if he can get a home easy, I hate to take 'im." She gave the little dog a hug, then put him back in the cage reluctantly. She stood looking at him for a moment, then asked, "Do you have somethin' little that could stay with me, but nobody else would want it?"

"What about a cat?" Joanna asked. "They're way harder to place than dogs are. The little kittens go faster, but it's nearabout impossible to find a home for an adult cat around here."

"Let's go see 'em," Kim said as she threw one last glance at Demon.

"Oh, look at 'em!" she gasped as Joanna opened the door to the cat room. "They're so sweet, it just breaks my heart to think nobody wants 'em." Paws reached out from several of the cages as the girls walked by, each one begging for attention.

"Hey, look at these little fluffy ones," Johnny-Vern opened the door to a cage containing a litter of Persian mix kittens and they assaulted him, climbing all over his chest and shoulders, digging tiny claws in through his shirt.

"They're beautiful!" Kim exclaimed as she took one that was crawling up Johnny-Vern's neck. "But I bet they'll get picked fast, won't they Jo?" Joanna nodded in agreement.

"Can we take some of the older cats out?" Kim asked. Returning the kittens to the safety of their cage, Joanna let the three adult cats out, and two of them began to rub against their legs, purring loudly.

"These two been here a right good while," Joanna said. "That there's Casper," she pointed to the white cat with blue eyes. "And this is Pandora, she's always gettin' into trouble, you know climbin' in boxes and stuff, makin' a mess." The beautiful Siamese mix looked up innocently, meowing as if to say, 'Who, me?'

"And this here feller, I reckon we'll call 'im Tiger, or somethin' like that. He just come in a few days ago." Joanna pointed to a plain orange tabby that remained in his cage, listless and depressed. "He's about five years old, his owner just decided she didn't want 'im no more. Said she had a new baby and he was too much trouble. Poor feller, I think he's right homesick. Wouldn't eat nothin' for the first coup'la days, and every time somebody come in, acted like he thought it was his owner. Soon as he saw it won't, he'd stop mewin' and lay down again. You'll be okay, though, won't you, Tiger?" Picking him up, Joanna gave him a little kiss on the top of the plain looking head. He responded by reaching up with his paw to give her a little pat on the face.

Kim took the tabby gently from her arms and caressed him as she looked around at the other cats. "I know everybody likes white cats," she murmured. "I never had trouble findin' homes for 'em. And the Siamese, she'll get picked. This one here'll probably be the last one in this room to find a home, won't he?"

Joanna looked at Johnny-Vern in amazement. "Dang! This girl has found homes for a lot of strays, ain't she? Vern, hang onto 'er, I believe she's a keeper!"

They filled out the paperwork as the orange cat lay on Kim's chest, his head completely still on her shoulder. Joanna loaned them a carrier and she promised to come back the next weekend to volunteer.

"How's that cat gettin' along?" Joanna asked when Johnny-Vern stopped by the house a couple of days later.

"Acts like a different animal," he answered. "He loves Kim to death. Follows her around the house, every step she makes. We named 'im Dandy Lion, call 'im Dandy. I ain't never seen a cat like 'im. You ought'a see 'im chasin' Stripper all over the house! And we took 'em both shoppin' to that new PetSmart store. Got 'em both one of them fancy collars, you know, with rhinestones on 'em. And a whole cart full of toys. Spent a hundred and fifty on one of them big cat condos, you know the things covered with carpeting and all the different little holes they can get in, and climb up high. Stripper looks mighty funny, sittin' up there near the ceiling like a cat."

"I believe Dandy got his'self a mighty good home," Joanna chuckled. "I sure like Kim, that girl ain't got one selfish bone in 'er body. Why don't you quit chasin' all them other women and settle down with 'er?"

"Oh, I think I am. Kim's special. I'm really in love this time."

"Ha! How many times have I heard you say that before?"

"Naw, this time's different."

"Seems like I've heard that before, too."

True to her promise, Kim was at the shelter bright and early on Saturday morning to volunteer. Eager to do anything she was asked, the young girl was soon a regular there. Joanna often found her just sitting and cradling a frightened animal in her arms, soothing it with tender caresses.

Joanna and Randy were sitting under the lean-to at Stumpy's one evening, when Johnny-Vern drove up.

"Hood Ornament! Come on in here, boy," Stumpy called. "Get you a cold one, there."

"Hey Vern! I hear you been dippin' your pen in the office ink," Haywood said and Johnny-Vern grinned sheepishly.

"Yep, that old Rita, she's got more moves than a bowl of jello, looks like to me when I go by the peanut co-op."

"Have you always got'ta tell everything you know?" Johnny-Vern asked.

"Y'all talkin' about that gal that works in the office there with you, Vern?" Joanna asked.

"That's her!" Johnny-Vern exclaimed.

"Dang, Vern! That old bleached-blonde floozy? She's still wearin' cobalt blue eyeshadow that went out'ta style twenty years ago. She's way older than you."

"Oh well, you know what they say in that old song: Older women make beautiful lovers! Don't you say nothin' to Kim, though."

"I ain't gettin' in the middle of all that," Joanna promised. "But I sure don't see why you'd want to mess with her when you got somebody like Kim. She's worth a hundred of that old Rita!"

"Yeah, forbidden fruit creates a lot of jams," Haywood shouted gleefully.

"Guess what," Randy came in a few nights later. "That girl of Vern's has done hired Snooper Cooper to scope 'im out."

"Hired who?"

"You know, George Cooper, the private detective. He's kin to Doc, second cousin or somethin'. Evidently she got wind that Vern was seein' somebody else. She hired old Snooper this mornin'. I got'ta tell Vern before he gets his'self in a mess."

"You ought'a let 'im get caught," Joanna responded.

Kim came out and asked Joanna about it at the rescue one day and she didn't know quite what to say. Even though she was irritated at Johnny-Vern, he was just being Vern.

"Are y'all supposed to be goin' steady or anything?"

"Well, he never came out and said that, but not long after we started datin', I told 'im I was goin' out with another guy and he got furious. Threatened not to see me no more, so I told that other guy I had to break it off. Don't that sound like goin' steady to you?"

"Yeah, but that's how these old boys are, they're livin' in the stone ages, when men could do what they want and women couldn't." Joanna didn't know whether to say anything about Rita or not, she didn't want to be a snitch, but it didn't seem fair for Kim to sit around waiting for a commitment she wasn't getting.

Joanna decided to talk to Miss Velvie about it.

"Well, I don't know honey. Seems like when you go tellin' somethin' like that, sometimes you do more harm than good."

"I know. They're both my friends and I hate to stir anything up. Vern's always doin' somethin' like this, though."

The old woman shook her head. "That's menfolk for you. Stolen waters are sweet and bread eaten in secret is pleasant. Proverbs 9:17. But he ain't a bad feller, not at all."

Kim came in one morning full of rage.

"I found out for sure that Johnny-Vern's seein' somebody," she fumed. "I hired a private detective, that Mr. Cooper and he found out it's a woman that works with 'im."

"Well, why don't you just go on and date other guys then? Vern ain't gonna dump you, I know 'im better'n that."

"Nope, I'm gonna fix 'em both," she declared.

"What're you gonna do?"

"I don't know yet. But you know that sayin'; don't get mad-get even. I'll think of somethin'."

About a week later, Tansey confided, "Somethin' funny sure is goin' on. Vern come in the clinic yesterday with the worst case of poison oak we ever seen. And guess where he had it!"

"Where?"

"On 'is ding-dong! I didn't see it, but Doc was teasin' Vern. Asked 'im what had he been doin', making love out in the woods? He had me give Vern an injection, double the regular dosage. That boy couldn't hardly walk," she smirked.

"And today, that girl, Rita, that works with Vern, danged if she didn't come in with it. And you can just guess where she had it. That's too big of a coincidence, don't you think?"

"I know so." Joanna told Tansey what had been going on.

"Well, he sure got what he deserved, for once in 'is life," Tansey laughed. "Doc must'a been right, they been out in the woods, I reckon. Gettin' some ground rations."

But the next time Joanna saw Kim, she discovered exactly what had happened.

"I fixed Vern good," she giggled. "Acted like I didn't know anything about what was goin' on. Then I sneaked over to 'is house while he was at work. I had picked some poison oak leaves and crushed 'im up, you know, got the juice out. Anyway, I took it over and opened a few of Vern's condoms, and put the liquid on 'em inside and out, then sealed 'em up again. And I put some on the toilet paper, too and rubbed it in their underwear. I found one of them skimpy red see-through bra and panty sets. Put it all inside the bra and rubbed it on the thong bikini real good. Boy, I bet you old Vern's doin' some scratchin' about now. And that old blonde bimbo, too."

"How'd you get them condoms sealed back up?"

"Used one of those hot air shrinkin' guns, you know like you use for wrappin' presents. Put that cellophane paper over a basket or somethin', then kind'a melt it closed. I know Vern. He gets in a hurry and don't pay any attention. He's not goin' to notice it."

Joanna broke down then and confessed what she knew. "Don't let on you know, 'cause Tansey, she'd get into trouble. Both of 'em had to go in and get shots. They were eat slam up with it!"

"I got 'em good!" Kim danced around gleefully. "I bet it'll be a while before they can even think about gettin' any action, now. I sure would love to see 'im sufferin'."

"Well, it's Thursday. He usually comes by Stumpy's. Why don't you come to the house with me and we'll ride over there and kind'a check 'em out?"

The girls ended up going with Randy and were sitting under the shelter when Johnny-Vern drove up. He stepped down out of the truck gingerly and came walking over slowly.

"Hey man, what's the matter with you?" Stumpy wanted to know. "Why you walkin' so funny?"

"Got poison oak, man. The worst case you ever saw."

"Oh, you poor baby!" Kim exclaimed.

Johnny-Vern looked up. "Kim! I didn't see you over there. What you doin' here?"

He tried to sit down at the picnic table then quickly stood up again, shifting his weight from one foot to the other.

"Where's your poison oak, Vern?" she asked innocently.

He cleared his throat. "Well, you know, on my private parts."

"Oh, how'd you get it there?"

"I don't really know. Must'a had it on my hands or somethin' when I went to the bathroom."

"You might want to check out your Trojans," she offered sweetly.

"Do what?"

"You know, that you keep in the nightstand there by the bed. I heard they were givin' people a deadly rash. Only certain people are allergic to 'em, though."

"I ain't heard nothin' about that."

"Well it seems that it's only assholes that are allergic."

"What're you talkin' about?"

"And that little red negligee outfit? If I was that strumpet, I wouldn't wear that no more, either. How's her rash? Bad as yours, I hope."

"How'd you know about her?"

"Old Snooper Cooper's been followin' you around, buddy!" Randy broke in.

"You lied to me Vern!" Kim said. "I came right out and asked if you were seein' somebody and you said no."

"Hey Vern!" squealed Randy. "She's done tied a knot in your tail! Get 'im, girl!"

"You're done for now, boy," Haywood laughed. "You can't get out'ta this one. You ain't got no more chance than a kerosene cat in hell that's wearin' gasoline drawers!" The color of red on Johnny-Vern's face deepened another shade.

"Honey, I'm right glad you got 'im," Haywood went over and put an arm around Kim. "He thinks he's so slick he could slide down a barbed wire fence without scratchin' his butt!"

Stumpy, Nollie and Joanna sat quietly, watching and listening.

"Come on, now baby!" Johnny-Vern pleaded. "It ain't like we're married, or nothin'. Let's get back together and I promise you things'll be different." He tried to get down in front of her on one knee, but the rash and swelling were too painful and he had to stand up again.

"You're darn right, things'll be different! Johnny-Vern, if I do start seein' you again, I'm gonna still date other guys. I'm through sittin' home while you're tellin' me you're workin' late and such. I can imagine what kind'a work y'all are gettin' done."

His face brightened a bit and Joanna knew what he was thinking. If he could just get her back, he'd work on the other issues later. He could be so persuasive to women.

"Just take me back, baby. I promise you'll be the only one, from now on out."

Kim gave him a black look and shook her head. "Vern, I'm learnin' about guys like you. Don't piss on my back and tell me it's rainin'!"

A TOUCH OF MAGIC

"Love and magic have a great deal in common. They enrich
the soul, delight the heart. And they both take practice."
—Nora Roberts

Joanna knocked on the door and called out, "Miss Velvie! Anybody
home?"

"Yoo-Hoo! I'm out here honey." She turned in the direction of the
voice and saw her friend out in the little cemetery, sitting on the stone
bench. As she headed that way, she could see that the old woman was
wearing a wide-brimmed straw hat and garden gloves and she held a little
trowel in her right hand. Abby and Doo-Dad were sitting beside her and
the larger animals were scattered around, some resting, others running and
playing. She could hear Nat King Cole softly singing "I Love You Truly".
The music from the old record was scratchy, but the high, sweet tenor was
still beautiful.

"I just love this boom box thing that you young folks gave me, "Miss
Velvie said. "Just imagine, bein' able to bring my music right out here
where Willie can hear it real good. Course, if y'all hadn't helped me copy
it from the records, I'd have never figgered out how to do it. I brought the
old hand-wound victrola out here a few times, but that thing's just too
heavy to lug from the house. And the modernized player, you know, you
got to have electricity for that. This boom box is perfect! Sometimes, I sit
out here for hours, just listenin' to all our favorite old songs and talkin' to
Willie. 'Course, he don't have much to say, but then he never did. I was
always the one did most of the talkin'.

"Here, Izzy. Move over a little bit and let Jo sit down here." The old
dog moved over from where she had been lying by the bench and put her
grizzled head in the old woman's lap. "That's a good girl. Come on, Jo. Sit
down here for a spell."

"You been plantin' some more flowers?" Joanna asked. Red and purple petunias hung gracefully from baskets, their sweet fragrance drifting over to where the women sat, and perky pansies peeked delicately from freshly turned soil. Marigolds and zinnias nodded their brightly colored heads in the slight breeze and hollyhocks grew tall and stately along the wrought iron fence.

"Yep. I got my petunias potted. Ain't they purty?"

"Sure are."

"I declare, I just love bein' out here. It's such a peaceful, quiet place. 'Course, most folks probably think my bread ain't quite done, they seem to think cemeteries are morbid places, but it pleasures me to come out here. I feel so close to Willie here. Mama and Papa, too." The wrinkled old hand reached down to caress the little dog that had crawled into her lap.

"Miss Velvie," Joanna said. "I wanted to see if you had some of that stuff for skin disease. You know my dog, Ruffles? The one that looks like he's got some Sharpei in 'im, all covered with loose, wrinkly skin? Well, Doc Cooper's tried several different things and nothin' seems to work. Reckon you got anything?"

"Let's go to the kitchen, there, and see what we can find," the old woman answered as she got up and the animals followed her. "I got some soapberry oil, might just do the trick. Why don't you use it for a couple weeks and see how it does?"

As she was rummaging through the cabinet, the screen door opened and Denise came in with the children. "Granny Velvie," Petey called. "We're comin' to see you!" He ran up to the old woman and flung himself into her arms, returning the shower of hugs and kisses that were bestowed upon him. Kayla approached more slowly, in her bashful way, smiling quietly until the old woman picked her up. Then she giggled as Miss Velvie tickled her under the chin.

"Well, now! How you little fellers doin' today?" the old woman asked. "I'm just so glad to see y'all."

"Guess what we saw, Granny Velvie!" Petey exclaimed. "The other day after it rained...we saw a rainbow! Just like you showed us. I told my Mama that means everything is A-Okay. Right?"

"That's exactly right, son," the old woman smiled down at him. "My, ain't you a fast learner."

"Yes ma'am," the curly blond head nodded.

"You been sayin' your prayers?"

"You should hear 'im," Denise laughed. "Every night when he gets through blessin' this person and that person, he's got'ta say and God bless my bubble gum machine that Granny Velvie gave me."

"Can we have one of them little Coca-Colas in the glass bottle?" Petey asked.

"Petey!" admonished Denise. "You know better than to ask for somethin' like that."

"Oh, p'shaw," retorted Miss Velvie. "The little feller's right at home, here, and he knows it. I want 'em to feel comfortable in my house. Ain't that right, Goober?" she smiled at Petey and gave him a wink.

The small, red face puckered up with a little frown as he puzzled over what she had called him. "Why do you always call me Goober?" he asked. "I'm Petey."

"Well, your daddy, Pete. Don't they call 'im Peanut?"

"Yes ma'am."

"A goober's a little, small peanut. Did you know that?"

"Oh."

"So your nickname can be Goober, just like your Daddy's is Peanut."

"Okay. I'll be Goober if you want me to." And with that, he was off to explore.

"What about me?" asked Kayla. "I need a nickname too."

"Let's see now," murmured the old woman. "What about Budgie, 'cause you're so tiny, just like a little budgie parakeet I used to have. And that sweet little voice of your's, it reminds me of the way she used to sing."

"I'm Budgie," Kayla said thereafter, to anyone that would listen. "Granny Velvie says so."

They heard a horn blow outside and looked out the window to see Randy and Johnny-Vern. "Hey, Jo," called Randy. "I thought you were comin' by here, so we stopped. We been down to Homer's, got some of 'is fresh sausage and I thought Miss Velvie might want some."

"That's mighty thoughtful of you, son," the old woman said as she gave him a hug. "And who's that with you, is that my boyfriend?"

"It sure is, Miss Velvie," grinned Johnny-Vern, as he came up the steps and grabbed her in a bear hug. "How's my best girl doin'?"

"Fine as frog's hair," she replied as he twirled her around. "And that's so fine, why you can't even see it! Why don't you boys take the young'uns out to the porch and us girls will bring out a little snack?"

A few minutes later, the women carried out saucers of chocolate cake, light golden layers sandwiched between the old-fashioned fudgy frosting. Johnny-Vern eyed the little bottles of Coca-Cola and asked, "How 'bout some of that scuppernong wine, Miss Velvie?"

"Well, all right, but just be careful and don't drink too much of it. We got little ones here today, you know."

"Tell us a story, Miss Velvie," Denise begged as they watched the children playing in the yard.

"Well-sir. Accordin' to Papa, there was this big old bass, lived in the pond yonder and couldn't nobody catch 'im. Folks hereabouts had been tryin' for years, but didn't nobody have no luck and that fish just kept growin' and growin'.

" Papa went out there one day and took a cant hook, you know, one of them great, big things they rolled logs with. He put a ham hock on it and tied to a big, loggin' chain, then hooked it 'round that pine tree, yonder.

"He went on 'bout 'is business and was plowin' the mules when, all of a sudden, he saw that tree begin to bend and tilt over, 'till it looked like it was gonna be pulled up by the very roots! He run them two big, old, strong mules over there and hooked 'em to the chain. Said he turned 'round to cut a switch to whip them mules, make 'em really go, don't you know. But when he looked back, all he could see was them four mule ears goin' underwater! And he never did get that big, old fish!"

"Oh, Miss Velvie!" cried Denise. "I can't never tell whether you're reminiscin' or just tellin' a tall tale, until you get to the very end. You sure know some good stories."

"Why, thank you, honey. They just kind'a get handed down from one generation to the next. Y'all remember 'em, so's you can tell little Petey and Kayla when they get big enough to appreciate 'em."

Later that night, Joanna and Randy were watching television when Johnny-Vern called.

"Hang on," Randy said. "I'm on the way over.

Joanna looked up. "What's wrong?"

"One of Vern's horses is hurt. He thinks she got into some barbed wire."

"Oh, no! How bad is it?"

"Must be mighty bad. Vern's voice was shakin', and you know that ain't like 'im. It takes an awful lot to get 'im upset."

"Has he called Doc Cooper?"

"I dunno. I'll be back after while." With that, he was gone and Joanna was left, watching the taillights of his truck winding down the path. She thought about driving over herself, but she knew the men could do more than she could. She sat and fidgeted for a little while, then tried Randy's cell phone. No answer.

It was after midnight before Randy came in. Joanna was dozing on the sofa, and sat up when she heard him. "How bad is it?"

Randy just sat down and shook his head.

"That bad?"

"I ain't never seen nothin' like it in my life. Whole shoulder's gone, slam down to the bone. It looks like raw hamburger or somethin', the way it's mangled."

"Oh, no!"

"I think he's gonna haf'ta put 'er down. Doc gave 'er somethin' for pain and he's comin' back out first thing in the mornin'. Said he hated to try to make a decision in the dark, like that."

"Which horse is it?"

"It's Sandy. You know the filly that was born a few years back. In fact, she was the first foal born there on Vern's farm. Remember how he spoiled 'er so bad? The one that acted like a puppy dog, the way she played and followed Vern around."

"Sierra's San Bar? The filly off that cuttin' horse, Sierra? The one Vern bought when he went to that sale out in Montana?"

"That's the one."

"Oh, she's such a sweet horse! Not a bit like 'er mama. Don't you reckon they can save 'er?"

"I dunno. I reckon we'll just haf'ta wait 'till mornin' to see."

Randy wouldn't eat the supper that Joanna had kept warm for him, and he didn't go to bed. The television was off, but she got up and found him sitting in the recliner, just staring at the walls.

"Ain't you comin' to bed?"

"Naw, not right now."

"Why?"

"Every time I close my eyes, all I can see is that horse. I just can't stand to keep seein' it, over and over in my mind. I wish it was somethin' we could do to help 'er."

The next morning, when Joanna rode over with Randy, she understood.

The young mare stood, head hanging low and didn't move when they drove up. "Well, at least she's standin'," Joanna said, but she knew it takes an awful lot to put a horse down on the ground.

Even after all Randy had told her, she was still unprepared for the horror when she walked around in front of the horse. The ragged tear went all the way to the bone and shreds of flesh hung almost to the ground. Maggots were already working their way into the tissue and a foul smell emanated from the wound. Blood and drainage had worked into the long, silky mane and clotted there.

"That don't look like it just happened," Joanna said. "It looks infected."

"Vern said it had been a couple of days since he'd seen 'er. You know this pasture's almost eighty acres. He tries to check on 'em every two or three days. Said he come out and when she won't with the rest of the herd, he knew somethin' was wrong. I ain't never seen 'im this upset over nothin' before. Poor Vern. You know they're gonna haf'ta put 'er down. I don't see how nothin' hurt that bad can make it."

Tears welled up in Joanna's eyes as she looked at the mare. "Remember how Vern acted when she was born?" she asked Randy. "So proud, almost like most men are when their wife has a baby. He spoiled 'er so bad, Uncle Otto told 'im she wouldn't never be no good for nothin' but a pet."

"Yeah," said Randy as he rubbed the horse gently on the neck. "And that first time he rode 'er, the way she was buckin'. Throwed 'im three times, didn't you, girl?" His voice was beginning to quiver.

"Look," Joanna said. "Here comes Doc, and Vern's in the truck with 'im."

The men got out and looked at the horse. Dr Cooper shook his head slowly. "Vern, I hate mighty bad to say it, but I think 'bout the only thing we can do is put 'er down."

Johnny-Vern didn't say anything, just stood stroking the mare's face and Joanna could see his Adam's apple working up and down as he struggled with his emotions.

"Doc, what about that big equine clinic up near Richmond?" Randy asked. "You reckon they might could do anything?"

"Well, now," the old veterinarian looked up. "You could give 'em a try, Vern. It's mighty expensive, but I know how much you think of this particular horse. Just don't get your hopes up, though. They're the best, but son, this is mighty bad."

Johnny-Vern looked at Randy. "Can we take 'er on your stock trailer? It's lower to the ground than mine, might be easier to get 'er in it."

"Okay, I'll run to the house and get it. Be back in a little bit."

When they got home, the old gray hearse was just pulling out the driveway. When Miss Velvie saw them, she turned around and went back to the house.

"Hey, honey!" she called. "I brought over some more soapberry for that dog you told me about."

"Miss Velvie!" Joanna slapped herself on the forehead. "Why ain't I thought about you, I bet you might could help."

"Help with what?"

"Johnny-Vern's got a horse that's tore all to pieces, got in the fence. Doc says he can't do nothin' much for 'er, it's so bad. They're gonna take 'er up to that big horse clinic, but Doc don't think it'll do no good."

"Well, I'll be glad to help, but I don't want to stand in the way of the doctors. You know they can usually do a mighty good job."

"What if they can't? Would you at least try?"

"You know I will. If Johnny-Vern wants me to, that is."

Randy called Joanna later that afternoon. "They can't do nothin' up here. Said about the same thing Doc did, we should put 'er down. I talked to 'im and he wants to let Miss Velvie look at 'er. Said he ain't gonna give up if there's the slightest chance. She's eatin' purty good, so he don't think she's sufferin' too bad to give it a try."

Joanna and the old woman were waiting at Johnny-Vern's barn when the men pulled in. They waited until the horse was unloaded, then walked closer.

"I ain't seen nothin' this bad but one time before," Miss Velvie said as she ran her hand down the horse's leg. "Papa had two stallions that got together, one of 'em got into the pasture where the other one was and like to have killed 'im. It must have happened a few days before one of the hands found 'im, he was infected like this. In fact, he was down and we really thought he was done for. Had to get the tractor and a lift to even get 'im up. But Mama mixed up medicine for 'im, and Papa worked on 'im night and day, until he got 'im well."

"So you think she might have a chance?" Johnny-Vern asked, hope in his voice for the first time.

"I ain't sure, but I think we might could save 'er," the old woman looked up at him. "But I'll tell you this. It's gonna take a lot of work. And I don't mean a few days. You're gonna need to work on 'er three times a day and it ain't no tellin' how long it'll take. Maybe six months. If you ain't gonna be able to commit yourself to doin' it, you need to get Doc Cooper back out here right now, and have 'im put 'er down."

"Yes ma'am. Whatever you think it takes, I'll do it."

"Jo, you want to run me to the house to get some stuff together?" the old woman asked. "We'll be on back in about an hour," she told the men.

When they returned, Joanna pulled her truck up to the barn and got a big cardboard box out of the back. Randy came out to help her carry it and Johnny-Vern helped Miss Velvie down.

"Give me those scissors, Randy," the old woman instructed. "The first thing we want to do is trim those loose pieces off. Now hold 'er steady, Johnny-Vern."

The horse stood still through most of the ordeal, barely feeling it when the dead tissue was debrided. Then she leapt sideways, knocking the old woman off her feet when she hit a sensitive area. Joanna and Randy rushed to pick her up as Johnny-Vern struggled to hold the horse.

"I'm all right," she assured them, as she laid a hand on the horse's neck. "Sorry old girl, I didn't mean to hurt you." Now she looked around. "Jo, hand me that can of white powdery lookin' stuff, and that big thermos of hot water. That's right. Easy now, old girl," she soothed. "We got to make a poultice and pack it down in here.

"Now, we need to leave this on 'bout a half hour," she instructed. "That'll kind'a draw some of that old bad stuff out." The horse danced in place for a moment, then actually leaned into Randy's hand as he packed the warm poultice into the wound. Her eyes closed and a look of tranquillity came over her face as she stood stock still.

"Dang!" exclaimed Joanna. "She acts like that feels good! I figgered it would hurt like the devil."

"Naw," the old woman smiled. "That stuff is real soothin' to 'em, makes 'em feel better right off. Got a numbin' agent in it." She busied herself, mixing up another concoction as Joanna looked over her shoulder. "This is old-fashioned healin' oil," she explained as she stirred the viscous liquid. "I've seen Mama use it many a time, and it's some good stuff."

After the poultice was removed, the old woman took a handful of gauze and swabbed down into the wound, scrubbing until healthy pink tissue appeared. The mare moved around a couple of times, but didn't appear to be in a great deal of pain. Eventually, she had a bucket nearly filled with soiled gauze, as the dead tissue peeled away.

"Now, hand me the healin' oil," she instructed. Dipping fresh gauze into the reddish liquid, she carefully applied it to the injured area, going up under the skin near the top, where the wound tunneled underneath. "You got'ta make sure to get up under here, real good like this," she instructed as Johnny-Vern watched carefully. "If you'll do it just like this, three times a day, I believe you can get 'er straightened out. I'll come back and take a look at it in 'bout a week."

"Yes ma'am. It sure looks like you know what you're doin'."

"Oh, well. When you get old as me, you ought'a have learned a little somethin', I guess."

Johnny-Vern worked on the horse faithfully and when Miss Velvie returned, she could see a great deal of improvement. "You're doin' a mighty fine job, son," she told him. "I know you're puttin' in a lot of time, I can tell how hard you've been workin' on 'er. If you can just keep it up, I think she may be sound again."

"Even if she ain't, I still want to keep 'er," he answered. "It don't matter whether she's any good for ridin' or not, I just want to get 'er well. Even if she don't do nothin' but stand out there in the pasture all 'er life. I kind'a figger I owe 'er that much. I should'a never let it happen."

"Now, son. Don't go blamin' yourself. You know how horses are. If there's anything within a hundred miles for 'em to get into, they're gonna do it. That's just horses for you. Shucks, she had near 'bout a hundred acres to run in, look at all that green grass and that cool pond. Why, it's horse heaven out there, almost like runnin' free. Just think, they's a lot of horses stays in a stall, or a little muddy paddock all their lives. They'd sure love to be somewhere like this."

"I just hope she can get well, to where she can enjoy bein' out there again," Johnny-Vern said.

"Just give me a holler if you need any help," the old woman called as she and Joanna pulled out the driveway.

"I swear, Vern's gonna kill his'self lookin' after that horse," Randy said a few weeks later. "He's workin' on 'er mornin' and night. Goin' home at lunchtime, too. Ain't even drinkin' nothin' on the weekends, scared he won't be able to see to 'er if he drinks too much. But it sure is workin'."

It was nearly two months before Joanna saw the horse again and she was amazed. The cavernous wound was filling in as the healthy tissue grew from the inside and it was a good two inches smaller in width. There was no drainage or odor and the mare pranced around the small corral when she was turned out.

"I ain't never seen nothin' heal up the way that's doin'," Joanna gasped. "You have been workin' on 'er, ain't you, Vern?"

"Yeah. I went and got Miss Velvie a couple of days ago," he said. "Brought 'er out here and let 'er look at it. She says I'll need to work on it a few more months, but it should be okay to cut back to twice a day now. That'll help, 'cause I won't haf'ta come home in the middle of the day no more."

"Boy, I believe you missed your callin'," Randy said. "You ought'a be a horse vet."

Johnny-Vern's face lit up in a grin. "I couldn't never have done it without Miss Velvie." He winked at Joanna. "I've seen it before, she can work pure magic."

A BEAU FOR TANSEY

"There are some people who live in a dream world, and there are some who face reality; and then there are those who turn one into the other."

—Douglas Everett

"Hey Tansey, ain't that Candice comin' down the path yonder?" Tansey and Joanna were sitting in the glider at the river, watching the men play horseshoes while Dixie rambled around with Tansey's dogs, Tequila and Kaluah.

"Looks like it. Who's that she's got with 'er?"

"Looks like a couple of guys."

The white camaro pulled up to the tin shelter and Candice waved, sticking her head up through the t-tops. She got out with Moses on her shoulder, followed by the two young men.

"Surprise! I thought we'd find you down here, Tan. Hey Jo, good to see you. This is my boyfriend Robert. Honey, you remember Tansey, don't you?"

"Who could forget her?" the young man grinned.

"And this is his best friend, Logan." The other man stepped forward to shake their hands. Dressed in a white button-down and kakkis with perfect creases, he looked a little out of place here, where the other men wore levis and bib coveralls. Blondish hair, streaked lighter by the sun was combed back, every strand in place, a little ducktail tapered to a vee in the back. Perfectly spaced white teeth contrasted with his deep tan.

"Logan had heard me talk about you guys so much, he said he'd sort of like to come here for a visit," Candice said.

"That's true," Logan agreed. "I've always lived in the city and I feel like I've missed out on a lot of things you people have here. I very seldom have a weekend off."

"What kind'a work you do?" Joanna asked.

"I'm a model." Tansey and Joanna looked at each other. "Have you guys ever heard of Harrison's Menswear?"

"Ain't that the real fancy place over at Tiffany Plaza on the north side of Raleigh?"

"Yes, that's it."

The men finished their game and walked over to join them. "Hey Randy, Johnny-Vern," said Robert. "Wildman! What's going on?"

"Drinkin' mash and talkin' trash," grinned Wildman. "When y'all gonna come ride four-wheelers with us?"

"One of these days," answered Robert.

Candice called Tansey the following week.

"Guess what! Logan wants to go out with you. He says you're to die for! Why don't you come up to Raleigh this weekend?"

"I dunno. He ain't exactly my type."

"What do you mean?"

"You know, he's kind'a sissified."

"But Tansey! He's so nice looking! And do you have any idea how much money this guy makes? He's loaded. Come on. Just go out with him once, I know you'll like him a lot."

"I ain't never been able to have the last word with you, have I? All right, I'll come Saturday afternoon."

"Great! We'll go out somewhere you like. How about the Lone Star Steak House, that's real casual."

"Sounds good. I'll see y'all then."

Joanna talked to Tansey when she came home on Sunday.

"You know, I was surprised but I had a real good time," she confessed. "Logan was mighty nice, and it was good to get away for a change."

"You gonna see 'im again?"

"I dunno. I'm a country hick and he's strictly uptown. Probably wouldn't work out too good."

But Logan called nearly every night and Tansey allowed him to come visit her the next weekend. He showed up with two dozen red roses and took her to the finest restaurant in town.

"Can you come up to Raleigh next weekend?" he asked.

"Sorry, but I'm gonna be workin' at the animal rescue. Maybe another time."

"Suppose I come down and help you? I've always wanted to do something like that."

"It's kind'a dirty work. I'll be cleanin' kennels and all."

"That's okay. You can probably find something for me to help with. I'd do just about anything in order to spend some time with you."

Logan showed up Saturday morning, all smiles and ready to go to work. "Here's a pooper-scooper," Tansey handed him the long handled object and he picked it up gingerly. "You take the kennels on the right and I'll get the ones on the left. Then we'll go back and hose it down good." She began working, while he stood there for a moment watching. Turning back to his side, he made one scoop, then began heaving.

"Tansey, don't you guys have somehing else I can do?"

"How 'bout walkin' the dogs?" "Buster there needs a strong hand, he 'bout drags us womenfolks all over the place."

Logan reached in to hook the lead on the big dog and Buster snapped at him. "What in the world's wrong with you?" Tansey asked as Logan quickly drew his hand back and stepped out of the kennel. "I ain't never seen 'im act like that before!"

"How about if I sit up at the desk? Perhaps I could answer the telephone and direct visitors back."

"Okay. Go on up there and tell Neecie you're gonna stay up there. Ask her if she'll come back here and help me."

"Maybe Buster could tell Logan was afraid of 'im or somethin'," Denise said as she and Tansey worked together. "Poor feller, he's really nice. Looks like he's tryin' his best to fit in, he just don't know how. I tell you one thing though. That boy's got it bad for you Tan! And he sure is handsome."

Logan tried each week to talk Tansey into going to Raleigh, but he didn't have much success.

"I don't care nothin' much about goin' up there all the time," she told Joanna. "Too many cars and people, it gets on my nerves. Then, he'll just pop up down here. But I swear, I need some space. That boy sticks to me like a fart in a phone booth!"

They all went out to eat one night and Logan pulled out a small box, wrapped in gold foil paper. "I've got a little somethin' for you, Tansey. Go ahead and open it."

She looked down at the box as if it were a poisonous snake. "What you waitin' for, girl?" Randy asked and she took it, opening it gingerly. Inside was a gold watch with diamonds embedded around the face.

"Logan, you shouldn't have done this. It's way too expensive, I can't take it."

"You'll have to. I'm not going to take it back." Tansey threw Joanna a furtive glance, wondering what she should do.

A few weeks later, they went over for a barbecue with Randy and Joanna. The girls were in the kitchen, making a salad, while the men went out to start the grill.

"I done got myself in a mess," she confided. "And I'm scared I'm gonna hurt Logan's feelings."

"What're you talkin' about?"

"You know that watch he give me?"

"I took it back and got me a lawnmower."

"You did what?"

"Yep. I looked around and saw it come from Sears. Almost three hundred bucks. Now, what did I need a watch like that for? It ain't really worth doodly squat, except to tell time." She held up her left arm, with the white nurse's watch by timex. "This one here's good enough."

"What did Logan say?"

"He don't know! What am I gonna tell im?"

"Beats me. Would he believe you lost it?"

"I dunno, but I got'ta come up with somethin'."

Meanwhile, Logan began to act possessive over Tansey. He called every night and if she wasn't home he questioned her about where she'd been.

"Look, let's us just be friends," Tansey told him. "I ain't wantin' to get serious with nobody."

"I swear, every time I run 'im off, he comes back with some fancy present," she told Joanna. "Gave me a necklace and some earrings, but I took 'im back and got a weedeater and one of them big dog kennels. I don't need that fancy stuff. I feel guilty with it sittin' in my jewelry box, when that money could go to help the animals. We can use the mower and the weedeater at the rescue, we been needin' 'em bad. And I can use that kennel to foster when we get full at the rescue."

"I'm gonna tell Logan to start shoppin' at the hardware store for your presents," Joanna laughed.

"Hey, we're gonna have a ride over at the Sugar Shack this weekend," Tansey told Joanna that night. They're gonna cook a big Brunswick stew."

"Sounds like fun."

"They's a big crowd comin' in after the ride. And guess what! Neecie's gonna go by and pick up Miss Velvie and Uncle Otto's gonna ride 'er in the wagon. Neecie said Miss Velvie told 'er she's so excited, she can't hardly wait."

"Is Logan comin'?"

"I dunno. He rides right good, but he don't really care nothin' 'bout it. I kind'a hope he don't even come. Seems like here lately he's been tryin' to keep me away from everybody. He won't like that at first, but I tell you, I'm gettin' tired of it."

"Whoo-eee! You'uns get down and come on in here!" Uncle Otto yelled when Randy and Joanna drove up on Saturday. He was standing on the steps of the shack, cowboy hat in hand, drinking a Natural Light. "We're gonna have us a large time today!" Aunt Emma stepped out to wave at them. She was wearing a white western shirt with turquoise ruffles and matching jeans.

"Don't you look purty, Aunt Emma?" Randy said, as he stepped up to give her a hug. "You better watch out, Uncle Otto, she's lookin' so good, some of these young bucks are liable to steal 'er away from you!"

"Aw, that ain't never gonna happen," Uncle Otto answered, putting an arm around his wife. "If she leaves me, I'm goin' with 'er!"

"You want some help gettin' them mules hooked up?" Randy asked.

"Sure do. Let's go get 'em."

By the time they hooked up the wagon, Denise had arrived. Petey and Kayla spilled out and came running over while Denise helped Miss Velvie out.

"Hey there, young lady," Uncle Otto greeted Miss Velvie. "You ready to get in the wagon?"

"I sure am," she grinned. "I'd have never thought I'd be goin' on another horse ride at my age."

Randy and Uncle Otto helped her into the wagon while Aunt Emma hovered anxiously. Denise and the children piled in and everyone lined their horses up behind the wagon. "Ya-Hoo!" Miss Velvie called as the wagon lurched forward and the children followed suit. Soon, everyone in the crowd was yelling, as they headed down the dirt toad.

"Hey, I brought somethin' for you'uns," Uncle Otto's nephew rode up between Tansey and Joanna.

"What you got, Cecil?" asked Tansey.

"Some good old homemade moonshine, straight from Mt.Pilot! Come on, you girls take a swig."

Soon, Tansey was well on her way to being inebriated. She put Cloudy into a slow lope and stood on his back like a trick rider. Then she would stop him, turn around backwards, and holding the reins behind her, urge him back into a lope.

"Stop doing that silly stuff, Tansey," Logan commanded.

"Aw, she does it all the time," Johnny-Vern rode up beside him. "Even if she does take a fall, it ain't gonna hurt that hard noggin of 'ers."

"And just who are you?" Logan wanted to know.

"Why, ain't you heard? I'm Hood Ornament, the man what rides naked on the front of trucks. Glad to meet you, buddy!" Reaching across his horse, Johnny-Vern held out a hand for Logan to shake.

Logan gave him a dirty look and loped off to catch up with Tansey. "Come on, let's turn around and go back. You're drunk."

Tansey looked at him, slightly cross-eyed.

"Don't worry 'bout the mule goin' blind
Just lean on back and hold the line!"

She galloped off, leaving him in a cloud of dust.

Joanna stopped to wait for Uncle Otto and before the wagon reached her, she could hear music. Miss Velvie had her harmonica out, and they were singing:

You are my sunshine
My only sunshine,
You make me happy
When skies are gray
You'll never know, dear
How much I love you
Please don't take my sunshine away

Petey was sitting in Uncle Otto's lap, holding the reins. Between verses he would yell, "Giddy-up!" Kayla sat with Aunt Emma, singing her little heart out, her pink cowboy hat pushed back from her face, pink boots tapping the seat.

"Hey Jo," Miss Velvie called as the wagon pulled up even with Joanna's horse. "I'm just havin' the best time! Don't you want a Coca-Cola? They're icy cold." She leaned over and pulled one out of the cooler behind Aunt Emma's seat and handed it to Joanna as she rode closer.

"Logan ain't too happy, is he?" Uncle Otto asked.

"Don't look like it. He's tryin' to get Tansey to go back."

"He'll be tryin' a long time," Uncle Otto laughed. "Evidently, he don't know 'er good as we do."

Joanna rode off to catch up with Tansey, who was up ahead with some of the other girls. The reins were wrapped around her saddle horn, while she held a cold beer in one hand and a burning cigarette in the other as Cloudy pranced along at a brisk pace.

They stopped under a big oak and the wagon soon rolled up. "Let's us'uns wait on here for a spell and give everybody a chance to catch up," Uncle Otto directed. "Miss Velvie, why don't you play us another tune on that thing?"

While Miss Velvie played Turkey in the Straw, Petey and Kayla held hands, jumping up and down in the wagon, dancing in the small space. "Go, Granny Velvie!" Petey yelled, as he stomped one little cowboy boot up and down, and clapped his hands.

"Come on, Mama!" Uncle Otto urged, as he pulled Aunt Emma down from the wagon and twirled her around under the big shade tree. They were still dancing when the others caught up. Petey and Kayla laughed and clapped their hands with delight. Tansey got down and joined in. Now Uncle Otto was clogging in a big circle with a woman on each arm. Logan rode up, scowling and didn't say anything.

When everyone had rested their horses for a few minutes, they set out again. Cecil passed the moonshine and soon Tansey was swaying dangerously in the saddle, eyes half closed. She loped her horse up beside the wagon and swung herself over, landing at Miss Velvie's feet.

"What's wrong with Tansey?" Petey wanted to know.

"She's just tired," Miss Velvie answered. "She's gonna take 'er a little nap."

"I wouldn't take no nap if my Mama didn't make me," he responded. "Is Tansey's Mama here? Did she tell 'er she's got'ta take a nap?"

"I don't think so son, she's just real tired," Aunt Emma laughed.

Cloudy headed across the field at a run. Joanna caught him and tied him to the back of the wagon and Logan rode up beside her. "Don't we need to do somethin' about her?"

"Naw, she'll be fine. Just let 'er rest a few minutes and she'll be good to go."

Logan followed behind the wagon, but didn't say anything else.

Just before they got back to the shack, Tansey woke up. Looking straight up, the first thing she saw was Miss Velvie's face. "Well, hey there honey. We thought you were gonna sleep all day. Don't you want a cold drink?"

"I sure do," Tansey started, but her grin faded when she saw the soft drink. "No ma'am, I need me a cold beer."

"Not in front of the young'uns!" Miss Velvie whispered. "Ain't you had about enough? I'm scared you're gonna be sick." Tansey sat up and drank the coke, then untied her horse. Pulling him alongside the wagon, she sailed onto the broad back and took off. "Hey Vern! You got anything to drink in them saddlebags?"

Tansey could barely stand up when she dismounted, so Johnny-Vern took her horse, while Randy helped Miss Velvie down. They got a lawn chair for the old woman and Tansey dragged herself up onto Brandon Tanner's flatbed, dangling her feet over the side. As everyone gathered around, she pulled off her boots and sat them beside her.

Miss Velvie pulled her harmonica out and began to play softly while the men were cooking. "Ma'am, do you know Foggy Mountain Breakdown?" Brandon walked over and pulled a banjo out of his truck seat and sat down beside Tansey.

"Let's see now, if I recollect how it goes." The old woman put the harmonica back to her lips and after a few tentative trys, they were off, the lively music drawing a crowd.

Tansey sat on the truckbed, clapping her hands softly to the music. When he heard the first notes of Dueling Banjos, Johnny-Vern grabbed Denise and they took off, two-stepping. Tansey patted her foot and clapped her hands, threw her head back and laughed in delight.

"Come on, Tansey! Let's go," said Logan

"I ain't ready. You can take my truck, if you want to and I'll get Randy to run me home when they come."

"I said come on, and I mean now," he turned to walk towards the truck and WHAM! One of the scuffed brown boots hit him squarely in the back of his head.

"Dam'mit Tansey! Don't you ever do that again!"

He turned around and the other boot hit him on the third step.

"I'm leavin!" he yelled.

"That's good," Tansey answered. "You're a party-pooper."

Logan got into Tansey's truck and pulled off with a dark scowl on his face, kicking up a little shower of gravel.

"Hey, y'all play the Orange Blossom Special! Tansey called. When the lively first notes sounded, she stood up on the flat bed of the truck and began to clog.

"Come on, Miss Velvie. Sing with me!" said Johnny-Vern, as he carried a chair over and sat down beside the old woman. "Y'all know she's my special girl."

"Oh p'shaw! You got enough girlfriends, you don't need an old lady like me! What do you want to sing?"

"How 'bout Down in the Valley? You got your guitar in the truck there, Brandon?"

Brandon reached into his truck and pulled a guitar off the seat. Johnny-Vern took a moment tuning it, then hit the first notes and began to sing in his deep baritone, then Miss Velvie's sweet soprano joined in as young and old voices blended in perfect harmony.

Down in the valley
Valley so low
Hang your head over
Hear the wind blow

When they came to the last verse, Johnny-Vern held up his hand and stopped for a moment. "Now this here's exactly how I feel about you, Miss Velvie." He looked into the faded blue eyes and continued the song.

Roses love sunshine
Violets love dew
Angels in Heaven
Know I love you

"That's right, Miss Velvie! The angels know how much I love you. Remember now, you're my sweetheart." He bent over and kissed the withered old cheek as everyone clapped and yelled out for more singing.

By the time they finished eating, Tansey had sobered up a little, but Cecil pulled the moonshine out again. "Take you a little nip," he urged. As the other women cleared off the picnic tables, she sat with Cecil, sipping out of the mason jar. Uncle Otto built a bonfire and Aunt Emma brought out a bag of marshmallows for the children to roast.

"You know, this reminds me of when we used to make a little campfire and sit around tellin' ghost stories," Miss Velvie said. "Weren't nothin' much to do for entertainment like television and all. And no matter how many times the same story got told, we loved to hear it, over and over."

"Tell us one," Joanna urged.

"Well, the one that stands out the most in my mind is when Papa Frank and Mama Martha were first married. They lived in a real small house, just one bedroom and another big room that served as livin' room and kitchen. Papa and a neighbor was goin' into town. You had to go by mule and wagon and it took two days.

"The neighbor's wife came over to stay with Mama. When they went to bed that night, the neighbor lady got into Papa's bed. Him and Mama had little twin beds, there in the same room. Well sir, the neighbor said the mattress was too hard for 'er. So Mama traded beds with 'er.

"Then, in the middle of the night, somethin' made Mama wake up. They was a bright light outside, looked like it lit up the whole sky. It started shrinkin' smaller and smaller, until it came through the keyhole. Then it grew again and formed into a ball, 'bout the size of a pumpkin or so, and it went to the foot of the bed where the neighbor lady was. It went back and forth from 'er feet to 'er head, did it three times. After the third time, it went back to the door, shrunk itself up again, and went out through the keyhole and dissapeared.

"Mama just lay there, too scared to move, but she called to the neighbor, 'Essie, did you see that?' Well, Essie wouldn't answer. Finally Mama got up and went over to the bed, shakin' the other woman. 'Essie! Wake up!' But that lady was dead as a doornail. The ghostlight had killed 'er. They always figgered it had really come for Mama, and if it hadn't been for 'er havin' company and switchin' beds, she'd have been the one got killed. That's the only thing saved 'er."

"Ooh! I've got goosebumps," said Tansey in a subdued voice. "Did that really happen, Miss Velvie?"

"That's what they always told me. And Mama was well known for bein' a truthful, Christian woman."

Joanna got up to load their horses into the trailer. "Tansey, you 'bout ready? Bring Cloudy on and put 'im in here." The big appaloosa stepped up into the trailer and they closed the heavy door.

"Uncle Otto, Aunt Emma; we sure enjoyed it. Thanks for havin' us."

"We're glad you'uns could come," Uncle Otto said as Aunt Emma handed them two extra plates of leftovers. As the truck pulled down the path, Joanna could see them still sitting around the fire, telling more stories.

At Tansey's house, Randy pulled the truck around to the front of the barn and opened the trailer door. Cloudy backed out and Tansey caught his lead line and started to the pasture. Just then, Logan came out the back door.

"Well, did you finally decide to come home? It's about time. I don't know why you want to be around those people anyhow. They're a bad influence on you!" Logan grabbed her by the arm, causing the big horse to shy out and pull the rope from Tansey's hands.

"Boy, I've 'bout had a belly-full of you! They're my friends and ain't nobody gonna stop me from bein' with 'em!" Tansey declared as she turned and pushed him back. He tripped over one of the big roots that sprawled out from a pecan tree and fell backwards into the old fashioned claw-footed bathtub that Tansey used for a water trough. He soaked himself completely and came up sputtering.

"You need to just get on back up to Raleigh," Tansey declared as she caught her horse and removed his halter. Then, ignoring Logan, she got some feed from the barn and put it into the feedpan.

Just as Tansey started to open the gate to the electric fence, Logan grabbed her again. The gate was merely a piece of electric wire, with a plastic handle that attached to the next section. Tansey had the handle in her hand and she jabbed the end of it into Logan's midsection. When the naked wire made contact with his soaking wet shirt, he let out a shriek and turned her loose.

"What's the matter with you?" he yelled. "Are you crazy?"

"Hell, no. I think I'm finally comin' to my senses. Why don't you go on back to Raleigh and stay there? Get you one of them city gals that'll act like you want 'er to. 'Cause I ain't never gonna! I'm just a redneck, country girl that raises quarter horses and hell!"

Logan stood for a long moment, looking at Tansey, then shook his head in disgust. Turning on his heel, he went into the house and came out a few minutes later, carrying a suitcase. He got into his little sports car and drove off without saying a word.

"Well, maybe now we can have a little fun around here," Tansey squealed as she did a little dance of glee. Tequila and Kaluah pranced around her feet and she reached down to hug them. "Looks like it's just me and you dogs again," she said.

Days, then weeks went by and Tansey went happily on her way, never mentioning Logan.

Tansey and Joanna were in Raleigh one day, picking up supplies for the rescue. "Let's run by and see Candice while we're here," Tansey urged. "I ain't talked to her lately."

She turned her truck in the direction of her cousin's apartment and they were soon there. Candice opened the door and gave them a warm hug. "Hi guys! Why didn't you let me know you were coming?" Her face suddenly clouded over a little. "Logan's here with his new girlfriend," she whispered. "They're in the kitchen with Robert." She looked at Tansey sympathetically. "I know this must be a little embarrassing for you."

"Well, hell no!" Tansey retorted. "I don't mind meetin' his girl."

Walking into the kitchen, she said, "Hey, Logan, Robert. How y'all doin?" Going over to the attractive young woman, she stuck her hand out and pumped the girl's hand up and down. "My name's Tansey, and this here's my friend Jo."

"Nice to meet you," the girl murmured softly.

They stayed long enough to have a cold drink and talk for a few minutes. It was easy to tell that Logan was extremely uncomfortable, but Tansey paid him no attention. .

The young lady was in the restroom when they prepared to leave and Tansey winked at Logan. "Looks like you picked a winner this time, buddy. Wish you the best of luck." He just smiled nervously and cleared his throat.

As they pulled into the heavy traffic on the freeway, Tansey said, "Dang! I didn't even realize how happy I was that boy was gone. Y'all were always sayin' 'let's go do somethin' and he was sayin' let's stay home'. Got so's I didn't know what to do. Kind'a like havin' one foot on shore and one foot in the canoe."

Tansey was quiet for a few moments, then grinning, she started to sing that old Janie Frickie song at the top of her lungs. Her enthusiasm was contagious and soon, Joanna was singing along with her.

She's single again
Hold onto your men
Look out, she's single again
Yee-ee-ha!!!

HOPE

"Where there is love, there is hope."
—Unknown

"J o?" It was her neighbor, Hope on the telephone. "I wanted to see if you could come over. April's got somethin' to show you. We got 'er a puppy."

Joanna usually tried to visit while Hope's husband was at work, because he wasn't very friendly. If Joanna was talking with her on the phone and Jeff came in, she would hang up abruptly.

Joanna had suspected that Jeff was physically violent. Hope seemed nervous whenever he was around and she often had bruises on her face or upper arms. She had confided to Joanna that he was very different from her first husband, Roger. "He was always so good to me and April," she had said, "and he made everyone feel welcome at our house."

But when April was two years old, Roger was killed in an automobile accident. Hope was so grief-stricken that it was several years before she would even think about becoming involved with anyone else. Everyone encouraged her to start dating again, but she had seemed content to remain single, with April as the center of her life.

Then she met Jeffrey and was swept off her feet. Standing six foot tall, with broad shoulders and sandy brown hair, he was very handsome. But soon he became possessive and ill-tempered.

Hope had finally confided to Joanna that she was afraid to leave. "I tried it once. Jeffrey threw a cinder block through the windshield. He snatched me out of the car and told me he'd mess me up real good if I ever tried to leave again."

Hope just continued to become more and more withdrawn. She had gradually become so isolated that Joanna was about the only person she ever saw. Over time, Joanna watched Hope change from the fun-loving girl she had been into this isolated woman who was afraid of her own shadow. It almost seemed as though this loveless marriage was gradually draining the very life from her.

Joanna went over that afternoon to see the puppy, a golden retriever She was a ball of blonde fur with big brown eyes that could melt the stoniest heart. The little girl would lie down on the grass and the puppy would crawl all over her, tugging at the long hair with the little teeth, making her giggle and squeal.

"Jeffrey got her from a lady that works with 'im," Hope explained as she pushed a strand of light brown hair up off her swanlike neck. "He does seem to want to do things for April sometimes."

"I've got'ta pick out a name for her, Jo," April said. "What do you think about Sissy? 'Cause she's gonna be like my sister!"

"That's perfect."

Hope and Joanna sat on the back porch swing, watching the two of them play.

"April, she sure loves 'er, " Joanna replied. Animals teach children so much."

Joanna saw Sissy several times after that. The little dog had a box full of squeaky toys and balls, and on hot days April would put on her bathing suit and she and Sissy would splash around in the little plastic pool. April always saved a little out of her weekly allowance to buy something for Sissy. She got her a bright red collar and lead, dog toys, and doggie treats. Joanna had never seen April so happy.

It was a Saturday evening and Joanna was exhausted after being at the rescue all day when she heard a gunshot. Then a child's voice screamed out, but she couldn't make out the words.

"Randy!" she called. "Did you hear that?"

"What?"

"Somethin's wrong over at Hope's!"

She and Randy peered out the window, but the big cedar trees blocked the view towards Jeffrey's house. "I'm goin' over there," Joanna declared.

"Wait, I'll go with you. I don't like you bein' nowhere around that Jeffrey."

Joanna was already halfway across the field on foot when Randy pulled up beside her in the truck. Now they could see the house up on the highway. Jeffrey was staggering across the back yard, brandishing a rifle. When he saw Randy turn into the driveway, he got into his pickup and pulled off, tires screaming.

"What happened, Hope? Did he hurt April?" Joanna asked.

"No. It was Sissy. Jeffrey had been out all afternoon, drinking with his buddies. He came home in a nasty mood, pickin' at me, just lookin' for somethin' to start a fuss over. He went out to the garage, and found Sissy chewin' on one of 'is fancy cowboy boots. He should'a never left 'em on the porch. I saw him goin' for the gun and I tried to stop 'im. But I never really thought he'd do it. I thought he was just gonna shoot up in the air or somethin', but he shot Sissy!"

Joanna walked around the side of the garage, and there she was, a shaggy golden form lying on the cement, her lifeblood spreading in an ever widening circle. She had been shot in her right side. As the young woman gently turned her over, she saw the large, ragged wound where the bullet had shattered on impact and exited her body.

Going back around the building, she saw that Hope continued to kneel on the ground, rocking April in her lap like a baby. "Jo, where's Sissy? Can't we take her to the vet?" April cried.

"She's gone, honey," Joanna whispered to April as she gently stroked her hair. As April looked up at her with fresh tears in those big blue eyes she thought her heart would break.

Joanna got Hope and April into the house, and settled on the sofa, while she went into the kitchen and made coffee and hot chocolate. When she got back to the living room, April was nearly asleep in her mother's arms, her chest still hitching every few minutes with gentle sobs. She looked so pitiful and helpless lying there, her long brown hair falling across the fevered cheeks. Hope continued to rock the child tenderly as she looked up at her.

Joanna handed her a steaming cup of coffee. "Hope, you know we need to call the sheriff and report this."

"No," Hope responded in a flat tone. "I don't want anyone to know about any of this. I just don't think my nerves could take goin' to court and all."

Hope looked up at her neighbor. "We've got to get out of here. Could we stay with y'all tonight?"

"Of course you can. Go on and pack what you need, I'll stay here with April."

Randy drove them home and after they put April to bed, Joanna sat up with Hope until the sun peeked over the horizon. At last Hope lay down on the sofa and closed her eyes and soon her breathing became deep and regular.

Joanna woke up a couple of hours later to the sound of the dogs barking, then she heard someone knocking. Opening the door, she saw Miss Velvie.

"Hey, honey. I brought y'all some homemade muffins. Did I wake you up?"

"That's okay. Come on in."

"Well, who's this?" Miss Velvie asked as Hope sat up.

"This is my neighbor, Hope. She and her little girl spent the night."

"Nice to meet you, honey."

Just then, a scream came from the bedroom and Hope went running to her daughter. In hushed tones, Joanna told the old woman what had happened the night before.

In a few moments, Hope came back, holding the little girl, still wrapped in a blanket. She had stopped crying, but her face was pale and drawn. Hope sat down and rocked her as they talked softly.

"Jo, I'll try to find a place to live as soon as I can. I'm goin' to have to find a job."

"Well, don't worry about that. Y'all can stay here as long as you need to."

"I know, but it's so close to home. I just want to get further away."

"I've got an idea," Miss Velvie said. "Why don't y'all come stay with me?"

"That's awfully kind," Hope smiled. "But we couldn't impose on you like that."

"Oh, p'shaw. If I thought you'd be imposin', I wouldn't have asked you. Nobody but me and Roxie there and she's all the time at work or school."

"Are you sure you have room?"

"She's got the room all right," Joanna laughed. "Enough room for all of us to move in."

"I'm gonna go on home and get a couple of bedrooms ready. Maybe cook us up a special supper. You girls come on when you get ready."

Randy went with Hope to pick up some more of their things, while Joanna kept April.

April was quiet on the ride over to Miss Velvie's house that afternoon, as she sat between Joanna and Hope. Joanna noticed how tightly she clung to her mother's hand as they got out of the truck.

"Come on in here," the old woman held the screen door open wide. "Let's take your bags and I'll show you your rooms." She reached down to give April a hug. "Oh, we're goin' to have such a good time. You ever been to a pajama party, honey?"

"No ma'am. My best friend had one, but Jeffrey wouldn't let me go."

"Well, we can have one tonight. We'll put on our pajamas and pop us some popcorn. Maybe watch a movie or tell stories. It'll be fun!"

They were putting their clothes away when they heard a truck with loud mufflers coming up the path. Hope looked out the window.

"Oh, no! It's Jeffrey!" Hurrying to the side door, she locked it. They watched through the window as Jeffrey got out of his truck and came up the steps.

"Hope!" he shouted as he pounded on the door. "I know you're in there. If you don't get out here right now, you're gonna be sorry!"

KA-BLAM! A shotgun exploded, then the girls heard a rat-a-tat-tat pinging noise as tiny dents appeared in the shiny chrome of Jeffrey's front fender. Miss Velvie stepped off the front porch, breaking the stock to load another round.

"You're the one gonna be sorry," the old woman said as she drew a bead on him. "You get your hindparts in that truck and don't never come back around here."

"You're crazy, Old Lady!" Jeffrey shouted as his eyes widened.

"Yep. That's what a lot of folks been sayin' for a lot of years."

KA-BLAM! The baseball cap flew off his head, peppered with holes and he ran for the truck. "Don't let me catch you back around here!" Miss Velvie called as his tires spun in the sand. KA-BLAM! Little holes appeared in his back bumper before he could gain traction, then the tires caught hold and the truck bounced down the long path at top speed.

"Miss Velvie!" Joanna exclaimed. "I didn't know you could shoot like that."

"Willie's old double-barrel," the old woman patted it. "It comes in mighty handy sometimes. You know for shootin' at skunks and such riff-raff."

April was upset and crying again, clinging to her mother like she would never let go. "Its all right, baby," Hope was murmuring.

Later that evening, when they sat down to supper, the little girl refused to eat. Hope fussed over her, but Miss Velvie told her, "She'll be all right, honey. She'll eat somethin' when she gets hongry."

"I got a job I could use some help with," she looked down at the child. "Reckon you could help me?"

"What is it?" the delicate lips trembled.

"Some tiny little kittens what need to be bottle-fed, I bet you'd be real good at it."

"Just like people babies? Drinkin' bottles?"

Taking the little bottles, they all went out on the porch and Miss Velvie gathered up a box of kittens. Hope got April settled in the big swing and Joanna placed a gray-striped tabby into her arms, showing her how to hold him.

"Do it like this," the old woman placed a bottle into the small hand. "Let me get you started. You got to be real careful, so's he don't get too much and get choked. They're greedy little fellers, ain't they?" April's face was transformed as she looked down at the tiny fall of fur and began to talk to him. Soon, she was chattering away.

"Where'd you get all these dogs and cats? What's his name? Look!" she giggled. "Those two dogs are kissin' each other."

Roxanne came driving up the path, got out and came up the steps.

"Go on in the kitchen and get you some supper, honey," Miss Velvie urged. "I got you a plate there on the table wrapped up in tin foil. This here's Hope and April, they're gonna stay with us for awhile."

Roxanne brought her plate out to sit with them while she ate.

After the kittens had finished their bottles, April got down to play with the other animals. Two cats crawled into her lap, a puppy jumped up on her shoulder, and soon she was hidden from view.

"How about a Coca-Cola?" the old woman asked a little later. "And maybe a piece of chocolate cake?"

"Yes ma'am!" the little girl answered. "That sounds good."

After she ate, April crawled into the old woman's lap.

"I guess I'm really too big to be rocked," she said. "But you know what? You remind me of my Grandma, and she always used to rock me. Before she went to Heaven to be with Grandpa."

"Oh, p-shaw!" Miss Velvie smiled down at her. "You don't never get too big to be rocked. Why, we had this lady helped us, Mammy Jenny her name was. I'd sit in 'er lap and rock with 'er after I was a grown woman!"

She hugged the child tight. "There's somethin' about rockin' together, I don't know, it makes you feel all safe and loved. Don't it?"

April smiled up at her and nodded. "I believe somebody's gettin' tired," the old woman said. "Lean back and rest your eyes, just for a few minutes."

Go to sleep, my little pickaninny
Brother Fox will catch him if he don't
Slumber on the bosom of old Mammy Jenny
Mammy's gonna switch him if he don't
Hush-a-hush-a-hush-a-lu-lu-lu-lu
Underneath a silver southern moon
Mammy's little hush-a-bye
Mammy's little baby
Mammy's little Carolina coon.

"Miss Velvie, you're so good with 'er," Hope said as she looked down at her daughter, sleeping soundly in the old woman's arms. "This is just like goin' home again."

"I want y'all to feel like this is home," the old woman smiled back at her. "And y'all are welcome to stay on here as long as need be."

MAX

"Eventually, you will come to understand that love heals everything, and love is all there is."
—Gary Zuvak

April and Hope seemed to thrive in the loving atmosphere at Miss Velvie's house, but Hope soon insisted on getting her own place. She found a job at a day care center, rented a little house on the outskirts of town, and bought a secondhand car.

Away from the comfort she had found with Miss Velvie, Hope became tense again. Now that she was alone, Jeffrey began to stalk her and she was forced to call the police and take out a warrant. When she left the house, she would suffer from severe panic attacks, causing chest pain and shortness of breath. Her illness began to affect April, and she would rush home from school. April's grades started to drop, and she constantly had nightmares about Sissy. When she was at home, she didn't want Hope out of her sight and would follow her from room to room.

Joanna went over as often as possible, and tried to get them out of the house. "Y'all come help me down at the rescue this weekend," she begged. "It'll do you both good."

Denise and Sadie were there when they arrived that Saturday morning, and they were helping Joanna dip one of the dogs. As soon as April caught sight of the girls, she ducked her head bashfully and clung to her mother.

"Why don't y'all show April that litter of kittens?" Joanna called to Sadie. She followed them and watched as Sadie opened the cage and they came tumbling out in a heap of brightly colored fur. Sadie plucked a few tiny balls from a bucket and threw them to the floor. The kittens scurried after them, knocking each other down, leaping to their feet, knocking over buckets and brooms. Soon April was rolling the little balls and pulling strings around for the kittens to chase, as she giggled up at them.

Hope looked at Joanna gratefully, a little smile playing on her lips. "Thanks," she whispered. "You were right. This is going to be good therapy for both of us."

"Let's go back and meet some of the dogs," Joanna said to April. There's some back there that really need your help. We need to give 'em a little exercise. If you and Mama each take one, it'll be a big help."

She took April's hand and gently led her back towards the dog runs. April was fine until she saw the litter of golden retriever /black lab mix puppies. They were all shaggy little balls of fur, three were black, and one was blonde. It looked a lot like Sissy had when she was very small. When April saw it, she began to cry. Joanna picked her up and walked further back.

"April, this is Max," Joanna said as they stopped in front of the last pen. "He's been here for a long time. Nobody wants 'im, because he's such a big dog. How 'bout helpin' me exercise 'im?"

April nodded and Joanna set her down, Hope close behind them. Taking a leash from her pocket, she stepped into the run to put it on the dog. He was a huge, black dog with long shaggy fur. Despite his size, he had a quiet, placid nature and she knew April could handle him, because he was so gentle.

Hope knelt down and she and April began to stroke the long, black fur. A big, wet tongue came out to lick their faces in a slobbery, friendly gesture. The big eyes were irresistible as the long tail wagged slowly.

Sadie and Denise came out with two dogs they had picked to walk, and Joanna and Hope watched for awhile as they and the dogs frolicked across the freshly mown field. Then Hope helped her with the cleaning and feeding until they were exhausted. After Sadie and Denise left, Hope and Joanna wanted to go in and cool off with a cold drink.

"Come on, honey. Let's go inside and rest awhile." Hope called to April.

"Oh, Mama, let me stay out here with Max. Please?"

"All right, but stay right here in the back, where I can see you from the window."

The women went in and sat at the break table with soft drinks, watching April and the dog playing outside.

"I guess I should think about gettin' 'er another dog." Hope said. "Maybe a little dog this time, that could stay inside."

"I know a lady that's got a Yorkie to give away She's the cutest little thing, with her hair pulled up in a pink bow."

Hope got up to look out the window for April, but she didn't see her anywhere. The women went outside and Joanna spotted her. April had pulled a blanket off the fence, where Joanna had hung it to dry. She had placed it in a shady place under one of the outside runs and she and Max lay there, fast asleep. She was dirty, sweaty and disheveled, but on her face was an expression of pure bliss. She was lying with her head pillowed on the big dog's shoulder. He awoke as the women approached, but he lay perfectly still, as if he didn't want to disturb the little girl. He just rolled his eye around to look at them and thumped the porch with his big tail a couple of times to acknowledge their presence.

"I think he might have some Newfoundland in 'im," Joanna explained to Rose. "Back in the old days, they were used for water rescue. I read somethin' Lord Byron wrote ... "courage without ferocity. And all the virtue of man without his vices." Miss Velvie told me people used to call 'em the St. Bernard of the water. Back around 1920, one of 'em saved over twenty people from a ship that went down and they gave 'im a gold medal. They sure are gentle creatures."

"Well, he certainly seems smart and well behaved," Hope replied. "I can't believe no one wants him."

"Seems like everybody wants a small house dog or a cuddly little puppy, or a registered dog. He's got somethin' mixed in with the Newfoundland and that makes it harder, too. I'm always findin' big dogs, ugly dogs or mangy ones that nobody wants. But, don't worry. Sooner or later I'll find the right person to give 'im to. He's such a good dog."

"Poor fellow," Hope murmured. "It must be hard on 'im having to stay shut up in that pen all the time." Joanna could tell she was thinking about her own recent confinement.

"Well, why don't you bring April over on weekends and let her spend some time with 'im?"

"I'll think about it," Hope promised.

"Neecie, where is Jo?" Tansey asked as she came into the office at the rescue. "I ain't seen 'er in a few days."

"I don't know," Denise answered. "It's really weird, I've been callin' and leavin' messages, but she's not returnin' my calls. Maybe I've been puttin' too much on 'er out here. Could be she's tired of stayin' out here all the time."

"Naw," Tansey answered. "You couldn't hardly drag 'er away from here, the way she loves these animals. Somethin' must be wrong. Let's ride over there and check on 'er."

There was no answer when the two women knocked on Joanna's door later, so they walked in and found her sitting in the darkened den. She was just sitting on the sofa, the television was off and the blinds were drawn. Dixie lay beside her, her silky, white head in the woman's lap.

"Jo?" Tansey said. "You okay?"

"I don't know." The answer was flat and lifeless.

Denise walked over and put a hand on Joanna's arm. "What's wrong?"

"I'm pregnant."

"Well shucks," Tansey spoke up. "Much as you love young'uns, I'd think you'd be happy."

"You don't understand. We tried for a few years to have a baby, but every time I got pregnant, I miscarried. The last time was really hard for me, because I carried it almost to term and we thought surely everything would be all right."

Joanna looked up at her friends and a tear rolled down her cheek. "It was a little boy and we had picked out a name, gotten the nursery ready and everything. The doctor said if I could have only carried 'im for a few more weeks, he would have made it."

"Oh sweetie, I'm so sorry," Denise said.

"I went into a really deep depression," Joanna said. "It lasted for over a year. Could hardly eat or sleep, I just wanted to crawl into a hole. It was so painful that I went back on the pill. I never want to take a chance on goin' through anything like that. Ever again."

"Maybe if you went to a specialist, they might could help," Denise began.

Joanna let out a short, bitter laugh. "I've been to everybody you ever heard of. My obstetrician referred me up to the state university and I went to all the clinics. There don't seem to be anybody that can help me.

Dixie pushed her nose up under Joann's hand and nudged it. Whining, she looked up at the woman with anxious eyes.

"Maybe this time it'll be different," Tansey said.

"If only I could believe that," Joanna answered.

"What about adoption?" Denise asked.

"We tried. But I had been takin' antidepressants and nerve pills. When the adoption agency saw my medical records, they said I was too unstable."

"Bullshit!" exclaimed Tansey. "Didn't they know the reason you were depressed?"

"It didn't seem to matter."

"Look, I know we can't tell you to stop worryin' about it," Denise said. "But try to think positive." She stood up. "Now," she said briskly. "What have you had to eat today?"

"Just some toast. But I'm not hungry."

"Well you've got to feed that baby," Denise went into the kitchen and opened the cabinet. "I'm gonna heat you up some soup and make some sandwiches."

There was a light knock on the door that evening, then Miss Velvie poked her head in. "Yoo-hoo! Anybody home?"

"Come on in," Joanna was still sitting on the sofa.

"Hey, honey. Tansey told me what's goin' on and I thought I might be able to help."

Joanna looked up at the old woman with anger in her eyes. "So they're goin' around, blabbing to everybody? I told them that in confidence."

"Now, don't be mad at the girls. They just want to do somethin' to help you. And they ain't told nobody but me. Shucks, it ain't nothin' to be ashamed of.

"Anyways, I think I might could help you. If you want me to."

"How?"

"It's an old folk remedy, honey. Mama used it on women that had trouble with pregnancies and it really helped 'em."

"But Miss Velvie," Joanna looked up with eyes full of pain and sorrow. "Didn't Tansey tell you about all the doctors and specialists I've been to? If they couldn't help me, how can you?"

"Well now, honey. Here's the way I see it. The folk remedies use plants and herbs. Now you know that's somethin' the good Lord hisself give us, and sometimes that's a sight better than modern drugs that are just a bunch of chemicals all mixed together."

"God!" Joanna spat out. "If there was a God, he wouldn't·let an innocent baby die."

"Oh honey, He's there all right. We don't always understand why things go the way they do, but that don't mean He don't exist."

An expression of wistfulness that Joanna had never seen before crossed the old woman's face for a brief moment. "You know, I always wanted children too, but the good Lord never saw fit for me to even catch pregnant. Some folks say that's why I do for the animals, that I'm tryin' to create a substitute. But I don't know, I just love 'em."

Reaching down, Miss Velvie pulled a bottle from the ever-present pocketbook.

It contained a red-tinted liquid that looked like cranberry juice. "Now what you need to do is take twenty drops of this every day. It's a liquid tincture made from crampbark. Relaxes the uterus and keeps it from pushin' the baby out."

"And that's all there is to it? Crampbark?"

"That's it," the old woman smiled. "Course if it makes you feel better, we could use the fancy name: virbunum opules, but Mama just called it crampbark."

"I don't know."

"Well, I don't want to push you. I'll just leave it here, then if you change your mind, you'll have it."

"I don't know, I don't want to get my hopes up."

Denise called Joanna the next day. "Did you try that medicine?"

"Not yet."

"What are you waitin' for? It can't hurt."

"I just don't believe it'll work."

"You know how good Miss Velvie's treatments are. Remember how she helped me? When I was so sick with my periods, bein' out of work and all. You know the doctors couldn't help. Those hormones didn't work at all."

"Yeah, and I do remember you felt so bad about takin' 'em. After we heard those horror stories about the way they keep horses pregnant to make the drugs, then kill the foals right after they're born."

"Yeah, I felt so guilty. And now they're sayin' those hormones are causin' cancer too. Takin' estrogen and stuff is givin' a lot of women breast cancer and heart problems."

"What was it that Miss Velvie gave you?"

"She went out to 'er garden and picked some raspberry leaves. Dried 'em and ground 'em up. And I ain't had a minute's trouble since I started takin' 'em. Don't hardly even know when I'm havin' a period, they come and go easy as can be. Just think, somethin' simple as raspberry leaves."

A few weeks later Joanna was back at the rescue. "Neecie, you know I've got to be really careful, but I thought maybe I could do some of the paperwork."

"That would be great, there's a mountain of it piled up in the office there."

Denise watched for a few moments as Joanna began to sort the papers into piles. "You know, you really look good. You're puttin' on weight, got roses in your cheeks and all."

"I feel good. I don't know if it's that stuff I'm takin' or not, but this pregnancy seems a lot different. I'm not havin' mornin' sickness, or spottin'. And I haven't had any abdominal pain, like I always did before. That Miss Velvie sure is somethin'."

"That she is," Denise nodded in agreement.

April and Hope came in a little later. April wanted to go straight back to see Max. Joanna brought him out and the little girl gave him a big hug as his pink tongue bestowed wet, sloppy kisses on her face. "Hey, boy, I missed you!" April cried. Hope and Joanna looked at each other and smiled. The big dog and the little girl romped and played until it was time for them to go home.

"We've been comin' right often," Hope confided to Joanna as they watched April lead the dog back into his run. "All April wants to do is come out here and see that dog."

"Bye, Max," said April, rubbing the dog's head. "I'll see you next weekend."

"April, we can't come every single Saturday," admonished Hope.

"Why not?' April asked. "The animals need our help."

"You know what?" Hope replied. "You're right, April! Just why not? There's nobody to tell us where to go, or what to do, or when to come home."

Hope grinned at Joanna over April's little head. This was the Hope she knew and loved. Full of love and full of life again. Joanna grinned back at her. They were both going to be just fine. She put a hand on her abdomen. And so was she.

From that time on, Hope and April were at the rescue at least once a week. No different from any of the other kids, April loved it. She became fast friends with Petey and Kayla. Whenever you saw April, the smaller children were usually close behind, always with Max at their heels. And one day, Hope had a delightful surprise for Joanna.

"Jo would it be okay if Max went home with us? I've been trying to talk April into getting a smaller dog, but she just loves that big old guy. She keeps saying if we don't take 'im , nobody will. It's getting harder and harder to say no."

"Would it be okay?" Joanna squealed. "It would be just perfect! Nothin' would make me happier."

As she watched them walking together to the car that day, Joanna smiled to herself, thinking how well this was working out. They had all reached out in need and found each other, three lost souls that had been hurt by human negligence, but now they had each other. The big dog had restored the spirits of both mother and daughter. And as Max hopped into the back seat of the little Mazda with April, his huge size seemed to fill the tiny car to overflowing, just as his love had filled their hearts.

THIRD TIME'S A CHARM

"Angels capture love and sprinkle it on our hearts."
—Unknown

Hope and April continued to be active with the animals, and it helped them tremendously. With the resilience of youth, April seemed to be completely normal again, but it was taking Hope a little longer. She still had nightmares and great difficulty sleeping at times. But she was beginning to get out and make friends.

Everyone encouraged Hope to start dating again but she wanted no part of it. The years with Jeff had left a bad taste in her mouth as far as men were concerned. "Takin' care of April and helpin' the animals gives me complete fulfillment," she would say.

They would always bring Max when they came over to Joanna's house, and he would have a great time gallivanting around with her dogs and swimming in the pond. April would take hold of Max behind his neck and he would pull her along effortlessly, as she floated behind him.

One day when Max jumped out of the car, he had a tiny friend with him. It was the little Yorkshire terrier Joanna had told Hope about. When Joanna's dogs ran up to greet them, the tiny dog ran back to Max and cowered under his legs, but it wasn't long before she was bossing the entire group around.

"We decided Max needed some company," Hope said. "I really wanted to get her ever since you told me about her. Isn't she the cutest little thing you ever saw?"

"We named her Minnie," explained April. "Now we've got Maxi and Minnie! One's big and one's little! Isn't that neat?" Joanna had to agree that it was very neat, indeed.

Max and Minnie soon became a regular sight around the farm, and everyone that saw them just had to laugh, as Minnie bossed him around. Max seemed to adore the little Yorkie, and was protective of her, just as he was over April.

One Saturday the girls were at the rescue, walking dogs, when a nice looking young man drove up. Tall and broad-shouldered, he had the rugged good looks of an outdoorsman. He was accompanied by a little boy. "We heard y'all would take in stray animals." He spoke southern slang, but lacked the slow drawl of the territory. "My son found a mother cat and a litter of kittens at that dumpster right outside of town. Evidently, someone put 'em out there. I told 'im he could have a couple, but we just couldn't keep 'em all. I hate to send 'em to the pound, and I was wonderin' if you had room for 'em?"

"Gosh, I don't know," Joanna began. "We've got about all we can handle right now."

He was very understanding. "Do y'all have any suggestions as to what I could do with 'em?"

Joanna took a deep breath. "Is there any way you could foster 'em, maybe give us some time to move some of these we already have here?"

The answer Joanna got was not what she had expected. "Sure, I guess we could do that. We're livin' with my parents on their farm, and there's plenty of room. Just so we can find 'em homes before too long."

"Well, I can't make you no promises, but we'll do everything we can to help," Joanna said.

Maybe Nick could volunteer out here," he said as he looked around.

"That would be wonderful, we can use all the help we can get."

"By the way, my name's Luke Tucker and my boy here is Nicholas. We just moved back here from New York, moved in with my parents. My Dad's got a farm, so maybe we could foster animals for you sometimes. I know large dogs are really hard to place, so maybe we could keep one or two at the time for you."

"You sure sound like you know animals."

"My Dad does know all about animals, he's a vet!" the little boy exclaimed.

"Well you'll come in handy, we'll be buggin' you to death."

"That's fine, I'd love to help y'all. I'm gonna be workin' with Doc Cooper."

He stayed a little while, answering some medical questions and giving the girls some new ideas. He had worked in a large practice in New York and had a great deal of things to tell them about the shelters there. His wife had passed away last year after a long illness and he wanted to come home.

"Nick loves bein' here with my folks. We lived in an apartment in Washington and only had one small dog," Luke said. "Now he can have a few more pets. Dad already bought a pony for 'im, and he thinks that's the coolest."

The Tuckers began to show up often to volunteer. Joanna was surprised that Luke had enough time to come so much.

"Well, Jo, I'll tell you. I feel like Nick needs me so much right now, with 'is mother gone. That's one reason I'm staying at Dad's, that way I can just work part time for a while, and spend time with 'im."

"That Luke has got a heart as big as all the outdoors," Hope remarked one day. "I've never seen a man that has so much compassion for animals. And he's so good with the children."

"Hey, he ain't a bit hard on the eyes, either!" Tansey shot back. "Y'all ever notice how all the young girls are always flirtin' with 'im? And he don't pay 'em no mind."

"Yeah," said Denise. "Seems like he's always pickin' up a stray or helpin' somebody."

"He does have the gentlest hands I've ever seen," Hope mused with a faraway look in her eyes."

"Whoo-ee! I think the love bug's finally bit old Hope!" Tansey screeched. Hope blushed and looked down, but she smiled like a young girl.

Joanna did begin to notice that Hope and Luke often joined up to do chores at the rescue together. And when they had cookouts, the pair was always sitting together. At first, they were always talking shop, Hope asking questions and eager to learn more about how to care for the animals. Gradually it became more personal and soon they were dating (if you could call an outing with two children a date). No matter where they went, the children were nearly always with them.

"You know, Luke likes a lot of the same things I do," Hope mused.

"Like what?" Joanna asked.

"Well...doin' simple little things with the children, picnics and stuff. He don't care much about goin' out and socializing at any of the fancy affairs. Sometimes we just take the kids for ice cream at the Dairy Queen or take 'is little boat out on the pond. And he just loves old John Wayne movies. When my Daddy was livin', we'd sit and watch 'em together for hours. And he even likes the old Elvis songs!"

"Well, no wonder you two are gettin' on, then," Joanna answered. "You got every record the King ever made!"

A few weeks later, Hope called Joanna with the news the entire group had been expecting. "Guess what, Jo! Luke asked me to marry him!"

"You don't say!" Joanna teased. "I had no idea."

Hope giggled like a schoolgirl. "I never thought I would have any interest in men again, but Luke is so different from guys like Jeff. He's so lovin' and completely unselfish. He spends every wakin' minute doing somethin' to help someone. And April just loves 'im."

"Heck, Hope," Joanna replied. "Everybody loves 'im. You just can't help it. I think you really lucked up this time."

The wedding took place on the Tucker farm, in the backyard of the huge old rambling homeplace. The back deck had been decorated with big buckets of magnolia blossoms from the magnificent old tree in the front yard. Home-picked bouquets of zinnias and lilies adorned the picnic tables, which were covered with gaily colored tablecloths. The sun shone down through the leaves of the mammoth oak trees, which provided deep, cool shade. The birds were singing, and squirrels scampered through the treetops. It was a perfect day.

Miss Velvie had made the wedding cake and it was a bit unusual. It stood tall and elegant, with white icing and pink flowers, but the top tier was covered with tiny figures. There was the traditional bride and groom, but there were also two children, three dogs, two cats and a horse.

Nearly everyone had come in casual dress. Most people wore jeans or shorts, a few of the older ladies wore dresses. Miss Velvie, of course, was clad in her signature suit of white velvet, with the rose pin. The men who worked on the farm were barbecuing on a big cooker out by the barn and the aroma was tantalizing. People were coming and going all morning. Finally, it came time to seat everyone in the chairs that had been borrowed from the church and lined up on the lawn.

Max, Minnie and the Tucker's big Sheperd mix, Knucklehead were running back and forth among the crowd, greeting the guests. The children had shampooed them that morning and twisted silk flowers into their collars. Suddenly, from a row near the middle, came a shriek of anger. Knucklehead had run up to Hilda and cocked his leg on her fancy, long, satin skirt. "Y'all are crazy, lettin' a dog come to a weddin'!" she cried as everyone tried to hide their laughter. Agnes just stood beside her, making eyes at Johnny-Vern.

Grabbing the dogs, Nick took them up to the front row and sat down. Two of the cats had decided to join the festivities, and they perched on the porch railing, tails flicking lazily, as they stared out at the crowd on the lawn.

The screen door opened and out stepped Luke, to take his place on the deck, followed by Mr. Tucker, his best man. Luke made a splendid sight in a western cut black suede jacket and pressed blue jeans. On his head was a black Stetson and the outfit was completed by a simple pair of black western boots.

"Wow!" breathed Tansey in Joanna's ear. "Talk about a sexy man! Lucky Hope!"

Luke took one look at the menagerie on the front row and began to grin. A few seconds later, Denise sat down at the keyboard and began to play the wedding march. Everyone turned towards the back of the lawn as Hope started slowly around the tall hedges to walk up the path. The form-fitting bodice of her dress was trimmed in tiny seed pearls and the wide skirt swept out behind her. Her hair was swept back in soft brown curls and held by tiny blue and white flowers. And walking beside her, holding her hand was April, dressed as a miniature bride, an exact replica of her mother.

"Well, I realize this wedding party is a bit unusual," the minister began. "But since it was the animals that brought these two people together, they should indeed be present." With the exception of Hilda, everyone there nodded in agreement.

Luke stepped over to Hope and took her hand in his as they exchanged vows. Then he moved over to April and went down on one knee, slipping a tiny ring on her finger, too. "With this ring, I take you to be my daughter, to cherish and protect you. I promise to guide you through life the best I know how, and to take care of you, until death do us part."

Eyes began to tear up as Joanna's sweet tenor rang out with The Wedding Prayer and some of the ladies were sniffling. But not Hope. She smiled up at Luke and he tipped his Stetson at her as Joanna began to sing.

Love me tender, love me true
All my dreams fulfill
For my darling, I love you
And I always will

"You can almost see an aura of happiness and love surroundin' those two," Joanna thought as their eyes held an embrace throughout the song. Then, as they stepped down from the deck, their children and animals bombarded them with hugs, kisses and slobbering. "This is absolutely, positively and without a doubt, the best weddin' I've ever been to," Joanna said and Tansey nodded in agreement.

After the couple had visited for a few moments with everyone, the crowd turned at the sound of rattling chains and hoofbeats. Uncle Otto had brought over his mules and wagon for a wedding ride. They had hidden it behind the barn that morning and draped it with the Christmas decorations Joanna had brought down from her attic. Gold and silver roping was draped around the wagon and intertwined through the harness. Tassels of braided red and gold hung from the bridles. Magnolia blossoms decorated the front of the wagon and the men had taped posters to the sides exclaiming: Honeymoon Express!

Everyone was throwing rice at the newlyweds as they ran towards the wagon. Luke picked Hope up as if she were a feather and tossed her into the back seat. The children rushed up, followed closely by the dogs. "Wait Daddy! We want to ride too!" Nick was shrieking. Laughing, Luke scooped up Minnie and the children as the larger dogs bounded in. He could hardly get himself in, as they swarmed over him.

Those of the group who rode horseback had trailered their horses over and now they ran to the barn to mount up. As they rode out of the yard, it was pure pandemonium. The wagon rattled, a horse whinnied, the dogs barked, and Tansey let out a rebel yell. As the wagon rolled by the onlookers, Hope tossed her boquet out and Miss Velvie caught it, causing everyone to shriek with laughter. One of the farm hands caught her up and spun her around in a do-si-do that made her blush.

"Hey Jo, the minister said. "Seems funny to see the crowd ridin' without you."

Joanna put a hand down across her swollen abdomen. "I'm not takin' any chances until this baby gets here."

Uncle Otto had stocked the wagon with a cooler full of champagne and beer and Aunt Emma had put in cokes for the kids. Uncle Otto's nephew, Cecil pulled a half gallon of moonshine from his saddlebags. "Hey Tansey! Remember this stuff? You want a swaller?"

"I dunno, it give me a mighty bad hangover last time," she began, then she rode over. "Oh, what the heck! If a weddin' ain't a good excuse, I don't know what is!" And she turned the bottle up.

The barbecue was ready when they came in and they had a feast complete with homemade hush puppies and slaw. There were gallons of sweet iced tea and lemonade. Then everyone gathered around to watch Hope cut the cake.

By this time, it was twilight and the strands of tiny white Christmas lights covering the shrubbery twinkled along with the fireflies. The band Mr. Tucker had hired arrived and began to set up. April and Nick held hands and skipped in a circle, pretending to square dance, followed by the leaping, barking dogs. In the center of the circle, Petey and Kayla jumped and whirled. The band broke into "Cotton-Eyed Joe" and the adults formed a larger circle around the children. Johnny-Vern was spinning Miss Velvie around like a young girl. "I ain't danced this much in thirty years or so!" she panted.

Hope and her new husband didn't go on a trip for their honeymoon. "Everything we want is right here," she confided to Joanna. "We're just gonna take a couple of days and stay here with our family and our animals. It's what we both want."

The couple moved in with Luke's family in the big farmhouse. "I just love Luke's mother," said Hope. "She's just like my Mama was. And Mr. Tucker's a real sweetie. Did you know he bought a pony for April, too?"

Hope sometimes went out with Luke on late night calls, while the children stayed with his parents. On weekends, the children would often accompany them.

"Hey, Jo, you know what I want to be when I grow up?" April confided one afternoon while they were walking dogs at the rescue. "A vet."

"Well, that's wonderful, sweetie. You'd sure make a great one."

"Yeah, I think so too. I've got the best teacher in the whole world. I sure do love Luke and Mama does, too. He's so nice to us. It was a good day when we found 'im. Right?"

"Right!" Joanna couldn't have agreed more.

THE LITTLE ROSE

"Some people come into our lives and quickly go. Others stay for awhile and leave footprints on our hearts so that we are never the same."
—Unknown

"Jo, I'll see you tomorrow," Tansey called through the office door. "You gonna be okay here by yourself?"

"Yeah, I'm fine." Joanna gathered a pile of folders and put them into the filing cabinet. "I'm quittin' for the day too. I'm gonna walk over to Miss Velvie's for a few minutes."

"Okay. I'll be here to feed up in the mornin'."

Following Tansey out, Joanna crossed the field to the big house and went into the kitchen. "Yoo-hoo! Miss Velvie, anybody home?"

"In here, honey," the old woman called. Joanna followed her voice into the living room. Miss Velvie was sitting in her rocker, watching the soap operas. One hand held a length of cloth, while the fingers of the other hand flew back and forth, working colorful thread in and out.

"I'm just workin' on a cross-stitch plaque, thought maybe we could hang it in the office over yonder." She held it up for Joanna to see.

ALL CREATURES GREAT AND SMALL
THE LORD GOD MADE THEM ALL

"Hey, that's from the James Herriot books," Joanna said.

"Yes," the old woman nodded. "So it is. And from the poet, Mr. Coleridge, long before that."

"That looks just like Abby and Doo-Dad," Joanna pointed at the likeness of a dog and a cat.

"They posed for me," the old woman smiled. "Look-a-yonder, they're doin' it now."

Joanna looked over at the sofa, where the two animals were snuggled up together.

"Come on in the kitchen," Miss Velvie got up. "I got some chocolate pecan pie bars. Made 'em up special. Didn't put no bourbon in this time. We can't be feedin' that little tyke no whiskey." She put a hand on Joanna's abdomen. "But I bet you'd like some chocolate, wouldn't you, little feller?"

"Chocolate really wakes 'im up," Joanna said. "Every time I eat it, he goes to kickin' like crazy."

They were just sitting down at the table when the dogs began to bark. A light knock came at the door and a deputy poked his head in.

"Tony!" Joanna exclaimed. "What are you doin' here?"

The deputy stood for a moment, scuffling his feet, looking down at the old-fashioned tile. "Hey Jo, Miss Velvie. I sure hate to haf'ta come out here like this..."

"What's wrong, son?" the old woman asked.

"Well...." Tony pushed an envelope across the table. "I've got a supbeona for you. Since somebody had to bring it, I asked the chief to let me come."

"What in the world?" Miss Velvie opened the envelope, looked at the document and handed it to Joanna.

"It means you've got to go to court," Joanna scanned the paperwork. "I should have known, that darn Hilda's behind this."

"Well, I ain't done nothin' to Hilda!" the old woman exclaimed.

"She's claimin' you're practicin' medicine without a license," Tony explained. "She's been down at the courthouse accusin' you of all kinds of things."

"Well, come on and sit down, son. Since you're here, you might as well have somethin' to eat." The old woman pushed the plate of cookies in front of the deputy. "Jo, get 'im a Coca-Cola, will you honey?

"How much trouble you think I'm in, young man?" Miss Velvie asked.

"I don't know, ma'am. We ain't never had a case exactly like this before."

"Don't worry, Miss Velvie," Joanna said. "We'll go with you."

Joanna, Tansey, and Denise sat with the old woman in the courtroom. Miss Velvie was wearing her white velvet suit. Hilda and Agnes kept glaring at them across the courtroom and Joanna could hear the grinding of teeth. Tony stood by the door with a cluster of deputies. Finally, the judge came in.

"Hilda Hawkins versus Velvet White," the baliff called.

"Miss Hawkins?" the judge looked out across the courtroom. Hilda raised her hand. "You may take the stand.

"Now, I understand that you have a complaint against Miss White for practicin' medicine?"

"That's right. Old woman's crazy, goin' around givin' everybody medicine and she ain't no doctor! They ought'a put 'er in one of those homes for old folks."

"Where Miss White resides is not the issue here today," the judge began. "Now exactly who has she been givin' these medicines to?"

"Everybody," Hilda snorted. "People, animals, you name it."

"You have to be specific."

"My sister, Agnes. See, that's her, on the front row there."

"All right, Agnes Hawkins. Take the stand. I want to hear this from the horse's mouth."

"Jack-ass, he should have said," Tansey whispered.

"Now, young lady, what kind of medicine did Miss White give you?" the judge asked.

"It...ah...it was for acne."

"You had a skin condition?"

"Yeah, real bad."

"It certainly seems to have cleared up."

"Well...yeah, it worked real good."

"Then I don't understand what the trouble is."

"The problem is that old woman ain't got no right givin' my sister medicine," Hilda stood up. Agnes sneaked over there behind my back. She knew I would have never let 'er go over there."

The judge looked at Hilda. "Miss Hawkins, the question was addressed to your sister."

"Well...," Agnes stammered. "There ain't really no problem, least not that I can see." Agnes kept her eyes down, avoiding Hilda's glare. '

"Miss White," the judge motioned. "Take the stand, please."

The old woman stood up, trembling a little. But she marched proudly up to the stand. Holding her patent-leather pocketbook in the crook of one arm, she adjusted her veiled hat, then placed a hand on the bible.

"I most certainly do swear to tell the truth," Miss Velvie answered the baliff. "Been doin' it all these years and I ain't gonna start tellin' no lies at this late date."

A low murmur and a few stifled giggles spread through the courtroom.

"Now Miss White," the judge began. "Did you give Miss Hawkins medication of any kind?"

"I sure did. She come to me, askin' for help. Said her doctor sent 'er to the dermatologist, but they couldn't get 'er skin cleared up. I give 'er some skin toner. See, what you do is melt some beeswax in a saucepan. Then you mix in some chamomile and rosemary, then while it's cookin' you got to whip it to keep if from..."

The judge held up his hand. "That's all right, I don't need to know how you make it."

"And she come back a few weeks later, got a little more."

"Have you taken some sort of classes on herbal healin', Miss White?"

"Classes?"

"You know, attended school?"

"Lord have mercy, no. Learned from Mama Martha, my mother-in-law, don't you know? I know folks don't believe in herbs much now-a-days, but some of 'em work real good."

"Well Miss White, I'm afraid you're goin' to have to stop administerin' these herbs to other people. And to other people's animals as well. I believe you have only their best interest at heart, but Miss Hawkins is right. You can not practice medicine without a license."

The old woman looked up at the judge. "And he showed me the tree of life and the leaves of the tree were for healing."

"Ma'am?"

"That's Revelations 22:1-2. Tells you right there in the bible what we're supposed to do to heal ourselves."

"Nevertheless, you can not do that. Now consider this a warning. If there are furthur complaints against you, I will be forced to impose a fine on you, perhaps even some jail time."

Miss Velvie looked up at him. "You mean I got to stop helpin' folks?"

"I'm afraid so. Now don't look at me that way. If it was up to me, I'd tell you to keep right on doin' it, but the law is the law and I must uphold it."

"Well.... I'll do as you say. But, it sure ain't right. The Lord give us these plants to use and you want me to just let 'em go to waste, when they could be helpin' people?"

"It's not what I want, it's what the law says."

They had started down the steps to the courthouse when Hilda caught up to them. "I reckon you'll haf'ta stop workin' your black magic now, old woman! And don't think I won't be watchin'. If you so much as give somebody a cup of herbal tea, I'm gonna find out and report it."

Tansey let go of the old woman's arm and started towards Hilda. "All right, you got your way. Now get out'ta here, before I kick your ass, right on the courthouse steps!"

Hilda backed away, eyes wide and breathing heavily. "Just remember, I'll be watching y'all," she promised. "Come on Agnes, let's go."

The group had barely reached the bottom of the steps when Joanna doubled over in pain.

"Jo, what's wrong?" Denise asked.

"I'm not sure, but....I think.... maybe I'm goin' into labor."

Twelve hours later, Joanna delivered a healthy, seven-pound baby girl. With her thick, auburn hair and fair complexion, she looked like a miniature replica of her mother.

"We decided to call 'er Rosie," Joanna beamed up at the old woman from her hospital bed. "I know that's your middle name, Miss Velvie, and we wanted to name 'er for you. After all, I really don't believe she would be here if it wasn't for you."

She handed the infant up to the old woman, who cradled it in her arms, "Lo, children and the fruit of the womb are a heritage and a gift that cometh from the Lord. That's from Psalms 127:1-6." She smoothed a tiny wisp of hair off the baby's brow. "Now ain't you just precious? Oh, but we're gonna have us some good times together, baby girl."

The baby shower was held when Rosie was two weeks old.

"We wanted to wait," Denise explained. "You know, just in case somethin' went wrong."

All the women had brought food and Miss Velvie made the cake. She was standing in the kitchen looking at Aunt Emma's eyes.

"Get you some eyebright," she said. "Press the leaves and get the juice out. Mix one part juice to three parts water and boil it up for about a half hour..."

"Miss Velvie!" said Tansey. "You can't be doin' your medicines any more."

The old woman looked at her with a gleam in her eye. "Now that judge told me I couldn't give 'em to nobody. He ain't said nothing' about tellin' folks how to do it themselves!"

Randy held the baby while Joanna opened the gifts. He sat on the sofa with Dixie at his side. "I believe Dixie thinks this is her baby," he laughed as he patted the dog gently on the head. "She gets so anxious every time little Rosie makes a peep."

The door opened and Stumpy and Johnny-Vern came in, struggling underneath the weight of an antique cradle made of cherry-wood and adorned with a huge pink bow.

"Jo," Miss Velvie began. "I'd like for y'all to have this. It was my husband Willie's baby cradle. Papa Frank carved it with 'is own hands."

"Oh, Miss Velvie!" exclaimed Joanna. "We can't accept that, it's a family heirloom, you can't give it away."

"P'shaw," the old woman replied. "All my kinfolk are dead and gone. Take a look around you, honey. All you young people are my family now. It ain't doin' nobody a speck of good up in my attic and it would pleasure me to see little Rosie in it."

Joanna nodded at Randy, who stood up and carried the infant across the room to lay her in the cradle. Dixie was close on his heels with every step and propped her front feet up on the side rails as the baby gurgled and cooed.

Pulling one of the folding chairs up close, Miss Velvie swung the cradle gently and began to sing the now familiar song. Denise, then Tansey joined in and soon everyone was singing.

Go to sleep my little pickanniny
Brother Fox will catch you if you don't
Slumber on the bosom of old Mammy Jenny
Mammy's gonna switch you if you won't
Hush-a-hush-a-hush-a-lu-lu-lu-lu
Underneath the silver southern moon
Hush-a-bye, rock-a-bye, Mammy's little baby
Mammy's little Carolina coon

Joanna and Randy stood behind Miss Velvie's chair, looking down at their daughter, smiling and crying all at the same time. "Oh, Miss Velvie," Joanna asked as she reached down and put her arms around the old woman's shoulders. "How can we ever thank you?"

The old woman smiled up at her, with eyes full of love. "Why honey, you already have. Just bein' a part of this celebration today means more than I could ever tell you. It's just like old times when I was a girl." She looked down at the sleeping infant and the dog that kept up the vigilant watch over her self-appointed charge. "Just remember, always watch over the young'uns and the animals."

TOMMY-CAT

"A dog, quick as a rowboat to your side, is your best friend in a minute. A cat, turning slowly like the great ocean liner, is your friend for life."

—Anonymous

Joanna was helping Miss Velvie with Dicey as Little Rosie gurgled and cooed in her carrier nearby. The dog had a large abscess on his abdomen and Joanna was holding him in her lap while the old woman examined it.

"This here black salve will get 'im fixed up in no time at all," Miss Velvie declared. "It's made from comfrey leaves and it's got a real strong astringent action. It'll pull that old bad stuff right out'ta there. I reckon I can still doctor my own animals." She dabbed on a thick cream that looked like tar, just as Bonnie drove up the path.

"Hey Miss Velvie, Jo!" she called as she went around and opened the passenger door. A young girl got out, carefully holding a small bundle to her chest.

"We got a favor to ask," Bonnie said as they came closer. "This here's Ginny, Doc just hired 'er a couple of days ago. She's gonna help us part-time. Anyway, she's the one really needs the favor. Doc was doin' a spay today on a cat that was real good and pregnant, it was almost time for 'er to deliver. Well, Ginny here just pulled this little guy right out'ta that womb." Pulling the towel back, she revealed a tiny marmalade kitten. "Now she don't know what she's gonna do with 'im. Done got 'erself in a fix, ain't she?"

Ginny stroked the tiny head with her index finger. "I was holdin' the basin for Doc to drop the uterus in and when I went to set it on the counter, I saw it move. I looked closer and sure enough, there it was again. Well, I couldn't stand it. I grabbed a scalpel and cut the sac open. Three kittens were dead, but this one gave a little kick. I picked up a little towel and started to rub 'im real easy. In a few seconds, I could see 'im begin to breathe on 'is own and then he gave a pitiful little mewl. I couldn't believe it, this little guy was gonna make it."

"Doc said he might let Ginny assist with neuters sometimes, but no more spays for 'er," Bonnie laughed.

"Well, the little feller can stay here if he needs to," Miss Velvie took the kitten and held him in her left hand, gently turning him over with her right. "Looks like he's developed right good, must've been just about time for 'im to be born.

"Jo, will you run in and fix 'im up a little bottle? You know where the stuff is." As Joanna headed towards the kitchen, Miss Velvie picked Rosie up and led the other girls around to the front porch.

When Joanna joined them, the old woman took the tiny bottle and squeezed a drop onto the little tongue. It took a few minutes, but she soon had him suckling greedily. "I don't know what I would have done if you couldn't help me," admitted Ginny. "I can't have pets in my apartment, or I would have taken 'im home. How can I ever thank you?"

"The old woman smiled and gave her a hug. "Just keep on helpin' animals honey, and that's all the thanks I need. And come back and visit us too!"

The tiny kitten thrived under Miss Velvie's care. As soon as he was able to walk, he followed her every movement and she began to lift him up to ride on her shoulder as she went through her daily chores.

"Miss Velvie, I believe you've spoiled that little feller rotten," Joanna exclaimed.

"Yep, my little Tommy-Cat," the old woman reached up to caress the golden ball of fluff sitting on her shoulder. "He sure thinks he's the big boss around here, even though he's the tiniest one."

"He is mighty spunky actin'."

"You know, that's how bottle-fed kittens usually are. They act a little different from the ones that're raised up by their mamas. Ain't scared of the devil himself!"

"Hey, you wanna ride over to Stumpy's with me?" Joanna asked. "They're cookin' a brunswick stew over there. Let's go get us a bowl."

"That does sound right good," the old woman agreed. "Let me take my apron off and get me a sweater. It's liable to get right chilly before we get back. Won't take me but just a minute."

When Joanna pulled into Stumpy's yard, Johnny-Vern rushed over to open Miss Velvie's door and help her down. "How's my best girl doin'?" he teased as the old woman smiled down at him. "Come on over here and let me get you a chair, we're just about ready to eat."

Randy helped Joanna take Rosie's carseat out and sat it on the long picnic table.

"You ladies want somethin' to drink?" Stumpy asked as he looked over from the big fryer where he was cooking hush puppies.

"How 'bout one of them little chocolate Yoo-Hoo drinks you always keep around?" Miss Velvie asked.

Haywood had just handed Miss Velvie a bowl of stew when she noticed one of the shetlands limping across the pasture. "Stump, looks like that pony yonder has done got foundered."

"Yes ma'am," Stumpy answered. "I didn't know what was wrong at first. Jo come over here and give me some of them bute tablets. Told me to cut out 'is grain and just give 'im hay for awhile. It helped some, but then I had to get Doc to come out and give 'im some real strong anti-inflammatory stuff. But he said it was a mighty bad case and he might not get straightened out."

"I know somethin' you might could try," Miss Velvie said.

"What is it? I'll be glad to pay you, if you can help 'im."

"Well, it's a mighty complicated treatment," the old woman said as she winked at Joanna. "Let's see, what should I charge you? How 'bout a quart of that good stew?"

"Oh shucks, Miss Velvie. You know you're welcome to all the stew you want. I'm serious."

"All right. Get you one of them iron stakes there, that's right, the big ones. Now, you got a hammer? Come on, bring it and follow me." She started down the hill, towards the pond. "Vern, come on and help us, son. You got those tall boots on.

"Here you go, now. Get out there in the water, Vern, 'bout ankle-deep and hammer that stake down. That's right.

"Now go catch hold of your pony, Stump."

"What in the world you gonna do?" he stared at the old woman.

"You just go get that pony and I'll show you. Go along now."

Stumpy let out a whistle and all the ponies came running except Buddyweiser, who trudged along slowly, head bobbing up and down as he limped along painfully. As the other ponies milled around, he stood and let his master take hold of his halter.

"Randy, get us a lead line, will you son?" Miss Velvie called. "All right, now. Let's take 'im out and see can we get 'im tied to that stake. If we can get 'im to stand in that cold water, it'll help that swellin' go down. Easy does it, little feller, that water ain't gonna hurt you none, it'll feel good to them old hot feet of yours." The pony balked a few times, but with Johnny-Vern leading and Stumpy pushing, they soon had him where they wanted him. As soon as Johnny-Vern tied him and backed away, the pony let out a huge sigh and closed his eyes as the cold water soothed his inflamed hooves.

"Now try to leave 'im there a couple hours or so," Miss Velvie instructed. "I wouldn't go off nowheres and leave 'im, but long as y'all are gonna be 'round the yard here, just keep an eye on 'im. If he was to get tangled up, he could drown hisself right there in that shallow water. Then put 'im back out here for a little while in the mornin' and again tomorrow evenin'. I believe it ought'a help 'im right much. I've seen Papa do it many a time and those horses of 'is always got right much relief."

"Tell Miss Velvie old Buddyweiser's right as rain," Stumpy told Joanna a couple of days later. "She sure is somethin'. I believe she could cure most anything."

Joanna agreed with him.

Meanwhile, Tommy-Cat kept growing in size and personality. He rode on Miss Velvie's shoulder as she did her chores and curled up in her lap whenever she sat down, purring like an outboard motor.

"I'll tell you a secret, Jo," the old woman confided. "I believe Tommy-Cat thinks he's a she."

"What do you mean?"

"Watch this," Miss Velvie lowered him down to the porch floor, near a box of kittens. Tommy crawled into the box and lay down, curling himself around them and began to lick them in a maternal fashion."

"He does act like a mama cat, don't he?"

"Just hold on, watch a minute."

Tommy stretched out on his side and pushed a kitten up under his belly, as if he were trying to encourage it to nurse. The kitten tried, but quickly got discouraged and crawled away. One by one, Tommy continued to push the kittens underneath him until Miss Velvie hauled him out of the box.

"You know, most of the time tom-cats won't have nothin' to do with little ones, unless it's to whip up on 'em. Oh, they'll try to kill 'em right often, if they can catch the mama gone. Not our Tommy-Cat though, he just loves everybody and everything."

When the spring chicks hatched, Tommy would carry them around in his mouth, but he never harmed one. He just gently placed them into one of the cat boxes and crawled in with them. They would flap their wings and flutter out of the box, running back to the chicken yard and Tommy-Cat would follow closely, trying to convince them to stay with him.

"He just can't seem to understand they want to scratch around for worms and such," Miss Velvie laughed. "You ought to have seen what he done the other day! Brought 'is cat food to 'em. He'd bring it out one little piece at the time and drop it for 'em. And they ate it, too. I've seen some strange things in my years, but I declare, little Tommy-Cat nearabout takes the rag off the bush!"

Petey and Kayla loved to watch Tommy-Cat as he mothered the baby animals. He was sitting in a box on the porch with a little dog and her litter that had been dumped near the road. The mother was bathing one tiny puppy and Tommy had another, a paw gently curved around it as he licked the little ears, cleaning them carefully.

"Granny Velvie, did Mr. Noah have cats on that big boat?" Petey asked as he picked Tommy up, and crawled into her lap.

"Well, of course he did, son. Two of 'em, a mama cat and a daddy cat."

Denise caught Joanna's eye and smiled. They knew what was coming next, for the children never tired of hearing the old woman tell the fascinating tale.

"Tell us the story!" Kayla urged as Rosie curled her tiny hand around Kayla's finger.

"Y'all love to hear about that, don't you?"

"It's our favorite," Kayla nodded.

"Well, let's see, now. As I remember, God was gonna send a great big flood, 'cause folks were all bein' so bad, don't you know? And he told Noah to build the arc, so's him and 'is family could live on it, until the water went away."

"And take the animals with 'em, right?" Petey asked.

"That's exactly right. And folks laughed at Noah, called 'im crazy, but he kept right on workin'. Then, when it was time, he got 'is family and all the animals and put 'em on the arc. The animals walked in two by two, and there weren't no fussin' and fightin' the way you might think it would be when a whole bunch of wild animals got together."

"Kind'a like your house?" Petey asked. "All the cats and dogs get along good together here, don't they?"

"I reckon so, son. Kind'a like around here.

"And then, after the water finally went away, God sent a sign. Remember what I told y'all it was?"

"A rainbow!" shouted Petey as he spread his little arms wide. "A great, big, beautiful rainbow! And it covered the sky!"

"That's right. Remember what it meant?"

"That everything was A-Okay. Right?"

"That's exactly right. He was tellin' Noah they should all be happy again, 'cause he was watchin' over 'em."

"Yes ma'am," Petey agreed. "That's right."

"So always remember, whenever you see a rainbow, that's a sign from Heaven. Right?"

"Right!" the children chimed in together.

Petey climbed down and placed Tommy-Cat on the porch floor, where he climbed back into the box with the puppies and resumed licking them.

"Boy, Mr. Noah should have had Tommy-Cat with 'im," Petey remarked.

"Why is that, son?"

"'Cause he looks after all the other animals. He would have made a good helper for Mr. Noah."

"I reckon you're right son," Miss Velvie chuckled. "I reckon you're right."

POSSUM

"The...dog; in life the firmest friend, the first to welcome, foremost to defend."

—Lord Byron

"**W**here'd you get that mutt?" Johnny-Vern asked as Wildman pulled in at the river. In the back of his truck, along with Wrangler was a big, yellow dog. The solid body wriggled with excitement as the dogs waited for Wildman to come around and let the tailgate down. Joanna walked up with Rosie on her hip. She ran her hand across the broad head and the dog looked up at her, a friendly grin on his face and an intelligent expression in his hazel eyes. Rosie reached down to touch the wet nose and laughed in delight as the dog nuzzled her.

"He just showed up at the house yesterday. I come out the door and he was out there, playin' with Wrangler. He sure loves to ride, every time I crank the truck up, he has a fit to go with me."

"He'll make a good partner for Wrangler," Randy said as he watched the two frolicking around.

"Naw, I ain't gonna keep 'im. Figgered if I caught y'all down here, maybe I could talk Jo into takin' 'im home."

"Don't even say such a thing," Randy shot back. You know how many dogs we already got."

"Why don't you keep 'im, Wildman?" Joanna asked.

"One dog's enough for me, I ain't gonna have no more'n that. Why can't you take 'im to the rescue?"

"We're full up down there. I might can get 'im in, but it'll probably take awhile." She rubbed her hand down the dog's broad back and the short, thick coat felt like wool. "Look how curly 'is hair is, looks like maybe he's got some Chesapeake Bay Retriever or somethin' like that in 'im. Maybe that and yellow lab, is that what you are, big boy?" The dog let out a tremendous "Woof!" as if to answer affirmatively.

"Come here, feller," called Johnny-Vern. "You want some redneck caviar?" The big dog quickly but gently took something from the man's hand and gulped it down.

"What you got there, Vern?" Joanna asked.

"Potted meat and crackers," he said. "Come on Wrangler, I got a bite for you, too."

They watched the dogs for a few minutes, then went to sit on the deck of Haywood's cabin, which overlooked the river. Johnny-Vern threw a stick into the water and the dogs dove in and raced after it, dragging it out together, one at each end.

"Y'all seen that purty little old gal Vern's been datin'?" Haywood asked Randy.

"Naw, who is it?"

"What's 'er name, Vern? Susie Glover?"

"What? I thought she was through with you, Vern! Told me she won't never goin' out with you again after she caught you with that Wendy Dawson."

"Oh, you know Vern," said Wildman. "That guy could talk a dog off a meat wagon. Said he was gonna do this and that, bought 'er one of them little pearl necklaces all the girls are goin' crazy over. Told 'er he'd stop seein' Wendy, if she'd just take 'im back."

"Ha!" screeched Randy. "That boy lies so bad, he has to hire somebody to call 'is dogs!"

"She sure is a purty little thing though," Wildman continued. "Boy, you ought'a see that set of love bubbles she's got on 'er." Looking over at Joanna, who was bouncing Rosie on her knee, he said, "Oop's, sorry 'bout that, Jo." Sitting up suddenly, he looked out behind the cabin. "Hey! Did y'all see that possum run across the path, there?"

The men turned to look where Wildman was pointing, but Joanna noticed the yellow dog suddenly drop, roll onto his back and stick all four feet straight up. She bent over to scratch his belly, then began to wonder.

"Hey, I think this guy's callin' his'self playin' possum."

"Do what?" Wildman asked.

"You know. Remember how we used to say play possum and act like you were dead? Like a possum does when somethin' gets after 'im, he just plays dead until they leave 'im alone. I think somebody's taught 'im to do that."

"Let's see," Wildman said. He called the dog over to his side, then ordered, "All right, boy. Let's see you play possum!"

Immediately, the dog fell to the deck and rolled over, even closing his eyes.

"Danged if you ain't right," cried Wildman. "That's exactly what he's doin'!"

"He sure is smart," Randy said. "I believe he's got a lot more sense than you do, Wildman."

Wildman just shot him a withering glance. "That'll make a good name for you, you want us to call you Possum?" Once again, the dog fell over and played dead.

"Ha!" screeched Johnny-Vern. "Every time you call that dog, he's gonna fall out, instead of comin' to you."

"We'll work it out, won't we boy?"

Joanna and Miss Velvie were down at the river a few weeks later, gathering herbs when Wildman drove up with the dogs in the truck. "Jo, ain't you found a home for this dog yet?" he called.

"Sorry, I talked to some folks, but you know how hard it is. The only person that seemed really interested wanted a guard dog and it didn't seem like a very good home."

"Well, he'd make a fine guard dog, wouldn't you, boy?"

"Yeah, but this guy was gonna put 'im on a chain and just leave 'im on it all the time. You know that ain't no way for a dog to haf'ta live. Said every time he lets 'is dogs off the chain, they end up gettin' run over. He's already got three dogs and no vet. He don't look after 'em very good."

"Well, I guess you're right. I don't want 'im to go nowhere like that. But I got to find somebody to take 'im, he's a terrible nuisance."

"What's he doin'?"

"Diggin' holes all over the place, I got craters in the yard nearabout wide as the river there. And destructive! Tears up everything he can get ahold of. Keeps me awake all night long, barkin' and howlin'. The neighbors are gettin mad, 'cause he's wakin' them up, too. And gettin' into their trash, tearin' their clothes off the line. I don't want nothin' bad to happen to 'im, but I swear! He's just about the most obnoxious dog I ever seen in my life." Even as he spoke, he reached down and rubbed a hand across the broad head in a fond gesture. "I do want 'im to go to a good home, though."

"Well, he can come stay at my house for awhile," Miss Velvie said as they watched the dogs cavorting around, running up and down the hill to the water. "I always say one more won't hurt nothin'."

"Hey!" Wildman jumped at the offer, knowing the dog would be in good hands. "That ought'a work out real good. How about that, boy? You want to go stay with Miss Velvie?"

Possum looked up at him and let out a deep woof, as if to agree.

"See there, I believe he wants to go with y'all."

"Okay," Joanna laughed. "Come on, boy. Hop in my truck and you can go with us."

"Hey, Wrangler!" yelled Wildman, as his own dog jumped into the truck with Possum. "Not you, don't you want to stay with me?"

"Wrangler knows a good thing when he sees it," Joanna teased as she buckled Rosie into her seat. Wrangler jumped out and Joanna closed the camper door and drove off. Possum poked his head through the sliding window and slobbered happily on Rosie, making her squeal. When they reached the house, there were a few minor skirmishes with the other dogs, but nothing serious. Miss Velvie was more worried about the cats, but Possum was fine with them.

"You know, somethin's been up here and killed one of the chickens," Miss Velvie confided to Joanna a few weeks later. "The dogs got to barkin' last night and before I could get out to the back yard, there was a terrible squawkin' in the henhouse. By the time I got the flashlight and got out there, poor old Corabell was layin' there, looked like 'er neck was broke. It must have been a fox, or somethin' like that."

"You'd think he'd be afraid to come up here, with all the dogs around, wouldn't you?" Joanna asked.

"Ain't had no trouble in many a year," the old woman answered. "Way back yonder, when Papa was livin', we'd have all kinds of trouble like that, you know after the livestock and all. Why, we even had a bear to come up once. Papa got 'im with the shotgun, but he killed a couple of calves first."

"What are you gonna do?"

"I'll fix that sucker, I'm gonna string up some electric wire 'round the chicken pen. If he hits that hot wire, he'll know somethin' then!"

Joanna helped the old woman hook the wire up and there was no more trouble for a few weeks.

Joanna had left Randy babysitting and was at Miss Velvie's late one night when the dogs began to bark furiously. "I don't see nobody comin' up the path or nothin'," Joanna said as she looked out the window.

"Lord have mercy!" cried Miss Velvie. "I bet somethin's after them chickens again."

Joanna ran to the back door but she could see nothing in the darkness. She could hear Miss Velvie slamming a door in the downstairs bedroom, then the old woman came into the kitchen with her shotgun. Thrusting a flashlight into Joanna's hands, she motioned for her to lead the way.

"Oh, God! It's some kind of wildcat!" Joanna cried. "And he's got somethin'!" Running as fast as she could, she left the old woman behind quickly and hurled herself headlong at the figure on the ground, but it refused to loosen it's hold on the smaller animal. Joanna brought the heavy flashlight down on the broad head and the light winked out, as the animal let out a chilling scream of fury.

Cornered between the henhouse and the barn, the animal had nowhere to go and it turned on Joanna. Claws slashed across her face and she threw her hands up, unable to see what was coming at her.

"Jo!" Miss Velvie shouted. "I can't see to shoot! What is it?"

Just then a heavy form lurched itself against Joanna, knocking the wild animal off her. It was Possum. He hurled himself onto the screaming ball of fury as Joanna stumbled backwards, trying to catch her breath.

"Possum! Possum!" she screamed over and over. She strained to see into the darkness, but could hardly tell one animal from the other. Then everything went silent.

She stood for a moment, afraid to move, then something brushed against her. Frozen with fear, Joanna heard a deep, throaty whine.

"Oh, Possum! Are you all right, boy?"

Joanna dropped to her knees to hug the big dog and his tongue bathed her face as a bright light washed over them. Miss Velvie had gotten into the old hearse and turned the headlights on. Looking down, she saw the animal laying on the ground as the old woman walked up.

"You okay, honey?" Miss Velvie asked. Joanna nodded, unable to speak.

"A bobcat!" the old woman exclaimed. "I should have known. There's still right many around here."

"What was he after?" Joanna asked and the women began to search the ground. It didn't take long for them to find out.

Tommy-Cat was lying in a pool of blood, his neck twisted grotesquely.

Possum sniffed at him and whined as they approached.

"Oh, my little Tommy-Cat!" Miss Velvie cried out. "Lifting him gently, she cradled the still figure in her arms and hugged him to her breast. "My sweet little Tommy, you ain't never hurt nobody. I'm so sorry I didn't do better for you."

Carrying the golden tabby, Miss Velvie went into the kitchen and sat down for a moment. The gnarled old hand trembled as she smoothed the bloody fur and Joanna saw a tear running down her wrinkled cheek.

"Poor little Tommy-Cat," she crooned. "I should have kept you inside, the way you were so gentle and all. I just never imagined somethin' like that would happen this day and time." She looked down at Possum, who was resting his head on her knee.

"But it sure is lucky for us you were here, old feller. That bobcat went crazy once he got cornered. Jo!" she looked up suddenly. "Are you okay, honey? Did he get ahold of you?"

"I just got a couple of scratches. I'm fine." But her hand trembled as she stroked the broad head. "I...I just couldn't see nothin', I...I....." she began to cry softly.

"It's all right, honey," the old woman hugged her.

"I just wish we'd have got there in time to save Tommy-Cat. I can't believe he's gone."

"I know, honey. I'm sure gonna miss 'im."

They buried the little body the next day, out by the pond. Joanna covered the grave and Miss Velvie put a boquet a fresh flowers from the garden at the head of the little mound.

"He sure was special," she said.

Miss Velvie called a few days later. "Jo, I'm worried to death. Hilda come over here and Possum bit 'er. She's tryin' to get animal control to come pick 'im up. Do you reckon they will?"

"Oh, thank goodness! Wildman took 'im in and got a rabies shot done when he had 'im. I had forgotten all about it, but I'll run by and get the certificate. We better call and let 'em know he's been vaccinated. But what in the world happened? That ain't like Possum at all. I ain't never seen 'im act vicious to nobody."

"I believe he thought he was protectin' me. She got to hollerin' and all and it scared 'im. He must have thought she was goin' to attack me or somethin'."

"What was she doin' over there? And hollerin' at you? What in the world ails that girl?"

"Carryin' on again, somethin' about me bein' a witch doctor. Talkin' about the doctorin' I do with my herbs. Said I'd been doin' voo-doo, and I was workin' spells. I tried to tell 'er, I ain't gave nobody a speck of medicine, since that judge told me not to. She acts like she's a little bit teched in the head."

"Was it a bad bite? Did it break the skin?"

"Just a little bit, I think. Soon as I hollered at 'im, he backed off. I don't think he wanted to hurt 'er, he was just tryin' to warn 'er back away from me."

"We might better do somethin' with 'im. She's liable to come over there and try to get 'im or somethin'."

"I thought about that, because she said she'd be back. Don't worry, he's stayin' right here in the house, I ain't gonna let 'im out'ta my sight. If she wants to get 'im, she'll be lookin' down the end of Willie's double-barrel shotgun! Ain't nobody gonna hurt this dog!"

"You be careful over there."

Joanna called to let animal control know what had happened and assure them that the dog had been vaccinated.

"Just run the certificate by here and let us make a copy of it," Albert said. "That Hilda Hawkins, she's always tryin' to stir up trouble somewhere. If she was over there, threatenin' that old woman, the rabies is the only thing we'd be concerned with at all. Sounds to me like the dog was protectin' that old lady."

Nothing further was heard about the incident and Joanna gradually stopped worrying. She was at Miss Velvie's one afternoon when Denise drove up with the children. In a flash, Petey was out and running towards them. Possum intercepted him and knocked him sprawling.

"Lord have mercy!" cried Miss Velvie as they rushed over to him. "Are you all right, honey?"

"Yes ma'am," Petey giggled as he lay on his back, Possum standing over him and licking his face eagerly. "I like this new dog of yours."

"I think he likes you too," Miss Velvie said. Joanna set Rosie on the ground and pulled the little boy to his feet. Rosie toddled over to Possum and laughed as the big, wet tongue bathed her face.

"So that's the vicious dog, huh?" asked Denise as she walked up with Kayla on her hip.

"Yep," confirmed Joanna. "Ain't he a mean one, though?"

"Hey! Look at those!" Petey shouted, pointing to the big, black and yellow worms crawling over the leaves of a tree.

"They're catalba worms," the old woman informed him.

"Can we get some and go fishin' with 'em?"

"Well, now. With catalba worms, it's a little bit different than regular old fishin' worms."

"Why?"

"Because you got to bite their heads off and turn 'em inside out before they make good bait."

"Yuck! I ain't gonna do that!"

"I thought not," Miss Velvie grinned at Denise and Joanna. "I got a much better idea. Why don't we go out to the goldfish pond and feed 'em some treats?"

"Can we see 'em when they eat it?"

"Well, of course. They'll come right up and take it out of your hands. And you know what the best part will be?"

"What?"

"Well, this way, why, we won't hurt no worms or fish, neither. Come on and help me." He followed the old woman into the garage and they returned in a few moments, carrying a small bucket.

"What y'all got in there?" Denise asked.

"It's dogfood!"Petey shouted. "We're gonna feed it to the fish."

"My goodness, they must be some big ones," Denise murmured. She pushed Rosie's stroller as they followed Miss Velvie through the pasture gate and around behind the big barn. There, at the bottom of the hill, was a small pond, filled with floating water lillies.

"Let's see can we draw 'em up," Miss Velvie said as she flung a handful of the dogfood across the water. The nuggets floated on the still waters for a few moments, then something broke the surface. Soon, flashes of orange were popping up all through the water. The old woman scattered food closer to the edge of the pond and Joanna gasped in surprise.

"Dang, Miss Velvie! That one there was near 'bout big as a bass!"

"Yep. They been in here growin', more'n thirty years now." She winked at Petey. "I expect it's the Purina makes 'em so healthy. Look here, son. Hold a piece right down to the water like this." A golden head broke the surface and took the nugget of dogfood from her hand. Petey and Kayla giggled as they repeated the performance and the fish tickled their fingers. Rosie squirmed in Joanna's arms, trying to get down and crawl into the water.

The women watched as the children fed the fish. Possum sat beside Miss Velvie and her gnarled old hand stroked the broad head. They could see Tommy-Cat's little grave with fresh flowers on it.

"Just think, Jo," the old woman began. "If it won't for old Possum here, that bobcat might have tore you up real bad, too. They usually run from people, but backed up in a corner like that, it ain't no tellin' what he would have done."

"It was right scary," Joanna admitted. "I just wish we could have got there in time to save Tommy. He was such a good little cat."

"Yes, he was," Miss Velvie agreed. "Mighty special." She laid a hand on the big yellow head and gazed into the brown eyes. "And so are you, Possum. So are you."

SISTERS OF THE HEART

"Each of us are angels with just one wing and we can only
fly while embracing each other."
—Unknown

Miss Velvie was sitting on the porch when Joanna drove up one
evening, Possum laying by her rocking chair. "Come on in
honey," the old woman said. "I declare, I'm about pooped, just
finished feedin' up. Go on in the house and get you a cold glass of tea."

Joanna came back with two glasses and lowered herself into the swing.

"Where's my baby?" Miss Velvie asked.

"I left 'er with Randy," Joanna answered. "She missed 'er nap this
afternoon and she was worn out."

The women sat and talked for a few minutes, then Joanna got up to go
to the bathroom. She was just zipping her jeans up when she heard a
commotion outside. Looking through the tiny window of the bathroom,
she could see the familiar lime-green truck, but she couldn't see anyone.

Suddenly, she heard Miss Velvie shout, "You leave that dog alone!"
and saw Hilda dragging Possum across the yard, towards the driveway.
The big dog was resisting with every ounce of strength he had, trying to
brace his paws against the ground to pull back.

"Ouch!" Hilda screamed. "You damn bastard! See there, old lady, he
bit me again!" She held her right hand up and even from where Joanna
stood, she could see blood running down to Hilda's elbow, to drop slowly
to the ground like pellets of red rain.

"Oh, no!" Joanna thought as she tore out the door and raced through the
house. "He really got 'er this time, now we got trouble."

Hilda was forcing the dog into the back of her Surburban when Joanna
reached the back door. Just as she slammed the tailgate closed, Miss
Velvie reached around her and opened it. "Here Possum, come on boy!"
she urged and the dog leaped out.

Joanna ran across the yard, feeling as if her feet were dragging in a mire of quicksand. No matter how fast she ran, she couldn't get there fast enough, as Hilda grabbed the dog once again.

But as she shoved him into the truck for the second time, a hickory limb came down hard on the back of her head and she swayed, dazed for a moment. Once again, the big dog gave a mighty leap and ran to Miss Velvie, who was standing with her feet spread wide, the heavy stick in her hand. Joanna was halfway there when the old woman crumpled and fell to the ground.

"Miss Velvie! No-o-o!" Joanna screamed into the stillness of the evening as Hilda jumped into her truck and roared off down the long driveway. Possum reached down to nudge the old woman with his nose as Joanna raced to her side. She was still breathing, but her face was pasty white and she was unresponsive.

Turning, Joanna flew back to the house and slammed into the kitchen, grabbing the old telephone. She dialed 9-1-1 and a calm voice answered.

"Send help to Miss Velvie White's house," Joanna screamed, her heart beating like it would burst from her chest, her mouth dry from shock. "It's Mimosa Plantation, do you know where it is?"

"Yes, I do. I'm dispatching a unit right now. Try to remain calm, ma'am."

"You have to hurry!" Joanna insisted. "I think she's had a heart attack!"

Joanna knelt over the old woman until the rescue vehicle arrived and the paramedics took over. She watched as they worked over her friend, stabilizing her vital signs. When they loaded her into the back of the ambulance, Joanna was allowed to ride with her to the emergency room, where she called Randy.

"Stay as long as you need to," he said. "I'll call Tansey and let 'er know."

Tansey and Denise came in to sit with Joanna and wait.

Several hours later, they were finally able to speak with a doctor.

"I'm afraid Miss White has suffered a stroke," he informed them. What's this the nurses were telling me about someone attacking her?"

"Actually, it was the other way around," Joanna explained what had happened.

"So she picked up a stick and hit that young woman, huh? She must be one feisty little lady."

"That would be an understatement," Joanna answered.

"Evidently, the excitement was what triggered the stroke," he said. "It seems to be pretty serious, but we won't know a lot for a few days. We need to perform some rather extensive tests, and of course, she may recover some of the use of her right side. There's a great deal of paralysis at this point, but people often recover. We'll just have to wait and see.

When they went into the intensive care unit the old woman lifted her head and tried to speak. Her mouth twisted grotesquely, trying to form the words but the only sound that came out was a gutteral moan. A tear of frustration rolled down the wrinkled, old cheek as Joanna grasped her hand.

"Don't try to talk right now, Miss Velvie," she soothed. "Just lay back and rest." But the old woman's eyes were trying to tell them something.

"I know what she wants!" Tansey said suddenly. "You're worried about your animals, ain't that it, Miss Velvie?"

The old woman nodded her head vigorously.

"You know me and Jo will look after 'em."

"That's right," Joanna agreed. "We've helped you enough times to where we can do it just like you do. They'll be okay."

But the faded blue eyes were still trying desperately to communicate as the girls tried to soothe the old woman.

"Is it Possum you're worried about?"

Again she nodded and uttered the deep, grunting sounds.

"We'll take 'im over to our house," Joanna promised. "We won't let Hilda get 'im."

Miss Velvie laid her head back on the pillow and her facial features relaxed. She closed her eyes for a few moments and her breathing slowed, becoming deep and regular. It wasn't long before a nurse came in and told them they would have to leave. They all kissed the withered old cheek gently and filed out.

The girls fed the animals and loaded Possum into Joanna's truck. It was nearly two A.M. when they left and Joanna fell into bed, exhausted, but she was unable to sleep. She tossed and turned until daylight, then got up and headed back to the hospital. Miss Velvie was sleeping peacefully and Joanna sat by the bed until she awoke.

"J-J-J-o-o," the old woman's voice was low and gravelly, but she was forming words now. "My c-c-crit-ters? They o-o-kay?"

"Yes ma'am, they're just fine. And you're talkin'! That's a good sign. I believe you're gonna get better fast." The old woman leaned back, her good hand grasping Joanna's.

Tansey and Denise arrived a little later and the girls waited, hoping to speak with the doctor. Randy and Johnny-Vern came in.

The old eyes lit up and the crooked mouth tried to smile when Johnny-Vern reached over and hugged the old woman gently. "M-m-y b-boy-f-friend," she rasped.

"Yep, you're still my sweetheart," the young man nodded. "Now don't you worry about nothin', we'll help the girls with everything over at your house."

It was midafternoon before Joanna was able to talk with the doctor.

"Miss White seems to be recovering rapidly," he said. "We'll be moving her into a room today. Her prognosis seem good."

The old woman continued to recover and was discharged three days later. Randy went with Joanna to pick her up and there were several vehicles in the yard when they got to her house. Johnny-Vern came out to help Randy get her inside, while Denise and Tansey hovered nearby. Haywood was on one of his small tractors, cutting the grass and Nollie was weeding the flowers by the back door. Wildman was putting a big garbage bag in the back of his truck and Stumpy was repairing the pasture fence, where Clyde and Grover had gotten out.

"Don't you want to lie down and rest?" Joanna asked, but the old woman wanted to sit in her rocking chair. She sighed as the men lowered her and Doo-Dad jumped into her lap. She soon began to nod and when Denise came in to bring Miss Velvie's lunch, she had to wake her.

The girls took turns staying with the old woman while she slowly regained her strength. Tansey kept her blood pressure checked and it just wouldn't stay down. Her medicine was changed several times, but it made no difference.

"You know what I believe I need?" Miss Velvie looked at Joanna. "Some hawthorne root. It works kind'a like a water pill, you know to get the extra fluid out. And it opens up your blood vessels, makes your heart beat slower and stronger. I saw some down at the river one day. Reckon we could ride down there and get some?"

They did and it seemed to help. Over the next few months, Miss Velvie gradually improved and her blood pressure came down. But then, she was sitting on the porch when Joanna drove up one evening and she didn't get up from her rocking chair. "Come on in honey," the old woman said. "I declare, I just don't feel up to par."

"What's wrong?"

"I dunno. Just been weak and kind'a faintified. Little bit short on breath. Had some kind of little spell this afternoon and had to lie down."

"We better get you in to see the doctor."

"Naw, I'll be all right."

"I'm not gonna take no for an answer. Sounds to me like you might have had another stroke."

The doctor wanted to admit her to the hospital for some tests.

"But what about my animals? I ain't left 'em for more'n a couple of hours at the time. I ain't spent a night away from home in nigh onto twenty years, except when I was in there right after I had my stroke!"

"You know we'll look after 'em."

Joanna took the old woman home to pack a bag. She held her head high and was quiet until they started out the back door.

"Izzy old girl, you look after everybody else. You and Beaucephus, y'all keep the young ones in line." Her top lip trembled as she patted the grizzled head. "I don't think I'll be gone but a couple of days. The girls will look after y'all just like I do." She straightened up and composed herself. "Now, make sure you soak Izzy's food. Poor old thing, she can't hardly eat that dry stuff, what with most of 'er teeth gone. And everybody gets a half can of food mixed in with the dry."

"I will," Joanna promised. "I got the list right there in the kitchen where you wrote everything down and we'll go right by it."

"And be sure you don't forget to put Ishmael's food on top of the freezer in the garage. You know the other cats won't let 'im eat if you try to feed 'im under the shelter with them. I don't know why, but they just don't like 'im."

"We'll see to it nobody don't starve 'fore you get back."

"I don't know what in the world I'd do if it won't for you girls," she said. "Before y'all come along, it won't nobody I'd leave in charge of lookin' after my critters."

After Miss Velvie settled into her hospital room, Joanna went to do some errands. When she returned, the old woman was sitting up in her lacy pink bedjacket, all smiles. "You know, they're mighty nice 'round here. They got the sweetest nurses!"

Joanna stayed for a little while, then Miss Velvie began to fidget. "Honey, it's sweet of you to stay with me, but I wish you'd run on to the house and see 'bout everybody."

"All right, I'll talk to you later on this evenin' and let you know how they're doin'."

Joanna called the old woman that night. "I just left your house and everybody's doin' fine. Had their supper and bedded down for the night."

"I appreciate that, honey. I been so worried 'bout 'em."

"Well, you can rest easy, 'cause they're all right. I'll talk to you tomorrow."

But Tansey called Joanna early the next morning. "Doc just called me, they can't find Miss Velvie! I called 'er house, but I didn't get no answer. Where in the world do you reckon she could be?"

Joanna dressed quickly and headed for the old woman's house. She could feel a knot in her stomach and her pulse was racing. But as she turned into the driveway, she saw the familiar figure shuffling across the back yard. As she pulled up, Joanna could see that she was in a light housecoat.

"Miss Velvie! What're you doin?"

"Just messin' with the dogs a little bit."

"Why ain't you at the hospital? How'd you get home?"

"I just couldn't sleep in that place. I got up and started on home, walkin'. Fore long, a nice young feller picked me up. On 'is way home from a date with 'is sweetheart, he was. They're plannin' on gettin' married in a couple of months. Anyways, he brought me on home and I got me some rest. Got up long 'bout daylight and come on out here. I'm feelin' right much better."

Joanna threw my hands up in exasperation. "But Miss Velvie, you're sick! How's the doctor gonna help you if you don't cooperate a little bit?"

"Oh, I'll be all right."

But in a few days, she was worse and Joanna took her back to the doctor. She expected him to be a little angry, but he just shook his head and smiled. "What in the world are we gonna do with you, Miss Velvie?"

"Couldn't you run your tests in the daytime and let me go on home at night?"

And that was what he ended up doing. She went in for three days worth of testing on an outpatient basis. On the fourth day, they returned to see the physician at his office.

"Miss White, some of your tests didn't turn out so good. I'm very concerned about the fluid around your heart."

"Can't you give me no medicine to set it right?"

"Yes ma'am, I'm gonna give you a beta-blocker for your heart, too. Keeps it from workin' so hard."

"That'll be just fine, young man. I'll take it just like you say."

The old woman kept her word and for a few months the medicine helped. But she gradually grew worse and the dosage had to be increased. She and Joanna were on the way back to her house from a doctor's visit when she first broached the subject.

"Jo, there's somethin' I'm right worried about. Bein' sick and all has done got me to thinkin'. Suppose somethin' was to happen to me? Who would look after all them animals?"

"Ain't nothin' gonna happen to you, don't be talkin' that way!"

"Well honey, I don't mean to sound morbid or nothin', but it's been on my mind. I ain't scared for mysef. Shucks, in a way, I'm kind'a lookin' forward to goin' on, you know, seein' Willie and Mama and Papa and everybody again. But it's my critters I'm worried about."

"We'd would take care of 'em, if need be."

"It's just too many of 'em. Y'all already got so many you're lookin' after. I couldn't put that kind'a burden on top of what you're already carryin'."

"We could try to find homes for 'em," Joanna answered doubtfully.

"You know as well as I do, there ain't enough proper homes 'round here. 'Specially not for the old critters like Izzy and Beaucephus and the ones that're crippled up or got health problems. Wouldn't nobody want 'em. Now I been thinkin', I got a little money saved up. That's why I'm so stingy, this has been way back yonder in the back of my mind for a long time now. Anyways, I want to talk to a good lawyer. What I wanna do is set up a trust fund to where there'll be enough in it for everything they need. Can you take me in to see somebody?"

"Yes ma'am, you know I will."

"And there's somethin' else I need you to do, a lot more important. We need to find somebody to come live here and look after 'em. It's got'ta be just the right person, mind you. But I'll will the house to 'em, long as they just take care of the critters. It's got'ta be somebody that loves 'em just like me and you do. And we got to keep kind'a quiet about it. If folks get wind of gettin' somethin' like this for free, they'll put on and just play like they love animals. You're the only person I can trust to help me find somebody."

"Well, let me kind'a look around and put some feelers out."

"That'll be just fine," she leaned her head back and closed her eyes as they turned into the long drive. "I didn't mean to upset you none, but it's a relief to finally talk to somebody about it. I feel better already."

As Joanna began the search, Miss Velvie's health grew steadily worse. "Her poor old body's just worn out," the doctor confided to Tansey. "There's not much more I can do for for her, except keep her comfortable."

In the meantime, Joanna wasn't having much success. The people that she would trust already had homes and families, or already had a yardfull of their own animals. They had their hands full now that Miss Velvie was barely able to take care of her own personal needs. Tansey, Denise, Sadie, Roxanne, Hope and Joanna took turns going to her house daily, initially to feed the animals, later to begin doing things for her.

At first, the girls would just see that she had meals and everything she needed, but as time passed it became obvious that she was going to need more care.

"Miss Velvie, let's see 'bout gettin' you a chore worker in here," Joanna said one night.

"You mean hire somebody to clean up and all?"

"They do a few little things, like helpin' with your bath, runnin' errands and all. Social services sends 'em in for half a day. I know the doctor will fill out the paperwork for you."

"Well, all right, I know it'll take a lot off you girls. Go ahead and see about it."

The young woman the agency sent was a disaster. Slovenly and rude, all she wanted to do was watch television and talk on the telephone as she wound her long, greasy, blonde hair around her forefinger. Miss Velvie didn't tell anyone though. Joanna began to question her as to why meals hadn't been cooked and she would just say that she wasn't hungry. But then the girl made a fatal mistake.

She and the old woman were having their afternoon snack as they watched the soap operas together. Abby jumped up onto the coffee table and snatched a cheese cracker from Jean's plate.

"You nasty cat! Get out'ta here 'fore I kill you!" Her foot caught the old tabby in the side as she started to jump down and she was tossed across the living room like a rag doll.

Miss Velvie struggled to her feet and crossed the room, trying to kneel down to pick the cat up, but Abby scurried behind a chair and she couldn't reach her. She turned to look the chore worker straight in the eye. "You can leave now, young lady. And don't bother comin' back. You're not welcome here anymore."

"I ain't goin' nowhere!" Jean replied. "I ain't givin' up this job, you're the easiest patient I've ever had. The only problem with this assignment is all them nasty old cats and dogs you got 'round here." Abby shot out from behind the chair, trying desperately to escape the big room, but the doors were closed. Jean kicked out at her again.

Miss Velvie limped over to the cold fireplace, lifting the iron poker. "If you don't get out'ta here right now, I'm gonna crack your skull just like a hickory nut." The chore worker gave a little shriek and fled, leaving her purse behind.

Joanna talked with the agency to see if they had someone else.

"You know, this sounds like just the assignment for one of my older employees. The animals won't bother 'er, she loves 'em. She's always pickin' up strays and takin' 'em home. Been late for work more'n once, on account of stoppin' to help an animal she sees on the road. She should fit right in with your patient. Perhaps we can switch them over and put her with Miss White."

A tall, stout black woman in her mid-fifties showed up the next morning. "I'm Mattie," she said in a deep, slow voice that sounded like molasses would sound pouring from a bottle, if molasses had a sound. "How y'all doin' this mornin?"

"Purty good," Joanna answered as she watched her lean down to pat Izzy on the head. "My goodness, you an old lady too, ain't you girl, you look nearaout old as most of my patients." The old dog took to her immediately. "Land sakes, y'all got more animals 'round here than anybody I ever seen in my life! It's a good thing I like 'em, don't I'd a been scared to get out'ta my car." As they walked into the kitchen, she stretched up to reach Abby, lying on top of the refrigerator and give her a loving pat.

"You and Miss Velvie's gonna get on just fine!" Joanna exclaimed with delight. "That's why the last employee didn't work out, she didn't like animals."

"You can tell a lot by the way folks treat dumb animals," Mattie stated. "Somebody that's mean to 'em, why, they ain't gonna think twice 'bout hurtin' their patients. 'Specially if it's one can't talk, like somebody that's had a stroke or somethin'. Lordy, I seen some mean folks workin' in the nursin' homes and all. They steals from 'em and beats 'em up, I even seen patients with broken bones and everybody knew the aid done it, just hard to prove, unless somebody be standin' right there lookin' when they do it."

"Miss Velvie, this is Mattie," Joanna called as they went through to the big living room. "I believe you gonna like 'er!"

And she did. It was a match made in Heaven. After Mattie would finish her few tasks, she would take the old woman out to visit with her pets. She was in a wheelchair now, and the men had built a ramp at her back door. Mattie would take her out and gently push the animals back so they wouldn't hurt her.

"Jo, you know what Mattie done today?" the old woman told her over the phone. "Baked homemade dog biscuits! I declare, I just love 'er to pieces. I've known some mighty fine colored people, but I don't believe I've ever seen one that loves the critters like she does. Shucks! Come to think of it, I ain't seen no white ones loves 'em that much except you girls."

Joanna was at the big house one Sunday afternoon, Rosie playing in the floor with Abby and Doo-Dad. Glancing through the window, Joanna saw Mattie's car coming up the path. "What in the world? She's supposed to have the day off. Did you know she was comin', Miss Velvie?"

"Nope, but I sure am glad to see 'er."

"Jo, I needs to talk to Miss Velvie," Mattie said in the kitchen. "I got a problem, come on out here and look." She opened the back door to her old Ford Tauras and Joanna heard the familiar sound of puppies whimpering. She looked down into a small cardboard box and there were five of the most adorable puppies. All but one were white with big brown splotches.

The fifth was solid black.

"Oh, ain't they precious! Looks like they might have some chow in 'em, maybe some collie or somethin. Where'd they come from?"

"I'm in a mess, here. My landlord's done threatened to kick me out if I bring any more dogs home. Oh, he ain't a mean man, but I ain't supposed to have no pets at all and he's been lookin' the other way for years. But he said enough's enough and he got no choice but to put the brakes on. I went to dump the trash and heard a noise. I looked behind the bin and there they were, in this box. I just couldn't go off and leave em!

"I swear, sometimes I feels like I ought'a just lock myself in the house, looks like every time I go down the road, I see some animal or another that needs help. Reckon we could keep 'em here? They won't be no trouble, I'll look after 'em and try to find homes if I can." Her face fell. "It ain't easy, though. Seems like it's so many mean people just wants to stick 'em on a chain and don't half look after 'em. But maybe we can find some homes."

"Come on in here and ask 'er. But you and me both know what she's gonna say. She wouldn't have it no other way, but for you to keep 'em here."

Mattie picked Rosie up and Joanna rolled Miss Velvie out into the yard. The old woman's face brightened with interest. "Well, hey there, little fellers! I reckon y'all are hongry, ain't you? Jo, will you heat some milk and get a couple of the little bottles out?" Joanna brought the supplies out and the puppies suckled greedily as the women sat in the yard feeding them.

"I declare, there ain't nothin' to make you forget your own ailments like havin' some babies to look after," the old woman stated. She finished feeding the last puppy, the black one, and he snuggled into her neck, grunting with contentment.

She watched as Mattie and Joanna got the puppies settled. "Now, I'll come on the weekends and look after'em too," Mattie promised. "I'm just so grateful for y'all takin' 'em in like this."

"We'll help you, Mattie," Joanna offered. "Neecie and Tansey and them will pitch in. Ain't no need for you to haf'ta come on your days off. Maybe we could get 'em in at the rescue. I'll go ahead and put 'em on the waitin' list. It's a whole lot easier findin' homes for cute little puppies like this than the older dogs."

"That's mighty kind of you, Miss Jo. I don't know what I'd have done if y'all didn't help me." She hugged Miss Velvie as she prepared to leave. "I'll see you in the mornin', sugar-pie."

Putting Rosie into Miss Velvie's lap, Joanna rolled the wheelchair into the kitchen and made two cups of cofee. As she sat across the table from the old woman, they both spoke at the same time.

"Miss Velvie, you know..."

"Jo, I believe we've done found..."

They looked at each other and burst out laughing. It was so good to see that old sparkle back in the old woman's eye. They each knew what was on the other's mind.

"Are you thinkin' what I'm thinkin'? Miss Velvie asked.

"Yes ma'am, you got it. She's perfect!"

"Hallelujah! The Lord does work in mysterious ways, don't he? Now here, if it won't for that mean old Jean showin' herself, we wouldn't have never found Mattie!"

"That's true, we wouldn't. And if anybody needs a home of their own, it's Mattie. I'm always so thankful to live on the farm and be able to have my animals. I'm all the time thinkin' how terrible it would be if I had to live in town, 'specially in a rented house and be scared all the time 'bout your pets."

"I'm gonna talk to 'er in the mornin! I want her to go on and move in right away and bring all her critters with 'er."

Before the month was out, Mattie was ready to move in. Randy and the men brought a couple of the big trailers and in no time at all, they moved all the boxes she and Joanna had packed up. She had the entire second floor for her living quarters. Joanna and Denise helped her decorate the upstairs sitting room to entertain her few friends.

"Now you and the ladies just make yourself at home 'round here," Velvie would say when they would come over on Saturday afternoons.

"Miss Velvie, would it be all right if we went up and used the piano, you know to practice on our hymns? Kind'a like to have choir practice here, if it wouldn't bother you too much."

"Pshaw! It'll be fine. I love to hear folks sing church music. And you don't haf'ta ask me 'bout nothin' like that. Remember, you live here too, and I want you to feel like you're at home."

"I just wish I could be up there with 'em," the old woman confided as Joanna sat with her one evening. They could barely hear the women up on the third floor, singing Rock of Ages. "They can forevermore do some singin'. I ain't heard nothin' like that since way back yonder when my church was full!"

Joanna talked to Randy that night. "Lemme get my crops in and we'll see what we can do," he promised. "Maybe we can get that piano downstairs, put it in the parlor, or somethin'."

But Nollie had other ideas. "You know I taught shop for a few years and it wouldn't take too much to put in a lift. That way, she could go anywhere in the house. And from the way she talks, she used to love going up to the ballroom so much. I believe we can do it."

In a few weeks the lift was completed and everyone gathered around to test it. The men lifted Miss Velvie into a rocking chair and had Joanna take the first ride up to make sure it was safe. "Come down here and let me hug your neck, young feller," the old woman said to Nollie. "You boys don't know what this means to me, now I can get back upstairs and all and I love you for it. There ain't a square inch of this place I don't love with all my heart. I had so missed bein' able to get upstairs and visit my house."

The following Saturday afternoon, Joanna took her up to the ballroom and the ladies got ready to practice. The mellow voices rolled out in praise:

What a friend we have in Jesus
All our sins and griefs to bear
What a privelege to carry
Everything to God in prayer

The old woman clapped her hands and her toes began to tap on the footrest of her chair, keeping time with the music. Soon, she was singing right along with them. Joanna hadn't seen her so happy since she had gotten sick.

Miss Velvie called the next morning. "Jo, there ain't no need in you comin' to sit with me today, honey. I'm goin' to church with Mattie."

"Well, that's wonderful. But are you sure you're up to it?"

"Oh, it'll do me a world of good to get out. I just know my sweet Jesus will send me the strength and I'm lookin' forward to it!"

From then on, Mattie took Miss Velvie with her every week and the old woman loved it. One Sunday when she wasn't feeling well, Joanna and Rosie went over. "I sure hate to miss services today," Miss Velvie said. "We just been havin' the best time! Why, the singin' and shoutin', you never heard such! It's like old times. Don't get me wrong now, I enjoyed church with Denise too, but they're a mite quiet. And they just don't put as much pizzaz into the music as these folks do."

"I'm glad you're enjoyin' it," Joanna said. "And it looks like it's workin' out fine with Mattie bein' here."

"You know, that Mattie is like the sister I never had! I love that girl to death." She suddenly looked serious. "She don't even know nothin' yet 'bout the final arrangements. I reckon' I ought'a go on and talk to 'er about it."

"Well, you got time. You been doin' better since she come to live with you."

"I believe you're right." She winked at Joanna conspiratorily. "We've been havin' such a good time, I think I'm gonna haf'ta stick around for awhile longer."

VELVIE'S RAINBOW

"I have set my bow in the clouds."
—God

"Jo, we're at the hospital. Reckon you could come up here?" Mattie's voice was trembling.

"Where are y'all? In the emergengy room?"

"Yeah, we just got here. I don't know if they're gonna admit 'er, or what."

"Let me just tell Randy, then I'm on the way."

On the drive, Joanna kept thinking how Miss Velvie's condition had deteriorated over the last few months. She could feel a cold little knot of panic in her midsection.

The old woman was lying on a stretcher in an examination room with her head elevated as much as possible, but she was still struggling for breath. "Hey honey," she gasped. "Won't no need for you to haf'ta come up here. I'm all right."

"I won't doin' nothin' much, noways. Just figgered I'd take a ride up here and see what was goin' on."

"I know when you're tellin' me a fib. You always got a' plenty to do."

The doctor came in. "Well! Hello, Miss White. I hear you're not feeling too good."

"A tad under the weather, Doc. But I reckon if anybody can fix me up some, it'll be you."

"I'm going to order some oxygen for you, Miss White. The tests show that your blood gases are a little low. And I think we need to see about getting some portable tanks for you at home, too. I'm going to increase your medication a little bit and I think you'll feel better in a few days. Let's keep you up here overnight and see how you're doing in the morning."

"All right, Doc. I got somebody here now that can tend to my critters while I'm up here." She squeezed Mattie's hand.

"You're not going to go running off on us again, huh?"

"I'm real sorry 'bout that, Doc. I was just so worried 'bout my animals and won't used to bein' away from home. But that ain't a problem no more."

The old woman felt much better the next day and was released. She went home with two bottles of portable oxygen and that seemed to help her. She was getting weaker though, and was beginning to stay in bed more. But she always had her hair pinned up neatly and a smile would appear on her face when someone entered the room. Joanna could tell it was a strain for her to sit up and talk, but she tried to hide it. The girls from the rescue were still coming by often, bringing savory dishes to try and stimulate Miss Velvie's appetite. Amanda's mother was there nearly every day with something she had made for lunch and Joanna would bring supper.

Denise brought Petey to visit one evening. "Settle down now," she warned as he jumped up on the bed. "Miss Velvie don't feel good. You can't be jumpin' around and actin' all wild."

He climbed gently to the head of the bed and looked the old woman in the eye. "I'm sorry you feel bad, Granny Velvie. I don't like for you to be sick." The little arms wrapped around her neck and he pecked her on the cheek. "You want some Coca-Cola? With ice all crushed up in it? That's what Mama gives me when I get sick and it makes me feel all better."

"Well, I believe that would be right good, little Goober," the old woman smiled down at him with love in her faded blue eyes.

"I'll go get you some!" he scurried off to the kitchen. "Can you help me, Mattie?" He came running back in a few minutes, carefully holding the glass half filled with the sweet, dark liquid. "Here you go, we put a straw in. That's how you haf'ta drink it when you're in bed."

"Why, thank you honey," she sipped on the cola and smacked her lips. "M-m-m-m, that's good."

They stayed for a little while, then Denise picked the little boy up. "Come on Petey, we've got'ta go, so Miss Velvie can get some rest."

"But I don't wanna leave 'er when she's all sick! She needs me to look after 'er."

"Mattie'll be here to look after 'er. She'll take good care of 'er."

"I'm gonna sing 'er to sleep," Petey put his arm around the old woman's neck and began the now familiar lullaby in his childish voice. He remembered most of the words.

Go to sleep, my little pickaninny
Brother Fox will catch him if he don't
Sling him up the bushel of old Mammy Jenny
Mammy's gonna switch him if he won't
Hush-a-hush-a-hush-a-lu-lu-lu-lu
Under the stuffy silver moon
Mammy's little hushabye, Mammy's little baby
Mammy's little Carolina coon

"That was wonderful," Miss Velvie said. "I believe I can go right on off to sleep, that was so relaxin'. You go on now, honey. I'm just fine," the old woman assured him. "You just made me feel so much better!"

"I love you, Granny Velvie," he said. "A bushel and a peck and a hug around the neck!"

"Well, I love you too! To the moon and back! You always remember that. And God loves you too."

"I will. Good night, Granny Velvie."

"Good night, son. And remember, always be kind to the other young'uns and the animals."

They were the last words the old woman ever uttered. She closed her eyes after they went out and fell asleep. Mattie went in to check on her later that night.

"She was just layin' there, with one arm 'round Abby and the other 'round Doo-Dad," Mattie explained when Joanna walked in and found them the next morning. "She had the most peaceful look on 'er face. Her mouth was turned up in a little smile and at first, I thought prob'ly she was dreamin'. You know how a little child looks sometimes when he's sleepin', all innocent and happy. That's just how Miss Velvie looked. Then I saw she won't breathin' and I knew. I tried to move Doo over to where I could get to Miss Velvie, and she went to whinin' and moved right back up under Miss Velvie's arm. It was just so hard to let 'er go, though. I love 'er so much. There won't nobody in the whole world like our Miss Velvie."

A single tear slipped down the mahogany-colored cheek now, as Mattie watched the younger woman fall to her knees beside the bed. Joanna took the cold, pale hand into her warm one, massaging it over and over, as if she could rub life back into the passive body.

"Please don't leave us now, Miss Velvie!" Joanna murmured softly. "There's so many things we've still got'ta do, so many things you've got'ta teach us about. I haven't had a grandma since I was little, and you were just like one. I didn't never even tell you I loved you but I do. Oh, why didn't I tell you? I'm so sorry."

"Hush, Sugar-pie. Miss Velvie knew how much you loved her," Mattie came up behind Joanna and put her arms around her. "She was always braggin' to me, tellin' me how her girls were always doin' this and that for 'er. Some folks can't come out and talk about feelin' for somebody. They show it in the little things they do. Every time y'all took 'er somewheres, or did somethin' to help 'er animals, you were showin' Miss Velvie how much you loved 'er. You didn't have to come out and say it, she always knew it."

Joanna turned and buried her face in the ample bosom, sobbing as if her heart would break. "I'm just not ready to let 'er go yet."

"Well Sugar, you know how she went down in the last few months. We should be rejoicin', 'cause now she's free from all that pain and torment. Miss Velvie tried to put up a brave front, but there's a lot of bad nights y'all didn't never know about. She told me one night that she was about ready to go meet 'er Master, she was so worn out. Said now she didn't have to worry 'bout the critters, she could rest peacefully. I know it hurts, but it would be selfish of us to want 'er to stay, she's gone to a better place."

"I know, but I want 'er here with us, I just can't help it. And as for God!" Joanna shook her head in disgust. "I don't believe in him. Anybody that loves us so much, how could he do things like this? You don't hurt somebody you love!"

"I ain't got all the answers, Sugar-pie. Ain't nobody walkin' around on this earth that does. But I do know one thing for certain. God is real. And He's got a reason for everything he does. What makes it so hard on us is, we don't never know what 'is reason is. But believe you me, He's got a reason for what He's doin' now, and it ain't our place to question 'im."

"Well, I am! I don't even think He exists."

"Hush now, Sugar. You musn't talk like that," Mattie's strong brown arms held Joanna tight and she cried softly until she was spent.

"She done told me she don't want no fancy funeral," Mattie said later that evening as she and the girls sat at the kitchen table where they had shared so many meals with the old woman. In all the years Joanna had known Tansey, she had never seen her cry. Until now.

Denise got up to pour more hot coffee as Mattie took Rosie from Joanna.

"Said it's just a waste of money," Mattie continued, "and we should only have graveside services here at the house. Wanted everything to be real simple."

"You think the choir would sing?" Tansey asked. "Ain't no reason we can't have some music just 'cause it's outside."

"I'm sure they would," Mattie answered. "She'd like that, you know how she did love to hear 'em."

"You know what preacher she wants?" asked Denise.

Mattie looked up. "She mentioned one time how much she'd like to have my preacher, Mr. Cofield. She sure did love to go hear 'im every Sunday.

"And she said don't go spendin' money on no flowers and all," Mattie continued. "Said there's plenty of 'em growin' out 'round the cemetery and she'd rather for people to just make a donation to the rescue. Maybe we could set up a special fund in 'er name."

The day of the funeral dawned bright and clear. The sky was blue, the sun was shining and birds were singing. The big kitchen was filled with home baked goods the ladies had brought and people began to arrive early. Miss Velvie lay in the pink casket in her parlor. She was dressed in the white velvet suit that had been her husband's favorite, her signature rose pin in it's place. Mattie had done her hair the way she always wore it and carefully applied light makeup, with a little rogue, bringing just a hint of a blush to the withered old cheeks. People drifted through the parlor, saying their final goodbyes.

Roxanne stood alone, looking down into the coffin, tears running down the high cheekbones. "Oh, Miss Velvie, how you changed my life! How can we go on without you?" Joanna put an arm around the slender, shaking shoulders and the girl leaned against her, sobbing softly.

Johnny-Vern came up to stand beside them, giving Roxanne a pat on the back. In his hand was one long-stemmed rose, white as ivory. "Our white velvet rose," he murmured with a catch in his voice. The sweet smell drifted up as he placed it in the casket.

Finally, the time came to carry the old woman to her final resting place. The men wept silently as they lifted the casket; Randy, Johnny-Vern, Nollie, Haywood, Stumpy, and Wildman. The news had been a hard blow for Johnny-Vern. He almost fell now, as his knees threatened to give way beneath him and Kim rushed over to take his arm.

"Vern, you okay?" Randy asked.

"I'm fine."

Mattie stepped up. "Vern, we can get one of the other men to fill in, if you want. This is a hard thing to do when you were so close to 'er."

"No, she would've wanted me, I know she would." He brushed a tear from his eye. "You know, Mattie, besides my Mama, Miss Velvie was the only woman I ever really and truly loved."

"I know, Sugar. You and her had a mighty special relationship. Shucks, ain't many old women like that could say they had a young sweetheart like you. Y'all young folks brought a lot of joy to 'er life in these last few years. She told me one time how lonesome she was before she met y'all." She gave the young man a hug. "Go on then, if you think you're up to it."

It was a short journey to the little graveyard as the mourners filed behind the pallbearers and entered the little garden, surrounded by the wrought iron fence, then looked around as they stood in the deep shade of the big oak trees.

Uncle Otto caught Aunt Emma's arm and helped her across the uneven ground where huge roots grew out from the trees. Amanda stood with her parents, Lazarus sitting at her feet. Randy's strong arm supported Joanna, as she held little Rosie, silent tears rolling down her face. The entire Tucker family crowded in and April buried her face in Luke's shoulder. Doctor Cooper and the girls from his office stood to the side.

As the pallbearers lowered their burden to the ground, Joanna noticed that several of the animals had followed them. Looking across the field, Joanna could see Clyde and the other animals that were confined to the pasture. Instead of continuously grazing on the green grass, they all stood quietly, looking over the fence towards the graveyard.

Izzy limped over to the stone bench, where she had spent so many hours with her mistress, as the old woman played music or simply sat quietly. The dog laid her head on the seat, and gave a little whine.

Everywhere Joanna looked, she could almost see the old woman, planting her pansies and petunias, pulling weeds from the edges of tombstones, filling the birdfeeder with seed, or picking up sticks and pinecones.

The choir gathered around in their red and gold robes and the sweet, clear notes of Mattie's voice rang out above all the others.

I've got a mansion
Just over the hilltop
In that fair land where
We'll never grow old
And someday yonder
I'll never more wander
But walk the streets made
Of purest gold

The beautiful music stirred emotions deeply and brought waiting tears to the surface. As people wept, the animals continued their silent and serious vigil.

"We are gathered here today to bid farewell to a very unique person," Reverend Cofield began. "Miss Velvet White. They say her husband used to call her his white velvet rose. A white rose is a very rare and special flower, one that stands alone, because it dares to be different. It dares to be different! I think that describes our Miss Velvie right down to a tee, because she was just about the most rare and special person I've ever had the privilege of knowing.

"Miss Velvie had a very good friend, Nollie Odom. Those of you who know Nollie will agree that he is famous around here for his knowledge of old legends. The day Miss Velvie died, he told me there is a Christian legend of the white rose. The Virgin Mary took off her cloak to rest, and draped it across a bush of red roses. The flowers turned white, symbolizing her purity and goodness. And that is why the white rose is so special.

"Miss Velvie taught us a great deal about kindness and mercy. As I look around now, I see many people whose lives she touched and changed. I don't believe she ever turned her back on any creature in need, be it animal or human, colored or white. She took in strays, fed hungry people and spread the word of God. And she was never ashamed of God, but proud to call him her friend and savior, always praising him to everyone she came into contact with.

"Miss Velvie gave us another gift, a glimpse into our past, back through a heritage that is rapidly disappearing in today's busy world. And she had the great gift of laughter. I think that's why people loved to be around her so much. I've often thought..."

"Preacher, look-a-yonder!" The mourners looked up in surprise that someone would shout out and interrupt at such a solemn moment. Tansey was pointing at the sky, her face aglow, even under the fresh tears. "It's Miss Velvie! She's showin' us she's okay!"

As Joanna turned in the direction Tansey was looking, she saw a great, vibrant rainbow, stretched wide across the sky, like the gates of Heaven.

"How could that be?" the thought flashed briefly through her mind. "It ain't rained for days. You got to have rain to make a rainbow!"

"She always told us 'bout the rainbow!" Tansey shouted. "Said it was a sign from above, to let us know everything was gonna be all right! Like when God sent it to Noah, to let him and all the animals know there won't gonna be no more trouble. It was 'er favorite story and she talked about it all the time. Now, she's sendin' that sign to us, that everything's okay!"

Reverend Cofield just stood quietly for a few moments, not saying a word as they watched the colors arch through the sky. The animals were all looking up, as if they too, knew it was their beloved mistress.

Tansey clapped her hands, jumping up and down, waving her arms up towards the Heavens. "We see it Miss Velvie! We see it! We're all right now, 'cause we see it!"

The people stood entranced, for perhaps twenty minutes, watching the sky, sure that it would fade any second. "I never saw a rainbow last so long," whispered Denise. "They usually come and go in just a few minutes."

Finally, Reverend Cofield spoke. "Well, I had a service prepared, but I believe it pales in comparison to what we just saw. Let's just join in singing Miss Velvie's favorite hymn, Amazing Grace.

As they sang the old familiar refrain, the light glowed and pulsated, keeping time with the tune, as if the hues of the rainbow were lending their colors, in place of the old woman's voice. The first verse was one everyone knew by heart; Amazing Grace, how sweet the sound, that saved a wretch like me. Then voices faded away leaving only Reverend Cofield and the choir singing; and the words took on new meaning;

Yea, when this flesh and heart shall fail
And mortal life shall cease
I shall possess within the veil
A life of joy and peace

As they sang the final notes, the colors began to fade from the sky. The animals began, one by one, to walk slowly back towards the house, as if they knew their mistress had just taken leave.

"I guess this concludes the service," Reverend Cofield began. "Mattie wants me to let everyone know they're invited back to the big house to share one last meal.

From that time on, the rainbow was all Tansey could talk about. Joanna tried to act excited for her sake, but she was only pretending. She still didn't believe in miracles.

The next day, the phone rang. "Jo, look out the window!" It was Tansey. "It's back!"

"What're you talkin' about?"

"The rainbow! It's back! Go look! I'm gonna call Neecie while you're outside."

Joanna went out onto the porch and looked around. Sure enough, there it was, just aboue the treetops. It was beautiful, and she stood watching it for a few moments before she went inside.

The phone rang again. "Did you see it?"

"Yeah, it was really purty," she tried to sound enthusiastic, but all she felt was hollow.

"And look what time it is! Three o'clock! Just like yesterday, it came back at the same time."

The next evening there was a message on the answering machine. "Jo! It's back, the rainbow's here again! If you're home, go look!"

Joanna called to tell her she'd gotten the message, but hadn't seen it.

"You don't sound real excited. You don't really believe it's her, do you?"

Joanna tried to deny it, but the silence following Tansey's question admitted the truth.

"It is, I promise you, it's Miss Velvie! I know it's her."

The next day, Joanna was at the rescue, cleaning out the dog kennels at the very back, when she heard the door slam. "Jo! Where are you?" She heard Tansey's voice.

"Back here," she answered.

Running down the aisle, Tansey grabbed her friend by the forearm and the water hose flew up in the air, drenching them both. "Come on," she shouted. "It's back! Her eyes were shining with a joy that was overflowing, and Joanna was dragged towards the front door, her feet barely touching the floor.

"There it is!" They stood in the parking lot, watching silently, until it faded away.

"Three o'clock again," she announced, beaming happily. "And just like the other times, it ain't rained nary a drop!"

Tansey saw the rainbow every day at the same time, and she made sure that Denise and Joanna saw it too.

Then, on the seventh day, the three of them were in the little cemetery, cleaning up the few flowers that people had insisted on bringing. They were beginning to turn brown, and the leaves had withered. Rosie toddled after the dogs as the girls worked.

"It don't hardly seem like a week's gone by already, does it?" Denise asked as she leaned over to pick up a bunch of wilted roses.

"Look!" Tansey shouted. "There it is!"

The three girls looked up, and sure enough, there the rainbow was, once again. Suddenly, a raw tension tore through Joanna's chest and throat. The gale force of her tears splattered against the necks of her friends as they held each other. Then, the rain of tears was exchanged with laughter. Softly at first, but it grew and grew. Tansey and Denise glanced at each other as Rosie looked up at them in surprise. But Joanna knew the answer at last and now she was free!

A few days later, the girls were at the rescue, walking dogs. Y'all know, I was really mad at God when Miss Velvie first died," Tansey admitted. "But Mattie just kept tellin' me he had a reason. She said we wouldn't know what it was, but I think now I do."

"What do you mean?" Denise asked.

"Well, just look at Jo. If it won't for Miss Velvie sendin' the rainbow, she wouldn't really know Christ. That was when she finally found 'er faith."

"That's right," Joanna nodded. "Y'all remember what Miss Velvie told us that time? About how you would always remember the day you were saved? I never really understood what she was talkin' about. But now I do!

"And it's really scary. If I hadn't had somebody that loved me as much as Miss Velvie did, maybe I'd have never really and truly believed."

"Well thank goodness she was determined," Tansey grinned. "It took 'er a whole week to get through to you. And y'all say I'm hard-headed!"

BATTLE OF THE WILLS

"Definition of the Golden Rule: He who has the gold makes the rules."

—Unknown

"Jo?" Tansey's voice came over the telephone. "I got a call this afternoon from Braxton Battle, you know the attorney that handled Miss Velvie's estate. He said the rescue should have a representative down at 'is office for the readin' of the will. He wants to do it next Thursday."

"You reckon she left the rescue some money?"

"I don't know what else it could be."

"That don't make sense, though. When I took 'er down there, she was havin' papers drawn up about leavin' the house to Mattie. And she told me she was leavin' 'er a little money, too. Surely that would've taken everything she had. You know how she was always scrimpin' and savin' every little penny."

"I guess we'll just haf'ta wait 'till Thursday to find out."

Leaving Rosie with Randy, the girls picked Mattie up on the way to the attorney's office. When they turned into his parking lot, they saw the familiar lime-green surburban.

"Oh no!" exclaimed Tansey. "Looks like Hilda's here."

"Wonder how she found out."

"I asked Janice to come. What with 'er bein' treasurer, I felt like she ought'a be here but she couldn't make it. I asked 'er to keep it quiet, but she must have said somethin' and it got back to Hilda."

"Good afternoon, ladies," the attorney greeted them as the receptionist showed them into his office. Hilda and Agnes were sitting to the right of his heavy walnut desk and barely returned Joanna's greeting.

"I'll get right to the point," he said as soon as the introductions were made. "As you know, the purpose of today's meeting is to settle Miss white's estate." Taking out a legal document, he began to read.

"I, Velvet White, do hereby bequeath my house, heretofore known as Mimosa Plantation to Mattie Cherry. Also to Mattie, I leave fifty thousand dollars."

Joanna could hear the familiar grinding of teeth coming from the right.

Mattie, always the strong one, began to cry now. "Lordy, that'll be plenty to carry me through retirement. "I'll be able to look after Miss Velvie's critters full time now." Joanna put an arm around the quivering shoulders as the attorney continued.

"It is my strongest desire that Mattie will remain in charge of all my animals. Special funds have been set up for them, five hundred dollars each, to be used in any way that Mattie deems fit."

"All that's just a waste of money," Hilda hissed between the big teeth she had been grinding together. "Those animals ought to just be put to sleep. They're just a pack of mutts with no breedin', most of 'em are missin' a leg or somethin'. Ain't nobody in 'is right mind would want none of 'em! That crazy old woman should have left us that money. We could put it to good use. I told y'all she was crazy, and this proves it. Leavin' her house to that nigger!"

Tansey half-rose to her feet. "You want to shut your mouth, Hilda? Or do you want me to shut it for you?" Mattie laid a hand on her arm and she sat down, but continued to glare at Hilda.

The attorney cleared his throat. "Actually, Miss White did make a provision for the rescue. If you'll just allow me a moment I'll read it to you."

"Big deal," Hilda snorted. "That old woman couldn't have had much more than you already mentioned. That old house was fallin' to pieces and she wouldn't even fix it up!"

"And to the Beagle Brigade and Small Animal Rescue," he continued. "I leave the remainder of my assets, to be determined after all my final expenses have been paid. The funds will be used in the way that the rescue desires. I have the utmost faith that it will be used for the welfare and protection of many animals."

"So how much is it gonna be?" Hilda wanted to know.

"After all the expenses have been deducted, the final sum is five hundred, fifty-three thousand dollars."

Joanna heard Tansey let out a little gasp.

"When do we get it?" Hilda demanded.

"You should recieve it in no more than sixty days. There's still a great deal of paperwork to be done."

"You hear that, Agnes?" Hilda's eyes were bulging and her mouth hung open. "Boy, can we do somethin' with that kind of money!"

"You know, I was worried to death about how we would treat the sick ones," Joanna interjected. "Miss Velvie saved us a lot of money on vet bills, the way she was always helpin' us with 'em."

"Hmmmph!" Hilda sniffed. "Crazy old woman, thought she was a doctor. And we can find somethin' a lot better than vet bills to spend money on."

"What could be more important than that?" Joanna wondered, but she turned back to the attorney. She didn't want to start an argument here and if she uttered one word, it would be enough to really set Tansey off. It was the attorney who spoke in the old woman's defense.

"Seems to me that Miss White was a very special lady. I've heard a lot of good things about her."

It was exactly two months later that Joanna drove up to the rescue and saw a truck from Sinclair's Furniture Store. Two men were unloading a sofa covered in soft white leather and Hilda opened the door for them to carry it in. Following them inside, Joanna gasped in disbelief. Pale pink carpeting covered the office floor and another employee was hanging a large painting on the wall.

"Careful with that!" Hilda snapped at him. "It's an original Monet. Cost more than you earn in six months." He threw her an angry scowl but said nothing.

"What in the world?" Joanna began, but Hilda cut her off.

"Now that we've finally got some money, we might as well fix this place up. It's such an eyesore."

"But why spend all that money on a paintin' when we could get one at the dollar store? And carpet! How will we keep it clean? You know how the dogs are always takin' a pee every time they come through here."

"You always criticize everything I do. I'm tired of the way this place looks. A room like this will impress people."

"Miss Velvie didn't want us to impress folks. She wanted us to use that money to help the animals."

"I don't know why you always think we should spend every penny on them stupid animals!"

Biting her tongue, Joanna turned and headed for the dog runs. She tried to avoid Hilda for the rest of the evening, but the building was small and every time she turned around, Hilda was there.

"I was thinkin'," Joanna said at the next meeting. "Now that we've got the funds, what about havin' Doc or Luke come out, maybe once a week. On a regular basis, and you know, pay 'em for it."

Several heads nodded in agreement as she continued. "They been teachin' me a lot about how to help sick animals, but sometimes I don't know what to do."

Hilda jumped up and pounded her fist on the table. "How many times have I got to tell you? Just put 'em to sleep! Doc Cooper should have never showed you how to do treatments like he did. You're just like that crazy old woman, think you're a doctor!"

The rest of the meeting was very tense and everyone dispersed quickly as soon as it was adjourned.

"Hey, have y'all noticed that paintin' is gone?" Denise said a few weeks later.

"I been so busy, I ain't really even looked," Joanna answered.

"Well, I went over to Hilda's last night to pick up some supplies that had been donated. What do you think was hangin' on 'er livin' room wall?"

"You got to be kiddin!" Joanna exclaimed.

"I don't know why you're so surprised," Tansey said. "I wouldn't put nothin' past 'er."

Joanna and Tansey stopped at Sylvia's on the way home. "You girls come on in," she opened the door, still wearing a cashmere suit and high heels. As Joanna explained what had happened, she began to twist the pearls that cascaded down over her silk blouse.

"I can't come out and accuse Hilda of takin' somethin' like that. It'll cause hard feelin's,"

"But it ain't right!" Joanna argued. "It was Miss Velvie's money paid for it. And the money ain't bein' spent the way she wanted. You know she wanted it to be used for the animals. What would a dog or cat do with a paintin' that cost all that money?"

"I know, but I told you before. I don't want to get into a conflict with

Hilda," Sylvia's hand reached up to smooth her ash-blonde french twist. Whenever she makes an enemy, she goes out and ruins their reputation. You know she did that to Evelyn last year, just because she doesn't like 'er. I don't want 'er to start doin' things like that to me. I've got my business to think about, I have to keep up a good image."

"Well, God-a-mighty!" Tansey shouted. "You're the president! If you can't do somethin', who can?"

"I don't know. Nobody wants to cross Hilda."

"You're always talkin' about how you want somebody to get rid of 'er, but you ain't got the guts to face 'er," Tansey declared. "Looks like you're all vines and no taters!"

"Why don't you do it yourself? You don't seem to be afraid of 'er."

"Because I ain't nothin' out there but a little peon!"

"Well, we don't even go out to the rescue, we only attend the meetin's."

"Why don't you bring that prissy butt of your's out there sometimes, then?"

"Come on, Tan," Joanna intervened. "Let's go."

"I just don't understand it," Denise said later. "The money's bein' spent on everything but the animals."

'Ain't there somethin' we can do?" Tansey asked. "Everybody knew Miss Velvie intended it to be used for the animals."

Joanna called Braxton Battle to ask his advice.

"Unfortunately, I don't see what you could do," he answered. "The will reads to spend the money as they see fit. It only says 'I have faith that it will be used to help the animals.'"

"So there's nothin' at all that we can do?"

"Well....you girls are just volunteers, so you don't have any authority over how the money is spent."

"It's just so unfair!" Tansey exploded when she heard the news. "I've had a belly full of them folks. I'm quittin'! You know this ain't how Miss Velvie wanted it. I wish she'd just left all that money to Mattie. Then we could just do more over there."

"I just wish we had realized before it was too late," Joanna sighed.

"Oh well," Denise summed it up. "You know what they say. Hindsight's twenty-twenty."

THE TRUTH ABOUT HILDA

"The end never really justifies the meaness."
—E. Duane Hulse

"Come on, Aunt Emma, you're purty enough," Joanna called impatiently. "You don't haf'ta primp so much to go to the rescue. Them animals don't care what you look like."

"Just a minute, darlin'. I'm almost ready. It took me a while to get them curlers out of my hair. Let me get my sweater and we'll go."

Aunt Emma had decided she wanted to adopt a kitten. A few months ago, her beloved cat, Skipper, had died. He had lived with Aunt Emma and Uncle Otto for nearly fifteen years. Joanna thought their hearts would break when the old feline's kidneys had failed and they had to put him down.

"I ain't gonna push y'all," she had promised. "But if you decide you want to get another one, let me know." It had taken a little time for them to get used to the idea. "Can't nobody take Skipper's place," Aunt Emma would say. "He was the only cat I've ever seen that liked to get in the little rowboat with Otto and go out fishin' on the pond. Started it when she was just a tiny kitten, that's where he got 'is name. I think I'll feel guilty if we get another one."

"I know, I've had that feelin' before," Joanna sympathized. "But if it's what you wanna do, ain't no reason you ought to feel guilty. Many animals as it is out there needs help, I don't think Skipper would begrudge 'em havin' a good home like he did."

So she had called one evening. "Jo, could you take me out to the rescue this weekend? I think I'm ready to get a cat. Or maybe I'll bring a little kitten home."

Now, Joanna was so excited she could hardly wait. There were twelve adult cats and two litters of kittens waiting to be adopted. "Aunt Emma would probably like the calico kitten in the top cage," she thought to herself. "Or maybe the slate gray cat with the white stockings.

Finally, Aunt Emma was ready, and started out.

"Tell Mama bye-bye," Uncle Otto urged as he held Rosie up for Joanna to give her a kiss.

"Now Otto," said Aunt Emma. "Her bottle's in the fridge, all you got to do is heat it up. We'll probably be back before she get's hungry anyway."

Uncle Otto looked down at the little girl. "They act like I ain't never took care of no young'uns before. Get on out'ta here now, me and Rosie's gonna have us a large time."

"You know, Jo," Aunt Emma said as they drove along. "I'm glad I decided to do this. It's been so lonesome around the house, it don't hardly seem right. 'Specially at night, when me and Otto are sittin' in the den, watchin' television. Seems like there should be a cat, curled up there by the fireplace, or draggin' my knittin' thread around, gettin' it all tangled up. It'll be so good to have one to keep us company again."

When they arrived at the rescue, Joanna took Aunt Emma into the cat room to show her what they had. "I like old Hobo here," she said as she took the black and white tomcat out of his cage. A lady found 'im down by the train tracks and he's sweet as can be." Hobo snuggled up and rubbed his head against her cheek as she took him in her arms. "He's been here for a couple months, I sure wish he could get a home."

"I declare, I wish I could take 'em all, darlin'. It's so sad thinkin' 'bout all the homeless kitties out there. Poor things, it just about breaks your heart."

"This here's Purvis," Joanna said as she picked up the gray cat. "See how loud he purrs?" The big cat sounded like an outboard motor humming as she held him.

They heard a vehicle drive up. Looking out the window, Joanna saw Agnes and Hilda getting out of their truck. They came inside, but didn't come to the cat room. Joanna could hear them talking, then they dissappeared towards the dog runs. Aunt Emma continued to look at the cats, stroking and talking to them.

Suddenly, the door burst open and Petey came running in, cheeks flushed and blonde curls tousled on top of his head. "Hey, Jo-Jo! I'm comin' to help you!" he cried as he flung himself into her arms and hugged her tightly.

"Well, hey there, Goober," she laughed in delight as she swung him up.

"Aunt Emma, I didn't know you were here!" the bright little eyes fell on the older woman and he had to scramble down and give her a hug too. "Are you helpin' Jo-Jo work?"

"No, darlin'. I came down here to adopt a kitty and take 'im home with me."

"You did? Can I help you pick one out?"

"You sure can," Aunt Emma responded, thinking he would encourage her to choose one of the lively kittens that were so much fun to play with, but Petey surprised her.

"You need to get Hobo. He's been here for a lo-o-o-ong, long time. I think he's sad, 'cause people always pick the little baby kittens and nobody wants him. I think it hurts 'is feelins' and he feels left out."

Aunt Emma looked at Joanna over the blonde curls. "Goodness Gracious, this little tyke's been learnin' some stuff out here, ain't he?"

"Yes ma'am, it looks like it. I didn't realize he was pickin' up on so much of what we said."

"I'm gonna be an animal helper when I get big!" Petey declared. "Just like Jo-Jo and Aunt Neecie."

"You sure are," Denise said through the little window to the office. "She had been standing there, holding Kayla up so she could see and they were watching Petey quietly. Now she opened the door and they came into the cat room.

"Jo-Jo!" once again, little arms reached up to embrace Joanna and she swung Kayla around.

"Hey, there, Budgie! How's my girl doin'?"

Kayla just ducked her head shyly and nestled into the hollow of Joanna's shoulder, as Aunt Emma came over to say hello.

"Come on over here, darlin' and see the kitties," Aunt Emma urged and the little girl allowed the woman to take her. The little hand reached out and stroked Hobo's head ever so gently and she began to talk to the cats, forgetting her bashfulness.

We just stopped by for a minute," Denise said. "I've got to run up to the grocery store and pick up a couple of things. You kids tell Jo and Aunt Emma we'll see 'em a little later."

"I want to stay here and help 'em," Petey declared. "They need me!"

"No, sweetie. They're busy workin'."

"Why don't you let 'im stay here while you go?" Joanna asked. "I'm not doin' anything much right now, we're just kind'a hangin' out to give Aunt Emma a chance to spend some time with the cats and pick one out."

"I dunno," Denise began doubtfully. "Petey, can you behave yourself and do what Jo tells you?"

"Yes ma'am, I promise!"

"Oh, go on," said Joanna. "He's always good as gold when he's with me. He ain't never a bit of trouble."

"All right, but you mind your manners, now. You hear me?"

"Yes ma'am, I will. I love to help Jo-Jo."

"Okay, I'll be back in about a half hour. Don't you be no trouble."

"I won't," the little boy declared as he watched his aunt and sister leave. Turning to Joanna, he asked, "What do you need me to do, Jo-Jo?"

"Well, we got some puppies in the back that sure could use some exercise. You want to go see 'em?"

"Yes ma'am! I sure do. I'll be real easy with 'em, too. Just like you always tell me. They're like little babies, right?"

"That's right," Joanna agreed, as she tousled the blonde curls. Aunt Emma was right, Petey was learning a lot about how to treat the animals.

"Here we go," she said as she stopped in front of a run filled with a litter of labrador puppies. They barked and squirmed with anticipation of the attention they wanted so badly.

"A-w, hey there, little dogs," Petey said. "Do y'all need to come out and play?" Reaching through the gate, he rubbed one gently behind the ear. Joanna opened the gate and the puppies tumbled over the boy, knocking him to the ground and swarming over him. He lay there for a few moments, giggling and squealing as they licked his face and ears. "Look, Jo-Jo!" he exclaimed when he was finally able to sit up. "They like me!"

"They sure do," she agreed. "You're a mighty good animal helper. "You're gonna be some kind'a good at it when you grow up."

"Yes ma'am, I sure am. I'm gonna help all the animals in the whole world!" The innocent eyes looked up at her as he stroked one puppy on the head and another climbed into his lap.

"I hope you can hold onto that innocent enthusiasm for a long time, little buddy," Joanna thought as she smiled down at him. Then she noticed that one puppy was still in the run, cowering down in the corner.

"Come on, little Runt," she said softly. "Ain't nobody gonna hurt you. She went into the kennel and sat down in the corner beside the puppy, watching Petey through the open door. She murmered soft nonsense to the puppy until it finally climbed into her lap, then sat quietly, stroking the soft ears, while she watched Petey playing with the other puppies.

"What are you doin' back here, you little brat?" It was Hilda, stomping up the hall. "You got no business in here by yourself. I'll teach you a lesson!"

Looming over the cowering figure, she raised the garden sprayer she was holding and directed the nozzle of the sprayer into the boy's face.

"No!" Joanna screamed as the long finger with dirty nails tightened around the nozzle. Scrambling to her feet, she slipped on the cement and fell, hitting her head on the concrete wall and nearly passing out. With doubled vision, she saw the stream of pesticide shoot into Petey's little face and he let out a shriek of anguish, as he clawed at his eyes. Joanna could barely hear Agnes in the background.

"Stop it Hilda! That stuff's poison! It could really make 'im sick!"

Now Aunt Emma was running down the aisle and Joanna saw her pick Petey up and clasp him to her breast.

"Get 'im under some water, and rinse that stuff off 'im!" Joanna screamed. "Go! Hurry, Aunt Emma!" she struggled to her feet, as the older woman started towards the bathroom with the child.

"You should'a kept 'im out'ta here!" Hilda loomed in the doorway of the run as Joanna finally stood up.

"You bitch!" Joanna shrieked. "How could you hurt that young'un? He won't even doin' nothin'!" Without thinking, she grabbed the flat-bottom shovel leaning against the cage and swung at Hilda. It connected solidly, knocking out a tooth, which clattered to the floor. Hilda's nose, streaming blood, now sat at a peculiar canted angle and both eyes began to blacken within seconds.

"Jo! Come quick!" Aunt Emma shouted. "He's stopped breathin'!"

Slinging the shovel down, Joanna went running towards the bathroom, where Aunt Emma was holding Petey, looking down at him helplessly.

"Give 'im here!" Joanna grabbed the little boy, and gave him two quick breaths, then started doing chest compressions, but he didn't respond.

"We've got to get 'im to the hospital!" Aunt Emma shouted.

"We ain't got time for that!" Joanna cried as she thrust the lifeless body back into the older woman's arms. "We're too far from town!" Running into the medicine room, she snatched the emergency box open and the contents scattered everywhere. Fumbling through the contents, she grabbed up a vial and syringe and quickly drew the amber liquid into the tiny chamber.

"Pull up the leg of 'is shorts," she cried as she ran back towards Aunt Emma. Leaning over, she injected the contents into the little boy's thigh. Within a few seconds, he began to shake violently. Joanna began the chest compressions again and Petey began to cough. "Thank you, God!" she cried over and over as she clutched the blond head to her chest, tears running down her cheeks.

Just then, Denise and Kayla came in. "Jo, what's wrong?" Denise wanted to know immediately.

Her face twisted in horror as Joanna and Aunt Emma told her what had happened. "Oh, how could she?" Denise asked the same question Joanna had asked earlier. "He's just a tiny little boy!"

"What was that stuff you gave 'im, Jo?" Aunt Emma asked. "It worked like a pure miracle."

"Epinephrine," Joanna answered. "He was havin' an anaphylactic reaction and 'is throat swelled closed, to where he couldn't breathe. We keep it here, 'cause we give the animals antibiotics, and you don't never know when you may have a bad reaction."

"Well, thank goodness!" Aunt Emma declared. "I don't know what would have happened if it hadn't been here."

"I do," Joanna replied bitterly. "He wouldn't have made it."

"I better get 'im to the hospital, don't you think?" asked Denise.

"Yeah, he's gonna haf'ta be checked over good," Joanna answered. "Come on, we'll go with you. She lifted Kayla, who was crying softly and started out the door. "Put 'im in your car, Neecie and I'll get Kayla in on the other side. Aunt Emma, you sit up front with Neecie, and I'll sit back here with the young'uns." She swung the little girl into the back seat. But just as they were hooking the belts on the car seats, a deputy's car charged into the driveway, sirens blowing and lights flashing. Hilda ran out the door to meet the lawmen before they could step out of their vehicle.

"Arrest that woman, officer!" she cried. "She's the one that attacked me."

Joanna looked up in bewilderment.

"You just wait a minute. We got a sick boy here, we got to get 'im to the hospital."

"'What's wrong?" one of the officers asked, concern written across his face.

"He had a bad reaction to poison that was sprayed on 'im!" Joanna shouted.

"Let me see if I can help," the man said as he leaned into the truck. "Well, he seems to be all right," he turned to look at Joanna as if she were making it up. We received a call a few moments ago from a woman that had been attacked with a shovel. Where is she?"

"I'm the one that needs help," Hilda declared. "Just look at my face!" She pulled the wad of paper towels down and blood flowed out of her crooked nose copiously. The eyes were now swollen, black circles and one tooth was hanging over her lip, ready to follow the one that had fallen out earlier.

"Well, I've got to say you do look you got the worst end of the bargain," the officer admitted. "Do you ladies want to tell me what's been goin' on around here?"

"We'll do that later!" Joanna said impatiently. "Right now, we need to get this young'un to the emergency room."

Hilda walked over to the car and pulled Joanna out. "You heard the officer."

"Get your hands off me, you bitch!" Joanna screamed and pushed Hilda backwards, causing her to fall in the mud under the car.

The younger officer immediately grabbed Joanna and started to handcuff her. The harder he tried, the harder she fought, and the other officer went to his aid. Denise was trying to comfort the children while Aunt Emma came over and grabbed the older lawman's arm.

"Please, sir! She's tellin' the truth. This little boy had a bad reaction and just about died. She gave 'im a shot and he came around, but we need to get 'im to a doctor."

"Lady, you can't be puttin' your hands on me like this," the officer said gruffly. Pulling handcuffs off his belt, he put them on the older woman and she began to cry.

"Now, ma'am, if you need to take that youngster to the hospital, go ahead," he said to Denise, "But we're gonna haf'ta take these two in for assault."

"I'll come down as soon as I can see to Petey," Denise cried as she pulled out of the parking lot. Joanna watched her turn onto the highway, then the officer took her over to the police car.

"Watch your head, now," he instructed as he manuevered her into the back seat. The other deputy was putting Aunt Emma in on the other side.

"Please, sir," Aunt Emma was weeping softly. "Don't do this, you don't understand. We're not criminals. Joanna was just defending the little boy!"

The older officer turned to look back over his seat at her. "I'm really sorry to have to do this to you, ma'am. But you probably won't haf'ta stay very long. Do you have a husband or somebody you can call to come get you out?"

"Oh, goodness," Aunt Emma sniffled. "I sure don't want Otto to see me, all handcuffed like this."

"We'll take 'em off just as soon as we get you there, ma'am. Don't be frightened, it probably won't be as bad as you think."

"Oh, Jo," Aunt Emma turned to the younger woman. "I'm so worried about Petey. Do you think he's okay?"

"Yes ma'am. I'm purty sure he'll be fine now. I just wanted Neecie to take 'im in to make sure."

"All the same, I wish we could be with the little feller," Aunt Emma sniffled.

"Me too," Joanna admitted. "I can't believe that Hilda! Why in the world would she do all this?"

"Well you know everybody says she's crazy," Aunt Emma responded. "I guess they're right. I always thought if we tried to be friendly to 'er, it would help, but I don't never want to be nowhere around 'er again. She's downright dangerous!"

When they arrived at the jail, the officers courteously escorted them inside, then took off the handcuffs. "Have a seat right here, ladies," the older officer informed them. "I'm gonna call a female officer to take y'all back. Would y'all care for anything? A cup of coffee, or maybe a coke?" When they declined, he left to find the other officer.

Soon, a middle-aged woman in uniform came into the room. "Okay, ladies, I've got to frisk you," she said.

Aunt Emma looked at Joanna , confusion written all over her face. "Does that mean what I think it does?"

"Yes ma'am," Joanna answered. "I think so."

Aunt Emma stood there for a moment, a deep flush spreading across her face. Then she spoke. "I'm sorry, but I can't allow you to do that. My own husband doesn't even touch me in such lewd ways, and neither is anybody else. You can put the handcuffs back on me, if you want."

"Well, I think we could make an exception this time," the officer said as she took in the gray curls, the old-fashioned dress, and button down sweater. "Don't tell anybody I didn't do it," she whispered, "but you look exactly like my Mama. What in the world did they haul you in here for, anyhow?"

"For tryin' to defend a little boy's life," Aunt Emma answered as she began to tell the story.

"That Hilda Hawkins, I know 'er," said the officer when she had finished.

"You do?" Joanna asked in surprise.

"Yep. She stays in trouble all the time. Either she gets into trouble herself, or trys to stir some up for somebody else. She's all the time takin' people's money, and then not deliverin' service. And, brother, I'm tellin' you, when you mess with them hunter's trophies, it's like declarin' war. Or she's haulin' 'er neighbors into court for petty little things that are downright silly."

"That sounds just like 'er," Joanna agreed.

"Anyway, I've got to have you ladies put these on," the guard handed each of them a pair of bright orange coveralls. You can take turns goin' in the bathroom there, where you can have a little privacy. After they had changed, she escorted them down the hall, to a small cell.

"I'm really sorry to haf'ta do this," she said. "Let me speak to the captain and I'll find out when I can take you up to use the phones." After she left, Aunt Emma sat down on one of the small bunks and folded her arms tightly across her chest. Joanna stood, clutching the cold, steel bars, still unable to believe this was really happening. Suddenly, she heard a familiar voice, singing in a low growl, sounding for all the world like a female Elvis and her spirits lifted at once. The calvary was here!

Goin' to a party at the county jail
My buddy Jo's here and the band began to wail
The band was jumpin' and the joint began to swing
You should've heard those knocked out jailbirds sing
Tansey rounded the corner and came into sight.
Let's rock, everybody let's rock
Everybody in the whole cell block
Was dancin' to the Jailhouse Rock

As Tansey continued to sing, Aunt Emma burst into fresh tears.

"Well, Aunt Emma, don't take on so," cried Tansey and Joanna turned to look at the older woman, then stepped over to put an arm around her.

"Please don't cry, Aunt Emma," Tansey begged. "I was just makin' a joke, you know, tryin' to make y'all feel better. We're gonna get y'all out'ta here."

"But I've never broken any kind of law before," Aunt Emma sobbed. "And now, I'm a... a... jailbird! Just look at me in this, this prison uniform!"

"How'd you know we were here?" Joanna asked.

"Neecie called me."

"Is Petey okay?'

"He's fine. But from what she told me, it sure is a good thing you got that shot in 'im right quick."

"Well, that's one thing we haf'ta be thankful for," Aunt Emma said, as she dried her eyes with a piece of toilet tissue. "Thanks be to the good Lord the little tyke's all right."

"Sorry it took me so long to get here. I had to go down to the Simmons farm to find Randy. He was on the tractor and didn't have 'is phone with 'im. He's gone to the bank and he ough'ta be on in just a little while to bail y'all out."

Tansey stayed to keep them company and Randy was there in less than an hour. "What am I gonna do with you two?" he asked shaking his head, but he was grinning the whole time. "Aunt Emma, you're a vision of beauty in that outfit. That color suits you perfect."

"Watch out, you'll have 'er bawlin' again," Tansey warned. "She's a might sensitive about it, ain't you, Aunt Emma?"

"Well, I guess I'm bein' a little silly. The good Lord knows we didn't do nothin' wrong, and that's what counts. It's just been so upsettin' and embarrassin'. But you know, they sure have treated us mighty nice 'round here. Almost as if we was visitors or somethin'. It won't near as bad as I thought it would be."

"That lady officer said she'd be on in a minute with your clothes. I've already paid the bail, so we can go soon as y'all get dressed."

After they dropped Aunt Emma off at home, Joanna admitted, "I was kind'a thinkin' you'd be mad, havin' to stop workin' durin' plantin' season, shellin' out all that bail money and everything."

"Maybe I ought'a be, but dog'gone! That Hilda's been askin' for it ever since I've known her. The onliest thing I'm sorry about is that I won't there to see it. I reckon I would'a been cheerin' you on. Hurtin' little Petey like she did, I wish you'd knocked every tooth in 'er head out. Serves 'er right. He's a good young'un and you done right by 'im."

Joanna looked up at her husband standing tall and handsome, his arm around her shoulder protectively. Solid as a rock, she could always depend on his support. Even now, in the middle of a fiasco like this, Randy always stood by her. And that was the reason she loved him so.

SAYING GOODBYE

"When you have an elephant by the hind leg and he is trying to run away, sometimes it is best to just let him run."
—Unknown

"Joanna?" The voice on the other end of the telephone line was polite but hesitant. "This is Helen Scott. Our neighbors moved away and just left their pony. They never did take very good care of 'im, but now the little fellow is starvin'. My husband bought some hay and gave it to 'im, but we really don't have a place to put 'im. Could you help?"

Jonanna strapped Rosie into her carseat and hooked up the horse trailer. A half hour later, she pulled into the driveway of a dilapidated mobile home. The grass was knee-high and a pile of garbage lay by the back door. In a small, muddy paddock stood a tiny, shetland pony. He was a brown and white paint, with a long, shaggy mane that nearly touched the ground. Velvety, brown eyes peered out at her beneath the long forelock as the pony nickered.

"Hey there, little feller," Joanna walked up to the fence. "How would you like to go home with me, where you'll have a big, old pasture to run around in?"

The pony nickered again and now Joanna could see how pitifully thin he was. His ribs stood out and there were sunken hollows above his eyes. The hooves had grown so long that they had turned upwards and it looked like water skis had been strapped to his feet. He moved along with a shuffling, stumbling gait.

"Poor little guy," Joanna led him slowly out the gate and over to the trailer. After three trys, the pony was able to step up into it. "Pony, Mama, pony!" Rosie cried with excitement. "Want to ride the pony!"

But when Joanna released the pony into the pasture later at home, the bigger horses nipped and kicked at him until she was forced to take him out. Putting him into a holding pen, she went in to call the ferrier.

Tansey pulled the pony's lips back and inspected his teeth that afternoon as the ferrier trimmed his back foot. "He's not as old as I thought," she said. "Just starved, probably wormy, too." She scratched him on the withers and looked at Joanna. "Wonder what 'is name is?"

"I don't know," Joanna shrugged.

"Look at this big, brown splotch on 'is side." Tansey ran her hand across it. "It's shaped just like a heart, we ought'a call 'im Valentine."

The ferrier finished with the last hoof and led the pony forward. Now he walked along briskly, long tail swishing back and forth.

"Wanna ride the pony, Mama!" Rosie squealed as she stretched her arms towards him. Joanna set her on the fuzzy back and walked alongside, holding her tightly as the ferrier led him around the yard.

"I don't know where to put 'im," Joanna said. "The horses were runnin' 'im so bad I had to take 'im out."

"Why don't we run some hot wire 'round the field down at the rescue?" Tansey asked. "All that bermuda grass is just goin' to waste. Then we won't haf'ta mow it so often."

Randy and Johnny-Vern put the heavy corner posts up that evening while the girls strung electric wire. When they released the pony, he ran through the thick grass, bucking and jumping.

"I believe old Valentine's gonna like it out here," Johnny-Vern said.

Denise called the next day. "I'm so worried about one of my students."

"What's wrong?" Joanna asked.

"Her mother abandoned 'er. She got to cryin' this mornin' and I finally got 'er to tell me what was wrong."

"Poor thing," Joanna responded. "And she doesn't have any idea where 'er mother went?"

"Laura thinks maybe she's stayin' with one of 'er boyfriends. She's a drug addict and she's done this before. I called Social Services and they're tryin' to find 'er a foster home."

"Why don't you bring 'er over here?" Joanna asked. "We've got that extra bedroom, she could stay with us for awhile."

"Oh, that would be great!" Denise exclaimed. "You sure it'll be okay with Randy?"

"If it ain't, he'll get used to it," Joanna answered.

Denise knocked on the door later that evening. When Joanna opened it, she was standing there with a frail looking girl. Her chestnut hair was pulled back in a ponytail and her hazel eyes were downcast.

"Jo, this is Laura," Denise introduced them.

"Hey there, honey," Joanna welcomed her. "Y'all come on in."

Denise nudged the girl into the living room where she took a seat on the sofa.

"How old are you, Laura?" Joanna asked.

"Eight." The girl kept her eyes on the floor.

Denise looked over Laura's head at Joanna and shrugged helplessly. They tried to make small talk for a little while, but the girl remained withdrawn.

Then a cry came from the bedroom. "Let me go get Rosie up," Joanna excused herself. When she came back to the living room holding the child, Laura looked up and smiled.

"Would you like to hold 'er?" Joanna asked.

Laura reached out to take the toddler in her arms. "Hi there," she cooed as Rosie pulled her hair. By the time Denise left, they were in the floor playing with a Tickle-Me-Elmo doll.

Joanna was sitting at the front desk of the rescue that Saturday morning filling out paperwork. Laura walked over to the window sill with Rosie on her hip, to play with the cat that perched there. Suddenly, the door opened and a shaggy head appeared. Valentine walked in with a clop-clopping sound as the tiny hooves hit the cement floor.

"Well, come on in!" Joanna exclaimed as Laura gaped at the pony. Walking over to the desk, he grabbed a paper in his teeth and shook his head up and down. When Joanna reached up to grasp it, he backed away. She got up, went around the desk and Valentine whirled to run out the door, still holding the paper.

"You little monster!" Joanna screeched as she ran after him. Laura and Rosie laughed as she chased the pony around the field until he finally dropped the paper and she picked it up.

"Where did you get 'im from?" Laura asked. "I've always wanted a pony."

"The people that owned 'im moved away and left 'im." Joanna explained. "The neighbors called me and I went to pick 'im up."

The hazel eyes clouded over as Laura rubbed the pony's velvety nose.

"I know how that feels," she said.

Joanna put an arm around the little girl. "I know it must really hurt," she said. "But you just remember...you can stay with us just as long as you want. I'll always be here for you. And so will Randy."

Laura suddenly turned and buried her head against Joanna's stomach. Her arms wrapped around the woman and she began to sob. It was the first time Joanna had seen her cry.

"I...I get so scared when my Mama goes away," the child stammered. "Sometimes she's gone when it's dark...and there's all kinds of sounds. I never go to sleep when she's gone, I just go get in 'er bed and wait for 'er to come home."

Joanna stood there with her left arm around Laura, Rosie on her right hip. The little girl cried until she was spent, then Joanna tipped her chin up and looked at the mournful, hazel eyes. "I meant what I said, you've got a home with us for as long as need be. Now come on, let's go in and get a cold drink."

Joanna was cleaning the cat cages one evening when she heard loud mufflers. Looking out the window, she saw Johnny-Vern's Dodge pull in. He had a two-wheeled pony cart in the back.

"Look what I found at the farmer's auction this mornin'." Johnny-Vern was already unloading the cart as Joanna stepped outside. "I figured the young'uns would have a good time with it. Let's hook old Valentine up and see if he's harness broke."

They harnessed the pony and he stood quietly as Laura climbed into the seat. When she flicked the reins lightly on his back he stepped out briskly and when she clicked her tongue, he broke into a trot. They circled back around and Joanna put Rosie on the seat beside Laura. The toddler laughed as they trotted around the field, waving at her mother each time they went past.

By now, Valentine had free run of the rescue, following the volunteers wherever they went. He snatched anything he could find: buckets, medications, the caps from people's heads. They soon found the easiest way to get the items back was to ignore the pony. If he couldn't entice someone to chase him, he simply dropped them on the ground.

Joanna stepped out to take the trash one Saturday and saw Laura with the pony. She was holding a plastic Mountain Dew bottle up and

Valentine was drinking from it. "Look, Jo!" the little girl laughed. "He likes it 'cause it's sweet."

As the months went by, Joanna's feelings for Laura grew deeper and she constantly worried that the little girl's mother would snatch her away from them.

"She's in a drug rehab program," Denise told her. "I guess that's the only reason we haven't heard from 'er."

Randy and I talked about adoptin' 'er," Joanna admitted. "But you know what happened before, when they refused us because of my depression."

"But that was a long time ago. And now...well you've been Laura's legal foster parents for a few months. It's a lot easier to adopt a child that you're already fosterin'."

Laura had to attend the court hearing. "I love my Mama very much," she told the judge. "But couldn't I live with Joanna and Randy? I...I feel safe with them."

The adoption was approved and Lori-Ann's mother was granted visitation rights.

"Do you think Mama will be mad at me?" Laura asked after the judge left the room.

"I don't think so, honey," Joanna replied. "Your Mama loves you, she just needs some help. How about if you and me go visit 'er this weekend?"

The little girl agreed, then fell silent for the rest of the way home.

"I've got a surprise for you, Laura," Randy said as they turned into the path at the farm.

"What is it?"

Randy drove past the house and barn. The small back field had been enclosed with white rail fencing and a small shed had been erected.

"What's this for?" she asked again.

Randy got out of the truck and hoisted Rosie onto his shoulders. Joanna and Laura followed him through the gate and around to the front of the shed.

There, above the door a name was etched into the fresh pine: VALENTINE. It was surrounded with dozens of little heart shapes.

Realization began to dawn in the little girl's eyes. "Valentine's comin' to live here?"

"That's right," Randy picked her up and swung her around. "He's gonna be your pony—we adopted you and now you're gonna adopt him! Now what do you think about that?"

"Oh, Randy!" Laura put her arms around his neck and squeezed tightly. "Thank you! I can't believe it, a pony of my very own."

Joanna looked at Randy over the little head. "I love you," she mouthed silently.

Laura turned to give Joanna a hug. "And you! You sure kept it a secret!"

Joanna looked down at her. "I didn't know, I'm just as surprised as you are."

Leaving Rosie with Randy, Joanna and Laura headed to the rescue, the horse trailer behind them. Laura chattered happily the whole way. "I still can't believe it. Valentine's the best pony in the whole world! I was so afraid somebody else would take 'im and I'd miss 'im so much."

When they pulled into the path, Valentine didn't run up to the fence to greet them with a nicker, as he always did. Getting out, Joanna whistled but there was still no sign of the pony.

"Maybe he's under the lean to," Joanna walked out to peep under the shelter, but he wasn't there either.

"He must have got out," she told the little girl. "Let's walk around the fence and see if it's down anywhere."

They walked the entire perimeter of the fence but it was intact.

"I can't figure out where he could be," Joanna admitted as they went back to the front of the building. "Let's walk over to Miss Velvie's and ask Mattie if she's seen 'im. Maybe he's over there in the pasture with the goats."

Mattie opened the back door a few minutes later, shoving dogs and cats out of the way. "Y'all come on in," she reached out to give Joanna a hug. "How you doin' today, sugar-pie?" She gave Laura a pat on the head.

When Joanna asked if Mattie had seen anyone around, the answer sent a chill through her heart.

"Yeah, I saw Jed Bullock over there early this mornin'. And Hilda's truck was there. I figgered Jed came to see about adoptin' a dog, or maybe he had one he wanted y'all to take."

"Mattie!" Joanna's voice rose with urgency. "You know he's a horse dealer...all the time pickin' up cheap horses to take to the killer sale! And Valentine's missin'!"

"Lordy, you don't reckon he took that pony?" Now it was Mattie's turn to look alarmed.

Pushing past Mattie, Joanna rushed into the kitchen and lifted the receiver to the old-fashioned wall phone. With barely concealed panic in her voice, she got the horse dealer's number from information.

A deep voice answered on the fifth ring. "Bullock's Livestock."

"Mr. Bullock, did you pick up a pony from out here at the animal rescue at Mimosa this mornin'?"

"Yeah, that Hawkins woman called me over there to get 'im."

"Well, don't take 'im anywhere! I'm on the way over right now to get 'im, there's been a terrible mistake!"

"Ma'am?" the voice on the other end of the line was hesitant. "I already run 'im up to Siler City."

"I'll have to go there, then." Adrenalin coursed through Joanna's veins and the hand she held phone with shook. "It'll take about two hours to get there, is he at the stockyards?"

"Ma'am," the voice stammered. "I...I'm mighty sorry about the mix up, but it's too late. They done killed 'im."

"How do you know?"

"They done it early this afternoon...while I was still there."

"But...maybe they didn't ," Joanna refused to accept it. "Ain't there a chance they might not have done it so fast?"

"I'm sorry, but I seen 'em with my own eyes. I feel mighty bad about this, I'll take the money I made on the deal and replace 'im for you."

"No..no," Joanna said flatly. "That's, that's , well..." Trailing off, she gently cradled the receiver and turned to Laura.

"Honey," she began. "I'm so sorry..."

The hazel eyes met hers. "They killed Valentine, didn't they?"

Mattie walked up behind Laura and stroked her hair as Joanna nodded. She didn't trust herself to speak, she couldn't get the words past the lump in her throat.

A single tear rolled down the little girl's cheek and she brushed it away. "But, why did they do it?"

Joanna's shoulders slumped and she just shook her head.

The sun was going down as they drove slowly up the path at home. Randy stepped out onto the porch.

"Hey, where's...?"

He stopped in midsentence when Joanna shook her head at him and followed them into the house.

"I've got some sausage and eggs scrambled up," Randy offered.

"I'm really tired," Laura said. "Is it okay if I just go on to bed?"

"Go ahead, honey," Joanna put a hand on her shoulder. "I'll be in to say good night in a little bit."

Joanna sat down at the kitchen table, but she couldn't eat either. As she told Randy what had happened, she could see the anger growing in his face.

"I'll buy 'er a pony," he said. "But I can't believe anybody could be so cruel."

"I told 'er on the way home we'd get 'er one," Joanna told him. "But she says she doesn't want one. I don't know...maybe we can talk 'er into it later. She's hurtin' too bad right now."

Joanna walked over to the telephone and dialed Tansey's number. "Hey girl, I need some help." She told Tansey what had happened. "I just can't do it anymore, I'm leavin' the rescue. But first, we've got'ta get all the animals out. If you can take a couple, I'll call everybody else."

They all met at the rescue the next evening.

"Hey, Catfish! You and Tadpole want to go with me?" Tansey opened the gate to let out a couple of labs and laughed as they jumped up to lick her.

"What about Domino?" Roxanne pointed at the Dalmatian. "Now that I've got my own place, I'd like to take 'im."

"Slick could come with me," Denise said. The speckled Bluetick hound sat back on his haunches and howled his approval.

"And guess what!" Denise continued. "I talked my sister into gettin' Skittles. You know how much the children love that dog."

Joanna smiled at the memory of Petey and Kayla running through the field with the shaggy, black and tan dog. "She looks like the Skittles dog on t.v!" Petey had exclaimed. "That's my favorite candy and she's my favorite dog." The name had stuck.

"Let's take Sunny, Mama," April pleaded. She handed the big, marmalade cat up to her mother and he gave Hope a pat on the cheek with his big paw.

"That don't leave but four cats," said Mattie. "I'll take 'em over to Miss Velvie's.".

"The boys said they'd take some of the dogs," Joanna told Tansey. "I'll take Rooster over to Johnny-Vern's. Can you run Otis over to Wildman's?"

Joanna walked back down the aisle. "Well, Crackerjack," she sighed. "Looks like you and Lollipop are the only ones left, so I guess you're goin' with me." She opened the gate and the brindled Boxer jumped up, throwing gobs of slobber all over her. "What am I lettin' myself in for?" she laughed as she wiped her face.

Finally, every animal had been loaded. Joanna stood in the parking lot and watched as everyone drove away. Going back to turn off the lights, she looked around and tears started to well up in her eyes. "It's hard to believe I'll never be back," she thought. She looked at the empty dog runs. No barking echoed through the building. She had never heard it so quiet in here. Turning, she squared her shoulders and went out the front door. It slammed behind her with a heavy and final sounding thud. Wiping a tear from her cheek, she walked over to the truck and pulled off slowly.

RAINBOW BRIDGE FARM

"Courage doesn't always roar, sometimes it is the quiet voice at the end of the day saying, I will try again tomorrow."

—Author Unknown

The phone rang early Saturday morning and Joanna turned over sleepily to answer it.

"Hey, Jo. This is Aubrey Hedgepeth. Did I wake you up?"

"That's okay."

"I hate to bother you, but there's a dog over here that needs some help real bad. Looks like he's eat slam up with mange, and nearabout starved to death. He's 'bout the most pitiful thing I ever saw."

"Where is he, on the dirt road?"

"Yeah, 'bout halfway between two-oh-five and the Sandy Swamp Road. Up near the gate to the Jenkins farm, where my peanuts are. I been feedin' the little feller most every day, but somethin' must be wrong with 'im, he's pure skin and bones. Don't put on a bit of weight. There was two of 'em, but somethin' must have happened to the white one, I ain't seen 'er in a nearabout a month. But the black one, he's always hangin' around that old tenant place, you know that shotgun house at the back side of the farm."

"I swear, I already got so many over here, Randy's gonna kill me if I bring another one home."

"I called the animal rescue, over at Mimosa and wouldn't nobody ever return my calls. I went by yesterday and saw Hilda's truck there, so I stopped. She said they ain't takin' animals in down there no more."

Joanna felt the rage boiling up all over again. "What was she doin'?"

"Had a deer head down there, workin' on it, gettin' it mounted. You know, she's done closed up 'er shop. I thought she had gone out of business, but evidently she's using the rescue for that."

"Okay. I'll run over there and see what I can do." Hanging up, she called, "Laura, will you get Rosie up and get 'er dressed?"

As they turned onto the dirt road a little later, Joanna saw Aubrey, way in the back of the field, spraying the corn that was already head high. She drove on down to the path leading to the Jenkins farm and stopped, but the dog was nowhere to be seen. She got out, calling and whistling, with no luck, so she got back into the truck and headed up the path. At the top of the rise sat a dilapidated old tenant house. Half the rotten, unpainted boards had fallen off and the porch canted sharply to the right. At the sound of the truck, a little black face appeared from underneath the house and the dog scrambled out to meet her, tail wagging furiously.

"Oh, my God!" was Joanna's first thought when she saw him.

He was a young dog, and the little body was completely covered with mange. Most of the shaggy, black hair had fallen out and the skin was severely infected, oozing a clear, foul-smelling drainage.

"Come on, little feller," she coaxed. "I ain't gonna hurt you. Don't you wanna go home with me and get you some breakfast?"

The dog must have been in terrible pain, but he was ecstatic that someone had come to get him. He was emaciated, his ribs were standing out and it was obvious that he must have been on his own for some time. Joanna tried to load him into the back of the truck, but he kept jumping out. Running over to the back of the house, he would whine, then run back to the woman.

Looking into the cab of the truck, she found half a cheeseburger, left over from yesterday's lunch. Looking up with eager eyes, the dog barked and wagged his tail. When she offered it to him, he snatched it quickly, but instead of gulping it down, he ran behind the house with it. In a split second, he was back, begging for more. Dumping out a pack of french fries, she watched as he grabbed them and carried them, one by one to the back of the old house.

Leaving Rosie with Laura, Joanna walked around behind the house. She spotted a shaggy white form, laying under what was left of the step. The dog's right hind leg was caught in a steel trap, held fast to a support post, where a long chain was wrapped around it. As Joanna approached, she whined, deep in her throat and her tail thumped the ground. The leg was swollen and infected and the earth surrounding the dog was bare, as if she had been there for quite some time.

"Oh God! You pore little thing!" Joanna knelt down and gently stroked the white head. Like the other dog, clumps of hair were missing and pus drained from the sores that covered her body. Taking hold of the trap, she tried to pry it apart, but it was much too strong for her bare hands.

"I'll be right back," she looked into the brown eyes that begged her not to leave. "I can't do it by myself." Getting into the truck, she headed back down the road to look for Aubrey. She flagged him down and he maneuvered the big tractor to the edge of the field and got down.

"Run me over to my truck, there," he instructed. "I got some heavy-weight grips in the toolbox. Maybe we can get 'er out with those."

Joanna stroked the trembling head as Aubrey pried the steel jaws of the trap off her leg. Rosie kept calling from Laura's arms, "Doggie, Mommy, doggie!"

As soon as the dog was released, she crawled into Joanna's lap, dragging the injured limb behind her. The black dog stood nearby, continuously nosing and pushing gently at her.

"So that's why you didn't gain no weight," Aubrey reached over to pet him. "You were bringin' all that food I give you to your sister, here. Is that what you were doin'?" The dog's pink tongue reached out to lick Aubrey's face as he knelt beside them, concern in his eyes.

"You think they need to be put down?" he looked at Joanna.

"I guess that's what anybody with good sense would do," she answered. "But I don't know. Looks like they've been through so much, tryin' to survive, it sure would be a shame to kill 'em now. I'm gonna take 'em over to Doc Cooper's and see what he thinks."

The veterinarian looked at the dogs. "I know you want to try and save 'em, don't you, Jo?"

"Yes, sir. If you think we can."

"Well..." looking at the mangled leg, he scratched his head. "I believe we can save that leg. Let's see if we can clean it up and put 'er on some antibiotics. And that mange. Looks like we're gonna haf'ta put 'em on a schedule for dips. They're gonna need it twice a week for awhile."

"Doc, you know these ain't even Jo's dogs," piped up Bonnie. "They're strays, and she's tryin' to get 'em well enough to find homes We trained 'er on a lotta other stuff down at the rescue. Can I show 'er how to do the dip?"

"Yeah, that's a good idea. Go on back there, Jo. Let Bonnie teach you how to do it, but be careful, that's some mighty strong stuff." He took

Rosie from Laura's arms.

"I was just fixin' to take a break. Come on Rosie, let's me and you go find us a Mountain Dew. You like those, don't you?"

The toddler smiled up at the old veterinarian and pulled his glasses off.

"Where in tarnation did you get them things?" Randy asked when she brought them home and put them into a pen that was set apart from the others.

"On that dirt road, you know where folks are always droppin' animals out." She told him the entire story.

"Well, you ain't keepin' 'em here! They're full of mange, before you know it, all the dogs here will have it. Anyway, you got too many dogs 'round here now. Why can't they take 'em down at the rescue?"

She repeated what Aubrey had told her.

"That figures." He looked at the dogs. "I feel sorry for 'em, but this ain't no animal shelter. You just can't keep draggin' up every stray in the whole county!"

Joanna ignored her husband and gave the dogs their breakfast.

A few weeks went by and although Joanna kept up the schedule on dipping the dogs, the mange wasn't getting any better.

"Them dogs are lookin' worse all the time," Randy said as he reached down to pet the white one. "I hate to say it, but don't you reckon' you better think about puttin' 'em to sleep?"

"Maybe you're right," Joanna said reluctantly. "But...I don't know... they've come through so much. If only there was something I could....."

"Hey!" Joanna broke off suddenly. "Let's ride down to that spot on the river! You know, where me and Miss Velvie used to pick plants. There's some sasparilla rootstock down there. That's what she always used for skin diseases."

"You know how to fix it?" Randy asked.

"I think so! I watched her do it lots of times."

Joanna used the herbal mixture on the dogs and over the course of the next few weeks, they showed a great deal of improvement. The skin healed and the hair began to come in, thick and glossy. What had been wretched, diseased creatures, now were two of the most beautiful animals you would ever hope to see. And even now, when they had plenty of food, the black dog would stand back and watch his littermate eat, waiting until she finished before he would touch a morsel.

"Smokey and Snowball, that's what you ought'a call 'em." Randy had forgotten that he wasn't going to allow them to stay there. He laughed as they played tug-of-war with a piece of rope, growling in mock battle. He reached down to pet the black dog. "I'm gonna miss you little fellers when you find a home," he admitted.

Smokey and Snowball were never far apart. When you saw one, you could be sure to see the other. Even though they interacted with the other dogs, they seemed to have a very special relationship. If Joanna tried to seperate them, they dug under fences, jumped over the railing of the deck, whatever it took to reach each other.

Joanna made an appointment to have Snowball spayed. When she took her out of the pen that morning, Smokey barked and hurled himself against the fence.

"You can't go this time, buddy," Joanna told him. "Snowball's gonna have to spend the night. She'll be back with you tomorrow." She thought the fence should contain him. Wire was buried under the ground to keep them from digging out and a strand of electric wire ran across the top. None of the dogs had ever been able to escape from this particular pen.

Joanna started into the animal hospital a little later, leading Snowball. Laura was behind her, Rosie in her arms.

"Jo!" Courtney looked up. "Randy's tryin' to reach you, wants you to call 'im on 'is cell phone. Somethin's wrong, he's mighty upset."

The telephone kept breaking up and it was difficult to understand what Randy was saying. He kept repeating the phrase that someone was dead, but Joanna couldn't make out who. "It must be Prissy," she thought. She was so old, and with her heart condition, Joanna had been expecting it for quite some time.

But Prissy had been spared, at least for a while longer. It was Smokey. Joanna's mind went numb and tried to deny what it was hearing. "How could it be true?" she wondered. Smokey was young and healthy and he'd been just fine when she left.

"He got to the road," Randy said. "I was tryin' to catch 'im. I saw the car hit 'im."

"How? He was right there in the fence when I left."

"He went crazy when you left with Snowball. Climbed the fence. I went to hollerin' at 'im, but he acted like he didn't even hear me."

"But it's six foot."

"I know. And when he hit the electric wire at the top, it must have shocked 'im, 'cause I heard 'im holler out. But he just kept comin', never slowed down. He tore off down the path, tryin' to catch up with you, I guess. I couldn't get 'im to come back. I got in the truck and started after 'im, but he never slowed down when he got to the highway. Ran right out and the driver never had a chance to hit 'is brakes. I tried to get 'im, honest I did."

"I know you did," Joanna tried to console him as her own heart was breaking. "It's my fault, you know how they act when I seperate 'em. I should have just let 'im ride with us. I'm comin' on home, I'll be there in 'bout twenty minutes."

As they came to the end of the long path, there was Smokey, lying on the ground, right behind the house. Randy was sitting on the steps,waiting for them. When Joanna opened the truck door, Snowball ran to Smokey and nudged him with her nose. Joanna tried to pull her away, but each time she let the dog go, she would run over to Smoky and whine, pawing at him and begging him to get up. They finally had to tie her while they wrapped Smokey in a blanket.

Eyes watery, Randy went to the barn and got a shovel. "I'll go ahead and dig a grave out behind the dogpens," he said.

"Naw, let's don't put 'im out there," Joanna answered. "It gets all grown up so bad in the weeds and all."

"Well, where do you wanna do it?"

"Let's put 'im in that spot on the hill beside the house."

"Out in the cedar grove, where the wildflowers are?"

"Yeah, I always loved that little place. It's 'bout the purtiest spot on the farm and it's so peaceful and quiet out there."

So they loaded Smokey's wrapped body into the back of the truck and pulled over to the east side of the house, trying to block out the sound of Snowball crying and howling.

"Let's put 'im right here," she instructed, pointing to a level spot on the very top of the hill. Randy began to dig, while Laura tried to keep Rosie out of the way. They heard a vehicle approaching and looked up to see

Johnny-Vern.

"Hey man, I'm sorry to hear 'bout Smokey. I was over at Stumpy's and he told me what happened." He took the shovel from Randy and began to dig. When he finished, Randy lowered Smokey gently into the little grave and Johnny-Vern began to cover him up. All the dogs except Snowball sat silently in a semi-circle, almost as if they knew something was wrong.

Suddenly, a flash of white came tearing around the clump of cedars and flew into their midst. It was Snowball. She launched herself against Joanna, then stood still for a moment, as she searched for her brother. Finally, she jumped down into the shallow grave and started clawing at the loose dirt. Joanna had to pull her away so that Johnny-Vern could finish covering it up. And the entire time, Snowball cried. It was a pitiful, wailing sound that almost made one's hair stand on end.

"Well, that's 'bout got it, I think," said Johnny-Vern as he finally straightened up.

"We sure 'preciate the help, Vern," Joanna said, and he stepped over to give her a fierce bear hug and pat Randy on the shoulder. Joanna had released Snowball and she immediately began to claw at the loose dirt, whining deep in her throat.

"Randy, you got anything we can lay over top of the grave, there, to keep 'er from diggin' it up?" Johnny-Vern asked.

"What about a sheet of plywood? I got some up at the barn."

Johnny-Vern thought that would do, so they got a piece and laid it on the ground, weighting it down on the corners with large, heavy rocks. It seemed to work, because Snowball couldn't get to the grave now. Finally, she stopped tearing at it and lay down, her head resting on the board and making that little whimper, deep in the back of her throat.

"Well, I'm gonna get on down the road," said Johnny-Vern. "Y'all lemme know if there's anything else I can do."

"We will, Vern," said Randy. "Thanks for the help." They stood there, watching him slowly drive away, then walked to the house, all the dogs but Snowball following them. As Joanna looked back, she could see the white dog lying there, still as a stone statue.

"Poor thing, I hate to leave 'er out there by herself," she said.

"Come on, she'll come to the house in a little bit," urged Randy.

But every time Joanna went to glance out the bedroom window, the little white dog was in the same position. She put together some sandwiches for supper, but none of them could eat very much. Randy turned the evening news on and lay on the sofa while Laura played with Rosie.

Joanna went to the bedroom and looked out the window. Sure enough, Snowball was still there. She went to the kitchen and got a can of vienna sausage. Going to the back yard, she shut the other dogs into the fence and walked over to the little gravesite. When she sat down and stroked the little dog's head, she paid her no attention.

"Come on, girl! I brought your favorite treat. Don't you want a bite?" she cajoled. But Snowball's grief was too deep. So Joanna simply sat with her for the better part of an hour, stroking the fuzzy head.

As the young woman looked around, she thought how right it was to have selected this particular location. Giant cedars grew across the back side of the little glen, their full limbs sweeping down to touch the earth and provide a windblock. A mammoth weeping willow shaded the side closest to the house, it's elegant, cascading branches lending a romantic look as the swayed in the gentle breeze. Soft clouds of pink and white dogwood were bursting forth under the pines and honeysuckle tumbled across the top of the hedge on the far side, sending it's heavenly fragrance through the air.

And the flowers! Oh, it was like a magical place, the colors and scents that surrounded the tiny grove. Daffodils were scattered across the little field like bright yellow trumpets. Groundcover flowers nestled underneath the trees, swaying as one of the cats slunk through them, pretending to sneak up on the woman and the dog.

Snowball and Joanna sat, looking down the hill to the pond, where the ducks and the single swan swam silently. A huge shadow crossed over the ground and she looked up, to see a huge white egret gliding towards the water. He landed at the marshy south end and waded slowly, searching for the silvery minnows that crowded the banks. He would stand, motionless on the long, spindly legs, then suddenly, the big head would dip down to scoop one up. She watched as two of the horses walked down to the edge of the pond for a drink. Suddenly, the big bird flapped his wide, leathery wings and the young sorrel colt spooked and bolted back up the hill towards them, tail held high and snorting nostrils heaving in and out. He circled the pasture, finally slowing down to a jaunty prance until she just had to smile.

"Life goes on, old girl," she said to the little white dog. "You've still got me, and all the other dogs. I know it ain't the same as havin' Smokey, y'all had a mighty special bond, but you're not alone. Come on, let's go to the house."

But Snowball refused to leave the grave for three solid days. She ate a little, but only if Joanna took food out to the glen, and hand-fed it to her. The third afternoon, Joanna and Laura were sitting on a log at the edge of the glen. Rosie toddled through the wildflowers. Gazing out across the pond, Joanna saw a rainbow. The brilliant colors stretched across the deep blue sky, like the threshold of paradise.

"Look!" Joanna cried. "That's Miss Velvie! She's doin' it again! She's tellin' us God will look after Smokey and everything's okay!"

She waved up towards the Heavens. "The Lord watch between me and thee, when we are absent from one another. That's what you always told me."

That night, Snowball began to come to the house at feeding time and return to the graveside later. Gradually she stayed away for longer periods of time. But Joanna would still look out the window sometimes and see her resting her head on the grave.

The weeks went by and spring turned into summer. Snowball, Joanna, Laura and Rosie would go out often and sit quietly by the grave. The ever-changing perennials had altered the appearance of the little glen, but it was no less beautiful. In place of the honeysuckle, running roses now rambled romantically through the shrubs, and black-eyed Susans danced across the open field.

Joanna was pulling up weeds beside the little grave as Lori-Ann chased Rosie. Picking the toddler up, the young girl sat down on the log and began to croon a lullaby. Dixie rested her head on Laura's knee and one of the cats sat beside her, rubbing his head on the girl's shoulder. Suddenly, Joanna smiled. She could almost hear Miss Velvie's voice, "Always watch over the young'uns and the animals."

"Hey, you girls want to ride down to the river with me?" Randy called one evening.

Joanna looked at Laura. "You want to go?"

The girl nodded and they piled into Randy's truck.

Rosie sat between Joanna and Laura on the glider while Dixie chased squirrels. As twilight descended, they began to see fireflies dancing through the trees. Randy opened the cooler on the back of his truck and handed Rosie a bottle of apple juice.

"Whoo-eeee! Pee on the fire and call the dogs!" The red Dodge was coming down the path, Johnny-Vern calling out the window. Nollie was with him. They ambled over under the shelter. Nollie picked Rosie up and sat down in a rocking chair.

"That wild coltsfoot certainly is growing on the riverbank," Nollie said. "Every time I see it, I can't help but think of Miss Velvie. I can almost see her down there picking it."

"I sure do miss 'er," said Joanna. "But you know, sometimes I feel like she's right here with us." She went on to tell Nollie about the way the rainbow kept returning.

"You know," Nollie began. "There's a legend about a place called the Rainbow Bridge. They say that animals go there when they die, to wait for their masters, then they enter Heaven together. I think perhaps it began with an old Indian belief. They used to say that when someone died, a huge rainbow would appear in the sky. One end touched the earth and the other end stretched all the way up to Heaven, providing the deceased with a bridge to reach the promised land. And you know, after what we saw at Miss Velvie's funeral, I think perhaps they were right."

Joanna couldn't get the legend off her mind for the next few weeks. She purchased a piece of heavy oak and wrote the words: RAINBOW BRIDGE. She went over the letters with Randy's old woodburning tool, then painted on a rainbow. She asked Nollie to come over and paint a picture of Smokey in the top right-hand corner and they glazed it with a protective finish.

"You know Jo, this really is a special spot," said Nollie as he looked around the little glen. "You've got a lot of plants here that have biblical legends."

"Really, like what?"

"Take the snowdrops, for instance," he pointed to tiny white blossoms that bowed gracefully from slender stems. "They say that snow was falling when Adam and Eve were expelled from the Garden of Eden. They were so miserable from the cold that an angel took pity on them and touched the falling snowflakes, turning them into these flowers.

"And the Jacob's Ladder," he knelt down to a shaded area beneath the cedars where tiny blue flowers swayed above apple-green stalks. "This is supposed to be the ladder that Jacob dreamed of.

"Look at the dogwoods, that's probably the most famous story of all. They used to be big as the oak trees. When Jesus was crucified, that's what they used for the cross. The tree was so ashamed that it changed to the small, gnarled trees we see today, too small to ever again be used in such a way. And the blossoms are in the form of a cross... two long and two short petals. Look, here," he plucked a bloom and held it up. "See the little spots on the edges of the petal? That's the nail prints, stained with red. And look at the very center." He pointed to the little cluster of golden beads. "That's the crown of thorns, and they say that all those who see this will remember, how Jesus suffered and died, that he might make life better for all of us."

"Just like Miss Velvie," Joanna thought as she stood there gazing at the bloodstains on the white blossom. "Oh, the pain those who loved us endured, in order to give us the gift of everlasting life. Jesus sent us the dogwood and Miss Velvie sent us the rainbow. What else could this place possibly be, but what she had in mind?"

Suddenly, she looked up at Nollie. "There's one plant that's missin'!"

"What's that?"

"Don't you know?"

A smile spread across Nollie's face. "The white rose?"

"That's right. I'm gonna get some and set 'em out."

"I think Miss Velvie would like that."

Nollie and Johnny-Vern came back to help Joanna put the oak plaque up in the little cedar grove, in front of Smokey's grave. Randy held Rosie and Laura rested a hand on Snowball's head. They all shed a few silent tears, but Joanna was experiencing a feeling of euphoria, that she had known only once before, for she knew that she and Snowball would see Smokey again.

In his memory, she would turn this place into a special sanctuary for animals that were sick or abused, a place much like Miss Velvie's house. If she could find proper homes, she would place them. If not, they would remain here.

Looking over at the little girl who was caressing Snowball, she thought, "And when people need help, we'll be there for them, too." She wondered how many lost souls Miss Velvie had taken in over the years.

Above all, she would never, never give up on any of them. There was no money, but she'd learned to do so many things with a shoestring budget and a lot of elbow grease. It wouldn't be easy, but it was something she had to do. Under no circumstances would any living thing that sought refuge here ever be turned away. And that was the beginning of Rainbow Bridge Farm.

On the anniversary of Miss Velvie's death, the friends all attended Mattie's church. Reverend Cofield announced that Joanna would like to sing a song in the old woman's honor. "This is a very special song," he began. "Jo wrote it herself."

Joanna walked up to stand in the sanctuary and her clear soprano voice rang out, charged with emotion.

She lived all her life, just giving her best
And now, she's gone up to Heaven to rest
She even made it easy for us to let go
When she sent us a sign, just so we would know
That all was well, up in Heaven above
And we still had her undying love
She painted the sky with a rainbow so bright
As we knelt by the grave, we were bathed in it's light
Not a raindrop had fallen, not a cloud in the sky
Velvie sent us this rainbow, and my heart tells me why
To give all she could had been her life's goal
Now, her greatest gift; on Heaven I'm sold

When the song was over, there wasn't a dry eye in the building. Mattie sat on the front row, her arm around Johnny-Vern. Her dark fingers reached up to smooth the curly hair on the back of his head, as his shoulders heaved with the sobs he held in.

Randy held Rosie in one arm, the other around Laura. Denise's bottom lip trembled and Tansey swallowed hard as they sat together, both swiping at the tears on their cheeks.

But Joanna was smiling and looking up at the light streaming in through the stained glass window. She spoke for everyone in the church when she held up her arms and said, "We love you, Miss Velvie!"